# GOOD GIRL FAIL

RONI LOREN

# A BIT OF GOOD GIRL
# INSPIRATION

I feel like this is my time to be rootless and just see where life takes me, and travel wherever there's a story to write.

— RORY GILMORE OF *GILMORE GIRLS*

Every relationship is just a big honking leap of faith.

— RORY GILMORE OF *GILMORE GIRLS*

# PROLOGUE

O'Neal Lory had been taught early on by her grandparents that one mistake could undo an entire life of right decisions. That it didn't matter if a person had been good ninety-nine percent of the time. One misstep, one snap judgment, could derail everything. She'd been that mistake for her mother. She'd witnessed the devastating consequences of what had followed. So O'Neal had listened. She'd taken a lot of right steps on the straight and narrow path laid out for her. Eighteen years of them, in fact. But the undeniable proof of her first stumble off that road arrived in her inbox on an otherwise unremarkable Thursday.

She was heading up the sidewalk to her grandparents' house after school when her phone dinged with an unfamiliar sound. She frowned, confused for a moment, and then remembered she'd reserved that sound for a private email address she'd set up. She quickly grabbed her phone from her pocket, almost dropping it to the pavement in her haste. *Oh God, oh God, oh God.*

She wasn't sure which result she was praying for. She opened the mail app she'd hidden two folders deep, and the

1

university's name glowed at her in all caps, the only new email in the box. Subject line: *Application status.* Her heartbeat picked up speed like she'd been caught committing a crime. *Had she really done this? What had she been thinking?*

She needed to drop the email into the trash, not even open it. The easiest way not to be tempted by something was to avoid the temptation altogether. Her teachers at St. Mary's always said that. If you don't want to eat the cake, don't bake the cake. In fact, don't even buy the sugar. But instead of dumping the email, she found herself tucking her phone into her backpack like it was contraband and glancing down the street to make sure her grandparents weren't coming home early.

They could *not* see this email. They'd already decided where she would be attending college. That plan had been in place since she'd moved in with them her kindergarten year and had scored freak-level on her IQ tests. Wainwright Women's College. Her application for the private religious school located thirty minutes away had been signed, sealed, and hand-delivered months ago—on paper, in person—because of course Wainwright wouldn't do something as gauche as *electronic* applications. Her place at Wainwright was probably already reserved with a star next to her name. With her honors-class-loaded 4.8 GPA from St. Mary's and her grandfather being friends with the dean, she probably could've drawn bunny rabbits and hearts all over her application instead of writing an essay and still would've gotten in.

Wainwright was where she was meant to go. That school made the most sense. She wouldn't have to live far from home. She'd get a stellar education and spiritual guidance. And it'd be familiar—a grown-up version of her current private school. Safe. Predictable. Exceedingly proper. No one would have the gall to bring up her family history. There'd be no guys to worry about. She'd be able to focus on her studies.

Growing up, she hadn't questioned her grandparents' plan

for her. *Of course* she would go to Wainwright like her grand-mother had. It would be a privilege, *an honor.*

But...when she'd taken a tour of the campus last year, O'Neal had discovered that they didn't have a dedicated jour-nalism program. She'd have to be an English major. Her heart had sunk at the news. An English degree could get her on the path to being a journalist, but the curriculum focused on reading the classics, not on digging up a story. They didn't even have a nonfiction class. And based on the pinched expression the lady leading the tour had given O'Neal when she'd asked about a journalism program, she suspected that this woman thought journalism wasn't exactly a respectable profession for a graduate of Wainwright. Too nosy. Too seedy. Too...impolite.

Her grandparents weren't cheering on O'Neal's choice of profession either, but they'd kept their opinions to veiled criti-cism. *An English degree from Wainwright will give you so many options for careers. You'll change your mind so many times before you graduate. You'd make such a wonderful college professor. Or an histo-rian. Journalists have to be so* aggressive. *And it can be dangerous.*

*Aggressive. Dangerous.* Literally the last words anyone would use to label O'Neal. *Smart. Focused. Quiet.* Those were the words normally used to describe her—if people bothered describing her at all. She suspected that if not for her mother being the subject of a regular rotation of cold case crime shows, no one would even spare her a second glance. She would just be *that girl who regularly screws up the grading curve.* Or *that girl whose grand-parents won't even let her go to a school-sanctioned dance.*

O'Neal checked the tree-lined street again, even though Nana and Pop wouldn't be home for at least another hour or so, and then hustled up the front steps of the two-story Georgian she'd lived in since she was five, its flat brick front and rows of windows somehow both welcoming and fortress-like. She unlocked the front door, turned off the house alarm, and grabbed a Coke from the fridge before heading upstairs to her room. Her heart was thumping in her ears, and sweat prickled her neck as she tossed her backpack onto the bed and locked her bedroom door behind her. The navy blue backpack sitting in the middle of her pale green quilt looked like a time bomb ready to go off, and she was suddenly afraid to take out her phone.

She stalled, kicking off her penny loafers and shrugging out of her school blazer. How had she put herself in this position? The night she'd created that new email address and had filled out the online application seemed like a dream now, an out-of-body experience. She'd been riding a rare wave of self-righteous anger and had been feeling a way she'd never felt before…reckless. *Daring.*

It'd been all *his* fault.

She'd gone over to her best friend Maya's house to hang out, wanting to maximize the last two weeks of summer before senior year started, but when she'd knocked, Maya's older brother, Auden, had answered instead. Home from summer-session college, fresh from swimming laps in the pool, and shirtless. The sight of him half-naked and the bright smile he'd given her had sent a rush of tingly heat through O'Neal's body that she was sure reddened her face.

She hadn't seen him in over a year because he'd stayed for the summer semester, and before that, she'd only seen him in passing. The days when he would hang out with her and Maya to play video games or watch a movie had ended once he'd entered high school and left them three years behind in middle school. The line between kids and adults had been drawn, and he'd stepped to the other side.

But the division hadn't stopped O'Neal from noticing how the once lanky and awkward Auden had morphed into something truly beautiful. Tall with shaggy light brown hair, hazel eyes, and a swimmer's body that made her imagine things she shouldn't. Any romantic book she snuck onto her e-reader ended up with her casting Auden in the lead. But, of course, she hadn't been the only one to notice. He'd gotten popular fast in high school and always had a pretty girl to hang out with, though he never seemed to have an official girlfriend. And none of the girls he dated were anything like O'Neal. Not that she would've had a chance with Auden anyway—even if her grand-parents *had* allowed her to date. She was just his little sister's BFF.

But that day at Maya's, Auden smiled with surprise and reached out to hug her. "Hey, Shaq. Long time no see."

O'Neal groaned at the old nickname. Auden had gone through a basketball phase before settling on swimming as his sport and had decided O'Neal's mom had secretly named her to honor Shaquille O'Neal. Her grandparents had told her that her mother had chosen it because it was an old family name on their Irish side, but really, how could O'Neal know for sure? Her mother had died before O'Neal was old enough to have a real conversation with her.

But feeling Auden's arms around her, his bare chest warm against her, his scent laced with chlorine and sunshine, it was too much. She had to clamp her lips together so that she wouldn't do something embarrassing like sigh—or worse, *moan*. She wasn't prepared for this. She had no armor built up for being this close to someone so…everything. Gorgeous. Hot. Male. She couldn't find the right word for Auden Blake.

She'd spent her high school years keeping her head down, her focus on her studies, and her attention away from boys. Her grandparents had ingrained in her that her school years were for schooling and that boys at that age never made things better, only worse. One wrong guy and you could ruin your whole life —or lose your life altogether like her mom had. And really, the restrictions against dating hadn't been that hard to abide by. The guys that went to St. Mark's, the all-male counterpart to St. Mary's, were…fine. Some smart. Some obnoxious. Some so rich they acted like having money was personality enough. She hadn't found herself drawing hearts in her notebooks over any of them. But during that brief hug from Auden, she wondered if a derailment might be worth the consequences.

"Hey," she said, breathless and realizing she'd held on to him a little too long. She quickly released him. "Didn't know you were back."

"Yep. Just for two weeks. But now y'all are going to have to share the pizza I know Maya will be ordering." He tugged her ponytail playfully before stepping back, the sting of it bringing her back into her right mind. Auden was about to be a junior in college. She was starting her senior year of high school. There would be no derailing. She was a kid to him.

"That means *pizzas*—plural—must be ordered because you're not good at sharing," she said, trying to regain her composure and not look at his chest.

He smirked, a little sparkle in his eyes. "You'd be surprised. I have a roommate now. I've gotten good at sharing these days."

Something in the way he said it made O'Neal feel like she was missing out on some private joke, but she returned his smirk as she stepped inside, and he shut the door behind her. "Guess you're learning *something* at college."

"You mean at a lowly state school?" he said as they walked toward the kitchen, a playful note in his voice. "Where all the common heathens go?"

She frowned. "It's not lowly. Bennette State is supposed to be a great school. My mom was taking classes there...when everything happened."

He nodded, and she appreciated that he didn't give her the standard sympathetic look people gave her whenever the topic of her mom came up but instead let the mention glide by.

"Yeah, well, it's not *Wainwright or Wellington*," he said, pronouncing the men's and women's branches of the college with a faux British accent. "Which my parents regularly remind me of. Like I can help that Wellington didn't have a swim team."

"But water polo…" she teased, knowing that was what his parents had kept saying he should do instead.

He sniffed and turned around, walking backward so he could face her. "Not for me. The whole scene. They wouldn't have wanted me anyway—at least not without a monster donation from the family. My math score on the SAT was somewhere in the range of drunk monkey with a calculator."

O'Neal laughed. "I'm sure it wasn't that bad."

"Bad enough. But Maya said you're a lock to get into Wainwright, that your junior year SAT scores beat all the seniors this year. Nice job, smarty pants." When she shrugged, trying to act like his praise didn't send little sparks through her, he gave her a wry look. "Maya, on the other hand, is convinced she's going to be waitlisted and that her life will pretty much be over."

O'Neal rolled her eyes at the familiar lamenting. "Maya will get in. She's as much of a lock as I am with all her extracurriculars."

When they stepped into the kitchen, O'Neal had expected Maya to be waiting for them, but the sunny room was empty, and the pool glittering outside the back windows was also quiet. Auden disappeared into the laundry room for a few seconds and came back wearing a navy blue T-shirt. He went to the fridge, grabbed two cans of LaCroix, and tossed her the tangerine-flavored one, remembering her favorite.

"Maya should be here any minute. She called and said she and Mom lost track of time shopping."

"Shocking," O'Neal said with a smile.

"Yeah, they turn it into a sport. I'd rather sit through ten math classes than get stuck shopping that long." He leaned against the kitchen island and took a sip of his grapefruit-flavored water. "So are you excited about senior year?"

She opened the can, the sound loud in the quiet kitchen, and shrugged. "Sure."

He lifted his brows. "Wow, with that level of enthusiasm, it's a wonder you're not on the pep squad. Is it because you're just ready to get it over with and get to Wainwright?"

"I'm definitely ready to get to college." She leaned back against the counter, the can sweating against her fingertips. "But I'm in the process of readjusting my expectations about what that's going to look like."

"What do you mean?"

"I don't know," she hedged, fiddling with the tab on her can. "We went on a tour at the beginning of summer, and I found out that they don't have a journalism program, so that kind of threw me. I guess I shouldn't have assumed they'd have one. I'm going to have to be an English major like Maya instead."

He frowned. "No, you don't."

"Uh, yeah. I do," she said between sips of water. "Nothing else really fits what I want to do. I mean, I guess I could major in history or something. That could be—"

"No, I mean, you don't have to do that because you don't have to go there," he said, his tone shockingly nonchalant.

She scoffed. "Oh, right. Yeah, I don't have to go to the school that my grandparents have been preparing me for my whole life, the one other people would give their right arm to go to if they could."

Auden set his drink down and eyed her, an oddly intense look on his face. "Key words: *grandparents* and *others*. Your *grandparents* want you to go there. *Others* want to go there. But maybe...you don't?"

She couldn't process the question. "What do you mean?"

"You know what I mean," he said, giving her a pointed look. "I'm not saying Wainwright isn't a great school. I know Maya will love it because their creative writing program is supposed to be top-notch, and it looks damn fancy on a resume or whatever. But that doesn't mean it's the school for everyone. Just because it's exclusive and expensive doesn't mean it's the right fit for you. If they don't have your major, then go somewhere that does."

O'Neal laughed because the idea was so ludicrous. *Go somewhere that does.* "I can't just pick a random school. My grandparents are paying my way. I think the only other thing they'd accept besides Wainwright is like a nunnery or something. You do remember my grandparents, right? They won't even let me group date or go to prom because boys and drinking and sin, oh my."

His flat-mouthed expression said he was unimpressed with her argument. "You're not dating anyone because you don't want to, not because your grandparents told you not to."

She stiffened. "What? You know how they—"

"I know you're smart, and there are ways around rules if someone wants something badly enough," he countered. "You've never wanted anyone that much, so you haven't bothered to figure out how to break the rule."

Her lips parted for a rebuttal but none came.

Auden gave her a knowing smile, and his gaze drifted from her face to her feet and back up, making her suddenly self-conscious of the white shorts and yellow sleeveless top she'd chosen. "Come on, O'Neal. You're seventeen, right?"

Hearing her real name on his lips instead of Shaq made a tendril of awareness move through her. Suddenly, she felt very young next to him. "Eighteen. I was held back in kindergarten because I missed so much school that year."

"So you're already legally an adult and will be nineteen when you graduate," he said matter-of-factly. "I get why your grandparents are overprotective. I know they've been through a lot. *You've* been through a lot."

She looked down, hating when the subject of her mother came up.

9

"But you're old enough now that they don't get to make the decisions for you anymore if you don't agree with them," he went on. "You can go to school wherever the hell you want."

She glanced up. "They won't pay for it."

"*That's* your excuse?" He rolled his eyes. "Come on, Shaq, you're smart as fuck."

The word startled her. She wasn't unaccustomed to hearing curse words. She *was* in high school—albeit a conservative religious one—but she couldn't remember Auden using that kind of language with her before. It did something to her, made her feel like he was showing her a glimpse of the real him, not the one who was the polite golden son in his family, but who he was at school with his friends.

"You can probably get a free ride to go almost anywhere," he continued. "*You* hold that power. You may upset your grandparents. You might piss them off. But it's your life you're making decisions about. When you graduate, you can do what you want. Go to the school you want. Date who you want. Maybe break a rule every now and then." He leaned forward like he was sharing a secret. "I love my family, but believe me, living a couple of hours away and not worrying about tarnishing the family name or people talking shit about you at social events if you make a mistake...it's a freedom you can't even imagine."

The picture he was painting was one she couldn't wrap her head around. Actual freedom. No one looking over her shoulder. No one making her endlessly check in. No one putting rules on her that didn't apply to everyone else. It sounded equal parts terrifying and magical. But she also knew that if she left, she'd break her grandparents' hearts—hearts that had already been shattered by her mom's behavior and then the tragedy of losing their only daughter.

"I don't know if I could do that to my grandparents. After everything they've been through, they've worked so hard to get me here."

"And they *have* gotten you here," he said. "But it's not like you're thinking of dropping out of school to go be a groupie for a rock band or something. You would only be choosing another great school to get the degree that you want." He flicked a hand toward her. "They wouldn't need to worry about you. It's not like you'd go to college and go wild. You're you."

She straightened. "What's that supposed to mean?"

He smiled. "Oh, don't get your hackles up, Shaq. I'm just saying, no matter where you go, you're the girl who's going to do her homework and go to her classes and get the As. You're not going to be playing beer pong and strip poker at the frat houses." He shrugged. "Your grandparents have already done their job. They've raised themselves a proper young lady."

She narrowed her eyes at the tone he'd used on those last three words. "You're making fun of me."

He chuckled, a soft sound that came from deep in his chest. "I like seeing you get a little mad. It's good to get mad sometimes. But I'm really not trying to tease you."

"Uh-huh."

"It's just, I know the deal," he said, expression softening into one more serious. "All that press your mom's murder got, the way she was painted in the media. It reflected on your grandparents, and they overcorrected with you. They wanted a different outcome, so they got really strict."

Bitterness bubbled up in her. The killer had taken her mom's life, but the press had added to the tragedy, destroying her reputation. "Well, I can guarantee that if someone were to kill me, it definitely wouldn't be dubbed the Party Girl Murder like my mom's was."

He grimaced. "For the record, I think that name is bullshit. So what if she was seeing a few guys at the same time? Who cares? Calling her a party girl is misogynistic."

Her gaze flicked upward, meeting his eyes.

His lips curved a little at her surprise. "Look at me, learning big words at college. But all I'm saying is that anyone with any sense can see that you're more responsible than most adults. If there were an encyclopedia entry for *Good Girl,* your picture would be right there."

She groaned, her face heating. "Speaking of misogynistic terms."

He grinned from behind his water. "Sorry. Not *Good Girl. Responsible Young Woman* who is going to be successful at whichever college she chooses."

"You make me sound like the most boring person on Earth." She tipped her head back and closed her eyes. "Maybe I am. My cold case episode would be called the *Who Was She Again? Murder.*"

Auden made a sound of displeasure, and O'Neal felt the air shift. She lowered her head and opened her eyes, finding him standing right in front of her. He put his hands on her shoulders. "Hey, none of that. No talking of your own murder, Ms. Morbid. And I didn't say you were boring. You're…"—he looked thoughtful—"stoic. My guess is that you have a whole lot going on behind the quiet. But if you keep letting other people make decisions for you, you'll become who *they* want you to be. Believe me, I've been there." He gave her a long look and then put his mouth next to her ear, his breath gentle against her skin. "Can I tell you a secret?"

She swallowed hard at his proximity, at the summery pool scent of him, and nodded.

The words tickled her neck as he whispered, "I'm really not that bad at math."

Her lips parted.

He lifted his head, hands still on her shoulders and gaze sparkling. "So if who they want you to be is not who *you* want to be, then you're going to have to piss some people off, Shaq. You're going to have to surprise them."

"Right," she said softly. *Surprise them.*

"I bet you could," he said, voice barely above a whisper.

The heat of his palms was burning into her bare shoulders, and he was close, so close. The sliver of space between them felt like it would spark if she brushed against it. Her longtime crush on him pulsed through her like a living thing. She'd never wanted to kiss someone so much in her life. What would he taste like? Would he kiss her back? Would he want more than that? Her grandparents always said kisses were dangerous invitations.

Auden held the eye contact, something new flickering in his gaze, something curious.

Her skin was warm, and she could feel things in her body tightening, tightening. She had no doubt that if she looked down, two embarrassingly obvious points would be visible against her tank top. This was what arousal felt like. Real, in-person arousal. Not the secondary kind she sometimes got from reading books or watching movies. She wet her lips, and his gaze drifted down to her mouth, lingering there before tracing back up.

*Whoa.* Was he actually *thinking* about it?

*You're going to have to surprise them.* His words came back to her, daring her. When would she ever be this close to Auden again? On a surge of bravery, she grabbed his wrists, his hands still on her shoulders, and she forced herself to hold the eye contact. She lowered his hands, bringing his body closer.

"What are you doing, Shaq?" he asked, his voice low and tense.

"Something surprising." She pushed up on her toes and pressed her mouth to his.

His wrists stiffened in her grip like he'd curled his fists, and he made a sound in the back of his throat. His lips were soft and tasted faintly of grapefruit and salt. She shifted even closer. Her chest brushed his, setting her nerve endings on fire. She had never kissed anyone and had no idea what she was doing or what to do next. All she knew was that she was kissing Auden Blake.

His lips parted hers, and the control shifted, his tongue sweeping into her mouth and gently stroking. Electricity crackled through her, and her hands went to his waist to steady herself, afraid her knees might buckle. He braced his hands on the counter on each side of her, trapping her there and deepening the kiss. She drank in the taste of him, his breath, the confident way he coaxed her tongue to move with his. She drew closer to him, needing contact everywhere. Their bodies pressed together, and his began to harden against hers—his very *male* body.

*Oh, God. Oh, God. Oh, God.* Every part of her clenched in anticipation of being touched, of being able to touch him.

But then a door slammed, and Auden broke away from the kiss instantly, taking a big step back and glancing toward the kitchen doorway like it was going to explode in their faces. He turned back to her, a slightly panicked look in his eye. "Jesus, O'Neal, I'm sorry. That shouldn't have—"

She cleared her throat, trying to find her voice again, trying to sound confident even though her knees felt like they were about to quit their job of holding her up. "Don't be. I started it."

"Fuck," he said under his breath. He raked a hand through his hair, looking ten kinds of uncomfortable, and then adjusted the front of his swim shorts to hide what she'd been feeling against her stomach. "No, that was my fault. I shouldn't have let that happen. I—you're a kid."

She'd been staring in stunned awe at where his hand had been, but at the word *kid*, she reared up like she'd been pinched. "No, I'm not. I'm eighteen. You just said—"

"You're in high school," he said, cutting her off but keeping his voice low. "And I'm—"

"Two years older than me. Big deal," she said, feeling bold.

"On the timeline, it's two years. In real life, it's a lot more than that." He sighed and gave her a look she could only read as pity. "Look, Shaq, that can't happen again. That was…a momentary lapse in judgment on my part. I'm glad you're ready to make some bold choices. But I can't be one of them. I'm not a boy who's gonna hold your hand in the hallway and ask you to prom. You've got lots of steps left to take on paths I've already been down."

Her cheeks burned, her entire being feeling stupid and chastised and childish. His words proved that he'd definitely been able to tell that she'd never kissed anyone before. He probably felt embarrassed for her. She'd never felt so silly and young.

But at the same time, a different emotion was surging up behind the embarrassment. *Anger.* Not really at him, but at all of it. That she was so ill-equipped for this. That she didn't have a mom to talk her through these things. That she was eighteen years old and this had been the first time she'd kissed a boy. That she was so sheltered, she didn't know how to interact with a guy only two years older than she was. That even if she wanted to go to prom with someone, she couldn't because she wasn't allowed to date or go to school dances.

She was eighteen, and all her life choices had already been decided for her. She would not be the party girl. She would not make teenage mistakes. She would always get the A. Her school would be this and her major would be that. She would be the proof that her grandparents could raise a fine young woman, no, *a good girl.*

She didn't *want* to be a good girl. She didn't want to be bad either or disappoint the people she loved. But in that moment, she could no longer bear the idea of going to a college that was just like her high school—insulated, protected, controlled. She didn't want to major in English and only go to classes with other privileged, protected girls. She wanted to experience life outside the bubble. She wanted to make her own decisions. She wanted to grow the hell up.

The noise of Maya and her mother dropping shopping bags in the foyer broke O'Neal out of her whirling thoughts. Auden was staring at her, looking concerned. "Shaq, say something. I feel like such a dick."

She reached out and squeezed his arm. "Thank you."

"What?" His brow wrinkled.

"Even if it was a mistake, I'm glad my first kiss was with you and not some random guy. And don't call me Shaq anymore."

Horror flashed across his face. "Your first—*Goddammit.*"

She handed him her drink. "Don't tell Maya I stopped by. I'll call and tell her something came up. I need to go."

Auden tried to say something else, but she was already heading for the back door.

A few hours later, her application for a new college and their journalism program was sent in and completed. There was a pit a mile deep in her stomach, and the next morning, she'd instantly doubted the move and had chalked it up to a moment of hormone-induced insanity. She'd almost let herself forget about it. She'd let the application process for Wainwright continue as normal.

But now the response from that night's rebellion was sitting in an inbox on her phone, and she needed to open it.

After taking another deep breath, she walked toward her bed and unzipped her backpack. The phone felt awkward in her hand, heavier somehow. She knew the email would say that she'd gotten in. But that wasn't the question she needed answered. She'd need more than an acceptance. She needed…everything.

With shaking hands, she sat on the bed and opened the mail app. Part of her hoped the answer was a no, that the decision would be yanked from her, that fate would tell her to stay put. That would be so much easier. Yet, her heart pounded with hope.

She tapped to open the email.

On top was the school's crest. Her eyes jumped around, skimming over random sentences and phrases.

*Dear Ms. Lory,*

*Congratulations! You have been accepted...*

*...full academic scholarship*

*room and board included...*

*College of Journalism.*

*Response needed by...*

*Look forward to seeing you this fall!*

The room was spinning, her phone trembling in her hands. She'd done it. She'd gotten a full ride. At a college hours from home. Journalism. At Bennette. Where her grandparents wouldn't be over her shoulder. Where she could be somewhere that her mother had once been.

Where Auden would be a senior.

The last part made her cringe. Bennette had seemed like the best choice for a number of reasons that night. Great journalism program. Still in the state. But she couldn't deny that Auden being there hadn't played some role. She'd know *someone.*

But he'd probably think she was a total stalker. A silly little freshman chasing after a nothing kiss on a summer afternoon.

An engine cut off outside her window. Nana and Pop were home.

Her gut twisted. She couldn't do this. This was a ludicrous idea. A selfish idea. She was going to crush them with this news.

She needed to delete the email. Decline the offer. Throw out the temptation.

She closed her eyes, breathed, thought about how she'd felt in that moment when she'd grabbed Auden and kissed him, when she'd taken control of her own life for just a blink, when she'd stepped outside of her safe world and taken a risk.

She nodded to herself, clutched her phone to her chest, and then went downstairs.

# CHAPTER ONE

*O*ne year later

Auden pressed his chin to the top of the boxes he had in his arms, hoping the whole pile wouldn't topple over as he bumped his hip against his car door to shut it. He was running late because he'd overslept and would definitely get an earful from both his mom and sister about it. He probably should've come up with some excuse for why he couldn't help Maya move into the Wainwright dorms, but she'd been forced to tag along when he'd moved into the freshman dorm at Bennette and had been promptly traumatized by Mo, the hairiest guy on campus, streaking down the hallway right past her, so Auden figured he owed her. Mo's furry ass was a hard image to erase from the memory bank.

And really, Auden didn't mind helping his sister. He just dreaded seeing Maya's roommate. The last time he'd seen O'Neal Lory was when he'd acted like a goddamn creeper and kissed her in his parents' kitchen. She'd kissed him first, technically, but he knew he'd made that happen. He'd gotten in her space, given her a look that crossed the line, basically dared her to do it. Then he'd taken it to a different level once she'd put her mouth on his, kissing her deeper, pushing up against her, *getting hard*. With the most innocent and sheltered girl he'd ever known.

That would've been bad enough, but the part that haunted him was that he'd liked it way too much. He hated the fact that her innocence had turned him on, hated that he'd *liked* that he'd been her first kiss. He was a fucking asshole.

When he'd told his best friend, Lennox, about it after he'd returned to school, Len had been unimpressed with Auden's crisis of conscience. *So you have a thing for virgins? Sounds like she was into it and she's of consenting age. No big deal. Add it to your list.*

But Auden didn't want to add it to his list. His *list* would already give his family heart attacks if they knew about it. He should've never acted that way with O'Neal. The girl had been through enough. After the kiss, she'd hauled herself out of the kitchen like the cops were on her tail, and whether it was purposeful avoidance or not, he'd never run into her at the house since. When he came home for visits, she was nowhere to be found. And at Maya's graduation, he'd only seen O'Neal walk across the stage and give her valedictorian speech. She hadn't stayed for the reception, so he hadn't even gotten a chance to apologize.

And she for sure hadn't told Maya what had happened because his sister would've not taken that news quietly. Maya would've set his shit on fire for even thinking about messing with one of her friends. Maya was a decent sister most of the time, but she liked her vengeance Old Testament style. He tried to keep the peace.

But he couldn't do anything about any of it now. O'Neal would be here, and he would have to be polite and act as if it'd never happened because their families were going to be there. *Hi, Mr. and Mrs. Lory, so good to see you again. No, I never stuck my tongue down your precious granddaughter's throat. I know she's not allowed to touch boys. No, of course I'd never get a hard-on in her presence and press it against her.* He groaned. He needed to get his sister moved in as quickly as possible and then get back to Bennette so he could get his apartment settled for senior year. He could deal with an hour or so of awkwardness. Probably.

He carried the boxes over to the two-story white brick building that served as the honors dorm at Wainwright and stepped through the double doors that had been propped open with cinder blocks. A whirlwind of noise engulfed him as soon as he entered. Dads asking how many more boxes. Moms directing foot traffic. Girls shouting greetings at friends they hadn't seen since last semester. Items toppling out of people's arms. Doors squeaking open and slamming. Christian pop music drifting out of someone's room. It was like an alternate universe version of his move-in experience at Bennette. Same level of noise, same crowded hallways, completely different vibe. No one would be streaking down the hallway here.

"Auden!" His mom's familiar voice caught his attention in the chaos, and he peeked around the boxes to find her waving at him from the other end of the hall. "Over here. Room 4B."

She disappeared into the room, and Auden weaved through the crowded corridor as best he could, dodging girls with carts and boxes. A few smiled his way, but he was too preoccupied to smile back. When he passed room 3B and knew his sister's was next, he took a fortifying breath. *Here we go.*

"Oh my gosh, what took you so long?" Maya asked, taking the top box off his pile. "You have all my makeup and toiletries. I thought I was going to end up at the meet-and-greet tonight looking like a troll."

Maya was dressed for moving day in an oversized gray T-shirt and a pair of black leggings, her blond hair in a high pony-tail. Despite her declaration, he could tell she already had makeup on. Ever since their mom had given Maya the okay on wearing it when she started high school, he rarely saw Maya without it. He guessed with her five-foot-one height, she didn't want to be accidentally mistaken for a twelve-year-old.

"The day is saved then. You're welcome." He set the boxes down on the floor. "I got caught in traffic."

His mom gave him a quick hug and peck on the cheek. "Thank you, sweetheart. I know your sister *greatly appreciates* you going out of your way to help get her settled." She gave Maya one of her mom looks. "Right?"

"Yes, ma'am," Maya said dutifully and then hugged Auden, pinching him in the side where his mother couldn't see. "You're a saint. A late one."

"Saint Tardy," he said, releasing the hug and stepping back. "Patron saint of students."

Maya smirked. "I remember doing this for you. This room smells better, thankfully."

"Not a high bar to cross," he said. "Boys' dorms are one of the official circles of hell. But I've upgraded now. Off-campus apartment with Lennox this year."

"Good. Maybe I'll actually visit you this semester." Maya kneeled to open the boxes he'd carried in. "How many more do you have to bring in?"

"Just a few." He glanced toward the empty bed on the opposite side, his shoulders tightening a little. "Are you going to have room for them? Where's O'Neal going to fit any of her stuff?"

Maya's attention flicked upward, her nose wrinkling. "O'Neal?"

"Yeah, you're rooming together, right?" Maybe he'd gotten lucky and O'Neal was moving in on a different day.

His mother clucked her tongue and shook her head. "Maya didn't tell you?"

He grabbed a bottle of water from the case his mother had brought in. "Tell me what?"

"She bailed on me at the last minute," Maya said with a huff. "Left me to roommate roulette."

Auden frowned, water bottle halfway to his mouth. "Bailed?"

"I mean, I guess she's having a moment or whatever," Maya went on, lifting her palms like she just *could not even* with the topic. "It was bound to happen at some point. The Lorys have been so crazy strict with her. But I expected her to, I don't know, like sneak out for a date or get tipsy on wine coolers or something. A little rebellion. Not like, burning every plan she ever had to the ground."

Auden wasn't tracking. "So y'all had a fight and aren't going to be roommates?"

"No, honey," his mother said. "O'Neal had a big falling out with her grandparents a couple of weeks ago. Said she didn't want to come here for college. She had applied elsewhere without their knowledge and had gotten a scholarship, but she didn't tell them or anyone else until the last minute because she was scared."

"She—" A smile broke out. "No shit?"

"Auden," his mother said firmly, glancing out toward the hallway. "*Language.*"

"Sorry, I just"—he ran a hand over his head—"wow, so she actually did it."

"She did it, all right," Maya said, sending him a look as she unloaded shampoo from the box in front of her. "Her grandparents freaked out and told her they would cut her off if she went through with it. Said if she was going to Bennette, she'd have to figure out finances on her own—*all* of her finances."

Brakes screeched in his head. "Wait, what? She's going to *Bennette?*"

Maya frowned and sat back on her heels. "Yes, apparently they have a great journalism program, which is all she's ever wanted to do. I mean, she's still my best friend even if she left me hanging here, so I support her one hundred percent. I just worry she's biting off more than she can chew doing this all on her own."

Auden was only half-listening. On one hand, he was strangely proud that O'Neal had taken his advice. On the other, she was going to *his* school. It was a decently sized campus, but he was bound to run into her. He'd still have to face that awkward apology, but more than that, he liked being at Bennette because there was no one there to connect him to home. He had a separate life there, a private one. He had secrets that needed to stay there. He didn't need someone with a direct line to his sister reporting back home.

"Auden, honey," his mom said, putting her hand on his shoulder, her blue eyes serious. "I know you're a senior and have a lot going on, but I want you to reach out to O'Neal and let her know that you're there if she needs anything."

He blinked. "What?"

His mom lowered her hand from his shoulder and pushed a stray blond hair that had fallen out of her twist away from her face. "I'm hoping the Lorys will come around and patch things up with O'Neal. I know what it's like to think your child is going to one place and then ends up going to another. It's quite a shock." She gave him an arch look. "But I think they're being too harsh on the girl. I know they think the threat of no money is going to force her into changing her mind, but she wouldn't have gone through all this trouble if it didn't mean something to her." His mother's lips pressed into a line. "My theory is that it has to do with her mom. She didn't get a chance to know Katie, and maybe she wants to go to the same school her mom did, have some connection. Grief can make people do weird things."

Auden released a long breath.

"But whatever her reasons," she went on, "she's never lived on her own, has never been to any school where she wasn't protected by iron gates. She's smart but sheltered. And if she has to manage her own money and be all by herself there with no family support…that's a lot. People might take advantage of her."

Auden's stomach twisted at the thought of O'Neal being out there in the world with no support from anyone. That was like sending a lamb into the lion's den. "I can't believe they just cut her off."

"I told her that she could call us if she ever needed help, and I gave her some money as a graduation gift to help augment whatever financial aid she's getting. And, of course, she's always welcome at our house for holiday breaks and things, but there's only so much I can do. I'm not going to be up there. You are," she said. "I want you to look out for her. Be the big brother she doesn't have."

He groaned inwardly. A big brother who'd stuck his tongue down her throat. He didn't want this job. He didn't want to be responsible for anyone. But what else was he supposed to do? O'Neal was partly in this situation because of his brilliant pep talk for her to stand up for herself. He was glad she had, but he hadn't thought through what those consequences would look like for her when she did. "I'll keep an eye on her."

His mother smiled and patted his cheek affectionately. "Thank you. I'll feel much better knowing she has you there. You're a good boy."

He tried not to cringe at the term.

"I can't believe I have to room *with a stranger,*" Maya said dramatically and flopped onto her bed. "Does it make me a horrible person if I'm secretly hoping O'Neal's experiment fails and she comes running back to me?"

A dark thread of temptation wound through Auden at the thought. Maybe that *would* be for the best. Maybe he shouldn't make it so easy for O'Neal to be at Bennette. Maybe she was better off here after all.

Safe. Protected. Away from him.

∽

O'NEAL HAD NEVER FELT SO ALONE IN SUCH A BIG CROWD. THE dorm hallway was packed with people and their families. Girls were chattering. Moms were hugging their daughters. Dads were dabbing their eyes as they left out the front door. And O'Neal had a backpack and a pile of boxes in her car outside.

She'd known this wouldn't be easy, doing this alone, but she hadn't anticipated the hollow ache in her chest. Not that her grandparents weren't here. She was still too mad at them to want to see them right now. But that her *mom* wasn't here. That the only first day of school her mom had ever gotten to bring her to was kindergarten, and O'Neal only had a vague memory of that. She could picture the rainbow painted on the kindergarten classroom wall more vividly than her mother's face. But she did remember that her mom had cried when it was time to leave her there. O'Neal had told her it was going to be okay.

That was one of the last memories she had of her mom. She'd moved in with Nana and Pop by then so that her mom could come here to Bennette to try and finish her education. After having O'Neal at sixteen, her mom had gotten her G.E.D. and a receptionist job, but she'd wanted more. Nana and Pop had agreed to take care of O'Neal so that her mom could get her degree and a better future for them both. But a few months later, her mom had been gone. Just like that. Not a better future. No future at all.

Had her mother felt this overwhelmed when she'd first arrived on campus?

O'Neal doubted it. From everything she'd heard, her mom had been one of those people who everyone wanted to be around. Outgoing. Popular. Pretty. She'd probably made friends with half the campus by the end of her first week.

O'Neal cringed inwardly. She was listing things she'd heard in true crime documentaries. Like her mother was some character, the Party Girl, who was going out every night and inviting whoever into her bed, instead of an actual person.

Her memories were tainted by the media's portrayal. She closed her eyes. Breathed. Tried to wipe the thoughts out of her head.

"*Excuse me.*"

Someone bumped into her and her eyes flew open. "Oh, sorry."

A blond girl rolled her eyes as she passed her. "You're in the middle of the hallway."

Another group of girls navigated around her, jostling her, and O'Neal quickly moved to the side. She was supposed to be finding her room, but suddenly she couldn't catch her breath. The walls seemed too close, the voices too loud. She spun back toward the main entrance and made a beeline for the door. When the sunshine and fresh air hit her face, she finally took a breath. She got out of the way of all the parents with boxes and walked around the side of the building, finding an unoccupied bench.

She pulled off her backpack and collapsed onto the bench, feeling like every decision she'd made over the last few months had been wrong. How did she ever think she could do this? She'd gone to school with the same people since she was five. Even if she wasn't popular, she at least knew her classmates. She wasn't living among strangers. She imagined Maya four hours away in some well-appointed room at Wainwright. The comfort of doing this move-in with her today would've been such a relief. Getting their room organized, making plans, laughing at inside jokes.

She lowered her head and pressed the heels of her hands against her brow bone, a headache forming. Her grandparents had known. They'd known this would happen, that she wasn't ready for something like this. They were probably waiting by the phone, expecting her to call any minute and ask them to let her come back home. She pulled her phone out of her pocket and looked at it. The temptation was a strong, pulsing thing.

With one phone call, she could undo this insanity. She could go to Wainwright. Live with Maya. Study…English.

She groaned and stared at her blank phone screen like it had the answers, but her fingers didn't move. Not yet. She couldn't call them yet.

She flipped the phone over and shifted to put it back in her pocket, but it vibrated in her hand. She turned it over, expecting a check-in text from Maya, but it was a *Hey* from a number she didn't recognize.

She frowned and unlocked the phone. It was probably a wrong number or spam. It vibrated again.

> Unknown: It's Auden. Are u on campus yet?
> Mom said u might need some help moving in

*Auden.* Auden was texting her. Butterflies crashed around in her stomach. She hadn't spoken to him since the kiss and had made a point not to be around when he was home on break. He'd made her feel like such a dumb kid that day. But he'd also been the inspiration for this trip down insanity lane. This was his fault.

The awkwardness was going to be off the charts, but right now, knowing *anyone* felt better than sitting on the bench alone. Plus, they'd have to clear out the awkwardness at some point anyway. They'd see each other on campus.

She bit her bottom lip, steeling herself, and typed.

> O'Neal: Hey. Yeah, I'm here. And that'd be great. I'm in Redmond – the honors dorm on the north side of campus

> Unknown: I can be there in 15. Where can I find u?

> O'Neal: There's a bench on the left side of the building

Unknown: Got it

He didn't say anything after that, and she programmed his name into her phone. She had no doubt that his mom, Clare, had put him up to this. Clare had been so great since she'd found out about Nana and Pop cutting off O'Neal's funds. But even if Auden was doing this out of obligation, she felt better knowing that she was about to see a familiar face.

She'd just ignore the embarrassment still burning in her stomach over the last time she'd seen that face.

And kissed it.

# CHAPTER TWO

*A*uden grabbed two bottles of water out of the fridge and tossed them into his backpack. He checked the time on his phone. If he was going to get over to O'Neal's dorm by the time he'd told her, he needed to get going—and get this over with.

Lennox stepped out of his bedroom, zipping up his jeans, his blond hair still wet from the shower and his T-shirt slung over his shoulder. The new tattoo he'd added over the summer, scrawled poetry lines that traced up the side of his left rib cage, seemed to dance as Lennox exhaled loudly. "Damn. Watch out for the hot water setting in that shower. It goes from cold to boil-your-nuts-off with one little twist."

"I'll call Doug about it. He said they'll take care of whatever we need here," Auden said, grabbing his keys. He'd hoped to slip out before Len was done with his shower but no such luck.

Lennox pulled his shirt over his head and nodded toward Auden's backpack. "Where you headed? Wanna grab lunch?"

He glanced toward the door. "Can't. I need to go to campus and help a friend get moved in. I told her I'd be there in a few minutes."

Lennox's eyebrows lifted in interest. "Which friend?"

"Just a friend of my sister's. My mom asked if I could help her out. Her family couldn't be here and she's a freshman, so you know how crazy move-in day is." Auden realized too late that he was talking too much, giving too many details.

"A family friend. A freshman." Lennox smiled that wolfish smile of his, the one that made it nearly impossible to ignore him. "Your poker face is shit today, Aud. I mean, I feel like I've taught you better, but you're showing your whole hand."

Auden groaned. "Shut up, man. I gotta go."

"It's her, isn't it?" Lennox looked all too proud of himself.

Auden's fingers flexed. "It's no one."

He laughed. "Oh shit, it actually *is*. Hell, I was just casting a line out to see if I could catch some trout. This is little sis's friend, isn't it? The high schooler who'd never kissed a boy and had you feeling all the guilty feelings?"

"Bye. I'm going." Auden gripped the door handle.

"Hell yes, you are. And I'm going too," Lennox said, swiping his Doc Martens from the side of the couch and meeting him by the door.

"No way," Auden said, tone sharp. "I'm just going to carry some boxes because my mom asked me to help her out and then I'm done. This isn't a social visit."

Lennox grinned unrepentantly and tugged on his shoes, hopping on one foot as he did so. "Get over yourself, man. I'm simply being a friendly graduate student helping out the underlings. The poor girl is brand-new to campus and probably doesn't know anyone. I can help with boxes too. I'm a great welcoming committee."

A ripple of trepidation went through Auden. Len was one of his favorite people in the world, but he could also be a weapon of mass seduction. In their kinky corner of the campus underground, that worked to Auden's benefit. Lennox had taught him a lot, introduced him to things he never would've known he liked. But Auden didn't need that world or anyone in it touching the one that O'Neal and his family occupied.

"Come on," Lennox cajoled and put his hands in a prayer position. "I'll be on my best behavior. Promise. An absolute choirboy."

He gave Lennox a look of warning. "Fine. You can come, but O'Neal is off-limits. Like one hundred percent off-limits. Beyond the fact that she's a freshman, she's a direct line to my sister. I can't have her knowing me as anything but the guy I am at home."

"Mr. Pious Goody Goody who accidentally-on-purpose kissed her and who secretly wanted to relieve her of her virginity in your parents' kitchen. Got it." Lennox nodded resolutely like he was memorizing the story.

Auden made a pained sound. "I'm serious, Len. No messing around. No flirting. No innuendo. She's…you'll see. She's smart as hell, but she's been wrapped up like fine china her whole life. She's never even been on a date. So don't freak her out. Being here on campus where they're handing out condoms instead of Bibles is probably overwhelming enough."

Lennox lifted his hands, his expression losing its jest. "I hear you, okay? I actually am capable of behaving myself when I need to."

Auden let out a breath and nodded. "Fine. Let's go and get this over with."

Lennox followed him out and locked the door behind them, but Auden's mind was already looping over the things Len had said. He *had* wanted to do more with O'Neal that day in the kitchen—things that O'Neal probably didn't even know existed —and that made him feel like an asshole all over again. He needed to apologize. And now he was going to have to do it with Len there.

Auden was quiet the whole drive over, trying to put together what he would say. When they got to the dorm, the parking lot was packed, and it took them longer to find a spot than he'd planned. He was already running late, and O'Neal was probably melting in the southern sun waiting for him. He turned off the engine and pulled out his phone to text her.

Auden: Here. Still meeting by the bench?

She replied instantly with a thumbs up.

"Come on." He grabbed his backpack, and Lennox followed him to the lawn in front of the dorm. It looked like an anthill had been kicked over, people everywhere, boxes in random places, people shouting at each other. He didn't miss living on campus. At all.

Lennox fell into step beside him. "I remember when we did this your freshman year." He put his hand over his heart. "The horrified look on your face when you saw I was your roommate is one of my fondest memories."

Auden snorted. "I remember my mom pulling me aside to make sure you were really a freshman because how could an eighteen-year-old kid already have a half sleeve of tattoos? When I told her you were a year ahead of me, you'd think I'd told her you were an alien."

"Now she loves me," he said with a grin.

"Because you bribe her with art."

He shrugged. "Bribery works."

Lennox was an art major and had started sending his poetry-loving mother pen and ink drawings inspired by famous poems. It'd worked like magic with his mom, and it'd also inspired Lennox. Some of the lines from W.H. Auden's "Lullaby" were now etched into his skin in the new tattoo.

"Left side of the building," Auden said, pointing. "Look for a brunette."

*You'll know the one.* For some reason, he had no doubt Lennox would spot her even if he'd never met her before.

Something about O'Neal made you want to look...and linger—which Auden absolutely shouldn't be thinking about right now.

They weaved their way through the milling crowd and rounded the side of the building. Auden tensed when he saw O'Neal sitting there all alone. Her knees were pulled up to her chest. She was looking down at her phone, scrolling through something. Her dark brown hair was piled into a messy bun, and her entire posture was curled inward like she was fighting off outside invaders. Like an Alice who'd fallen into the rabbit hole and didn't want to look around to see where she'd landed.

"That's her, isn't it?" Lennox asked, keeping his voice low.

Auden swallowed past the knot in his throat. "Yeah."

"She looks like she's trying to disappear," Len said, a frown in his voice.

O'Neal looked up then, her lips twitching into a tentative smile when she spotted Auden. She lifted her hand in a little wave and put her feet on the ground.

Auden raised his hand in response and picked up the pace.

"Fuck, man," Lennox said under his breath as he kept stride next to him. "Now I know how you got yourself in trouble. She's—"

"Off-limits," he repeated.

"I know, I know. I'm nothing if not a man of my word," he said quickly. "Besides, it's not me she's smiling at."

Auden's shoulders relaxed a little. Len was a wild card and could be a handful, but he was right. He'd never broken his word to Auden.

When they got close enough, O'Neal stood, hugging her elbows like she was cold. "Hey."

Auden smiled back as he took her in with her loose white T-shirt and army green shorts. If he'd hoped that his attraction to her that day in the kitchen had been a fluke, his hopes were dashed immediately. If anything, she was even more beautiful now. Bright blue eyes, glossed lips, and legs that seemed to go on for miles.

"Hey, Shaq."

She frowned.

"Sorry," he said, clearing his throat. "I'm not supposed to call you that anymore." He stepped forward and gave her a quick, totally platonic, no-chests-touching hug. "I can't believe you're here."

"Me neither," she said, her voice a little shaky.

Auden jutted a thumb toward Len. "This is Lennox, my roommate. He offered to help too. Len, this is O'Neal, my sister's friend."

Len put his hand out to give hers a shake. "Nice to meet you, sister's friend."

"Same," she said, "and thanks for offering to help."

"Of course," Lennox said, still holding her hand. "Always happy to help a friend of Auden's. Plus, I've always wanted to see how the other half lives. Guys aren't allowed in the under-classmen girls' dorms except on move-in day. It all feels very scandalous."

"Right," she said with a nervous smile.

Auden was about to elbow Lennox for even the hint of innu-endo, but he caught the way O'Neal's gaze swept down over Lennox, taking in the tattoos, the black jeans, the Docs. She rolled her lips together and looked down, her cheeks taking on a pink tinge. He couldn't get a read on if it was because she was uncomfortable with Lennox's look or if she was into it, but he knew Len had to have noticed the natural submissiveness in the move. The guy picked up on that stuff like a bloodhound catching scent.

Auden wished in that moment that O'Neal wasn't so inno-cent, that she wasn't his sister's best friend, that she was someone who wouldn't be traumatized or horrified by what he was into.

Lennox put his hand on Auden's shoulder. "Why don't we get started? We can knock this out in no time and then take O'Neal to get some decent food off campus. You don't want to start off your college career with cafeteria food. Trust me."

Auden sent Lennox a look. They weren't supposed to be inviting her anywhere.

O'Neal's gaze jumped to Auden as if seeking permission. She must've read something in his expression because she quickly said, "Um, no, y'all don't have to do that. I'm sure you have other things to do today, and I have to meet my roommate and stuff."

The fact that she'd deciphered a *no* on his face made him feel like a jerk. She was here alone on a campus she didn't know. He forced a smile. "We're going to be grabbing food anyway after this, so you're more than welcome to join."

She still looked unsure, but she grabbed her backpack from the bench. "Thanks. Maybe."

Lennox put his hand out to take her bag for her, and then she led them both to her car. She didn't have much beyond two heavy duffel bags and a few boxes, so they had her loaded into her room in about twenty minutes. O'Neal didn't say much beyond where to put the boxes, and she kept glancing to the other side of the room. Her roommate's bed was already made up with a colorful flowered comforter, so the girl was around somewhere.

"Do you know who you're rooming with?" Auden asked while he helped her unload some books from a box.

"I know her name. We've exchanged a few texts. She seems nice," she said, putting her books on a shelf in an order that apparently only she could understand. "It will be weird living with anyone at all, though. I'm so used to having my own room."

"Yeah, it was weird for me too," Auden said.

Lennox laughed. "Especially when he walked in and saw me. I think he suspected I was a Satanist or something. I was going through a goth/guyliner phase."

36

O'Neal looked surprised for a moment and then laughed. "Not a worshiper of the Dark Lord then?"

"Nah," he said, sitting on the edge of her bed. "More of a Stoic these days. I think schools of philosophy offer better guidance than organized religions most of the time."

Auden snorted and sent O'Neal a conspiratorial look. "Did I mention that art majors are the worst? They say things like *schools of philosophy* in regular conversation."

She gave Auden a half-cocked smile that sent heat straight downward. "I hope I get along as well with my roommate."

Len made an amused noise in the back of his throat. One that seemed to say, *you have no idea.*

Auden sent him a warning glance and then turned back to O'Neal. "Aiming for not wanting to murder each other is a good first step. Set the bar low."

"Got it." She held his gaze for a moment as if she wanted to say something else then turned back to her bookshelf.

Silence stretched for a long moment.

"So," Lennox said, slapping his thighs and standing up. "Looks like we're done. I'm going to bring these empty boxes out to the recycle bin, and then let's get that food."

"Yeah, sure," Auden said. "We'll meet you out front in a minute."

Lennox grabbed the boxes and gave him a little nod as he passed. "No rush."

Auden realized then that Len was making himself scarce so that he could talk to O'Neal alone. Clear the air. "Thanks."

Lennox headed out, whistling a tune that sounded suspiciously like Billy Idol's "Rebel Yell."

O'Neal watched Lennox go, tracking him like she was a scientist who'd discovered a new species, and then sat on the spot he had vacated. When she looked back to Auden, her blush was back. He sat down across from her in the desk chair.

"So thanks for this," she said, her hands together in her lap, her fingers turning the little silver ring on her left hand. His sister had the same kind. The two of them had been part of the same church purity ring ceremony when they'd turned twelve. The fact that she was still wearing it was a blatant reminder of why he and O'Neal needed to move past what had happened last summer and reset. "I know your mom probably gave you marching orders. But you didn't have to do this."

"She did," he said. "But that's not why I'm doing it. I wanted to help. I know this has got to be...a lot." He let out a breath. "Plus, it gives me a chance to say I'm sorry."

She met his gaze, surprise there. "Sorry? For what?"

He gave her a *come on now* look. "You know for what. For what happened last time we saw each other. I was way out of line."

She shrugged, the move tight instead of casual. "It wasn't your fault. I told you. I kissed you. My mistake, not yours."

"You started it, but I took it too far. I'm not sure what I was thinking. And I'm sorry. I hate that it was your first kiss." He rubbed a hand over the back of his head, the guilt rolling through him again. "I stole that milestone from you. I feel like shit for that. Your first kiss should be like a special thing."

"What? Like with the guy I'm supposed to marry?" she said, sarcasm heavy.

"No, I'm not your grandparents, but you know what I mean." He shrugged. "It should've been with some guy you were dating or really liked or whatever. A guy your own age, for starters."

"Auden," she said with a huff. "Stop being so dramatic. Yes, the whole thing ended up turning into an embarrassing and awkward moment, but I'm guessing that's pretty common for first kisses. And you're forgetting the other part of that day."

"The other part?"

"Yes. You're the reason I'm here. You gave me a push when I really, really needed one. I went home that day and filled out the application for Bennette." She grimaced. "Which is totally going to make me sound like a stalker. But I didn't do it because you were here. I did it because you were the first person to say, *why can't you?* And it gave me the courage I needed to do it."

Something tightened in his chest.

"And I don't know if it was the right call or not. I'm completely freaked out about what I'm doing," she said, giving him a stark look. "Like have almost called home to undo this twenty times today, but I haven't. And I haven't because I know I need this. I need to prove to myself and to my grandparents that I'm capable of being an adult and taking care of myself in the real world. That the minute I'm free, I'm not going to go on some wild bender or become another person."

"Of course, you're not," he said, meaning it.

"You don't know what it's like, to have this legacy following you around. My mom had a wild streak, and everyone thinks that's what got her killed. So maybe her daughter is destined to be the same way unless carefully monitored at all times. Like rebellion is genetic."

"You know that's crap, right?" he said. "Victim blaming at its finest? Like getting murdered was *her* fault."

"Does it matter? People think what they think. My grandparents think what they think." She blew out a frustrated breath. "I've never given anyone any reason to doubt me. I'm not sure what else I could do to prove that I'm not her. Until this, I've done every single thing they wanted me to do. What else do I have to do?"

There was a catch in her voice, a shine in her eyes.

He couldn't take seeing her that way. He got up and sat next to her on the bed, putting his arm around her shoulders, and then gave her a squeeze. Suddenly, all those thoughts he'd had about scaring her back home evaporated. "You don't have to prove anything to anyone, okay? Fuck everyone else's opinion."

Her head turned his way, a startled look there.

"I'm serious. Fuck 'em."

She laughed. "It's so weird hearing you curse. Your mother would have a fit."

He smiled. "The joys of living hours away." He lowered his arm and turned his body toward her. "Maybe you should try it."

She lifted her brows. "What?"

"Say the words." He grabbed her hand and manipulated her fingers until only her middle one was straight. He lifted her hand for her and met her gaze. "Say *fuck everyone else's opinion.*"

She wrinkled her nose. "Come on, Auden."

He grinned. "No, I'm serious. It can feel really good just to say it. Cursing is cathartic." He kept her hand in place so that she was flipping him off and tried to ignore how soft her skin felt against his. "Repeat after me. Fuck. Everyone. Else's. Opinion."

She licked her lips nervously, but there was a sparkle in her eyes. She held the eye contact. "Fuck everyone else's opinion."

Her voice was almost a whisper, but the words wound through him.

"Again," he encouraged. "Louder."

He watched as her throat worked, and then she straightened her spine. *"Fuck* everyone else's *fucking* opinion."

He laughed and released her hand. "Beautiful. How'd that feel?"

"Like a lightning bolt might strike me down," she admitted with a sheepish smile. "But also really good."

He peeked up at the ceiling. "No lightning bolt. I think God has bigger things to worry about than salty language."

She let out a breath. "Thanks."

"No problem. I know you can do this," he said. "You should be proud of yourself. Coming here took a lot of guts."

She gave him a wry look. "So you don't think I'm a *Felicity-*style stalker?"

"Noooo, because then I'd have to admit I've watched *Felicity.*"

"Oh, you can't hide that. Maya told me you totally got

hooked when she was bingeing all the retro teen dramas. I know your dark secrets, Auden Blake," she teased.

*Dark secrets.* A little warning bell sounded at that. He wanted to help O'Neal, but he needed to keep the boundaries clear. "Fine. I may have watched a *few* episodes. So let's clear the air. Did you come here because you think I'm your Ben and wanted to stalk me?"

She tilted her head, expression droll. "The kiss wasn't *that* good."

He laughed, relief filling him. "Ouch."

She smiled. "Their journalism program is, though. It's totally worth stalking."

"Good. We are stalker-free then." He stood, feeling lighter now that they'd talked, and cocked his head toward the door. "Ready to grab something to eat? Lennox is probably asking incoming freshmen if they have any snacks he could buy off them by now."

She laughed and stood, grabbing her keys and student ID off the desk next to her bed. "Let's go."

They wound their way through the hall, dodging people with boxes, and he found himself putting his hand on the small of her back to guide her through. He told himself he'd do the same for his sister in a crowd.

"So Lennox is a good guy?" O'Neal asked as they neared the exit.

"The best," he said without thinking. "And you don't have to worry about him hitting on you or anything."

"What?" she asked, sending him a confused look.

"He can be a flirt," he explained. "I told him you were off limits."

She stopped and turned to him, annoyance there. "What? Why?"

He winced inwardly. He should've kept his damn mouth shut. "Because Len can be a lot. And he's in grad school and you're a freshman. And you're Maya's friend. And just…so many reasons."

"Uh, hi," she said, tone as pointed as he'd ever heard her. "Last I checked, I was a grown person. You don't get to make those decisions for me."

He sighed, feeling like a jackass. "You're right. I don't. I'm sorry. But just…trust me on this one, okay? Advice from a friend. You're going to be experiencing a lot of new things here. Start slow. Lennox is…not that. He's graduate level in more things than his transcript."

Her eyes widened a little, and her throat worked as she swallowed, nervousness flickering in her expression. He'd gotten through. She started walking again. "Fine. I get what you're saying, and I wasn't even implying that I would *want* Lennox to flirt with me. I'm just—I'm tired of other people making decisions for me. I'm here to make my own choices. I don't need another person protecting me from the big, bad world."

He peeked over at her. "Message received."

She jutted out her chin. "Good."

Lennox was leaning against Auden's BMW when they made it to the parking lot. He smiled at the two of them. "Table for three then?"

"Yep," O'Neal said, the tremor in her voice giving her away. She was probably weaving all kinds of sordid stories about Lennox in her head now. But no matter what she could come up with, they wouldn't come close to the truth. "You guys lead the way. I don't know what's good around here."

Lennox's smile curved wider, and his gaze flicked to Auden's as he opened the car door for O'Neal. "We can definitely do that. We know all the best-kept secrets in town."

# CHAPTER THREE

*L*ennox loved playing poker. Any game where you could have a losing hand and still win big was his kind of game. His whole life had been an ongoing game of poker, a shit hand dealt to him from the start. But right now, watching Auden and O'Neal chat over burgers was as entertaining a poker game as he'd ever watched.

Auden was being Hometown Auden, the guy Lennox had first met when they'd gotten paired together as roommates. The rich kid from the small southern enclave. The upstanding young man who'd been bred to be exceedingly polite, God-fearing, and people-pleasing. Lennox was well aware that this side of Auden still existed when he went back home, but it was fascinating watching it in action.

Auden was trying to act like some kind of big brother, telling O'Neal the easiest routes to get to her classes, the best dining hall, explaining where the nearest church was—because, of course, he assumed sweet, sheltered O'Neal would want to be nowhere else on her Sunday mornings. Lennox had his doubts that someone who would sever a relationship with her family and give up all that old money to be here was looking to recreate the same life she'd had at home, but he didn't interrupt. He'd promised Auden he'd be good.

He definitely didn't want O'Neal bringing back info to Auden's sister. If Lennox did anything to jeopardize Auden's relationship with his family, Aud would never forgive him for that. Despite the differences he had with them, Auden loved his family and had a whole life waiting for him in his father's company when he got out of school. Blowing that up meant blowing up his future. Part of Lennox wished he'd do that. Then Auden wouldn't be leaving here at the end of this school year, but that wasn't his call to make.

He had a sneaking suspicion that Auden thought these years were just an experimental college phase and that when they were done, he'd return to where he came from, get a job, find a girl, and do the marriage, kids, and mansion thing his people did. Lennox pushed away the grim thought. They still had this year to have fun. Lennox still had time to prove to Auden that who he was here was who he was at his core.

And as he watched Auden laugh at something O'Neal said, he began to wonder if this pretty freshman could help with that. Her being here put Auden squarely straddling the border between his two lives. O'Neal might be the tipping point that made Auden fall to one side or the other. Based on the way Auden was looking at O'Neal right now, no one else would be able to tell that the guy wasn't thinking the most wholesome of thoughts. Auden was good at poker too. But Lennox knew his friend's tells. Auden's jaw kept flexing, and his fingers were curling and uncurling against the tabletop, like he was doing everything he could not to reach out and touch her in some way.

Lennox was riveted, watching his normally calm and collected friend struggle. This girl tugged on some string in Auden that he *really* didn't want tugged, some part of himself he didn't want to admit he had. The part of him that saw O'Neal's sweetness and naïveté and wanted to *ruin* it. To tear at it with his teeth.

Auden didn't want to admit that he was one of those guys all the people in O'Neal's life had warned her about.

Lennox had no such qualms. "How old are you, O'Neal?"

Her head turned his way, her blue eyes a little startled. Auden sent him a look that could've burned a fresh tattoo into Lennox's skin.

"Nineteen," she answered. "Why?"

He smiled his best innocent smile. "Just curious. Some freshmen come in at seventeen. It can restrict which clubs and bars around campus you can get into. Wanted to make a note for future reference in case you ever come out with us."

"Oh," she said, shifting in her chair, uncrossing and recrossing her legs. "I don't know if I'll be going to any clubs or bars, but yeah, nineteen. Had to repeat kindergarten, so I'm always a year older than my classmates."

"Ah, those ABCs can be tough," he said with a nod.

"O'Neal didn't fail it," Auden said, clearly annoyed.

Lennox lifted his palms. "I didn't mean—"

"No, it's fine." She had tucked her hands beneath the table and glanced at Auden. "My mom died when I was five. I missed a lot of school days that year."

Lennox frowned, taking in O'Neal's wary expression and feeling like a jackass. "I'm sorry. I didn't mean to bring up bad memories. I lost my mom young too. It sucks."

Her gaze flicked upward, meeting his, the unveiled empathy there catching him off guard. "I'm sorry for your loss, too, then. And yeah, it does. It sucks a lot."

She held the eye contact for a beat, and he found himself wanting to ask more questions. He'd been aware that O'Neal was beautiful from the start. He'd noted it, but lots of people were beautiful. Beautiful could be boring. He was more attracted to complicated. But something in her eyes belied the pretty, naïve church girl role he'd assigned to her in his head. There was depth in that gaze—pain, weariness, sadness. An old soul.

"Thanks," he said softly.

"Sure." A self-conscious smile touched her lips. "Sorry, didn't mean for lunch to take a dark turn." She sent Auden an affectionate look. "But thanks for defending my reputation. Can't have anyone thinking I didn't get straight As one year."

Auden winced. "Sorry. I wasn't thinking. Didn't mean to put you on the spot."

She tucked a lock of hair behind her ear. "It's okay. I'm used to everyone knowing my family history back home. I'm hoping for a clean slate here." She glanced at Lennox. "But Lennox doesn't look like a gossip."

Lennox leaned back in his chair and smirked, opening his arms. "I am a human vault."

"He is," Auden agreed. "He's nosy as hell, so don't feel obligated to answer anything you don't want to, but he won't be telling anyone else your business."

O'Neal took a sip of her iced tea and gave Lennox an evaluating look. "Good to know."

They finished up lunch, talk returning to casual things, and before Lennox knew it, they were dropping O'Neal back at her dorm.

"You sure you don't need anything else?" Auden asked, leaning out the driver's side window as O'Neal rounded the front of the car.

She stopped next to Len's side and crossed her arms like she was chilled. "I'm good. I should probably find my roommate and finish unpacking. Thanks for everything, though. It was nice to see a familiar face today." She leaned down and looked at Lennox. "And to meet a new one."

"Happy to be part of the welcoming committee," Lennox said.

"And I'll tell your mom and Maya that you were really help-ful," she said to Auden. "I'll make sure you get all the brownie points."

Auden laughed. "I didn't do it for the brownies. But seri-ously, text me if you need anything."

She straightened. "Will do."

"Good luck on your first day of classes," Lennox called out.

She gave them a little wave and then turned to head back to the dorm, the bun on top of her head bouncing with her purposeful stride and strands coming loose.

Auden watched her the whole time.

When she was a good distance away, he leaned back against the headrest, closed his eyes, and let out a long, beleaguered breath.

Lennox had pressed a knuckle to his lips, but now he lowered his hand and let his chuckle escape. "*I didn't do it for the brownies?*"

Auden flipped him off without lifting his head.

"Man, your wholesome act is *so* entertaining to watch. What a perfect big brother for her to count on," he teased. "One who definitely wasn't picturing her naked at any point today."

Auden turned toward him, a defeated expression on his face. "Off-limits."

"Hey, I was on perfect behavior today," he said, affronted.

"No, I mean for me too. I'm reminding myself." There was a tired note in his voice. "She's got at least a minor crush on me—or at least on the guy she thinks I am. She'd say yes if I asked her out. She trusts me. It wouldn't take much to get her to sleep with me, especially since she's feeling a little rebellious. I remember what that felt like when I first got here—that first real taste of freedom."

Lennox's mouth hitched up at the corner. "I remember too. I took full advantage of your blossoming rebellion."

"But she's not me. I didn't walk in here innocent. My parents had rules and made me go to church and all, but I dated. I knew how to sneak out. I'd had sex. O'Neal...she's basically been in lockdown her whole life. A PG-13 movie was considered scandalous at her house."

Lennox rubbed his jaw, watching the dorm entrance door where O'Neal had gone in. "Damn. Sounds like the girl could use some fun. Maybe you *should* make a move. I bet she'd be real good at following *your* rules and saying *yes, sir.*"

Auden groaned. "No fucking way. No kink. She can't know anything about that stuff. I don't need that shit getting back to my family, especially Maya. And even if I went vanilla with her, if this is some kind of virgin fetish for me, then once I sleep with her, the appeal will be gone. I'm not looking to be someone's boyfriend, especially not someone from back home. And I won't use her like that."

"I know." Neither of them was going to manipulate someone into bed. If kink had a religious doctrine, it was the *safe, sane, consensual* rule. "But are you sure it's just a virgin thing? I mean, I get it. Introducing someone to things can be hot as fuck. Can be a power trip too."

Auden sent him a *you would know* look, and Lennox's blood heated remembering how delicious it'd been when he'd first given Auden a peek into his tastes. When Auden had accidentally walked in on Lennox watching a very particular type of porn...and then hadn't left the room.

"But are you sure that what you're feeling isn't something specific *to her?*" Lennox asked. "You two have history."

He snorted. "History? What? Sharing popcorn while we played Scrabble with my sister? Teaching her to swim at summer camp? That's childhood history. She was always just *my little sister's friend.* I don't even really know her as an adult."

"Maybe you should, then," Lennox said with a shrug. "Maybe that will dampen some of the appeal. Right now you're seeing her as a representation of something. If you get to know her as a real person, you'll probably realize she's just another pretty undergrad. Campus is full of them."

He gave him a skeptical look. "You think?"

"Sure. You know, like idolizing a celebrity, and then you see some candid tabloid shot of them bloated and passed out at a bar or a video of them being rude to waitstaff." He snapped his fingers. "The fantasy is shattered."

Auden looked back toward the dorm. "Maybe you're right."

Lennox smiled. "I usually am."

Auden rolled his eyes and started the car.

"Good. Then it's settled. We'll be O'Neal's honorary welcoming committee and ease her into college life." Lennox pulled out his phone. "Text me her number."

"No way," Auden said, backing out of the parking spot. "You don't need her number."

"What?" Lennox asked, tone full of wide-eyed innocence. "Too soon for dick pics?"

The deadly glare Auden sent him made Lennox laugh. This was going to be a blast.

# CHAPTER FOUR

*O*'Neal pulled up short when she swung open the door
to her dorm room and found a girl with pink-streaked
black hair and clear-framed glasses sitting on the other bed. She
had earbuds in her ears and a hardcover book open in her lap.

The girl looked up, apparently sensing a disturbance in the
force, and smiled. "Oh. Hey." She tugged the earbuds out.
"O'Neal?"

"Uh, yeah," she said, shutting the door behind her. "I'm
guessing you're Quyen?"

"Yep. Yay, you're here!" She tossed her book to the side and
stood. "Welcome, fellow inmate."

O'Neal smiled at the girl's genuine enthusiasm and set her
keys on the desk. "Thanks."

"I'm so glad you're here." She tightened her spiky ponytail
and rocked to the balls of her feet like she was a moment away
from literally hopping with excitement. "I tried to go out to the
lounge to meet people, but everyone is paired up with their
roommate already like they've exchanged vows or blood oaths
or something. I felt like the girl without a prom date. And I've

*been* the girl without a prom date, and I definitely am not ready to repeat that experience."

O'Neal laughed lightly. "Sorry about that. I didn't see you around when I moved in so I left to grab some lunch." She put out her hand. "You're officially paired off, roomie. But maybe let's wait on the blood oath."

"Sweet." Quyen shook her hand like they were making a business deal. "But no blood oath? Man, I can't believe I spent that money on the upgraded ceremonial knife." She put her hands on her hips. "I always do that, you know? Go just a little too far, put in a little too much effort. I guess I should probably cancel our appointment for matching tattoos as well."

O'Neal snorted, a little nervous and overwhelmed, but glad she at least had a roommate who wanted to be friendly and who had a sense of humor. "We'll work up to that."

"Hashtag roommate goals," Quyen said with a wink and then grabbed her phone from her bed. "I know this is going to sound weird, but can we take a selfie?"

"Uh...sure?"

"Awesome, thanks." She stepped next to O'Neal and lifted her phone. "Smile and look responsible!"

*Look responsible?* The phone clicked before O'Neal could puzzle that one out.

"Perfect," Quyen said as she analyzed the photo. "I can now text this to my parents and reassure them that I am not rooming with a boy. They saw your name and thought there'd been a mix-up."

"Ah. Gotcha. I get that a lot. Did your parents move you in today?"

Quyen plopped back down on her bed, sitting cross-legged, and brushed her bangs away from her face. "Yeah, bright and early. They like to be first for everything. Told me if we didn't get here by seven sharp, I'd get the bad side of the room." She gave her a droll look. "It's a dorm room. There are no good sides of the room, but at least we beat the crowd."

"You could've had whatever side you wanted anyway. I'm not picky." O'Neal sat on her bed, trying not to marvel at the bright pink streaks in Quyen's hair. Her grandmother would've had a heart attack if O'Neal had even put in highlights.

"I totally cared what side, but I would've pretended not to while coercing you into letting me have it," she said brightly. "I'm both nice and crafty. You've been warned."

"Noted."

"And I saw you earlier, I just didn't realize you belonged to this room or I would've said hi. You were with two guys." She glanced toward the door. "Were they your brothers or something?"

"Brothers?" O'Neal shook her head. "No, just a family friend who's a senior here and his roommate. My grandparents couldn't make it up here so Auden and Lennox were helping me out."

Quyen gave her a conspiratorial look. "Well, you definitely had the hottest help. I mean, wow. Glad they're not your brothers."

O'Neal's face warmed. This was new territory—openly talking about how hot some guy was. She'd rarely talked about boys with Maya. It was like an unwritten rule that since O'Neal couldn't date, Maya wouldn't regale her with stories of the dating life. Not that Maya had dated all that much anyway. "Yeah, they're...nice."

"Nice? *Girl.* The guy with the ink?" She fanned herself. "Yes, please."

O'Neal rolled her lips together, remembering the focused way Lennox had looked at her over lunch, like he could see right into her head. He was equal parts fascinating and terrifying. When he'd asked how old she was, her mind had gone to places it shouldn't have. She'd felt like a mouse being teased by a very clever cat, but of course, he'd only been asking to see if she'd be able to go places with them. He was only being friendly.

O'Neal cleared her throat. "Lennox is…scary hot."

"Oh my God," Quyen said, pointing at her. "That's the perfect description. He's one of those guys you know is like totally out of the realm of possibility and would probably be way too much anyway. But it's fun to think about." She leaned back against the wall. "For real life, I prefer my guys nerdy and awkward. I like a level playing field."

O'Neal laughed. "Level playing field?"

She shrugged. "You know, some guy who's kind of in the same place as I am. I don't want to be with a guy who I have to always be on my toes with. I want to be able to say something stupid and not feel like an idiot, you know? Because he's being awkward too."

O'Neal considered her reasoning. "That makes a lot of sense."

Quyen reached over to her desk, grabbing an already open bag of brownie-flavored M&Ms. She lifted the bag. "You want?"

She lifted a hand, her stomach still a little queasy from the excitement of the day. "I'm good."

"So what's your type?" Quyen asked before popping a few candies in her mouth.

"My type?"

"Yeah. We should get this out of the way now so that when we meet all the guys we're definitely going to meet here—because you and I are going to become super best friends obviously—we can figure out which of us is going to go for which dude."

O'Neal laughed again, Quyen's ease and openness like a ball of sunshine after her mostly stormy day. "Um, right, my type." *Auden.* She reached back and adjusted the pillow behind her back, searching for a non-weird answer. What would a guy on her level of playing field be like? A monk? "I haven't dated much, so I'm still figuring it out."

"Oh man, I'm being a total jerk about this, making assumptions, aren't I?" she said looking mildly horrified. "I mean, you may not even be into guys and I'm just blabbering on about it. Look, you don't have to share your preferences with me. Unless you want to, but you don't have to, you know? I totally support whatever part of the rainbow you're on. Love is love."

Quyen had said all the words so fast that it took O'Neal a second to process what she was implying. When it registered, O'Neal felt her neck flushing. At her old school, things like this would only be discussed in whispers. She'd heard that some churches had become more open-minded about LGBTQ relationships, but hers had not, and St. Mary's had no students who were out. It was implied that it wasn't okay to live that kind of lifestyle.

O'Neal had never felt comfortable with that stance, but she also had never spoken openly about the topic. "I'm not…I like guys. But my grandparents were really strict. I haven't had a chance to find out my type yet." She lifted her hand, figuring she might as well get it over with, and showed her purity ring. "I come from a place where Love Is Love is not taught. True Love Waits is."

Quyen's brows went up. "Oh. Wow. So have I already offended you like eight different ways?"

"No, I came here against my family's wishes. I'm supposed to be in a private religious college," she admitted, hoping this new information wouldn't put Quyen in self-edit mode around her. "So I'm completely out of my comfort zone and will probably out-awkward you on a regular basis, but you don't have to watch what you say around me. I came here to experience new things and to find out where I stand on things instead of my stance being told to me."

Quyen's lips curved into a pleased smile. "That is super

badass." She did a little fast clap with her hands. "Yay. We're going to rock our freshman year, O'Neal. One awkward step at a time. I'm glad we got paired up."

O'Neal's shoulders sagged in relief and she smiled. "Me too."

"Good. Now get your schedule out. Your friends threw me off and made me fail the Bechdel test. That nonsense stops now."

"The Bechdel test?"

She grabbed her phone. "Yes, two women only talking about guys, like they're the only worthwhile topic of conversation. I'm ashamed of myself, frankly. I blame the tattooed dude's hotness. It momentarily blinded me." She turned her phone screen toward O'Neal, showing her schedule. "Let's see if we have any classes together, and then I want to know everything about you."

O'Neal snorted softly. "That might be a boring list."

Quyen tilted her head, giving her an evaluating look. "Not a chance. I can feel it. You've got stories."

She didn't. Not really. But maybe she was at the start of one. The thought made her feel lighter inside.

COFFEE, COFFEE, COFFEE. *I NEED COFFEE.* O'NEAL WAS MAKING UP A song in her head about her desperate need for caffeine as she walked out of her American History class when her phone buzzed in her pocket. She shifted her backpack and grabbed her phone, assuming Quyen was probably texting her with the same need. They'd met up yesterday at one of the coffee kiosks on campus. But that wasn't whose name was lighting up her phone.

> Auden: We're going to do a movie and pizza at our place tonight. Wanna join?

Her step halted, and she stared at the phone, unable to

process the words for a moment. Movie. Pizza. Tonight. *Auden was inviting her over?*

That seemed out of left field. She hadn't seen him since the day she'd moved in. He'd checked in with her once by text, but she figured he'd considered his obligation to her over. He had a whole life here—classes, friends, swim team. None of that involved babysitting a freshman. But she should've known better. The Blake family had always been there for her. Auden's mom was probably calling him and making sure he hadn't bailed on her.

> O'Neal: You know I released you from any and all obligations, right? I've survived almost a whole week with no babysitter at all. I've even managed to clothe and feed myself.

> Auden: *eyeroll emoji* Don't be a brat. I'm not trying to babysit you. I'll be babysitting Len and that's enough work. I just know you like movies and every college student appreciates free pizza

Free pizza *would* be nice. She'd eaten every meal in the dining hall this week because that was what was included in her scholarship, and their pizza tasted like it was made of plastic and sadness. But going over to Auden's place when only he and his roommate would be there? The idea sent old ingrained thoughts rising to the surface.

She hadn't been allowed to be alone with boys her own age since she was twelve because "a girl shouldn't put herself in that position." But the thought of it being dangerous to be with Auden was laughable. Yes, she'd once kissed him, but that had been a moment of insanity. This wasn't a date. Lennox would be there too. This was simply friends having her over for a movie, trying to be welcoming.

Her thumbs hovered over the screen. Finally, she shoved away the looping thoughts.

> O'Neal: Sounds good. Can I bring anything?

> Auden: A quart of vodka, a keg, and some fireworks

She blinked at the screen.

> Auden: Kidding. Just bring what you like to drink. You can bring your roommate if you want

She bit her lip, staring at the screen. He was giving her an out. She wouldn't have to break a "rule" if she brought Quyen with her. But suddenly, she wanted nothing more than to prove to herself that this was a dumb rule.

> O'Neal: Thanks. She has plans but I'll be there.

> Auden: Cool. I'll send you the address. It's a building right off campus. See you around 7

O'Neal didn't realize she was smiling like a fool until some girl passing her on the sidewalk gave her a strange look. She quickly straightened her expression and tucked her phone back into her pocket.

As she made her way to the coffee kiosk and then the library to work on homework, her step felt lighter and a rush of pure, unadulterated freedom moved through her. She'd made a choice, and no one was going to stop her from going. No one was going to shame her about it or make her feel guilty. This was why she'd come here. She didn't want to dismiss all the things she'd learned growing up. She knew some of those things were useful, some of them would protect her from bad situations. But when your life was filled with nothing but rules, it became harder and harder to decipher which ones were smart and which were ridiculous. Her gauge for that had been broken because she'd had no real choice but to obey them all.

Maybe it was time to take a hard look at each one.

When she arrived at the library and found an unoccupied table in the philosophy section, she sat down and pulled out a fresh notebook. She wrote a number one on the first line, and for the next hour, she wrote down every rule her grandparents or the church had expected her to follow. She put stars next to the ones that were obviously good advice. *Don't steal. Don't murder. Be kind to others.* She drew a line through the ones that didn't feel right to her. *Love is only between a man and a woman. Only men can lead the church.* But the ones that were hazier, she left with no mark at all. When she wrote down *Don't be alone with boys* she put a checkmark next to it. She would mark the ones she'd tried and make a decision afterward on if it was good advice or not.

The list was almost five pages long when she finished it, but she felt like a weight had been lifted off of her. Seeing it all in black and white made her feel better about her decision to come here than she had all week. This was not about rebellion or hurting her family. This was her running an experiment.

She wanted to prove that she could do this and go back to her family and say—*see, I can handle myself. I didn't go wild. I didn't become my mother. I didn't get pregnant like she did. I didn't end up dead after some party with three men's DNA all over me like she did.*

*I can live in the real world and not let you down.*

She leaned back in the hard library chair and rubbed the spot between her eyes. Bad thoughts about her mother made her stomach hurt. She couldn't deny the facts of the case, but it still felt wrong, thinking about her mom that way. She didn't remember much of her, but what she did remember was good. Her mom had given great hugs. She'd read her bedtime stories at night. And before she'd left to get her degree at Bennette, she'd told O'Neal that she would call her every morning before school. And she had. Until one day she hadn't.

O'Neal had trouble wrapping her head around that version of her mom that she had known and the version those cold case shows painted. That her mother was going out all the time. That she was sleeping with multiple men. They said *party girl.* They meant *slut.* She'd overheard her grandparents using the terms *wild* and *loose* when they didn't think she could hear them.

She leaned forward and opened her notebook again. At the end of her rules and beliefs list, she turned to the next page and added one more thing she needed to work out in this experiment. The thing she knew her grandparents believed. *My mom was reckless and was punished for her behavior.*

She hated seeing the words, but they were important ones. She wanted to know the truth. She glanced around, wondering if her mom had studied here, in this building. She could've sat at this very table. The men she'd been seeing might still live here. Answers could be here. An idea came to her.

Maybe she could do a little investigating. Ask questions she'd never been able to ask. If she was going to be a journalist, maybe this would be her first assignment.

She closed the notebook and shoved it into her backpack. She would have to give this more thought later.

Right now, she needed to get back to the dorm and change. It was time to start marking items off of her list. She had a movie night to attend.

# CHAPTER FIVE

*O*'Neal parked on the street in front of the pale blue refurbished Victorian her navigation app had led her to. Seeing Auden's BMW in the driveway at the side of the house sent a dart of anxiety through her, but at least she'd found the right spot. Not giving herself time to chicken out, she got out of the car, grabbing her grocery bag on the way, and looked up at the house. Auden was definitely living better than she was in the dorms. She texted him that she was there, and he replied instantly.

> Auden: Side staircase. We're on the second floor

As she made her way toward the stairs, Auden stepped out onto the second-story porch and leaned against the railing, smiling down at her and looking like a dream in his black track pants and a blue Bennette swim team T-shirt, his light brown hair wind-blown. Man, maybe she *was Felicity*-ing him.

"Hey, freshman," he called out, a teasing note in his voice.

"Ugh." She reached the top of the stairs and gave him a look. "I finally get rid of Shaq, and you give me a new nickname."

He looked completely unrepentant. "You know when you get a nickname in sports, it's a sign of respect."

"Uh-huh." She arched a brow at him. "I bet that depends on the nickname."

He laughed and took the grocery bag from her. "True. But *freshman* isn't an insult, just a statement of fact." He peeked inside. "Ooh, ice cream. And Oreos. I told you that you didn't need to bring anything."

"Movie nights with no dessert are sad movie nights. And everything is better with ice cream."

"Ice cream?" Lennox leaned out the doorway, sending O'Neal a smile that could've melted the ice cream in its carton.

"And cookies," Auden added, handing the bag to Lennox.

Lennox peeked inside. "Nice."

"I figured vanilla was safe," she added. "I didn't know what y'all liked."

Lennox made a sound in the back of his throat, some sort of half-laugh half-choke, and then smiled toward Auden. "Vanilla is a good place to start. Then you can add whatever kind of extra flavors you want."

Auden rolled his eyes and then turned back toward O'Neal. "Come on in. Pizza should be here any minute. Len, get the ice cream into the freezer."

Lennox headed inside with the bag, and O'Neal followed.

"Welcome to our humble abode," Auden said.

O'Neal stepped into the main room, which was painted all white and had a mishmash of furniture, living room stuff on the left, a small dining table on the right, a drafting-style desk that she assumed was Len's. The floors were well-worn wood, and things looked surprisingly clean for two college guys. But what caught her eye was a wall in the living room that was striped with clotheslines. Postcard-sized black-and-white drawings hung from them and fluttered in the draft coming in from the door.

She walked toward the postcards to get a better look as Auden shut the door. Her gaze scanned over the drawings—a woman's face, a bird stretching its wings, a decrepit barn—then her attention landed on a postcard at the end of one of the lines. It was of a bare-chested man sleeping, his face turned away, hair falling across his face, the sheets draped low over his waist, barely concealing what was beneath. The lines of the drawing were so intricate and precise, so lifelike, that she almost expected the man to roll over and look at her.

"Lennox keeps the place classy with his art wall."

O'Neal startled slightly, having not heard Auden walk up behind her. "They're beautiful."

"Yeah." He touched the clothesline, making it bounce a little. "He carries these cards everywhere and sketches when something catches his attention."

Her gaze lingered on the man in bed, awareness dawning and awkwardness winding through her. Lennox drew what he saw. Now she knew why she'd been most captured by this one. It was Auden caught in sleep.

"He's really talented," she said, turning around so quickly she almost bumped into Auden.

"He is," he said with a nod. "And prolific. The wall is ever-changing. When he draws something new, he just tosses out an old one and replaces it."

She gasped. "Like *in the trash?*"

Lennox stepped out of the kitchen. "Not in the trash. I don't care if they do end up there. I'm sure most do. But I like the idea of ephemeral art."

"Ephemeral," she said, leaning against the back of the couch.

The doorbell rang, and Auden turned. "I got it. O'Neal, feel free to tell him you don't want an art lesson."

She waved off Auden. "No, I'm curious."

Lennox smiled and came over to her, looking toward the art wall. "Usually the term ephemeral is applied to art created in

nature that eventually washes away or to a one-time perfor-
mance or something. Art that is only there for a moment in
time and then disappears. But I'm experimenting with the idea
with my drawings. So I'll leave them places. On a park bench,
on a table at a restaurant, on the floor of a classroom. Or I'll give
them away to friends and strangers and never ask what they're
going to do with them."

"But you could sell these," she said, gazing at the wall again.
"They're really...captivating."

Lennox gave her a little smile, looking surprisingly humble.
"Thanks. But I like the idea that they'll only exist for a limited
amount of time. It's how life is. You only get to experience the
good stuff, the beautiful stuff for a tiny sliver of time. That
perfect sunset. A childhood friendship. A first kiss. But those
moments are there and then they're gone, slipping through your
fingers whether you like it or not. So you have to appreciate the
beauty when it's in front of you and be thankful you had the
experience instead of being sad you can't keep it."

The words drifted over her, landing softly but making her
feel heavy.

He laughed under his breath. "And soon, I'm going to sound
like some inspirational quote on a T-shirt. *Don't be sad it's over,
be happy you were there.* Ugh. Sorry. Auden's right about art
students. We're insufferable."

"No," she said, looking at him. "I think there's something
really beautiful about your art being temporary. Like this might
be the only time I ever see these drawings. It makes me want to
look longer."

His pale green eyes held her gaze for a moment like he was
trying to figure something out, then he smiled. "Well, you can
pick your favorite and take it with you when you leave."

"Oh, no, you don't have to do that," she said, shaking her
head.

He tucked his hands in the pockets of his hoodie and

leaned in a little. "The only payment required is that you promise to get rid of it at some point. Leave it somewhere."

The door shut, startling O'Neal from the quiet moment with Lennox, and Auden joined them, carrying three pizza boxes. "Y'all ready to pick a movie?"

O'Neal eyed the stack of food in his arms and laughed. "How many people did you invite over?"

Auden gave her an innocent look. "Wait, are you planning to eat pizza too?" His lips curved. "Kidding. Top one's yours. Pepperoni and all the olives."

The spicy scent of pepperoni wafted her way. "A pizza a person? Are we having some sort of eating contest?"

"We're growing boys," Lennox said, taking the boxes and heading to the couch.

She huffed. "It's exceptionally unfair that you guys can eat like this and still look..." She realized she'd walked herself into awkward land a few words too late.

Lennox grinned and set the boxes on the coffee table. "Still look like what?"

She glanced back and forth between the two of them and then rolled her eyes, trying to play it off. "Like the freshman fifteen is a myth."

"I swim for hours every day," Auden said with a shrug. "I'm almost obligated to eat a whole pizza."

Lennox sank into an armchair and propped his feet on the corner of the coffee table. "And I just wake up this way."

"I hate you both," she declared.

"Don't know why. Your body's perfect," Lennox said matter-of-factly.

She made a choked sound.

"*Len*," Auden said, annoyance edging his tone.

Len shrugged. "What? Just stating a fact. You've got a great body. And it'd still be great with the freshman fifteen or twenty or whatever. Thinness is a social construct. Enjoy food for the sensual pleasure that it is."

Her face was getting hot. She knew Len was making a point, not flirting, but she still didn't know what to do with the comment. She jutted her thumb toward the kitchen. "I'm going to grab the drinks. What do y'all want?"

"I'll come with," Auden said. "Since we have a lady present, we should probably break out the paper plates and some napkins and not lick grease from our fingers."

"How civilized," Lennox said. "I'll take a water."

O'Neal followed Auden to the kitchen, which was through a door past the dining table. The space was small but functional, clearly added after the original house had been built.

"Sorry about Len," Auden said as he opened a cabinet. "He says stuff sometimes that…well, he just doesn't have much of a filter. He didn't mean anything by it."

"It's fine," she said quickly. "I mean, it's kind of…nice. The thought that everyone's body is perfect however it is. You think he really sees people that way? Or is he blowing intellectual smoke and only dates supermodels?"

Auden looked over, his gaze flicking down the length of her so quickly she almost missed it. He turned back to the cabinet and cleared his throat. "Len's much more interested in what makes people tick than their body type. That's what flips his switches." He sniffed and shook his head. "And why the hell am I telling you this? Don't worry about what Len likes or doesn't like. Remember what I said."

"Yeah, yeah, yeah," she said with a flick of her hand. "I wasn't fishing for dating advice. Just curious." She opened the fridge to grab the drinks. On the top shelf, there were three kinds of soda, bottled waters, the tangerine LaCroix she'd brought in with her groceries, and beer. She glanced at Auden. "What should I grab for you?"

"Water's fine."

She straightened, her hand braced on the fridge door. "You know, if you guys usually drink beer with your pizza, you don't need to change that because I'm here. I'm not going to like, tell on you or something."

He frowned. "I don't think that."

She gave him a *don't lie to me* look.

He sighed. "Okay, fine. I do feel a little weird drinking in front of you. I don't want you worrying about my immortal soul while we watch a movie."

Their church didn't prohibit alcohol, but she'd been taught by her grandparents that drinking was a gateway to sinful behavior, so she understood why he might think she'd judge him for it. But it made her realize that if she was going to hang out with Auden at all, she needed to be more open with him about what she was going through. She closed the fridge door.

"I think we need to talk."

He leaned back against the counter and set the paper plates aside. "Okay."

She took a breath. "I know how I must look to you."

"How you look." A wrinkle appeared between his brows.

"Yeah, like the naïve girl from your church who's going to faint at the mere thought of breaking any rule," she said.

He remained silent, neither confirming nor denying.

"I'm not going to lie," she went on, mustering up the courage to have this conversation. "This is all very new for me. But I'm also not a child. I'm not at school with your sister because I *wanted* to experience life outside that walled garden. I'm... feeling out where I stand on things. Investigating. Making my own decisions."

"Where you stand on things," he said, his gaze intent on her, like he was trying to figure out what she *wasn't* saying in between all things she was managing to say aloud.

"Yes, like right now, I'm not tempted to have one of those beers. But I also don't care if you and Lennox drink. So my stance on beer is apparently—not for me at this moment but fine for those who want to." She tilted her chin upward. "And my grandparents had a rule about not being alone with guys. I've clearly decided to break that one tonight."

Auden gave her a look of warning. "Rules like that last one need to be on a case-by-case basis."

She narrowed her eyes at his firm tone. "What do you mean?"

"Being alone with me is fine. You're safe with me," he said, pushing off the counter and coming a little closer. "But if some new dude you meet at school asks you to come over to hang out with just his guy friends like this, bring a friend with you."

She shifted and crossed her arms, uncomfortable.

"Your grandparents assume every guy has bad intentions. They don't. But they don't all have *good* intentions either," he said, expression serious. "You need to be smart about it and protect yourself. Usually, an extreme rule has a grain of truth worth paying attention to at the heart of it. At least that's what I've found."

"Like which ones?" she asked.

"Like drinking, for instance," he said. "Drinking a little can be fun or relaxing. But too much and you make stupid decisions or get yourself in bad situations. So if you ever decide to drink, drink around people you trust, make sure someone sober is driving, and never leave your drink unattended because people can slip stuff into it."

She rubbed her arms as goosebumps prickled. The information wasn't news to her but was a stark reminder that some of the things her grandparents had warned her about had some scary truth to them.

"I'm not trying to freak you out," he said gently. "But we came from a black-and-white world. This world is gray. In some ways, the extreme rules are easier because there's no room for error. If you're never allowed to drink or be around a guy, you never have to worry about someone slipping something into your drink. But it also means that you miss out on the good parts of having fun with friends, going out, dating, and all the stuff that goes along with that." He shrugged. "The price for this kind of freedom is that there aren't always clear answers, and you'll make some mistakes along the way." He smiled. "Ask me how I know drinking too much leads to stupid decisions."

She smirked. "What happened?"

"It involves waking up freshman year on the soccer field wearing the head of the Bennette Bears mascot and nothing else."

She put her hand over her mouth, snort-laughing. "Oh my God."

His hazel eyes were sparkling with humor. "Wasn't pretty. I think I traumatized the groundskeeper. Landed myself the nickname the Bare-Assed Bear for the remainder of freshman year."

"Your sister would die if she heard that story," she said, still laughing.

"Which is why you definitely won't tell her," he said with a cocked brow.

She sobered at that. "I wouldn't. Seriously. What happens at Bennette, stays at Bennette."

His dimple appeared, making her stomach flip-flop. "Good. And if that's the case, grab me a beer and a water for Len."

"No beer for him?" she asked, turning back to the fridge, thankful for a way to hide the heat in her face.

"He doesn't drink. Too much of a control freak."

"He doesn't seem like a control freak." She grabbed the drinks and bumped the fridge shut with her hip.

"You don't know him that well yet," he said, napkins and plates in his hands. "Trust me."

She nodded. She did trust Auden. The nerves she'd been feeling since she arrived started to settle a bit.

They went back into the living room, where Lennox was

already working on a slice of pizza and scrolling through the streaming services. Auden took a spot on the couch, and O'Neal was left with the other side of the couch, the one nearest Lennox's chair. She handed out the drinks, then grabbed a plate and a slice of pizza and settled in.

"So what are we watching?" she asked before folding her pizza slice and taking a bite.

Lennox looked her way. "We play movie roulette."

"We're not doing that tonight," Auden said, twisting off the cap of his beer. "We can let O'Neal pick."

She looked back and forth between the two of them and swallowed her bite. "Wait. What's movie roulette?"

"It's nothing," Auden said, sending Len a look.

"Oh, it's not nothing." Lennox set down his slice and leaned forward, bracing his arms on his thighs like he was ready to tell a story. "It's Auden's super nerdy system for movie watching."

O'Neal glanced at Auden, who was studiously focusing on dipping his pizza into a container of ranch dressing. He clearly didn't want this discussed, so she turned back to Lennox. "Tell me everything."

Lennox grinned, delighted. "About two years ago, Mr. Film Geek decided that he wanted to make a movie bucket list of all the 'best of' lists. Best movies of all time. Best comedies. Best horror. Oscar winners. That kind of thing."

"I knew you liked movies, but I didn't know you were a film buff," she said to Auden and he shrugged.

"He's minoring in film studies actually," Lennox offered.

The revelation sent a dart of surprise through her. All she'd heard from Maya was that Auden was majoring in business so he could work at his father's company. Film studies seemed far outside of that realm, but maybe he was just doing it for fun.

"And so Auden made this enormously long list and put it in a spreadsheet," Lennox went on, "because the man *loves* a fucking spreadsheet."

Auden snorted.

"And now for movie nights, we use a number randomizer app. Whatever number comes up corresponds to a movie on the list. We're obligated to watch whatever comes up. No vetoing," Lennox said. "Even if it's an incredibly boring old western that should've never won any awards ever."

Auden sent him an affronted look. "It wasn't *that* bad."

Lennox gave O'Neal a meaningful stare and mouthed, "So. Bad."

She laughed. "That sounds really fun actually. If that's what you usually do, I'm game. I don't care what we watch."

"She's game, Auden," Lennox said, leaning over the arm of his chair and grabbing a laptop from the lower shelf of the side table. "Let's pull up the list."

Auden set his plate aside and shook his head. "It's a bad idea. We don't know what's going to come up. I'm not going to torture O'Neal with my project."

Lennox ignored him and opened the laptop, bringing up the list. He handed O'Neal his phone. "Here, you do the honor of the randomization. Just press the go button."

O'Neal looked down at the phone. There were four red boxes where numbers would appear. "All right, here goes." She pressed the button and watched as the number popped up. "And the winner is…number four hundred and seventy-six."

Lennox chewed his lip in concentration, scrolling through the spreadsheet. "Looks like tonight we will be watching… drumroll, please…the 1987 classic, *Fatal Attraction.*"

"The hell we will," Auden said.

The outburst caught O'Neal off guard, and her attention snapped toward him. "What's wrong? I thought you couldn't veto in this game."

"It's violent," Auden said.

She made an exasperated sound. "So? I assume if we rule out all violent movies, that's going to really shorten the list."

"And rated R," he added.

"Um, hi," she said with a little wave. "I'm nineteen."

"Yeah, Aud," Lennox chimed in. "She passed R-rated legal age years ago."

Auden sent Lennox a quelling look. "That's not the point. *You know* that's not the point."

"Then what is the point?" Lennox asked, a *poke the bear* tone in his voice.

O'Neal looked back and forth between them, confused by the tension.

Auden's jaw twitched. "The *point* is I'm not inviting my baby sister's friend over to watch a movie and then make her sit with two older guys while we watch what is basically an erotic thriller." He turned to O'Neal, tense expression softening. "Pick another number."

*Erotic thriller.* O'Neal swallowed hard. "Is it a good movie?"

Auden frowned. "There's sex on-screen with nudity. It will make you uncomfortable."

"That's not what I asked," she said, feeling bold.

"It got a pile of Oscar nominations and is considered a classic eighties thriller," he said, a frustrated note in his voice. "But that's also not the point."

"What *is* the point?" She shifted her body toward him, fully annoyed now. "To protect me?"

"Yes," he said like it was the most obvious answer in the world. "You're not ready for this kind of movie. You're…"

"What?" she challenged. "What am I, Auden?"

He raked a hand through his hair, frustration all over his face. "A babe in the goddamned woods, okay? A girl who doesn't know what she doesn't know. A virgin with a purity ring who doesn't realize that watching people fuck on-screen while hanging out with two guy friends is going to be really, really uncomfortable."

She gasped at the harsh words.

The chair squeaked as Lennox shifted in his seat. "Hey, let's take it down a notch, all right? Aud, you didn't need to go there. O'Neal..."

She turned to face Lennox, her heartbeat quickening from a combination of anger and embarrassment.

His expression was sympathetic. "Look, Aud clearly feels protective over you. I think his concern is coming from a good place even though he's being *a major dick* about it," he said, sending a pointed look at Auden and then focusing back on her. "But I believe in letting people make their own decisions. You're an adult who can make up her own mind. He's right. This movie will probably make you feel things. There's sex and it's not the sweet kind."

Sweating. She was sweating.

"But," he went on, "if you want to try out that kind of movie, you're safe here with us. To feel awkward. Or embarrassed. Or turned on."

"*Len,*" Auden said, his voice sharp with warning. "What the hell?"

O'Neal couldn't speak. Her mouth had gone dry.

"To tell us to stop the movie if it's too much," Lennox continued, ignoring Auden. "To ask questions. I have literally zero shame about any of this stuff. I'm an open book. So if you want to watch it, knowing you don't have to be cool about it, that's your decision. If you don't, that's fine too, and we can pick another movie."

She nodded and tried to swallow as she turned to look at Auden. He was staring at the TV screen, his jaw set, his skin a little flushed. She wet her parched lips. "If I don't know what I don't know, how will I ever learn anything if I don't do something different than what I've always done? Someone has to be willing to show me the things I don't know about."

Auden closed his eyes like he was pained.

"I want to watch the movie," she declared.

There was a long moment of silence, a standoff.

She won.

"*Fine.*" Auden got up and grabbed the remote. "If there's a hell, I'm definitely going there."

He wouldn't look at her.

He found the movie and hit Play.

# CHAPTER SIX

*a*uden didn't make it twenty minutes into the movie before he was scrambling for the remote. But in his rush, the damn thing slid off the side table, and he had to get up to grab it, cursing under his breath the whole way. Meanwhile, Michael Douglas was ripping Glenn Close's panties off and fucking her on a kitchen counter. Auden hit pause right as Douglas put his mouth on her tit.

"Shit." He hit a button to exit the screen completely.

"What's up?" Lennox asked, sending him a mild look and then sipping his water. "Bathroom break?"

"We're not doing this," he said, purposely not looking O'Neal's way. "*I'm* uncomfortable."

Len's expression was pure innocence. "Why? You've seen this movie before."

"It's me," O'Neal said, her words cutting through the middle of the conversation like a knife. "He doesn't want *me* to see it."

Auden finally looked her way, his teeth clenching.

She was curled up against the arm of the couch, her cheeks and neck tinged with pink. She swung her legs to the floor. "I'm

gonna go. I'm obviously getting in the way of your movie night.
You don't want me here."

"Not true," Lennox said, tone as calm as a summer breeze.
"I'm enjoying the company. I think Auden here has just
forgotten again that he's not your daddy."

"Shut up, Len," Auden bit out, giving his best friend a barbed
look at the word choice. "I'm not trying to be her dad. I'm trying
to be…responsible."

"For what?" O'Neal said, her frustration obvious. "My moral
standing? Should I only be allowed to watch cartoons? Maybe I
should've brought a juice box and some Goldfish crackers."

Lennox snorted in amusement.

Auden stared at her, trying to keep himself in check, trying
to stay cool. Failed. "Who gave you the sex talk, O'Neal?"

She blinked, obviously startled. "What?"

"Your Nana sit you down and tell you about the birds and
the bees?"

"I—no. But I know what sex is, Aud. I had access to books
and the internet. I educated myself. I know how babies are
made. I know about STDs. I know about org—" She stopped,
cleared her throat. "The pleasure aspects of it."

"See," he said, jumping on her stumble and pointing at her.
"You can't even say orgasm."

She narrowed her eyes. "*Orgasm.*" She tipped her chin up.
"Which I believe is what both of those people on-screen were
about to have until you started clutching your pearls and threatening to faint."

Lennox chuckled. "O'Neal, you're officially my new favorite
person." He looked to Auden. "Care to continue that pearl-
clutching, darling?"

Auden sent Lennox a bullet of a look. "Shut up, man. I'm not
pearl-clutching." He turned back to O'Neal. "And I get that you
might know the biological and technical aspects of things, but if
you've never…done anything with anyone and you've never

watched sex on-screen, you should start with something…
milder. More romantic or whatever. Not two people going at it
on a counter."

Her blush deepened.

"I don't know," Lennox interjected, his tone the kind professors use when they're trying to get the class to ponder something. "I mean, *Fatal Attraction* is basically a morality tale. Erotic
on the surface but pretty puritanical in the message. Don't cheat
on your spouse or else. This might not feel too different to you,
O'Neal, than those scary stories your grandparents have told
you about the dangers of sin or whatever." He shrugged. "Plus,
who says romantic sex is the correct sex? I'd argue it's just one
of many types of sex."

"Len," he warned.

Len gave O'Neal a little smile. "And neither of us has any
idea what you'd be into. You might not know yet either, which
is cool. That's what college is for, right? Experimenting. Finding
yourself. All that jazz."

O'Neal looked down at her hands.

"But, Aud, if you're going to cut her off at the pass, you're
not giving her a chance to even consider the possibilities," he
went on. "For instance, screwing on a kitchen counter." He
looked to O'Neal and put his hand on his chest. "For me, that's a
no-go. Too much of a germaphobe. I don't want anyone's ass on
my countertops."

O'Neal gave a small half-laugh, her tense posture easing up a
little.

Len looked to him. "Auden, thoughts on countertop sex?"

O'Neal turned to look at him, eyebrows lifted.

Auden's back teeth were grinding together, but he tried to
regain his composure. If he didn't calm the hell down, O'Neal
was going to realize there was more to this reaction than big-
brother intervention. He breathed out slowly and lowered his
arms at his sides.

"Haven't tried it. Will reserve judgment."

"Fantastic," Lennox said, looking all too pleased. "O'Neal, any initial thoughts?"

She cleared her throat. "Uh, I think I'd be afraid the guy would drop me onto the floor."

Len laughed. "Valid concern. Pro tip—no stand-up sex unless your partner has solid upper body strength."

O'Neal's neck was fully red, and she put a hand over her face. "I can't believe this is the conversation we're having."

Lennox reached out and patted her arm. "Exposure therapy, Sweets. Shame is a learned response. It can be unlearned. I mean, look at how far Auden's come since he showed up here all wet behind the ears."

O'Neal turned his way, questions in her eyes. "How far have you come?"

Auden grunted and sat back down, lifting the remote. "Let's just watch the damn movie."

O'NEAL WAS TRYING HER LEVEL BEST TO BE COOL. *BE. COOL.* Watching the very R-rated movie was an exercise in both breath and body control. There was no way—*no way*—she was going to give Auden the satisfaction of letting him see that she was shocked by the movie. Yes, she'd read some mildly sexy books that she'd snuck onto her e-reader in high school, and she knew the basics of sex. But never had she seen two people, like, trying to rip each other's clothes off. The franticness of the sex on-screen, the roughness, it was...intimidating but also making her really, really warm.

What had she been *thinking* when she'd agreed to this?

She was terrified Auden or Lennox were going to look over at her and be able to tell just how much her body was responding to the movie. She had no shot at controlling her internal reactions. Even the scary parts had her heart racing and did nothing to tame the pulsing between her legs. Her heartbeat had apparently relocated there, and her breasts had turned into a million nerve endings, every brush of her bra against them sending a shiver through her.

There was also an acute awareness that she was sitting there between two really gorgeous guys. She'd had a crush on Auden for a long time so that felt familiar, but to her horror, she also found herself sneaking glances at Lennox. He was just so...out there. The casual way he'd talked about things that had been so taboo in her world, that complete lack of shame or filter...the effect was heady. She felt like if she got him alone, she could ask him literally anything and he would answer. He wouldn't try to soften it or sweeten it for her. The journalistic part of her brain was hungry for that kind of resource.

She startled at a violent part of the movie, and she caught Auden glancing her way, obviously gauging her reaction. She grabbed a throw pillow and hugged it to her chest, hoping it would block any evidence that she was still turned on even though this was definitely not a sexy part of the movie.

A few minutes later, the movie ended and the credits started to roll.

Auden grabbed the remote and turned off the TV but didn't turn on the lights. They were left in the silver glow of the moon shining through the main window. He peered over at her. "So? What'd you think?"

She rolled the piping of the throw pillow between her fingers. "I think that was some Old-Testament-level consequences for adultery."

"Told you," Lennox said. "A morality tale."

"But..." She frowned.

"But what?" Auden asked, angling his body to face her so that one leg was on the couch, one on the floor, expression openly curious.

She picked at the piping a little more, trying to put together her thoughts. "The one who paid the real price was the woman. He got off easy in comparison, and *he* was the one who was married."

Auden nodded. "Yep. The guy gets a do-over, but the woman gets painted as crazy, a bitch, and deserving of the ultimate punishment. Movies reflect society's views, especially when they're morality tales." He jerked a thumb toward the TV. "This movie originally had a different ending, one where Alex dies by suicide and Dan ends up in jail, accused of murdering her. But it was the Reagan era, and test audiences didn't like it. They preferred the psychotic bitch angle."

"Ugh, really?" she asked. "How do you know all this?"

Lennox leaned forward to join the conversation. "Told you. This one's a total film geek."

O'Neal smiled at Auden. "I love that you get nerdy about something. You always seemed so cool and popular."

She winced. She needed to stop babbling. Next, she was going to tell him he was really neat-o.

Lennox laughed under his breath. "Auden, the golden boy. I remember that version of him. He showed up here freshman year with the sparkle still on him."

Auden grimaced. "Not golden. Just clueless."

She looked between the two of them, some silent exchange going on. "That's what y'all think I am, isn't it? Clueless."

"Nah," Lennox said. "There's a difference between clueless and sheltered. You had no control over the sheltered part. The fact that you're here at a school your family doesn't want you at, hanging out with someone like me who I'm sure they wouldn't approve of, and watching dirty movies with us even though that was probably a stretch for you proves that you're pretty damn brave." He glanced at Auden. "So was Auden. Still is."

She hugged the pillow to her chest. "Thanks. I don't feel brave. I just feel…overwhelmed more than anything else. Other people get to ease into adult life. They get to make some decisions in high school, get more freedom, get to practice being independent. Get after-school jobs and go on dates and stay out too late or drink too much and learn from it. I didn't get any practice tests. I'm doing it...all at once. All on my own. With no study guide. I don't know how to get an A in this class."

"Hey." Auden reached out and squeezed her shoulder. "You're not all alone. I know I freaked out a little tonight, but you've got me in your corner."

"And me too," Lennox said.

"Plus, you don't have to get an A at this," Auden went on. "No one does. You're going to screw up. That's part of the process. And so what if you're going through that process a little later than other people? You're nineteen. When you're thirty, it's not going to make a difference if your first date was when you were fourteen or when you were twenty. No one will care."

"I guess not," she said, looking down at the pillow.

"All I care about, at least when it comes to the guys and the drinking and stuff," Auden said, "is that you're careful. You end up on a date with someone and you get a bad vibe from them, you call me. Or Len. You drink too much at a party and need a ride, call us."

"Thanks," she said quietly.

"You want to see if counter sex is all it's cracked up to be," Lennox interjected. "Call me."

Her head snapped up, and a breath caught in her throat.

"Len, *what the hell?*" Auden said, shooting him an angry look.

Lennox lifted his palms. "I'm just saying." He looked to O'Neal, gaze gentle. "Sweets, I would never make a move on you without your permission."

Her heart was in her throat, pounding.

"But if your first experiences are messing around with freshman boys, it's going to be a shit show. They don't know what they're doing yet," he said with a matter-of-fact tone.

80

"You'll end up giving your V-card to some three-pump chump who has no idea how to make you feel good. You'll be left wondering what all the fuss is about." He shrugged. "I could show you the fuss."

A flood of prickly heat washed over her, and she couldn't determine if that was embarrassment or pure, unfiltered lust. She squeezed her thighs together.

"Or Auden could," he added with a smile. "I've...heard he's pretty good at the fuss too."

"Oh my God, *stop*," Auden said, lacing his fingers behind his neck and squeezing. "What part of off-limits did you not understand, Len? *Jesus.*"

O'Neal's voice came back to her at that. She looked between the two of them. "Off-limits?"

Auden stood. "Yes. What you are. For him." His jaw flexed. "For both of us."

Her lips parted, irritation whipping through her. "You've like...*discussed* me?"

Auden's hands were still laced behind his neck, and he looked pained, his dark hair falling into his eyes. "I'm trying to look out for you. Len's not looking for a girlfriend and neither am I. Sex for us is different. You need to take your time. Get used to school. Meet some people. Go out on dates. Eventually, find a boyfriend and then let things progress how they progress."

She got to her feet, righteous indignation giving her strength. "Are you kidding me right now?"

Lennox leaned back in his chair, folded his arms, and looked just shy of getting popcorn.

"The only part of the sentence you left out was 'get married and then consummate your love only enough times so you can have babies,'" she said, making angry air quotes. "I thought you'd moved past what we were taught, but apparently you can only identify misogyny in movies." She put her hands out to her sides. "Why do I need to follow some prescribed path and you don't? Why would sex be different for you than for me? Because I'm a girl? Maybe I'm not looking for a boyfriend either. And what right do you have to tell anyone I'm off-limits? What if I want Lennox to give me exactly what he offered? What if I *want* to know what the fuss is about?"

She did. She didn't. She was mostly terrified. But mad enough to let the reckless words fly anyway.

Lennox half-coughed, half-laughed. "Oh shit."

Auden lowered his arms and got very, very still. "You don't want that."

She crossed her arms and jutted her chin, her confidence faltering but not wanting to let him see that. "How would you know? You're not in my head. You only think you know me."

"Is that right?" His hazel eyes had gone dark, and the effect sent a little shiver through her. He took a step forward, holding her gaze. "Okay. Then take off your shorts, O'Neal."

The words were like shots fired, making her ears ring. Her throat went dry. "Wh-what?"

She could feel Lennox in her periphery, watching them in rapt silence.

Auden cocked a brow at her, only an arm's length away now. "You said you want to know the fuss? Fine. Take off your shorts and panties, and I'll show you." He leaned a little closer, never breaking eye contact. "I'll get on my knees and put my mouth on that sweet, untouched pussy of yours and lick you until you're well and truly fussed."

All her air left her.

"I bet you're already wet from the movie," he went on in that smooth-as-butter tone. "All slick and ready. You'd come against my tongue in no time."

Her whole body shivered, and her stomach tried to fold in on itself. She'd never heard those kinds of words even spoken aloud, and she'd definitely never been talked to like that. To have those erotic threats coming out of Auden's mouth… She was both scandalized and very, *very* hot.

The silence stretched between them, the air electric. She flexed her fingers at her side, trying to regain her bearings. "You're trying to scare me off."

"You think?" he said, a little hitch in his lips. "Then call my bluff."

Part of her was tempted to reach for the button of her shorts just to prove a point. Strip down, fear be damned, and win the argument. She knew what he was trying to do. He was trying to shock her, to scare her, to show her just how naïve she was in comparison to them. She didn't want to concede.

But she also knew there was no way she could even take off her shirt in front of these guys much less anything else. Panic was inching in.

She stared at Auden, trying to come up with what to say to save her pride, but then an idea hit her. She turned to Lennox, who was sitting there, seemingly enjoying the show unfolding in front of him.

She put out a hand to him. "Can you come here a second?"

Lennox looked surprised but grabbed her hand and smiled, getting to his feet. "Of course."

She turned to Lennox, feeling Auden's intense presence a few feet from her. She swallowed past the nerves in her throat. "Can you show me what a good kiss is like? I want to learn."

Len's eyes widened, and his hand tightened on hers. She didn't know much about guys, but she could see the interest there. But before he answered, he looked to Auden. "I'd be happy to, Sweets, but not without Auden's okay."

"What?" she snapped. "He doesn't get to make that call. He doesn't get to decide who I'm on- and off-limits to."

Lennox gave her a gentle look. "He doesn't. But he's also my friend, and I made a promise to him. I take that seriously." He eyed his friend. "Auden?"

O'Neal turned her head to find Auden with a stony expression. He met her gaze. "You don't want to kiss him. You're doing this to get me back off."

She gathered her courage and threw his words back at him. "Then call my bluff."

He folded his arms. "Fine. Permission granted, Len. Make sure you make it good."

O'Neal blinked, startled by the response. That wasn't how it was supposed to go.

Lennox put a gentle hand on her cheek and turned her face back toward him. His green eyes were full of mischief. "Time to say no if you don't want this, Sweets."

She bit her lip, taking in the sight of him that close. The guy really was beautiful. And intimidating as hell. She had zero idea what she was doing. She'd kissed exactly one person one time. He was probably going to laugh at her, or feel sorry for her or—

"Yes."

The word had come out on its own, her body answering for her.

Lennox smiled, slid his hand beneath the curtain of her hair, and tipped her face up. Before she could panic fully, he lowered his mouth to hers. His lips were soft against hers, tasting of vanilla from the ice cream and something uniquely him. He tugged on her bottom lip gently and teased with the tip of his tongue. Her lips parted and his tongue slipped inside, sending heat zipping up her spine. His grip on her neck tightened just a little, controlling the angle, the pace, coaxing her where he wanted. *Teaching* her. His tongue stroked against hers, and his other hand went to her hip. He kneaded her there, the gentle pressure sending waves of aching need straight downward. She sighed into his mouth, her body melting like ice on hot pavement.

When he pulled back, he smiled and kissed the tip of her nose. "Beautiful. Thank you."

She blinked up at him, dazed and shivery. "Uh, thanks back?"

He laughed softly. "I don't think you need much practice on the kissing. That was hot."

A throat was cleared. "No, she doesn't. She was good at that the first time out of the gate."

O'Neal tensed and turned, remembering they had an audience. Auden was standing there with an unreadable expression on his face.

Reality hit her like cold water. *What in the heck was she doing?* She'd just kissed a virtual stranger in front of the only other guy she'd ever kissed. She wasn't…that type of girl. God, what must they be thinking about her? What must Auden think?

Who was she turning into?

She took a step back. "I, um, better get going. It's late."

Lennox frowned. "Everything okay?"

"Yeah, sure," she said in a rush, grabbing for the tennis shoes she'd kicked off earlier. "I just have homework and stuff to do and I shouldn't have stayed this long and—"

"O'Neal," Auden said, putting a hand on her arm, the touch making her flinch and halting her for a moment. "Take a breath. You're freaking out a little."

"I'm fine," she said, shaking off his arm and reaching for her other shoe, her heart racing like rabbit feet.

"Look, I'm sorry about what I said, what I just did," Auden said quickly. "I was trying to show you why you should take things slow. I shouldn't have said—I don't want to scare you. That was a dick move. I don't want you leaving upset."

"And if I took the kiss too far…" Lennox started.

She straightened and turned to face them, her shoe left untied. "You didn't take the kiss too far. It was nice. And Auden, I'm fine. Obviously, neither of us likes to lose an argument, and we said some dumb things—you said more dumb things than I did, but I pushed too. I just…need to go."

Auden's concerned expression deepened. "Okay, but

promise me you'll let me know if you want to talk about this. Because tonight was…a lot. I know how it is to push yourself farther on something than you were ready for. Tonight got out of hand. That was one hundred percent my fault. I left you with no way to save face unless you did something to shock me back. I feel like I made you kiss Len."

She took a breath, trying to calm her thumping heart. "You didn't make me do anything. Tonight was my decision. I'm okay. I promise. I just need to go."

"Of course. Just know you're safe with us," Lennox said, no playfulness in his voice. "If you're leaving because you need to go or need some space, no problem. But if you're leaving because you think watching that kind of movie or exchanging dirty words with Aud or kissing me sets up some kind of expectation, you have nothing to worry about. Worry about that with other guys," he said, giving her a pointed look.

She stared at him.

"Some guys are pricks. But neither of us would ever push you to do anything you didn't want to do. And you always have the right to tell us to fuck off—which is what Auden deserved when he was being an asshole."

Auden grunted.

"I love that you swung back at him. Friends keep each other in line—and we're not the easiest friends to do that with." Len gave her one of his customary smirks. "You may have been sheltered, O'Neal, but you're tough. I think you're going to be just fine out in the world."

The words warmed her from the inside out.

"He's right," Auden said, tone softening. "You were right to push back. I'm sorry about the off-limits thing. You're an adult. That's not my call."

Her nervous energy smoothed out a little. "Thanks."

He laughed self-consciously, the old Auden she recognized returning. "I wish I could blame this whole night on being drunk, but I only had two beers. Can we just say I had a momentary lapse in sanity?"

"You think?" She let out a breath and then shoved him in the shoulder, hard. "I cannot *believe* you said what you said to me. The mouth on you. Maya would literally die if I told her."

"Which you *will not* do," he said, giving her a firm look.

"Of course, I won't. I can't even…" She pressed her lips together in consternation. "Say those words out loud."

Lennox smiled and rubbed his palms together. "Ooh, another thing we can practice one night. Dirty talk."

"Shut it, Len," Auden said with a snort.

"Auden's good at it. Could melt the paint right off your car," he added.

She looked to Lennox in surprise. "How would you even know?"

Lennox gave her a sly smile. "I've been his roommate a long time. Not a lot of privacy in a dorm room."

She waved her hand. "You two know way too much about each other."

"You're not wrong," Auden said, giving Lennox another *shut up* look. "Come on, I'll walk you out."

"Okay." She crossed the room and grabbed her purse from the dining table, happy that this was ending on this note instead of her running out in a panic.

Lennox had followed, and when she turned around, he gave her a little salute. "'Night, Sweets. It's been fun."

She stepped closer, and on a little surge of bravery, she gave him a hug, expecting it to feel awkward but only feeling comfortable warmth instead. "Good night."

He gave her a gentle squeeze and then released her.

Auden opened the door for her and then walked out after she did, joining her on the stairs, his hands deep in his pockets. The night air was humming with mosquitos and the distant sound of someone's TV playing.

87

They walked to her car in silence, and she pulled out her key fob to unlock it. He reached for her door, but before he opened it, he turned to her, expression pensive. "I really am sorry about what happened tonight. I was way out of line. I guess I'm not used to...thinking of you as a grown woman. I have this pretty intense urge to protect you, and when I couldn't get through, I went to shock tactics. It was uncalled for."

Her chest tightened, his concern for her taking some of the edge off of how he'd acted. She reached out and grabbed his hand, squeezing it. "I'm not your little sister."

He cleared his throat, and a muscle in his jaw ticked. "Yeah, I'm aware of that now. *Super ultra* aware."

She released his hand, confused by the emphatic tone. "What do you mean?"

He tucked his hands in his pockets, his shoulders stiff. "Because when I thought for half a second that you were actually going to call my bluff..."

She swallowed. "Yeah?"

He looked off to the side and squinted like he couldn't quite get the words out facing her. "I was prepared to make good on my threat."

Her heart dropped into her stomach, and any chance she had at speech left her.

"*That* wasn't a little sister thought." He looked back at her, his dimple flashing in a quick, self-deprecating smile. "Good night, freshman. Text me when you get home so that I know you got there okay."

He left her standing there, stunned and a little weak at the visual he'd left her with.

She may be tough.

But she was in way, *way* over her head.

# CHAPTER SEVEN

*L*ennox was aimlessly flipping through stations with his feet up on the coffee table when Auden came back inside. He watched as Auden shut the door and then leaned back against it with his eyes closed. Every muscle in his shoulders looked to be bunched tight beneath his blue T-shirt. Lennox grimaced.

He'd expected Auden to come back inside ready to argue with him after he'd pushed things with O'Neal tonight, kissed her, but the guy just looked beat down instead. He cleared his throat. "You okay, man?"

Auden let out an audible breath, then opened his eyes. "I don't even know what the fuck that was tonight."

Lennox clicked off the TV and lowered his feet to the floor, bracing his forearms on his thighs. "Well, let's recap. I kissed your little's sister's very virginal BFF at her request while you watched, and you, my friend, threatened to lick her pussy until she came—while *I* watched. That last part was implied—because I definitely wasn't going to leave the room if she'd taken you up on the offer."

Auden groaned and banged the back of his head lightly against the door. His hand went to his crotch and adjusted the obvious state of his dick. "When she gets back to her dorm and replays what happened tonight, she may rethink her stance and never speak to me again. I basically pushed her into a corner and made her kiss you. I didn't give her any good outs."

"Meh," Lennox said, shrugging. "You're giving yourself too much credit and her not enough. She wouldn't have kissed me if she didn't want to. I asked again before I did anything. And she kissed me back—and was into it." *So was I, way more than I should've been.* But he didn't think Auden would appreciate that tidbit. "Honestly, I think she liked that you were watching."

"Len…" he said, warning in his voice.

"You know, I've never really shared your hard-on for the innocence thing," Lennox continued. "I like my partners with some experience under their belt. I'd rather someone just role-play innocence if we want to play those types of games. But with her…I get it."

"Get what?" Auden pushed away from the door and walked over to the couch, collapsing onto it like his bones were too heavy to remain upright. He reclined and eyed Lennox.

Lennox laced his fingers together, thinking back over the night and trying to pinpoint what it was about O'Neal that was so intriguing. "O'Neal is naïve and inexperienced, but she's got a spine of steel in there. She's innocent and could play up that blushing virgin thing for effect, but she doesn't. In fact, she's kind of mad about it—that she's been left out of the loop. She's hungry for knowledge, and she's not afraid to stand up for herself." He sighed and decided to just be honest. "It's sexy. *She's* sexy. She can hold her own. Like if she ever were to submit to someone, you'd know that person earned it."

"She won't be submitting to anyone, Len," he said, warning in his voice. "She almost had a heart attack over a few dirty words."

Lennox smiled. "Yes, but she also almost took off her shorts. She was closer to calling your bluff than you think. She was shocked *and* turned on. I bet her panties were soaked through."

"Please don't paint that picture," he said with a beleaguered moan.

"Sorry, but it's hard to ignore. I could see the confusion on her face. She was scared but wanting what you were offering at the same time." His own cock twitched at the memory. "She's humming like a live wire and has no idea what to do with that feeling. You can feel that energy coming off of her. I could feel it in the kiss."

Auden lifted a skeptical brow. "Energy?"

"Yeah, you know how Melissa is always talking about how some guys walk around with Big Dick Energy?"

Auden snorted. "I believe she says *you* walk around with that."

"If the shoe fits." He smirked. "But I think what's pressing your buttons is that O'Neal is eager to learn, to feel, to experience things. She hasn't chosen her innocence. It was chosen for her. Tonight, with the movie, it was obvious she was anxious as hell but also too curious to let the nerves stop her. And that bravery, that desire to learn, *feels* kinky. That energy she's giving off is pressing those dom buttons of yours. Mine too, honestly. That feisty streak she has, going toe-to-toe with you? *Hot.* I was ready to take her in my lap and hold her thighs open for you while you made good on your threat. The three of us could have a whole lot of fun."

*So. Much. Fun.*

Auden made a pained sound and rubbed the spot between his eyes. "But we can't. You don't throw someone that green into"—he motioned between the two of them—"this."

Lennox let out a breath, his blood fully rerouting south at the thought of O'Neal between them, following their orders, maybe even fighting back a little. "Which is a damn shame," he said, grieving the fantasy already. "She'll go the traditional route. Good girl away at college and on her own for the first time gives her V-card to the first fumbling idiot who takes her out on a few dates, tells her she's special, and knows how to shove his fingers in her panties decently enough to trigger all that pent-up lust she's been carrying around since puberty. He'll blow his load in five minutes, she won't, and she'll wonder *wow, is that what I've been waiting for all this time?* Or she'll drink too much one night out with her friends and will wake up with some guy whose name she can't remember and realize she waited that long and has no memory of her first time."

"Fucking hell, man." Auden sat up. "Can you not draw those pictures either? I want to murder both those guys now, and they don't even exist."

Lennox gave him a sad smile. "Aud, those guys exist everywhere. They're kind of the main templates of college bros. O'Neal is going to have to deal with them. They're not *not* going to notice that she's hot. She's going to get hit on. And probably have no idea how to navigate that. She'll learn, but it'll take some time."

Auden pressed the heels of his hands to his eyes like his head was hurting. "I don't want this kind of responsibility."

Lennox would never admit it out loud, but seeing Auden this knotted up about a woman was rather enjoyable. Auden was usually Mr. Play It Cool in their hookups, never getting too attached, but O'Neal flipped some new switches Len hadn't seen before.

"She's not your responsibility. She's just your sister's friend. And an adult."

"An adult with a genius IQ and zero real-world experience," he said. "I know she's tough, but someone needs to have her back."

"Can I take her front?"

Auden sent him a murderous look, and Lennox smiled an angelic smile. "You walked right into that one."

"I think it's best that we don't have nights like this with her again," Auden said, collapsing against the back of the couch, knees wide. "If we hang out, it should be completely platonic, probably in public places. And no movies with sex scenes. And no more kissing."

"Yawn. Sounds boring," Lennox said, leaning back and hooking his ankle over his knee, disappointed but knowing he could only push Auden so far. "But she's your friend, and I'll play it however you want."

He glanced over. "Thank you."

"Of course." Lennox eyed Auden's unrelenting hard-on, and a little smile played at the corners of his mouth, the sadist in him unable to pass up the opportunity to needle. "So do you think she's going to wait until her roommate goes to sleep tonight and then slide her hand under the covers and imagine her fingers are your mouth?"

"Goddammit, Len." A tortured expression crossed Auden's face. "Shut up. I'm already hard as a fucking rock."

Len was about to annoy his best friend a little more when a horrifying thought passed through his brain. "Oh, man. Do you think she even knows how to get herself off? Because if not, holy shit…the built-up tension. How is she even functioning?"

Auden grimaced and adjusted himself again. "I don't want to think about it. Well, *I do,* in great detail actually, but I won't. My guess is she's figured out the basics just like anyone else does, but probably only does it when she absolutely can't resist anymore and then feels moral guilt afterward. That's how I was growing up. Orgasms with a guilt chaser."

"Fuck," Lennox said with a head shake. "I wouldn't wish my childhood on anyone, but at least I didn't feel bad when I beat off. Repression sucks."

"You don't have to tell me. Speaking of which." He lifted his

93

head and made a *gimme* motion with his hand. "Toss me the lube. I'm going to admit defeat right now and deal with this or I'm going to be up all night."

Lennox opened his mouth to make an offer. He was hard as hell and antsy after tonight too. The two of them could get each other off, fool around, but he shut his mouth before he could slip up. He already knew the answer. Auden spoke of repression like it wasn't a thing he dealt with anymore, but Len knew that was bullshit.

When there was a woman between them, Auden didn't flinch if he and Lennox touched, but if it was just the two of them, the line for that kind of thing was drawn in cement. Watching was okay. They'd crossed the jerking-off-in-the-same-room line a long time ago when they'd shared a dorm room and both discovered they had an exhibitionist streak, but beyond that, no.

Despite Auden's pronouncements about being free from the beliefs of his upbringing, Len suspected Auden still thought there was something wrong with him because of what he liked. That his kinks and blurry sexuality were an experimental phase he'd grow out of. That one day he'd be the family man his parents expected him to be.

And Lennox couldn't do a damn thing about it. So he played by the rules. Enjoyed the small sliver of his best friend he did have access to, knowing he'd always want more but accepting he'd never get it.

"Want me to leave?" Len asked as he reached over to the side table and pulled open the drawer where they kept supplies.

"You know I don't care if you watch." He glanced at Len's crotch, a little smirk appearing. "Or take care of things too. That shit looks painful."

It was—even more so after that invitation. Len unbuttoned his jeans and shoved them down to free his dick, knowing it would be ten times hotter if he stayed there with Auden than if he took care of things alone. He grabbed the bottle of lube from the drawer, tipped some into his palm, and then tossed the bottle to Auden.

Auden caught it one-handed, already having shucked his T-shirt and opened his fly, giving Len a killer view. Lennox slicked up his own cock, a snap of pleasure going through him, as Auden reached down and took his thick erection into his hand, the head already glistening with pre-come. When Auden drizzled the lube into his palm, he looked over at Lennox and let his focus trace downward before wrapping his hand around himself. The look sent heat traces through Len's body. Auden let out a long, shaky exhale and a zap of *fuck yeah* went through Len. Auden said he didn't care if Len stayed because Aud liked to believe that about himself—but what his actions said was that it turned him the fuck on when they did this together.

Too bad their new friend O'Neal couldn't be here to join in too.

Lennox wet his lips, the grip on himself feeling like too much and not enough all at the same time. He imagined rewinding the night a little, having O'Neal standing between them again. What would she think of this? Would she be appalled? Offended? Or...would she push her shorts down like she'd been so close to doing, slide her fingers between her thighs, and join in? Maybe follow their instructions as they guided her exactly how to get herself off? A grunt escaped him, and he squeezed the base of his cock so he wouldn't go off too soon.

Auden's hand was moving slowly, but the muscles in his forearm were flexing, the grip tight, the sound of slickness obscene. "You're thinking about her."

The words weren't accusatory. Just knowing.

"So are you," Len said, voice coming out strained. "She may be doing this right now too, you know? So quiet. So secretive. Pushing her panties down and peeking over at her sleeping roommate. Terrified at getting caught but too turned on to resist. Her hand sliding down her stomach, her pussy throbbing, aching for something she's never had."

Auden made a sound of appreciation. "Her fingers sliding over her clit and her other hand exploring, her teeth biting into her lip so she won't make any noise." Auden's voice had taken on a drugged quality, lost on pleasure. "The scent of how turned on she is filling the room."

Len tipped his head back, the images driving him to the brink. "I bet she's always had to be silent when she comes. All gasps and choked whimpers as she tries to hide the sound of hot fingers sliding into dark, juicy places."

Auden made a low sound in the back of his throat. "*Fuck.*"

"She probably has bite marks on her pillow from holding it all in," Len said. "I bet she thinks of you when she comes. Fantasizes you're fucking her. Imagines what your cock would feel like inside her."

That was all it took. Auden made a guttural sound, and Len opened his eyes in time to see Auden's head arched back in pleasure, neck muscles straining, his thighs spread wide, and his cock shooting his release all over his chest.

Everything in Len's body tightened, and he went over the edge with Aud, the view and the fantasy they'd just painted pushing all his buttons. Hot jets of fluid painted his stomach and T-shirt, pleasure rolling through him like a summer thunderstorm. He slowed his hand as his cock turned overly sensitive and breathed through the rest of the orgasm, draining every last bit of pleasure out of it and then melting back against the chair, spent.

When he gathered the energy to open his eyes a minute or two later, he caught Auden staring. Len glanced down at his disheveled state and laughed under his breath. "Can you call O'Neal and ask her if it was good for her too?"

Auden smirked without humor and grabbed his T-shirt,

using it to clean himself up. "I hope it was good for you because this is all we're going to get." He tossed the T-shirt to Len. "This —what just happened—further proves why we can't cross any lines with her."

Len cleaned himself off with Auden's shirt and yanked his pants up, leaving the fly hanging open. He huffed. "And why exactly is that?"

Auden stood, pants still unzipped and skin flushed. "Because this isn't about her. We're...I don't know, fetishizing her virginity or whatever. That's the appeal." He let out a tired breath like he was annoyed with himself. "The shit we just imagined about her? All about her innocence."

Lennox pressed his lips together, trying to be patient. "Aud—"

"No, I'm not doing that to her," he said, tone like a hammer strike. "I *like* O'Neal. I've known her for a long time and I care about her. As a friend. As a fully formed person who I find interesting and who deserves better than that."

Len kept quiet, gave a little nod for him to go on.

"I know I could get her into bed," he said. "She trusts me and has a crush. Hell, I could probably even open up her mind to some kink if I spin it right. But then what? I take something that I can't give back to her, and then the stuff that got you and me all keyed up—that innocence factor—is gone. We're ready to move onto the next adventure, and she's left feeling used—by a friend she trusted."

"You wouldn't use her," Lennox said gently. "You're not that guy. The fact that you're even thinking about this shows that you're not that guy. I'm not that guy either."

"What else would you call it beyond using her? I'd have nothing to offer her besides a non-terrible first time. Neither would you. It's not like either of us is looking for a relationship." He put his hands out to his sides. "There is no next step in that scenario."

"You're thinking in extremes. There are other stops between a one-night hookup and exchanging rings. Did you listen to some of what she said tonight? Maybe she wants to use *you*."

He scoffed, shaggy hair falling in his face. "No way."

Lennox sighed, suddenly exhausted, and stood. He put his clean hand on Auden's shoulder. "She's your friend. I'll respect what you want, but just keep in mind, *someone* will be that guy. If not you, someone. I haven't known O'Neal long, but after kissing her tonight, I know one thing for sure." He leaned closer, holding Auden's gaze. "She's *starving*, man. For touch. For experiences. For a chance to finally live her life without looking over her shoulder or up at the heavens to get permission."

Auden blew out a breath. "That's doesn't mean she needs to start by getting involved with two guys who are into sharing and dominance."

"Maybe not." Lennox straightened and crossed his arms over his chest. "But it's only a matter of time before someone slides a plate in front of her and offers her a bite. It's going to be hard to resist. Because when you're starving, even the cheap, flavorless shit starts looking good."

His jaw ticked. "Go to bed, Len."

He smiled. "We're going to relegate her to sad, gas-station-donut sex, Aud. You want that on your conscience?"

Auden rolled his eyes

"Stale-popcorn sex," Len went on.

Auden shook his head, a smile peeking out at the corner of his mouth now.

"*Fat-free-frozen-yogurt sex.*"

Auden laughed. "You're not going to win this debate. Frozen-yogurt sex won't damage her. It's sweet and—"

"Flavorless," Lennox filled in. "And leaves you unfulfilled and thirsty. So thirsty, dude."

"*Good night*, Len."

Lennox sniffed derisively, knowing that there was no getting through the Auden blockade, at least not tonight. He headed toward his bedroom. But when he was a few steps away, he called out, "Poor O'Neal, doomed to plastic-wrapped-processed-cheese sex!"

A throw pillow hit him in the back of the head.

# CHAPTER EIGHT

*O*'Neal stared at her laptop screen, chewing her thumbnail and trying to come up with a great closing line for her history paper. She'd already written four versions of the line and erased them. Nothing sounded right, and she refused to use *So, in conclusion...*

The door to her dorm room burst open, startling her and almost making her knock her laptop off the bed. "What the—?"

Quyen came in like a whirlwind, dropping her backpack by the door with a thunk and texting with the other hand. She smiled O'Neal's way as she disentangled herself from the earbuds in her ears. "Oh my God, hey."

O'Neal laughed. Quyen always had this vibe like she was rushing in to tell everyone some piece of urgent good news. "Hey, yourself."

Quyen tossed her phone and earbuds onto her bed and then plunked herself down on the foot of O'Neal's bed. "Guess what?"

"What?"

"It's Friday and you're done with studying and we're going

out to a club." She tapped the top of O'Neal's laptop. "Save your work and shut her down."

O'Neal gave her a look that she hoped conveyed the message: *have aliens taken over your body?* "Um..."

"No, no, no, don't give me that look." She shook her head. "We've been in school a month, and all either of us has done is study and work. These guys from a frat—really cute guys, I might add—invited us out. Said it's kind of a freshman welcoming party. The club lets in eighteen and up."

"A freshman welcoming party?" O'Neal said dryly. "Yeah, that sounds legit."

"I know, I know. It's probably a pickup line, but who cares? Cute guys! Dancing! Possibly people to buy us drinks. We're supposed to be doing this. It's college." She pressed her hands together in a prayer position. "Please, please don't make me go solo. I need a wing woman."

O'Neal snorted. "You realize I will be the absolute worst wing woman, right? I wasn't allowed to be alone with guys my own age. Or dance. I don't know how to flirt. I don't know... what to do with any of it. I didn't even get a chance to be a wall-flower because I wasn't allowed within the walls."

"Oh, come on," Quyen said, undeterred. "You're not that bad off. You have your friend's brother and his roommate. You hang out with them sometimes."

Yeah, she did. At public restaurants or the dining hall. Since the night at their apartment, Auden and Lennox hadn't invited her back to their place, and she hadn't asked to go. All they did was check in on her, making sure she was okay. They may as well pat her on the head and call her *good girl* at this point.

"I—"

"You could invite them," Quyen said. "Maybe that would make it easier since you already know them?"

"There's no way Auden and Lennox are going to want to go to a frat's freshman welcoming party," she said, wrinkling her nose. "I think that would be their idea of hell. They might break out in hives at the mere mention."

"You don't know if you don't ask." Quyen pummeled the bed in an excited little drumroll. "Come on, roomie. Let's have some fun! Text them."

O'Neal sighed, not wanting to go but unable to withstand the hopeful look on her friend's face. Quyen really had been a godsend these last few weeks, helping O'Neal feel less alone on this big campus. So she saved her paper, closed her laptop, and then reached for her phone, feeling a little ridiculous but forcing herself to text anyway.

> O'Neal: You said I could ask you for advice. Thoughts on frat boys inviting me and Quyen to a club for a freshman welcoming party?

The instant she sent it, her cheeks heated. Why would Auden want to weigh in on something so trivial? But it only took a few seconds for the phone to buzz.

> Auden: Freshman welcoming party, my ass. Which frat?

O'Neal looked up. "He wants to know which frat?"

Quyen waved a dismissive hand. "I don't know. Alpha Beta Hot Guy? Who knows? All I know is that it's at the Railway Club."

> O'Neal: She doesn't know. It's at the Railway Club. I think I'm going to go because she's really excited and doesn't want to go solo. She wanted me to ask if y'all wanted to come but I know better.

> Auden: You want us to go?

> O'Neal: You don't want to go hang out with frat guys and freshmen

> Auden: Not my question

She sighed, appreciating that he would be willing to go if she needed him but hating that he'd only be doing it for all those big-brothery reasons.

> O'Neal: I'll be okay. I don't need a babysitter or anything. I just wanted to make sure I wasn't missing something. Some secret code.

> Auden: The invite is code for "I think you and your roommate are hot, come get drunk and sweaty on a dance floor with us." Advice: don't drink more than two drinks, watch your drinks poured, and don't let them out of your sight. Call me if you need a sober ride

Huh. Actual advice and not a lecture. That was progress.

> O'Neal: Thanks!

"So?" Quyen asked, bouncing a little on the bed. "Are they coming?"

"No." O'Neal took a breath and gathered her courage. "But I am. Gotta rip the Band-Aid off some time, right?"

She lifted a fist in victory. "Yes! Now let's see what I have in my closet that you can wear. Because I love you but…jeans and a T-shirt aren't going to cut it tonight."

"I—"

But Quyen was already grabbing O'Neal's hand and dragging her toward her closet.

THE MUSIC WAS POUNDING WHEN THEY ARRIVED, AND O'NEAL'S heart rate was outpacing the beat. Quyen had lent her a little black dress that hit her above mid-thigh and had a halter neck, so no option for a bra. After years of dressing in school uniforms on weekdays and jeans and T-shirts on weekends, she felt basically naked. Her entire back was just...out there.

She'd protested that it was too much—or *too little*, actually— but Quyen had *ooh*ed and *ahh*ed over her so much that O'Neal had gotten a burst of borrowed confidence and had given in. Quyen had also done O'Neal's makeup, teaching her how to wing her eyeliner a little and bring out her eyes with the shadow. The only battle O'Neal had won was over the shoes. Quyen had wanted her in heels, but O'Neal had insisted on a pair of strappy black gladiator-style flats. She wanted to have fun tonight, not end up in the hospital with a broken ankle.

Quyen hooked her arm with O'Neal's as they waited in line at the door. Quyen had chosen a green strapless dress that hugged her body and brought out the pretty, warm tone of her skin. She also had heels high enough to bring her almost to O'Neal's height. She leaned into O'Neal, bumping shoulders with her.

"Thanks so much for coming with. I know this is out of your comfort zone. If you hate it, we'll leave."

O'Neal smiled despite the butterflies in her stomach. "I'll do my best not to hate it."

The door guy checked their IDs and waved them in, denying them the twenty-one-and-up wristband. O'Neal kept ahold of Quyen as they entered the darkened confines of the club. The place was busy already, loud with the music but also with voices. A few couples and groups were on the dance floor, bouncing around and grinding against each other in the flashing shafts of colored light. Was *that* what they were here to do? Because O'Neal wouldn't even know where to start. She resisted the urge to turn right back around and hightail it back to the dorm. She'd wanted to go to prom. She'd wanted to experience this kind of thing, but it was...a lot all at once.

"Ooh, there are the guys who invited us," Quyen said, pointing to the back left corner near the side of the dance floor. "Let's go say hi."

They snaked their way through the club, tension making O'Neal's movements tight, and one of the guys caught sight of Quyen and waved. When she and Quyen reached the table, she felt her shell closing around her. There were four guys at the table—two were drinking beers, one had a mixed drink in his hand. Only one had the twenty-one-and-up band, so she knew who was buying drinks.

"Hey, you made it," one of the guys said, standing up to hug Quyen. He was tall with longish dark hair, light brown skin, and dark eyes that crinkled when he smiled. Cute.

Quyen returned the hug and then looked toward O'Neal. "Daniel, this is my roommate O'Neal."

Daniel smiled and nodded her way. "Glad y'all could come."

"O'Neal?" One of the guys at the table, a burly-looking dude with red hair and bright blue eyes, laughed. "That might out-Irish me." He put his hand out to O'Neal and leaned forward so she could hear him. "Connall."

O'Neal took his hand and smiled. She noticed he didn't have a wristband, which put her more at ease. "Nice to meet you."

He released her hand, and the other guys shared their names, though she missed one because the music was so loud. Quyen was already chatting away with Daniel.

Connall touched O'Neal's elbow. "Want something to drink? Seb is our designated drink obtainer tonight."

She remembered what Auden had said about watching her drinks. "Uh…"

"How about shots?" Seb, the tallest and lankiest of the group, announced. "I'll be back."

Connall smirked. "I hope you like shots then."

She couldn't tell him that she had absolutely no idea what she liked, but she didn't say no.

A few minutes later, Seb returned with a tray of sloshing shot glasses filled with a golden liquid. There was also a plastic cup filled with lime wedges. "Tequila!"

O'Neal bit her lip. Auden had told her to watch her drinks poured, but this was a whole tray and everyone was going to have one. She figured that was safe. The question was did she want to drink at all?

"You like tequila?" Connall asked.

"Never tried it." At least that was the truth.

His eyebrows went up. "Well, then, your virgin run. It's the cheap shit so be warned but..." He grabbed a lime wedge and the salt shaker. "You take the sting off with this."

"We're not going to get in trouble for being underage?" she asked, the old anxiety angel on her shoulder whispering urgently in her ear.

"Nah, they check at the door and up at the bar for optics but don't really give a shit. They make all their money on college students." He handed her the shot glass. "You game?"

She took the little glass, eyeing it, nerves jumping in her stomach. She'd told him she'd never had tequila, but she hadn't mentioned she'd never had alcohol at all. She glanced over at Quyen, who was already tipping back her shot and wincing.

"Yeah, okay," she said, trying to be in the moment. She came to school to try new things. Why not this? "How does it work?"

He took her by the wrist, the touch gentle and friendly. "First, you lick the spot between your thumb and forefinger, sprinkle salt on it."

She did as he directed, noticing that he was watching with interest. The attention made her face heat.

He sprinkled salt on the damp spot on her hand. "Now, lick the salt, kick back the shot in one gulp, and then suck the lime wedge. Like this."

He went through the motions for himself, knocking back the

106

shot, and then ending with the lime. He squeezed his eyes shut as he sucked and then coughed. "Damn."

She inhaled deeply, steeling herself for whatever was to come, then licked off the salt and tipped the shot back, the alcohol turning to liquid fire on the way down. She shrieked a little, flapping her hand, and Connall laughed. He pressed the lime wedge into her mouth, his eyes sparking with humor.

"Suck!"

She dug her teeth into the lime, and the sourness eased some of the astringent taste of the alcohol. Her whole chest was aflame as the tequila went down.

She released the lime and pressed her fingers to her lips, still wincing a little.

Connall was still chuckling. "Sorry. Told you it was cheap."

"Why would anyone drink that *on purpose?*" she asked, laughing with him. "That's kind of awful."

"Because it's quick and effective." He cocked his thumb toward the dance floor. "Plus, it makes dancing easier because you forget you have no rhythm. Or that might just be me."

She glanced at the people dancing. Quyen was already making her way to the dance floor with Daniel. "I don't think it's going to get me out there."

"One more shot and you'll probably change your mind." Connall handed her another glass. "Take it from someone who wouldn't even be able to talk to a pretty girl like you if I hadn't already had a few."

The compliment threw her off for a minute, and she dipped her head. "Uh, thanks."

He lifted the salt shaker, asking the question. She could already feel the alcohol working, her muscles loosening, her nerves softening. It was like…magic.

She licked her hand.

# CHAPTER NINE

"*W*hat the hell are you doing?" Lennox asked, sounding vaguely horrified as Auden pulled up in front of a brick building with a flashing sign and peeling paint. "I thought you had an errand to run."

"I do." Auden parked the car on the street and shut off the engine. "We're going to the Railway Club."

"The Rail—have you hit your head? Taken a narcotic? How many fingers am I holding up?" Lennox waved both of his middle fingers in front of Auden's face. "This is the worst of the campus bar scene. I don't even drink and I know that. Crawling with frats and football players."

Auden gripped the steering wheel, trying to talk himself out of this and failing. He looked toward the front of the club. "O'Neal's here. Frat guys invited her and her roommate to a freshman welcoming party."

Lennox groaned. "God. Do those lines actually work?"

"I think she went to be nice to her roommate. She texted because Quyen wanted her to ask us if we'd go, but she basically told me she didn't need a babysitter. I was going to let her be." He unlocked his phone. "Until I got this."

Lennox looked at the screen. It was a text of gibberish—all *b*s and *f*s from O'Neal. He squinted. "I think this says….*wow, I'm super fucking drunk.*"

Auden took the phone. "Right, so…"

Lennox was already opening the door. "Yep. Let's go knock the flies off her because you know those bastards will be circling."

Auden was out of the car a second behind him, happy that Len was on the same page. He didn't know if it made him feel less like a stalker, but it made him feel less alone in his stalking at least.

The line at the door of the club was massive, and Auden could feel his worry growing like an oil spill inside him. What if O'Neal had already left? She hadn't texted him back after he'd responded to hers.

"This is going to take fucking forever," Lennox said, eyeing the line, his fists clenched at his side.

"Screw this." Auden stepped out of line and strode to the front, Len following. It took him approximately eight point two seconds to find two kids near the front who were willing to take fifty bucks to switch spots with them.

Once he and Len got into the club, it took a minute to adjust to the colored lights and the noise. Lennox grimaced. "Goddamn, it smells like armpit and asshole in here."

"You're being generous. Look for her," Auden said, trying to crane his neck and see over the crowd.

"I'm looking. Everyone looks the same. Sweaty and plastered."

They walked around the left side of the club, but neither of them spotted her. The place was too crowded with too many flashing lights. And the heavy bass of the club music made it hard to concentrate. "Where the fuck is she?"

"Isn't that the roommate?" Lennox asked, pointing toward a table off to the side of the makeshift dance floor.

Auden looked that way, spotting Quyen chatting with some guy, and relief flooded him. "That's her."

They maneuvered their way over to the table, the press of people around them making it difficult to move quickly. Quyen saw Auden first. She broke into a big, lopsided smile and stepped away from the guy she'd been talking to. "Oh wow, y'all came," she said with open enthusiasm. "O'Neal said you couldn't make it."

"Plans changed," Auden said, trying to talk over the music. "Do you know where she is?"

She pointed past them. "She's been dancing with Connall."

He wanted to say *who the fuck is Connall,* but when he turned that way, it didn't take a genius to figure it out. A dude with curly red hair was dancing up on some girl on the dance floor. No, not some girl. *O'Neal.*

"Whoa," Lennox said next to him. "She's...damn."

It was as if Len had spoken Auden's thoughts aloud. If Quyen hadn't pointed O'Neal out, he would've never recognized her. She was pressed up against the redhead and wearing the shortest dress he'd ever seen her in. The dude's hand was half on her naked back, half on her ass. By the way they were moving, he could tell that O'Neal was partially leaning into him for support, not quite steady on her feet.

A rush of *oh hell no* went through Auden, making him see red. Quyen was talking again, but he couldn't pay attention to the words. He muttered a thanks to her and stalked forward, winding through the people between him and the dance floor. Lennox followed right behind.

When Auden reached the handsy redhead, he tapped him on the shoulder. "Can I cut in?"

"Fuck off, dude," Connall said. "She's with me."

Auden's fists clenched as he barely resisted taking the guy by the collar and physically dragging him away from O'Neal.

As if sensing the tenuous hold Auden had on his temper,

Lennox stepped next to Auden, all placid expression, but when he spoke, the tone was laced with frosty menace. "I strongly suggest you get your hands off my friend's girlfriend, or we're all going to have a problem."

O'Neal lifted her head and squinted like she wasn't quite sure of the language in this country. "*Auden?* Len?"

"You know these guys?" Connall's gaze was wary now, his tone unsure.

"Heeey...what are y'all doing here?" O'Neal asked, her words sloppy.

Auden inhaled a calming breath and put out his hand. "Dancing with you. Come on. My turn."

"O'Neal?" the redhead asked, sending her a hopeful look.

She patted his shoulder. "S'okay. I'll meet you back at the table."

Connall looked confused and then annoyed. He shot Auden and Lennox a withering look but was bright enough not to pick a fight with two taller, much more sober guys. He rolled his eyes. "Whatever."

Auden took O'Neal's hand, guiding her closer to him. She braced a hand on his shoulder and leaned toward his ear, the smell of cheap liquor on her breath. "Wha's goin' on?"

Lennox stepped up behind her, his gaze meeting Auden's in silent solidarity, and he began to move to the music, putting his hands lightly on her waist. "You drunk texted Aud," Lennox said. "We wanted to make sure you were okay."

"I'm s'okay. I tried tequila!" she said with a goofy, triumphant smile.

Auden couldn't help but laugh. Now that he knew she was safe, he could relax—and enjoy the view because...*fuuuuck*, she looked hot. Even if silly drunk. "I can see that. How much of this tequila did you try, Ms. Lory?"

She wrinkled her nose like she was trying to concentrate.

"Three shots? Four? I think? Connall told me it'd help me dance better."

"I bet he did," Lennox said. "He also knew it'd increase his odds that you'd dance with *him*. You're way out of his league."

She made a *pfft* sound.

Auden slid his hand onto her back, the bare skin burning his palm and making him want to touch her everywhere. It was driving him crazy that there was nothing but a thin piece of fabric keeping her from him, not even a bra. He took a deep breath. "You shouldn't drink that much if you don't have someone sober looking out for you."

She frowned, a line appearing between her brows. "Wait, did you jus' tell Connall you're my boyfriend?"

"No, I did that," Len said.

She turned, giving Auden her back and facing Lennox. He could see her shoulder muscles stiffen. "*Why?*"

Len gave her a disarming smile. "Because a few more drinks, Sweets, and you might've woken up with an Irish surprise in your bed tomorrow. We figured we'd give you an out."

"What if I didn't wants...*want* an out?" She turned back to Auden, all of it looking like some on-purpose group dance. "I told you...*noooo* babysitter."

Auden lifted a brow at her drunken indignation. "I'm not going to stop you. You want to go home with the redhead? Have your first time be sloppy, drunk sex with some random frat guy who fed you cheap liquor? That's your call. But I'd like to wait until you're sober enough to make that actual decision."

She pursed her lips. "I'm not...drunk."

"Mmm-hmm." He leaned in and lowered his voice. "Spell your name backward, Shaq."

"O no L..." Her jaw clenched, and she lost the rhythm for a minute. "Fine. I might be...lil' drunk. But I had to do *something*. You don't know how hard it is. To do all this stuff. For the first time. It's scary. I hate..." Her voice caught. "I hate feeling like I don't know what I'm doing. No one's ever told me how all these things are s'posed to work. I just have to figure it out all by myself, no instruction manual. I feel like an alien."

Her words cut into him, making him hurt for her. He reached out and pushed her hair behind her ear. "You're not an alien and you don't have to figure it out all by yourself, okay? I'm here. And Len. Whatever you need. And I'm sorry. You're right. It's not fair that you were kept from so much. But drinking to get past the nerves is a dangerous game. I just don't want you to do anything you'll regret. We can stay with you until you're clear-headed enough to make your own decisions tonight. Even if that decision ends up being the Irishman. Okay?"

The last part tasted sour on his tongue, but he forced himself to say it.

"Okay." She stared at him for a long moment and then blinked, her eyes going shiny. "I don't want to go home with Connall. He's nice and he asked me to, but… I don't know. I just don't know…*anything*, it feels like."

Relief coursed through Auden at the declaration, but he hated seeing her upset. "Hey, shh, it's okay. You don't have to know everything."

Lennox met his gaze over her shoulder, concern there, and a silent conversation seemed to pass between them.

Auden nodded, took a breath, and then gently grabbed O'Neal's wrists and hooked them around his neck. "Here. Let's not overthink it. We can show you what a night out can be like. You want to dance tonight? Let's dance. You want to get shit-faced? Get shit-faced and we'll take care of you. You want to see what a hangover's like? We'll have hair of the dog ready in the morning."

"Hair of what dog?" she asked, looking thoroughly confused.

"I'll explain later," he said. "Just…stop worrying for a little while. I've got you. Will you trust me on that?"

She nodded and tightened her arms around his neck, bringing her body closer. "Okay."

"Yeah?" he asked, the warmth of her against him sending ripples of awareness through him.

"Yes." Then she put her head on his shoulder. "Make sure Quyen's okay too."

Lennox squeezed her shoulder. "On it."

Auden sent him a silent thank you, and Lennox went back toward the table. Auden rubbed his hand along O'Neal's back. He meant it to be a soothing motion, but the silky feel of her skin beneath his fingertips was making his blood relocate southward. She made a soft, needy sound against his neck, and he started reciting the Latin prayers he'd learned as an altar boy to try to keep himself in check. *Agnus Dei, qui tollis peccata mundi: miserere nobis...*

*Have mercy upon us.*

He needed all the help he could get right now.

They finished out the song, and when another blended into the last and changed beats, they stayed on the dance floor. The new one had a heavier, pulsing beat, letting them slow down some. A song meant for grinding languidly against each other. Something he probably shouldn't do.

He ignored the internal warning and pulled her a little closer, inhaling the scent of her hair.

"You look great tonight, by the way," he said, tracing the curve of her spine with his fingers. "Your grandmother would have a heart attack."

She laughed, her breath coasting against his neck. "It's Quyen's dress, would kill Nana for sure. Couldn't even wear a bra—which feels weird. And she made me wear a thong because the dress shows panty lines. Like, who even cares if lines show?"

He groaned at her loose, drunken tongue. "Things you don't need to tell me."

"Why?" She lifted her head, the lights flashing blue over her skin and that wrinkle between her brows appearing again. He couldn't tell if it was the liquor blocking the obvious answer or her inexperience.

"Because I'm pressed up against you, and the last thing I need to be thinking about is that all you're wearing underneath that dress is a little strip of dental floss." That if he slid his palms up that hem, there'd be nothing in the way if he wanted to give her ass a nice little smack, see her skin turn pink. His cock flexed against his fly. *Shit.*

Her eyebrows lifted. "That...turns you on?"

"No, O'Neal," he said, dipping his head closer, the sex music getting into his bloodstream. "*You* turn me on. I can usually put that aside, but telling me about what kind of panties you're wearing makes that harder. Makes *me* hard, actually, so maybe let's talk about the weather or the stock market or nuclear physics. How 'bout that Pythagorean theorem?"

She blinked. "You're...hard?"

The way she said the word, with such wonder, sounded absolutely obscene to his ear. Against his better judgment, he slid his hand to her hip, and pulled her fully against him, nestling her against his stiffening cock.

She sucked in a sharp breath, and he shuddered at the painfully good feel of her brushing against him. *Fuck, fuck, fuck.* He eased his grip on her, giving them both a little space.

Her eyes had widened, and she rubbed her lips together, looking nervous but also way too intrigued. That combo of curiosity and want was what Lennox had been talking about. It was fucking irresistible. She was triggering fantasies inside him that he hadn't been aware he had.

Without a word, O'Neal held the eye contact for a moment as if debating something and then adjusted her arms around his neck and got close again, their bodies now touching everywhere. Bold. Brave.

He was going to lose his mind.

She closed her eyes and danced.

They stayed that way for song after song, losing themselves to the beat of the music and the feel of each other until he was so hard against her, he thought he might explode right there on the dance floor. He breathed deeply through his nose, reminding himself that she was drunk, that he needed to be the responsible one.

He lost track of time. Of how many songs. At some point, Lennox brought them bottles of water and danced with Quyen nearby. The redheaded guy had found a new partner, and before long, he was sloppily sucking on that girl's neck in the middle of the dance floor. But Auden barely noticed. He didn't want to break the spell of the moment. O'Neal was getting what she wanted. She'd let go of her nerves and was enjoying herself, being free. And Auden had never seen her look sexier.

When the DJ started playing "Late at Night" by Buffalo Tom on repeat, Auden realized they'd danced all the way until closing time. O'Neal lifted her head as if just noticing that the song was playing for the third time. Her hair was clinging to her neck, and her skin was damp with exertion. This was what she'd look like after a night with him in bed. Flushed and sweaty and undone. He wanted to lick the salt off her skin, taste how turned on she was. But he kept his thoughts and tongue to himself. He was supposed to be the sober, responsible one tonight.

She met his stare. Her gaze was as clear as he'd seen it all night. She'd sobered up. The carriage was about to turn into a pumpkin. Reality was going to creep in.

"We should probably go," he said softly. "It's past last call."

She nodded and opened her mouth to respond but then shut it again. She pressed her lips together.

"What's wrong?" he asked. He braced for her to tell him he was a jackass for interrupting her night with her friend, for

116

breaking in on the dance with the redhead, for holding her closer than a friend should, for—

"Why do you put it aside?"

The question threw him, and he tried to find which thread of this conversation he'd missed. "What?"

Her throat bobbed. "If I turn you on, why do you put that aside? You know I...like you. I'm not great at hiding that. I mean, stuff got pretty personal on movie night. But ever since, you've avoided acknowledging anything happened." Her gaze shifted off to some spot over his left shoulder. "Is it because you'd think I'd be terrible at...everything?"

He stopped swaying to the music. "Are you being serious?"

Her gaze darted back to his briefly, and she gave him a look that told him all he needed to know. Even with the slightly smeared mascara and the exhaustion of hours on the dance floor, he could see the vulnerability there, the insecurity.

He cupped her jaw, tilting her face toward him, making her look at him. "O'Neal, that's not it at all. I have no doubt that it'd be amazing to touch you, to show you things, to see you come apart. I haven't thought about much else tonight...or honestly, since movie night," he admitted. "But it's not a deficit in you. It's a deficit in me. I put it aside because you deserve better than what I could give you."

She held his gaze this time, brave. "What if what you could give me," she said so quietly he barely heard her over the music, "could be exactly what I need?"

He stopped breathing for a moment, searching her face. "What do you mean?"

"You assume I want a boyfriend." A flush was darkening her cheeks. "Maybe I just want a"—she swallowed hard like she wasn't quite sure which word she wanted—"*teacher* I can trust."

His muscles tightened, his blood flashing hot.

"I'm tired of being in the dark," she said, her courage obviously gaining steam. "And I'm tired of being scared of the unknown. In my life, when I wanted to know about a topic, I always knew where to go—how to research, how to learn. But with this...physical stuff, there's no easy way to do that. I mean, I'm not dumb. I know I could find porn on the internet, but that's not going to give me what I need to know. I want to know what things are like. To feel what they're like." She slid her hands to his waist, tentatively slipping her fingers beneath the hem of his T-shirt, her fingertips grazing his skin. "To touch. To be touched."

His stomach dipped, and his cock flexed. "O'Neal..."

"And I want to do that with someone who's a...trusted friend, someone who isn't going to make me feel stupid if I do something wrong or don't know the right way. The guy who, when he got a drunk text from me, came all the way out here to make sure I was all right." She slid her hands back up to his shoulders as if the skin-to-skin contact had been too much, and he already missed the feel of her hands on him. "You keep trying to save me from bumbling freshmen and drunken frat boys. But if you don't want my first experiences to be bad, then why not guarantee that—by being the person who gives them to me?"

He closed his eyes, breathed. She was going to kill him. Outcome: death on the dance floor. Weapon: words.

"If you know anything about me, you know I'm one hell of a student," she said, a smile in her voice. "I always get an A plus."

*Fucking hell.* He had strong willpower, but every man had his limits. She was flipping switches in him left and right. *Show me. Touch me. Teach me. I'll get an A, and you can tell me what a good girl I am.* The erotic pictures she was painting for him without even knowing it were melting his brain.

"You're killing me, Shaq," he said, one last-ditch effort to keep him from jumping off the cliff. "I'm trying to do the right thing."

"Maybe that's overrated." She visibly swallowed but her chin tipped upward. "You want me to beg?"

*Yes. Fuck, yes.* On her knees without a stitch of clothes on, those pretty lips asking for all the salacious things he wanted to show her, his fingers tight in her hair.

But no. That he couldn't have. But this? Just a little taste. Maybe this.

He slid his palms along her arms and gripped her wrists, stilling her hands against his collarbone and feeling her pulse beating against his fingertips. He held the eye contact, trying to come up with the right words to say. But the open want on her face was too damn much. He lowered his head and did what he'd been wanting to do all night. He kissed her.

She seemed to melt the instant their lips touched, like he'd offered her the greatest relief, and he held her wrists tight. Her lips parted, and he dove into the kiss, his tongue tangling with hers, a groan escaping him. She stayed where he held her, letting him control the pace of the kiss, and that only made it hotter. He wanted to find a dark corner and shove her dress up, slide his hand between her thighs and rip that fucking thong off, tuck his fingers inside her and feel just how badly she ached to have him there.

But before his baser instincts could fully take over, he felt a hand on his shoulder. He startled, pulling away from O'Neal, and turned his head.

"Sorry to interrupt, kids, but they're kicking us out," Lennox said, cocking his thumb toward the bar, expression inscrutable. "Y'all are the last ones left on the dance floor."

O'Neal blinked and looked around, surprise registering on her face at the sight of the empty club. "Where's Quyen?"

"She caught a ride with a girl from one of her classes a while ago," Len said. "The friend was sober. I told her we'd make sure you got home all right. After a lengthy interrogation, she agreed to let us give you a ride."

"Oh," O'Neal said, still looking a little dazed.

"Ready to head back to the dorms?" Lennox asked.

"Um." O'Neal looked to Auden, questions in her eyes.

"Or...not?" Len glanced between the two of them, eyebrows up.

"Not," Auden said, keeping his focus on O'Neal, the decision smoothing something jagged inside him. He put his hand out to her. "She's coming home with me."

Some combination of relief and trepidation crossed over her features, but then she smiled and put her hand in his. "I'm coming home with you."

Lennox sent Auden a look over O'Neal's shoulder, and a slow smile crept up his friend's lips. "Okay then. Let's get out of here."

# CHAPTER TEN

$\mathcal{O}$'Neal knew she should be freaking out as she sat in the front seat next to Auden on the way to his apartment. She was supposed to be nervous. And somewhere in her psyche, she probably was. But as soon as Auden had put out his hand and asked her to come home with him, a deep level of calm had moved through her.

If she could pick any person in the world to walk her through this experience, it would be him. She'd known for a while that she didn't want to wait until she was married for sex. She wasn't sure if she'd ever want to get married at all. But there was so much she didn't know that the thought of trying something with someone was too overwhelming and intimidating to fathom—to even fantasize about. Except with Auden. She'd long been able to imagine it with Auden. He wouldn't let this be scary or bad for her. If she had questions, he'd answer them. If she did something wrong, he'd show her the right way without making her feel bad about it. She trusted that with one hundred percent certainty. She trusted *him*.

And no, this wasn't the conventional way to go about things. They weren't going to date. He wasn't going to be her

RONI LOREN

boyfriend. She knew that. He was going to be her...teacher. But she imagined she could do a lot worse when it came to first times. Plus, something about the thought of having Auden be in charge of things made her skin tingle. She knew how to be a student. It was what she'd always been best at.

So, in her gut, she knew this was the right choice. She had yet to regret him being her first kiss. Auden was gorgeous and funny and kind. He made her hot all over, but she also felt safe with him. She'd rather experience first-time things with her trusted friend than to roll the dice with some guy she met randomly.

If she'd gone home with Connall tonight, she'd be in a full-blown panic by now. She'd be afraid of embarrassing herself or feeling awkward or making a mistake. Or worse...putting herself in a dangerous situation. She hadn't gotten a bad vibe from Connall, but she also didn't *know* him yet. Her mom had gone somewhere with some guy and had never made it home. She needed more experience and tools in her arsenal before she could tackle those situations with guys who actually could be potential dates or boyfriends.

With Auden, she could take those unknown factors out of play. She *knew* Auden. Had grown up with him, had seen him be goofy and weird and sexy and smart, had seen him be good to his sister, sweet to his parents. He was a straight-up nice guy.

One who was about to relieve her of her virginity.

A ping went through her at that, some weird combination of anticipation and anxiety. A roller coaster climb.

She must've made some sound of distress because Auden glanced over at her, the glare from the streetlights flashing across his face. "You okay? You're pretty quiet over there."

She forced a tight smile and nodded. "Uh-huh."

"Least convincing uh-huh ever," Lennox said from the back-seat. "The silence is killing me, you guys. You two decide to hook up, and suddenly everyone has forgotten how to talk."

"Len," Auden warned, sending a glance to the rearview mirror.

"No, it's okay," O'Neal said, turning to look at Lennox. "You're right. We're making this awkward. Sorry."

"And we're not *hooking up*," Auden clarified. "Don't make it sound like that."

"Oh. Dating?"

Auden sniffed. "Not your business, Len."

But O'Neal felt weird leaving Lennox out of the loop. No, it wasn't his business, but he'd been so open with her since they'd met—not to mention that she'd kissed the guy—that she felt the desire to share. "It's not dating," she said. "I asked Auden to... teach me things."

Lennox's lips parted, and he quickly glanced at the rearview mirror to look at Auden. "Fucking hell." He let out a long breath and ran a hand over the back of his head. "*You* asked *him?* To teach you things in bed?"

She nodded, confused by his response.

He shook his head. "Damn, Sweets, you're the boldest virgin I've ever met."

The words made her stiffen.

He must've read her expression because he quickly added. "I don't mean that as a bad thing. It's a beautiful thing. A fucking sexy thing. Now I know why Aud's not talking. His head is about to explode because he can't believe his luck."

Auden laughed quietly, and her gaze shifted to him. He reached out and squeezed her hand. "He's not wrong."

"Of course, I'm not," Lennox said. "I rarely am. But good for you two. Count me jealous."

O'Neal looked toward the back seat, her ears catching on the word *jealous*.

Lennox's lips hitched at the corner. "Don't look so surprised. I didn't kiss you that night just to piss off Aud. I would've happily taught you anything you wanted to know too." He gave her a full smile, a wicked gleam in his eyes. "Feel free to reach out later if you want. You can get your bachelor's degree with Auden. When you're ready for your master's, come and find me."

Her mouth opened, the shock of his words leaving her speechless for a moment, and a ripple of something she *did not* want to acknowledge moving through her.

She looked to Aud, expecting him to be pissed, but he simply snorted and playfully flipped Lennox off with his right hand.

O'Neal looked between the two of them. "Is this normal? A guy's friend flirting with the girl he's with?"

"Not really," Auden admitted. "But Len and I don't do the territorial thing. A woman can make up her own mind on who she wants to be with. That's not a decision for us to make."

"Exactly," Len said, leaning back, his inked arm stretched out over the back seat. "Him. Me. Both. Whatever."

Her breath caught, her brain short-circuiting for a second.

"But if the flirting makes you uncomfortable," Lennox added. "I'll shut up. I'm not trying to woo you away from Aud. I saw you two on the dance floor tonight. I know what's what."

She probably should feel uncomfortable that Lennox was putting all this out there, but for some reason, she couldn't break eye contact with him. He was almost daring her not to look away. This whole dynamic felt foreign to her, like she'd landed on another planet, but after a lifetime of being locked away from boys and avoiding their attention, feeling the weight of two guys telling her they wanted her was quite a rush.

"I don't mind," she said, impressed she kept her voice steady.

His lips curved ever so slightly. "Excellent."

This was just a game. A fun one to play. It wasn't like she was going to pursue anything with Lennox. He'd called her bold, but she had her limits. She had a feeling he wasn't lying about the master's degree. Lennox was full of charm and easy smiles, but some instinctual part of her recognized the sharp teeth beneath, the edge. He was not the boy next door like Auden. He was like jumping into the deep end with no lifeguard in sight. She didn't even know how to tread water in this pool.

She turned back to Auden and took his hand again, lacing her fingers with his, the touch grounding her.

"Still with me, freshman? You can always change your mind at any time."

She took a deep breath and smiled. "Still with you. Nervous as all get out. But I don't want to change my mind."

He brought her hand to his mouth and kissed her knuckles. "It's okay to be nervous, but I promise I'll take it as slowly as you need. Things might not go very far tonight, and that's totally fine."

He slowed the car as an unexpected line of traffic appeared around the next turn. The side street was dark, but a parade of taillights stretched in front of them.

She groaned. "How is there traffic?"

"Looks like a fender bender." Auden peeked at the rearview mirror. "Damn. And now we're trapped. Two cars behind us. I can't back up."

"Fantastic," she said, her brain trying to whirl and spin with thoughts of what could go wrong tonight. What if she completely embarrassed herself? Her knee started bobbing up and down, the jitters turning physical.

A hand touched her shoulder. Lennox. "You okay, Sweets?"

She swallowed past the tightness in her throat. "Sorry. I'm fine. Just…"

"Starting to panic?" he asked, tone gentle.

She peeked back at him. "Not panic so much as overthinking. It's a bad habit of mine. It's like when they gave me ten minutes in a room alone before I had to give my valedictorian speech. By the time I got to the stage, I had already pictured myself tripping on my gown, forgetting how to speak, passing out, losing my notecards, crying, and/or burping mid-sentence."

RONI LOREN

Lennox chuckled and gave her shoulder a gentle squeeze. "Hey, if it makes you feel better, some of those would be good results from sex. I mean, if Auden can make you forget how to speak for a little while, job well done. And cry? Sometimes even better."

Her lips parted and a little sound of surprise escaped her. "People *cry?*"

It was still strange openly talking about these things. That Auden's best friend had just casually suggested Auden might be able to give her an orgasm strong enough to make her lose speech or cry and it was fine.

"You're going to make her more nervous," Auden said with a sigh. He put his hand on her thigh and rubbed gently, the touch both soothing and sending hot shivers through her. "I'm not going to make you cry."

"You don't know that," Lennox said, a teasing sparkle in his eyes as he looked at O'Neal. "The lovely Miss Lory may be a crier. We don't know what she's like when she comes. How's it go for you when you're alone, Sweets?"

O'Neal put her hand over her face. "Oh my God, we *are not* discussing this."

"Len, stop freaking her out," Auden said, his palm warm against her leg.

When O'Neal lowered her hand, Len gave her a tilted smile. "I'm not trying to freak you out. Just trying to keep you from overthinking things while we sit here. When I touched your shoulder, it was like touching steel. You're as tense as a bowstring."

"I know. I'm sorry," she said, frustrated with her automatic reactions.

"You don't have to be sorry. It's completely understandable. But I bet we can help. Or Auden can at least," he said. "Want some help getting back in the right headspace?"

She considered him. "What do you mean?"

126

He cocked his head. "Get in the back seat, Sweets."

She shivered at the suggestion, but his calm expression had her taking another deep breath. "Why?"

"I'm going to take over the wheel for a while," he said. "Let you and Auden hang back here. I bet he can make you forget to be nervous."

She glanced at Auden. He was looking at her intently and he gave a little nod. "Might help."

She swallowed hard, butterflies alighting in her stomach. "What might help?"

"Trust me?" he asked.

The question was a loaded one, but the answer rose in her without edit. "Okay."

Auden put the car in park since they weren't moving anyway, and they all got out and switched seats. She was relieved to feel steady on her feet as she made the move, the effects of the alcohol having faded considerably after switching to water and dancing with Auden for hours.

When Lennox clicked his seat belt and shifted into drive again, he peeked back at them. "Auden can help you get out of your head and remind you how you were feeling when y'all were pressed up against each other. You both have my word I won't look."

Her heart thumped at the implication, and Len turned back toward the road.

"He's right." Auden shifted toward her, his voice low and intimate, creating a private space between them. "I can help." He tucked a stray lock of hair behind her ear and then pressed a soft kiss to her lips. "Len won't look. He'll keep that promise. Is it okay if I touch you?"

"*Here?*" She glanced out the darkened window.

"No one can see in," he said, cupping her jaw. "Let me make you feel good."

Her throat was tight like a fist, her mouth dry, but she found herself nodding, mesmerized by the suggestion and the way he was looking at her. "Okay."

"Tell me to stop at any point if you want me to stop," Auden whispered against her ear. "I'll always listen." When she didn't say anything more, he nipped at the lobe of her ear. "Close your eyes, freshman."

Her eyelids fluttered shut, her heart hammering.

Auden's hand slid onto her knee, and she startled, slamming her knees together.

"Shh," he said softly. "You're okay. Just breathe and try to focus on what you're feeling. Forget everything else except how it feels where I'm touching you."

She inhaled deeply and nodded, loosening her clamped knees.

His fingers traced lightly over her knee, circling and lingering on the inner side, sending trails of heat upward.

"I know you're nervous about tonight and that's okay. It's normal." He kissed her behind her ear. "But I promise you, I'm going to do everything I can to make you feel good." His fingertips tracked higher, tracing up her inner thigh just a little and sending an electric shiver straight to her core. "I've been thinking of almost nothing else since I saw you in this dress tonight. I've damn near lost my mind imagining all the things I want to do to you. You're so fucking sexy, O'Neal. You have no idea how lucky I feel to be the first one to touch you, the first guy who gets to make you come, the first to hear what sounds you make when someone's deep inside you. When *I'm* deep inside you."

He traced a blunt fingernail up her thigh, and she let out a soft gasp.

"I lied that night we watched the movie," he said, his hot palm now flat against her inner thigh, spreading her legs wider, opening her. "I know I'd be into countertop sex because that day you kissed me in my family's kitchen, I wanted to strip you naked right there in the sunshine and take you."

Her body twitched in response, an ache going through her and a steady throb settling between her legs.

"That night, I slicked up my hand and imagined it, imagined you," he said, his voice low and full of gravel. "Me tugging off those shorts you were wearing, spreading your legs open to see how wet you'd gotten for me, tasting you. Hearing you beg for me to do more, to fuck you, to fill you up."

She licked her lips, the scene painting across her imagination and her blood rushing to all her most secret places.

"Have you thought of me that way?" he asked, his fingers brushing along the tender skin of her upper inner thigh, close, so close to where she ached most. "When you've touched yourself?"

Self-consciousness flooded her, but after an internal pep talk, she managed the barest of nods.

"Say it to me," he said, voice cajoling. "Nothing to be ashamed of."

She forced herself to breathe slowly, to find her voice, to trust that she was safe with Auden. "Yes."

"Good girl."

The words should've sounded patronizing but breath-stealing arousal punched her in the gut. *Whoosh.*

His hand ventured higher. The car was moving again, but she didn't open her eyes, didn't want to break the spell. His finger traced over the front of her now-damp panties, and her nails dug into her palms. "You know how to make yourself come?"

His touch was making it hard to concentrate. "I...I think so. Maybe?"

He let out a little grunt, and there was a slightly pained sound from the front seat.

"That's a no then," Auden said. "I'd like to say I'm sorry to hear that, but I'm selfish enough to be happy that I get to be the one to show you."

He dragged the little swath of fabric aside, and his fingers traced over her slippery skin. She let out an embarrassingly needy sound as her hips lifted, seeking, seeking.

He breathed out a soft *fuck.*

Hearing him lose his cool a little gave her a surge of reassurance. He wasn't fully put together either.

He circled her little bundle of nerves with his fingertip, and her back arched, the unfamiliarity of someone else touching her there amplifying the sensation by a thousand. She'd touched herself before, but that was always chased with so much shame that she couldn't fully enjoy it. This…this felt different.

The scent of her arousal drifted on the air, and shame tried to well up, but his circling fingers kept chasing away any thoughts. "Look how pretty you are here," he said, his fingers expertly drawing whimpers from her. "All slick and swollen and probably desperate for me to slide my fingers inside, give you some relief."

Her thighs tensed, her body bracing for something. But just as she was reaching for whatever that was, he moved his hand away and shifted her panties back over her.

She let out a sound of protest, and her eyes popped open. It took a moment for her vision to clear, but she saw they were in the driveway of his place. How had they made it all the way home? She turned to Auden. His gaze was heavy on her, his neck flushed and damp.

"Why are you stopping?" she asked, her voice a whisper.

He reached out and brushed his fingers across her lips. The scent and taste made her gasp. Had he just used the same fingers —*yes, yes he had.* He leaned over and kissed her gently, sucking the taste from her lips.

"I'm stopping because we're home and I don't want your first real orgasm to be in the back seat of a car. But…still nervous?"

Awareness dawned. Her nerves had been chased into a dark corner. All she wanted right now was more of Auden, more of whatever he was giving her. If he'd tried to strip her naked in the back seat, she probably would've let him.

"No."

"Good." Auden smiled. "Len, you mind heading up and unlocking the door for us?"

*Lennox.* She'd forgotten. *Oh my God.* Mortification burned up her body, fire settling in her face.

Her horror must've been evident because Auden cupped her chin. "Don't do that. Don't be embarrassed. Nothing to be ashamed of."

"He's right," Len said from the front seat, the quality of his voice different, deeper.

She forced herself to look his way.

He met her gaze, a quiet intensity there. "Thanks for trusting me to be here for that. I kept my promise and didn't look, but listening...that was hot as fuck." He gave her a chagrined smile and reached downward. "I'm hard as a goddamned rock."

Without realizing how it'd look, she leaned over, her attention going downward. A thick erection was outlined beneath his hand. The spot between her legs where she was already throbbing squeezed tight, and her teeth dragged along her bottom lip.

"Yeah, you did that," Len said, no ire there. "Now, I'll leave you two kids to it. Obviously, I have something to take care of if I want to be able to walk straight tomorrow." Lennox gave her a playful wink and then climbed out of the car. "Don't do anything I wouldn't do."

As she watched Len saunter off, she could feel Auden watching her, studying her.

She adjusted her dress, pulling the hem down and feeling suddenly awkward. She ventured a glance at Auden, finding a pensive look on his face. "What? Why are you looking at me like that?"

He tilted his head. "You like that you got Len hot and bothered."

She stiffened, the words making her want to backpedal. "What are you talking about? I—"

"It's not an accusation," he said with a little smile. "Just an observation. If you want to learn, then we need to pay attention to what turns you on. Some people...like to be watched. Others like the power trip of knowing they can tease someone. Maybe you fall into one or both of those categories."

Her mouth opened and closed, probably making her look like a guppy. "You're making me sound like some kind of freak."

He laughed. "Not at all. Everybody has their turn-ons. Sometimes they're common, sometimes they're quirky, sometimes kinky. As long as everyone involved is a consenting adult, nothing wrong with any of it."

She rubbed her hand over her forehead, the sheer amount of possibilities overwhelming. "I don't know what I am."

"That's okay." He took her hand and ran his thumb across her knuckles. "How do you feel about the fact that he's definitely going upstairs to jerk off to thoughts of what he just witnessed?"

She rolled her lips together, shyness trying to take over.

"There's no wrong answer," he said.

She took a breath and glanced at the house, thinking about Lennox inside. "Seeing him like that made me feel...warm. But I don't feel powerful. I maybe feel...bad for him? Like it's not fair that he has to be alone."

Auden's eyes narrowed. "Hmm. Good to know."

A laugh escaped her, surprising her, and she poked him in the chest. "*Good to know?* What is that? You pull answers out of me and then don't tell me what they mean?"

He smiled and bent forward to kiss her. "I'm gathering information. Final results to be determined later. But for now, let's note that maybe you have a little exhibitionist streak hiding in there. Wouldn't have guessed that."

She huffed. "Right. Thanks. So I'm a freak. A virgin freak, no less."

He reached for the door and sent her a teasing look. "Hey, look on the bright side, we can handle one part of that soon enough. Then you'll just be a freak."

"Ugh!" She tried to smack his arm, but he was already out of the car.

Auden walked around to the other side and opened her door, an unrepentant smile on his face. "Come on, freshman." He put his hand out to her. She took it, still stewing in her righteous indignation, but then he slid a hand onto her backside and pulled her to him. "If it makes you feel better, I'd take you right here on the hood of the car for all the world to see if you were into it. You might have a baby exhibitionist streak." He touched his forehead to hers. "Mine is full grown."

Her eyes widened.

"But tonight," he said, brushing his lips against her ear, "I want you all to myself."

# CHAPTER ELEVEN

*a*uden felt the weight of responsibility pressing down on him as he led O'Neal upstairs. The two sides of himself were warring—the small-town kid who wanted to do the right thing, who wanted to make this experience sweet and special—*traditional*—for O'Neal, and the other side of himself that was frothing at the mouth at the thought of having her fully under his tutelage, that student/teacher dynamic a kink he hadn't realized he had until O'Neal showed up. That was a different flavor of dominance than he was used to. Most of the women he played dominance games with were older than he was and more experienced. *He* learned from *them.* Those women could've played the role of the eager student if he'd asked, but O'Neal embodied it.

Her putting her trust in him was both the ultimate gift and a heavy burden. He didn't want to screw this up for her. He'd already let things go too far in the car. Bringing her to the edge of orgasm while Len was driving had been sexy as hell, but it'd also been out of bounds. O'Neal didn't know enough to realize that the dynamic he and Lennox had was outside the norm, that most guys weren't going to finger her in front of their roommate. And if they did, it would be because they were using her for entertainment, objectifying her.

Auden didn't pretend that his and Len's kink for sharing was noble by any means, but he liked to think that the woman was an equal partner in it, someone who also got off on the sharing aspect. O'Neal probably didn't even know menage was a thing, much less know enough about it to decide whether or not she was into it. He'd only gotten lucky that she hadn't been horrified that Len had been there.

"You okay?" O'Neal asked, her hand twitching in his as they made their way up the stairs. "Now you've gone quiet."

He looked over at her, her face silhouetted by the cloudy night sky, and smiled what he hoped was a reassuring smile. "I'm good. Just lost in thought."

They reached the landing in front of the door. She turned to him, a little wrinkle appearing at the bridge of her nose. "About what?"

He sighed and grabbed her other hand, facing her. "Just that I need you to promise me that you feel comfortable telling me no at any time. Literally any time."

Her brows twitched upward. "You don't think I would?"

He pressed his lips together, trying to find the right words, trying to smooth that jagged worry that kept cropping up inside him. "I just...I know you like me. Maybe had a little crush when you were younger?"

A flicker of panic crossed her face. "Uh..."

"It's okay. It's fine. I just, you're so new to all of this, and I'm in the driver's seat and I don't want you to feel like you have to...impress me or prove something to me. Or be a certain way. I don't want you to ever think...well, he asked me to do this thing or that thing and other women probably do this and so I should because that must be the way things are. Or whatever. I'm not explaining myself right."

She frowned, her gaze searching his face. "Okay..."

She sounded confused, and he hated that he couldn't get the point he was trying to make to come out the right way. "I guess if we're calling what we're doing lessons, I want your first lesson to be to only say yes to things that honestly turn you on or excite you. And if you're not sure and we start something and you decide in the middle of it—nope, not for me—you need to tell me. Immediately."

A self-conscious laugh escaped her. "What are you planning to ask me to do, Aud?"

He didn't smile. "We've barely even started, and I asked you to let me touch you in front of my roommate. That's not a typical thing people do on dates."

"I figured." She stared at him for a long moment. "Why'd you do it then?"

He swallowed past the constriction in his throat, not wanting to say it but knowing he owed her that much. "Because the things I like...aren't always typical."

The glimmer of surprise was there for a moment, but she covered it quickly. "Oh."

"I'm not going to—that's not what I plan for us. I want to make you feel good. I want to show you the basics, give you those first experiences. But I'm asking for your promise because in the heat of the moment, like in the car tonight, I might get carried away and push boundaries. This whole *teach me* vibe you're throwing at me really presses my buttons. Like *really* presses them. So I need to know you're not just going to go along with something if you're not into it. Do nothing that you don't want to do. I need to be able to trust you as much as you need to be able to trust me."

She stared at him for a long moment, and he could tell her genius brain was trying to put the puzzle of him together, but it couldn't—she didn't have the right pieces. Finally, she stepped closer to him and kissed his cheek.

"I promise."

He let out a breath and lifted their joined hands to press his lips to her knuckles. "Thank you."

"And I'm okay," she said. "What happened in the car wasn't something I expected but...it helped me turn my brain off for a little while. I don't know how I knew, but I knew Lennox wouldn't look if he promised he wouldn't. I felt...safe to just experience it. Because you were there. I wouldn't have done that with anyone else."

"Yeah?" A warm sense of satisfaction coursed through him, filling him up.

"Yes. I doubt your ego needs any stroking, Auden Blake," she said wryly. "But those times in my life when I did let myself think about what certain things might be like, what they would feel like, when maybe I tested a few things out on my own..." She flashed an embarrassed smile. "You were the one I pictured doing it to me."

He gripped her hands, the admission like gasoline on a fire. O'Neal sneaking touches in the dark, trying to find pleasure, wishing he were the one lying next to her. Part of him worried that she could get complicated feelings about him after this if she'd been into him for a while, but the more selfish part of him was just rolling around in the knowledge that, in some ways, she'd already been his. He touched his forehead to hers.

"You've starred in a number of my solo sessions lately too, freshman. You're always very, very eager to learn."

She laughed, her eyelashes dipping down. "Guess you should teach me some things then, huh? See if I can manage not to mess up the fantasy?"

Her gaze dropped at that, that old shyness of hers surfacing, but the words were like a drug being injected into his bloodstream.

"I know you won't. You're doing everything right," he said softly. "Just being you."

"You too." She lifted her head, and he could feel her hands

trembling in his, but her eyes were sparkling. "What's next, Teach?"

He gave her a slow smile and reached for the door handle. "Just do as I say, and I promise I'll take good care of you."

O'NEAL'S STOMACH WAS DOING SOMERSAULTS AS SHE FOLLOWED Auden to his bedroom, but the sensation felt like anticipation more than fear. Auden had looked so concerned outside, so worried that he'd taken things too far already, that now, more than ever, she knew she'd made the right decision. With someone else, she'd have to worry she was being used or manip-ulated. She'd have to worry that she'd picked the wrong guy like her mom had and risk ending up hurt or assaulted or dead.

But not with Auden. He was her friend first before anything else. He wanted to make this good for her. He didn't want to push her further than she wanted to go. And apparently, he didn't want to freak her out with some of the things he liked. She was going to lose hours of sleep trying to figure out what those things could be. He'd admitted to an exhibitionist streak, but she got the sense it was more than that. Her sexual vocabu-lary wasn't large enough yet to even brainstorm the possibilities but…she was intrigued. Before tonight, she would've never fathomed that Mr. Hometown Golden Boy had any real secrets. He always seemed like such a confident, *what you see is what you get* kind of guy.

They passed a closed door in the hallway. Auden caught her looking.

"Len's room," he said and then stopped at the next doorway. "And mine."

She inhaled a deep breath as he guided her inside. The room was larger than any college student deserved but decorated simply. Pale wood floors, light gray walls, a dresser, a basic black bookcase filled with books and framed photos and what looked to be a few of Lennox's drawings, a matching desk with a laptop, and a row of swimming medals hung on pegs on the wall above. But what drew her eye the most was the unmade king-sized bed with rumpled white sheets and a black-and-white pin-striped comforter.

"This is a nice room," she said, taking it all in, the gravity of what was about to happen making it a little hard to take a full breath.

"Sorry," Auden said, walking over to the bed and flipping up the sheets and comforter to smooth it. "I left in a hurry this morning."

She smiled. "Don't worry. I won't tell your mom you don't make your bed."

He laughed and walked back over to her, taking her in his arms. "We're not going to be telling my mom a lot of things, I think."

She bit her lip.

He brushed the tip of his nose against hers. "Still with me, freshman?"

"Nerves are back," she admitted. "But yes, still with you, Teach."

He lifted his head and gave her a heated look. "I probably shouldn't like you calling me that nickname so much, but…" He grabbed her hand and gently guided it between them. He pressed her hand over his crotch where the steel of his erection pressed against her palm. "But it totally does it for me."

She sucked in a shallow breath, the feel of him even through his jeans sending an electric pulse through her. She tentatively cupped her hand, mapping him, marveling that she was doing this with him…with *Auden*.

He groaned softly. "It's okay to use some pressure. You won't hurt me."

This was news to her, and she was eager for more information. She looked down between their bodies, dragging her teeth across her lip, a little spark of boldness flashing inside her. "Can you show me how to touch you…without the jeans?"

His gaze met hers, steady fire burning there. "Sit on the bed."

The smooth command sent awareness rolling through her, but she found she wanted to do exactly as he said. She walked over to the edge of the bed and sat.

He took his time, slipping off his shoes and socks, balling up the latter and setting them aside. He watched her the whole time, like he was thoroughly enjoying making her wait. He put his hand on his waistband, and she held her breath. He walked slowly toward her. By the time he stopped in front of her and flicked open the button on his jeans, her heart was beating like a hummingbird's wings. The outline of his erection filled up her vision.

He reached out and cupped her chin, tilting her head upward and making her shiver.

"Unzip me, O'Neal," he said in that calm, commanding voice he had. "Take off my jeans."

She held his eye contact, her breath speeding up, and then lifted a trembling hand. She watched her fingers tug his zipper down as if they didn't belong to her. It wasn't enough, though. She wanted to see him, feel him. She rallied her courage and slid her hands to his waistband, pushing his jeans down. When she got them to his ankles, he stepped out of them. She raised her head and took in the view of the snug pair of black boxer briefs, the sheer maleness of him pushing against the thin fabric. He was hard. For *her*. She could barely wrap her head around that. She looked up again, catching him watching her with intense focus. He nodded, answering the question that must've been on her face.

With a slight tremor going through her, she lifted her hand and slipped it inside the fly of his boxers. The steely heat of his...*cock*—she forced herself to think the word—brushed her palm, and she let out a little gasp.

She wasn't the only one. When she wrapped her fingers around him, Auden made a low rumbly sound in the back of his throat. She used her other hand to push aside the fly, and then he was out, the most private part of him in the palms of her hands. She stared in awe as she gave him a tentative stroke. She would've never guessed his skin would be so velvety, so different from anything she'd ever felt. She kind of wanted to rub her cheek against it just to see how it would feel, to kiss the head of it to taste him. But she wasn't feeling quite that brave yet.

"The look on your face might kill me," he said, reaching out to run his fingers through her hair. "You have no idea how fucking sexy you are."

The compliment traced over her skin like a touch, leaving goosebumps in its wake. She wet her lips and slid her hand along his length again, marveling. "Is this okay? Does that feel good?"

He closed his eyes briefly, like he was pained in some way, but she got the sense it was good pain. "I'm not sure you could do anything to me right now that would make me feel bad, but stroking it is better when there's some sort of lubricant."

She eyed the little bead of fluid at the tip but figured that wouldn't be enough. "Do you have some?"

He put his hand over hers. "You don't need to worry about making me feel good right now. And honestly, I've been turned on so long tonight, if you give me a hand job or put your mouth on me, I'm not going to last long." He gave her a disarming smirk. "We can save those lessons for another day. Unless you want tonight's lesson to be how to get come out of your hair—not a fun lesson."

She laughed, a little awkwardness lingering but a shimmer of anticipation there too. They had time. This would get more comfortable. She would have access to his body and him to hers for more than tonight. "Okay."

"Tonight, I want to focus on you," he said, deftly tucking himself back into his boxers. "Stand up. I've been wanting to peel you out of this dress since the moment I saw you in it."

She stood on wobbly knees. "The moment you saw me in it, I was dancing with someone else."

"You're right. The moment I saw you in it, I wanted to physically remove the redhead from the building. And *then* strip you out of this dress

"So much for you not being possessive," she teased.

He grabbed the straps of her dress and leveled a look her way. "I'm not possessive around Len. Other dudes who put their hands on you? I might get a little caveman over."

A hot shiver went through her, the words pushing buttons she didn't know *she* had.

Auden slid her straps down her arms. He paused right as the dress was almost exposing her breasts as if giving her time to change her mind, but when she didn't move, he pushed it farther, baring her.

"Jesus," he whispered, his gaze scanning over her breasts, devouring her.

Her nipples tightened under his perusal, and she had to stop herself from arching toward him, the need to be touched rising in her like hunger. Gently, he ran a knuckle down the curve of her left breast and then circled her nipple, making goosebumps break out along her skin. A soft moan escaped her, and he lowered his head, pressing a soft kiss to the tip of her right breast while still circling the other.

Liquid desire flooded her, making her legs tremble. "Oh, God."

"Easy," he said, voice quiet as he lifted his head. "I want to see all of you."

The dress was still resting at her waist. She reached for it, but he nudged her hands away, wanting to do the undressing himself. He pushed it down in one smooth motion, and it pooled at her feet.

When she stood there in only her gladiator sandals and a black thong, reality rushed in and she had a knee-jerk desire to cover herself. She'd never been so exposed in front of anyone but a doctor. She had hips, a soft belly, stretch marks from a growth spurt on her thighs. Her list of physical insecurities ran through her head like a ticker tape. But then Auden cursed softly and cupped her breast again.

"You're so fucking beautiful." His finger traced down her sternum, sending a tight, needy feeling downward. "Perfect."

She looked away. "You don't have to say those things. I know I'm not—"

"No." He pressed a finger over her mouth, giving her a look that had her choking back her words. "Next lesson: *trust what I say.* I don't say things I don't mean. And if any guy ever tells you you're anything less than perfect, kick him in the balls and leave."

She smiled beneath his finger and nodded.

"Good girl," he said, voice gentling. "Turn around for me."

He lowered his hand, and she slowly turned to face the bed. He made a sound of approval and then traced his blunt fingernails down her spine, ending at the edge of her panties. He hooked a finger in the band, then pulled them down and off, cool air drifting over her and making her hyperaware. She toed them off and flicked them aside, a little stunned that she was now naked except for her shoes.

Auden's T-shirt went sailing over her shoulder, landing in a ball next to the bed. She wanted to turn and look, to see him, but she got the sense he wanted her to stay where she was.

His hands slid onto her hips, and he drew her body back against him. The heat of his chest warmed her, and his cock pressed against her backside—his *bare* cock. The silky feel of him had her knees wobbling.

"You're trembling," he said softly.

"I'm sorry," she whispered.

"Don't apologize." He wrapped an arm around her, splaying his palm along her belly, and his mouth dipped to her neck. "Breathe for me."

She inhaled slowly.

"You're okay," he said, voice soft and comforting. "I'm going to take good care of you. You're safe. It's just me and you. Two longtime friends. We'll go at whatever pace you need. We can stop here if you want."

She exhaled slowly and shook her head. "Please don't stop here. Please."

"Such good manners," he said, a hint of a smile in his voice. He kissed the spot where her shoulder met her neck. "Just try to focus on how you feel. Be in your body instead of your head." His tongue traced lines of sensation along her skin, making her shift against him. His teeth grazed the curve of her shoulder, and after a few more kisses, his other hand dipped low. Closer, closer… Her teeth dug into her bottom lip when he found the place where she was sensitive and slick.

She leaned back against his shoulder and moaned softly. His mouth teased her earlobe. "There you go. That's good. Feel how wet you are for me, how much your body craves this. It knows what to do."

Her muscles loosened, his words just what she needed to hear, and her attention zeroed in on the slightly callused tips of his fingers brushing over her with just enough pressure to make her feel a little crazed.

His breath tickled her ear. "Tell me where I'm touching you, freshman."

The command startled her, and she found herself pressing her lips together, giving a barely-there head shake.

He kissed her neck, and his finger circled that sensitive little button that made her feet arch. "Is that a no?"

She squeezed her eyes shut, the sensations making it hard to process her thoughts. Part of her wanted to do what he said, but the words wouldn't come. "It's not a no—it's an I don't know if I can."

He dipped his finger lower, sliding just the tip inside her, and her body clenched around him.

"The words can be a turn-on. And freeing. Claiming them can feel powerful." He rubbed his cock against the small of her back, slowly, slowly, that velvety heat obscenely sexy. "How did you feel the night I challenged you? Threatened to lick your pussy?"

"Shocked," she said quietly. "And turned on. Len said you had a dirty mouth."

"He wasn't wrong," he said, amusement in his voice. "I'm a fan of the fun words."

"Why?" she asked, her stomach tensing as he slid two fingers over her, spreading the slickness and waking up every nerve ending she had.

"It's fun to know the power they can have," he said. "That I could get you wound up without even touching you. I could call you one day. You could be in the library surrounded by people, and I bet I could get you wet with a few choice words. And you could do the same to me. Hearing those kinds of words roll off your lips one day? Might kill me."

She smiled at that, liking the idea of affecting him that way.

"But I can be patient," he said, turning her in his arms. "Only say it when and if the spirit moves you. You mind me saying them?"

"Not even a little bit."

He smiled and gave her a wicked look. "Good. Because I'm about to spread your legs and lick that pretty cunt of yours until you come against my tongue."

She gasped and lightning crackled through her. "Get on the bed, freshman. I'm ready to teach."

# CHAPTER TWELVE

*O*'Neal turned and sat on the end of the bed, finding
Auden wearing only those black boxer briefs. He'd
tucked himself back inside as if sensing she needed to take this
in doses, but the boxers didn't hide the gorgeous lean muscle of
his chest and stomach or the very prominent state of his
arousal. She'd seen him in the barely-there bathing suit that he
wore for swim meets, had weaved many erotic fantasies about
him in that outfit, but that couldn't compare to this, seeing him
hot and hard and ready to do sexy, dirty things to her. Right
now, Auden was all hers.

"I like how you look at me," he said.

Her tongue pressed to the back of her teeth, staunching the
desperate sound that had tried to escape at the thought of
touching every last bit of him. "I like looking."

"Good. Lie back on your elbows," he said, tone full of calm
command. "I want you to keep your eyes open. Watch for as
long as you can. I want you to see what I'm doing to you."

She bit her lip, an illicit thrill zipping through her, and
leaned back, keeping her gaze on him. Part of her brain
wouldn't accept that this was the reality in front of her—Auden

looming above her naked body. Her schoolgirl fantasies couldn't have conjured this. She'd known what he looked like in his swimsuit, but she never would've been able to fathom this expression on his face, that dark sexual confidence, that look that said he could absolutely unravel her.

Before this, if casting a TV show, she would've put him into the good guy role, the easy-to-smile boy next door. That was who she'd always known him as. The Dean Forester to her Gilmore Girl. But *this* Auden? He'd need to be on an entirely different show. One where characters drew blood—or drank it.

He stepped forward and touched her knee. She jumped like she'd been bitten, and her thighs clamped together tightly. She squeezed her eyes shut, breathed. "Sorry."

"Look at me," he said, reminding her of his earlier command.

She forced her eyes open, catching his stare and holding onto it like an anchor. Even though she wanted this, she couldn't stop trembling.

"Remember, you can always tell me to stop," he said gently.

She shook her head. "I don't want you to. I'm just, I can't stop shaking."

He squeezed her knee with more pressure, the heavy feel of his hand grounding her a little, and he lowered down to his knees. He grabbed the back of her calves, massaging them, and he kept his gaze on hers. She could feel her locked muscles starting to soften.

"Spread your legs, freshman," he said, voice as smooth as glass. "There's no decision left to make. You know you want my mouth on this pussy. So you're going to give me what I want, and I'm going to make sure you love it."

The words probably should've bothered her, gotten her hackles up, but for some reason, they had the opposite effect. *There's no decision left to make.* What if that could be true? What if she just followed what he said without the mental debate? She took a breath and tried. Her knees parted.

"That's it. Good girl," he said, his hazel eyes flaring at the view and the pleasure evident in his voice. "Beautiful."

His praise coasted over her exposed body and lit her up inside, making her want to spread her legs even wider, do even better for him. She put that concerning reaction in a box in her brain and locked it for now. She'd worry about that later.

He kissed her inner thigh, his hand still stroking her calf, and then moved his mouth a little higher. She watched his dark head move closer and closer until she could feel her pulse pounding everywhere. Her hips tilted upward, her body seeking relief. His gaze flicked up to meet hers, his mouth hovering above the center of her, and he gave her a barely-there smile as if daring her to look away.

Auden. *Auden* was between her legs smiling up at her like she was the most delicious meal that had ever been put in front of him.

She made herself hold the eye contact and feel the electricity sparking through her. Whenever this ended, if she ever needed fantasy fodder, this moment would keep her going for a long time.

Auden didn't look away as he lowered his mouth and touched her with his tongue. A sharp cry escaped her, and she nearly levitated off the bed at the first stroke, but his hand shot out, pinning her thigh down as if he'd anticipated the move.

He spread her fully again, his grip firm, and open-mouth kissed her between her legs, his eyes still on her, his tongue and lips surrounding her clitoris like it was hard candy he was going to suck slowly until it melted away.

*Oh. God.* However she'd imagined this would feel, she'd been wrong. So very wrong. The heat. The pressure. The slickness. The sound. Never had she experienced anything so...*everything.* Touching herself hadn't even come close. This was primal and messy and...*delicious.* A choked whimper passed her lips, and it took everything she had to keep her eyes open and focused. The view was downright obscene. Auden Blake was between her thighs, his lips and tongue painted with her arousal, his eyes burning her to the ground, letting her know just how much he liked it.

He bent forward and draped her legs over his shoulders, giving himself ultimate access, and her heels dug into his back. Her whole body felt like it was going to dissolve.

Then, his finger eased inside her. The added pressure made her muscles clench like a fist, and he sucked on her flesh, sending sparks through her system. She moaned low and long like a desperate thing, but she couldn't help it. Her reactions were no longer in her control. He *mmm*ed against her like he was swallowing down the embarrassing noises she was making, and the vibration of his lips made her thighs tighten, clamping his head between them.

Her elbows collapsed beneath her, and she fell back onto the bed, her eyes closing and her heartbeat thumping between her legs. She reached down, her fingers latching onto his hair, and he grunted. But he must've taken her reaction as encouragement because soon, he'd pushed another finger inside her, and his tongue was doing things to her that were making her see colors behind her eyelids.

The sense of something growing, a balloon inflating, pulsed through her body. She rocked her hips and held onto his head, moving him where she ached most. She didn't know exactly what she was seeking, but she knew she needed to find it. He curled his fingers inside her, pressing against some perfect new place, and then it was all lips and tongue and exquisite pressure. Everything inside her ignited. Her back arched, and a sharp cry rushed out of her throat, the sound pulled out of her by force.

She couldn't stop the noises she was making, and he didn't relent. Her body was rocking now without conscious thought, the sensations too much to process all at once, and the springs in the bed squeaked. She was a passenger now, at the mercy of one singular goal. Her body knew what it wanted and was going to take it. When he sucked her clitoris between his lips again, she detonated. A shriek scraped against her throat, and she held onto his hair, afraid her grip was the only thing keeping her from launching off the bed.

Auden gripped her thigh hard, holding her in place for his mouth, and the pleasure bloomed and bloomed, exploding and renewing, until she was gasping for air and finally scrabbling backward up the bed like a crab because she was afraid her body couldn't take any more.

She found herself against his pillows, the comforter balled in her fists, and her body pulsing with sensations she'd never felt before in her life. If she'd thought she'd given herself an orgasm on her own, it hadn't been *this.* This was...world-tilting.

She glanced down the bed, breathing hard and still a little out of her mind, but needing to see him. Auden braced his forearms on the foot of the bed. His hair was a mess, his lips slick, and his tilted smile was as sexy as she'd ever seen it.

"I..." She tried to say something intelligent but nothing brilliant would form. "That was..."

"A thousand times hotter than I could've imagined—and I'd imagined it was going to be blazing hot." He shook his head in chagrin. "Goddamn, O'Neal. *Fuck.*"

"Really?" Her brows lifted. "I mean, that was...wow, but I'm the virgin here. This is all new to me."

He got up and dipped his hand into his underwear, squeezing his cock like he was trying to rein himself in. "You get an A plus at coming, freshman. And extra credit for the moaning."

She laughed, the little joke exactly what she needed right now. "Shut up."

His gaze drifted over her, and she could see the strain there, the tension in his muscles. "Come 'ere."

She climbed off the bed, her knees like jelly, and tried to

shake off the self-consciousness of being naked. He'd just had his mouth between her legs. What secrets did she have to hide at this point?

He took her hand and tugged her to him, his eyes dark.

"I feel like I should say thank you?" she said, feeling unsure and off-balance.

His dimple appeared in an almost smile. "You're welcome. But believe me, the pleasure was mine. I could spend hours eating that pretty pussy of yours and having you try to pull my hair out to get me just where you wanted. You are so fucking sexy when you get close to your edge."

Her face flamed hot, and she looked at the floor even as something blossomed within her. She couldn't get enough of his words, his compliments. Each one sent a warm shower of pleasure over her. She felt silly being that...needy, but she couldn't help the reaction.

He put a finger beneath her chin, bringing her gaze back to his. "Kiss me. I want you to taste how sweet you are."

The request probably should have shocked her, but she found herself just wanting to say yes. She pushed up on her toes, pressing her lips to his, the earthy flavor of her arousal making the connection so much more intimate. The kiss started off gentle, but Auden soon took it deeper, stroking his tongue against hers like he'd stroked between her legs. She melted in his hold, his erection rubbing against her belly and the aftershocks of her orgasm still thrumming through her. But need stoked anew.

A frantic ache pulsed between her legs, her craving for Auden an insatiable thing. She had to have more, needed him skin-to-skin. She wanted to make him feel as good as he had made her feel, but she didn't know what to do. She broke away from the kiss, rallying her bravery. "Show me how I can make you feel good."

He cupped her face, his gaze tender but his jaw tight. "You

already are making me feel good. More than good. I want to be inside you so fucking much right now, I can barely breathe."

She swallowed past the fresh lump of nerves trying to form in her throat. This was a big step, but she wanted this. Wanted him. "Then what's stopping you?"

He brushed a thumb along her cheekbone. "I don't want to hurt you. This first time…"

"I know," she said, nodding. "I know that can be part of the deal. I can handle a little pain. It's okay."

"It's not just that. It's that there's no going back," he said, watching her closely. "I know you said you were ready, but you have to really be sure this isn't just a temporary whim." He reached down and grabbed her hand, lifting it between them. The shiny promise ring she'd worn since she was a preteen glinted in the light of his bedside lamp. "I don't believe in this purity till marriage thing—or that sex is impure in the first place—but you have to make sure that's where your head is at too. You'll no longer be saving this experience for your future husband. I'm not him."

A ripple of apprehension went through her. Her grandparents' beliefs had so long been a part of her life that she sometimes didn't know where their beliefs ended and hers began, but she'd thought about this for a long time, about *him*. She looked up at Auden and checked her gut one last time. *Did she want to do this?*

Auden was taking care of her, making sure she didn't make a rash decision, and that concern made her want to hug him. She wasn't naïve enough to think this would turn into some romance, that he would fall in love with her and they'd live happily ever after. This was a friendship, though, and having her first time be with a trusted friend…

She stepped back a little, and he instantly released her, his expression turning resigned. But before he could say anything, she gave him a look. "Virginity is a social construct."

His eyes widened and then he let out a startled laugh. "Len would be proud."

She straightened her spine and then twisted that little gold band on her finger, slipping it off. She reached for Auden's hand and pressed the ring into his palm. "I want this. I want my first time to be with you."

Auden let out a slow breath, and his fingers curled around the ring. When he looked up, there was something unreadable in his eyes. He slipped the ring onto his pinky. "Thank you. I don't take that trust lightly."

She gave him a little smile, relieved. "I know. That's why I want it to be you."

He wrapped his arms around her and kissed her again, a tenderness there that had her chest tightening. But before she could overanalyze that feeling or let the nerves crawl back into her system, he was lowering her to the bed. Her head landed against the pillows, and Auden shucked his boxers. He stared down at her for a moment from the side of the bed, his hand stroking himself.

Her gaze roved, taking in every detail of his body, consuming the view like it was the most delicious of meals. He was so beautifully built, all hard lines and angles, skin smooth and tan. He shaved everything for swim season so nothing was hidden from her, everything she'd imagined in her fantasies was here for the taking. A desperate urge to lick the vee-shaped lines of his pelvis overtook her. How many times had she tried and failed not to look at that vee when he was at swim meets? How many times had she found herself imagining completely inappropriate things while sitting there with his family in the stands? Now here he was.

He smiled. "Keep looking at me like that, freshman. You're good for my ego."

She laughed. "Like that needs any help."

He leaned over and pulled open his bedside drawer. She

watched with rapt attention as he rolled on a condom, encasing the now intimidating length of his cock. When he finally climbed onto the bed with her, her body was revving like she'd never had any relief at all.

He braced himself on an elbow next to her and dipped his fingers between her legs again. Slowly, he coaxed her body back to a fully frenzied state. She closed her eyes, already feeling on the edge of orgasm again. "Aud..."

"The more turned on you are, the better it will be, the easier," he said, stroking her with deft fingers. Then he lowered his mouth to her breast, sucking lightly. His mouth on her nipple seemed to have a direct connection to the spot where his fingers rubbed.

Her heartbeat picked up speed and her breaths shortened. "*Aud...*"

"There we go," he said, his quiet words falling over her and his fingers curving inside her. "I want you so desperate you're begging for it."

"Please," she said, the word coming automatically. "I need... I want..."

"Come again for me, gorgeous."

As if her body were waiting for permission, her muscles coiled and pleasure crashed through her once again. She gasped and closed her eyes. Before she realized what was happening, Auden had moved, positioning himself above her. His cock nudged against her opening, his fingers sliding to her clitoris. Every part of her felt alive, but a bolt of apprehension went through her. When he pushed against her, the size of him felt impossible.

"Auden—"

But then he lowered his head and took her nipple between his teeth, using enough pressure to get her attention. A cry of pain/pleasure escaped her throat, and just as she was trying to catch up to what was happening, he pushed fully inside. A hot pinch of discomfort shot through her abdomen, rippling outward like a wave, but then it was over, already a fading memory, and he was pumping into her, her slickness easing the way and her body stretching to accommodate him. They were joined. Auden was inside her. She was no longer a virgin.

"Good girl," he whispered. "So good. The hard part's over. You did great."

Triumph shimmered through her.

His lips found hers, and he kissed her long and deep, his hips pumping slowly and steadily. She wrapped her legs around him, losing herself in the novel sensation of being joined this way. What a marvel that one person could take another inside their body. He tucked his hand between them, stroking her, chasing all remnants of pain away and just leaving pleasure.

Soon, she was panting into his mouth, the previous orgasm still echoing through her, and a new one on its tail, one that seemed to be building deeper in her muscles.

He groaned and picked up speed, his breaths turning to gasps, his own desperation something to behold. She wanted to snapshot the moment, hold onto it. Auden seeking his pleasure, giving himself over to it, giving himself *to her* even if only for a moment. The muscles in his neck strained, perspiration dampened his skin, and then he cried out, his head dipping and his body going tense and hard all over. The sound he made was a surrender, a primal call. She bathed in that sound, reveled in it, and then she moaned along with him, the feel of him swelling thick inside her making her eyes roll back in her head and orgasm envelope her again.

"O'Neal." The grinding way he said her made her come harder. She held on to him tight, her fingers at the nape of his neck.

*Auden. Auden. Auden.*

They were flying. Together. In that moment, no one else existed in the world.

When they finally drifted down and he sagged against her, spent and sweaty, she buried her face in his neck and breathed him in. *Aud.*

Only when she felt the dampness on her cheeks did she realize she was crying.

He lifted his head. "Oh, Shaq." He pushed her hair away from her eyes, a concerned expression on his face. "Talk to me. Are you okay? Are you hurting?"

She couldn't stop the crying, but she managed to shake her head. "I'm fine. I'm good."

He frowned, looking altogether unconvinced. "Give me one sec, okay?" He eased out of her and quickly removed and tied off the condom before tossing it into a trash can by his desk. He grabbed a few tissues and gingerly cleaned her of the little bit of blood their lovemaking had caused. When he rolled back toward her after tossing the tissues, he pulled a blanket over them and tucked her hair behind her ear.

"Tell me what's going on. Did I hurt you? I'm sorry if—"

She shook her head and swiped at her tears, trying to find the right words. "I promise I'm okay. It hurt a little, but that was only for a minute. That's not why I'm crying. I think I'm crying because I'm..." The truth came to her in a rush. "*Relieved.*"

His eyebrows arched. "Relieved?"

"Yes. I made a promise to save myself for marriage when I was too young to really understand what that meant. I was taught my virginity was the ultimate gift." She reached out and touched the ring he'd put on his pinky. "And that promise is the thing my grandparents used to keep me from...everything. From life. I was the fine china kept wrapped up in the attic and never used." She looked up at him. "Now there's nothing left to protect. The china is shattered. I feel...free."

His hazel eyes turned tender. "I wouldn't say you're not worth protecting, and you're not broken or used, but I think I get what you're saying. There's no more debate. The decision is made, and there's no undoing it. Even I went through a little bit of that. The first time I had sex, I thought I was for sure going to hell."

"Really?" she asked, surprised.

"Yep, one hundred percent." He gave her a mischievous smile. "Then I decided it was worth it. I was at peace with my eternal damnation if it meant I got to have sex."

She laughed.

He propped his head on his fist. "You sure you're okay?"

She lifted her head, feeling the answer deep in her gut, and kissed him lightly. "I'm sure. No regrets. That was...wow."

He looked pleased. "Yeah?"

The little hint of vulnerability he was showing sent a flutter through her chest. She wasn't the only one who needed reassurance. She hadn't thought about the pressure on him—being someone's first. "It was great. I don't have anything to compare it to but yeah, wow. Is it always like that?"

His dimple appeared. "Sadly, no. I mean, sex usually doesn't suck, but chemistry matters, and sometimes you just don't have the right mix with someone."

She looked up at him. "And we have good chemistry?"

He let out a soft sound, half laugh, half disbelief. "Not good, Shaq. Explosive. I knew it the second you kissed me in the kitchen. Which is why I was supposed to stay away from you, little sister's best friend. Look what happens when I hang around you too much. I corrupt you."

The confession made her happier than it should. "I'm a willing victim."

"Thank God." He cocked his head toward the door. "Want to continue your downfall and join me in the shower? We can have some fun getting clean."

She grinned. "Another first? It's like a two-for-one deal tonight."

He chuckled and climbed off the bed. "I wouldn't mind

smelling like you all night, but smelling like a college dance club? Not so much." He pulled on his boxers and then opened one of his drawers. He tossed her a soft gray T-shirt that smelled like his laundry detergent. "Come on."

She sat up and slipped it over her head. When she stood, it hit her at mid-thigh. She glanced toward the door. "What about Lennox?"

"He should be in bed by now. And he showers in the morning." Auden opened his door and peeked into the hallway to check. "We're good."

He put out his hand, and she joined him. But when they'd taken a few steps down the hall, Lennox appeared at the other end, apparently having gone to the kitchen for a glass of water.

All three of them froze.

Lennox, standing there in his pajama pants and nothing else, was the first to snap out of statue mode. His gaze quickly scanned over the two of them, and the corner of his mouth twitched up a little.

"Hey."

"Hi." O'Neal was suddenly super aware that all she was wearing was a T-shirt. She tugged at the hem.

"Everything okay?" he asked.

"It was great." She cringed at the blurted words, realizing too late that she'd said *it* was great instead of *everything's great.*

Lennox chuckled. "I heard. Congrats."

"You need the bathroom for anything?" Auden asked, all business.

"Nope," Len said, closing the distance between them. He took a sip of his water and gave O'Neal a playful look. "So he took good care of you, Sweets?"

She took a breath, tamping down the awkwardness trying to ruin the moment, and gave Auden a considering glance. She looked back to Lennox. "Solid bachelor's degree level, I'd say."

Len choked at her deadpan delivery, nearly spitting out his water.

"Hey!" Auden said with mock offense.

Lennox leaned forward and kissed her cheek. "I like you, O'Neal Lory. Any woman who could come that loudly and still give the guy shit about it is my kind of person." He reached out and patted Auden's cheek. "Better luck next time, champ. If you need tips or an extra hand, you know where to find me."

With that, Lennox walked past them and into his room.

Auden shook his head. "You shouldn't encourage him, you know."

She smirked. "Why not?"

He opened the door to the bathroom. "Because he's not kidding about the extra hand."

Her lips parted as a new, brain-breaking thought hit her, other previous comments piecing together in her head. "Wait. Have y'all ever—"

He put his fingers over her lips. "Get in the shower, freshman. No more lessons tonight."

# CHAPTER THIRTEEN

*A*uden stared at the slowly turning ceiling fan in the morning light, listening to the soft sound of O'Neal's breathing. He wasn't used to waking up next to someone. His and Len's hookups were always with people who had crystal clear boundaries and expectations about the night. No one slept over. But after last night, there was no way he was sending O'Neal back to her dorm. Not after her first time.

She already knew he wasn't going to be her boyfriend. He didn't need to underline that by letting her wake up alone after their night together. But now, in the quiet, his brain was going into overdrive. He'd fucked *O'Neal Lory*. Virginity might be a social construct, but first times were a big deal, especially for someone like O'Neal, who'd grown up in a world where her sexual purity had been lauded as her most prized possession. He had never been with a virgin, even when he'd been a virgin. The weight of that felt so much heavier in the morning light. He'd been her first kiss and her first lover. And she'd admitted that she'd had a crush on him at some point. The risk of hurting her was real.

But he couldn't be the kind of guy she needed even if he

wanted to do the boyfriend thing. He'd discovered things about himself over the past few years that he couldn't ignore. Things that he was still working through. Some he'd happily share with O'Neal, but others...others would change her opinion about him. She'd never look at him the same way. He'd scare her. He'd already crossed too many lines with her last night.

He'd enjoyed the hell out of every minute because goddamn, she was something, but the dynamic was uneven. Her inexperience gave him too much power. He could tell her anything was normal, and she'd probably believe him. He had resisted doing that last night, had tried to be honest about what had happened in the car, but the temptation was strong. *Sure, O'Neal, lots of people give their lovers orders and get off on being in charge. Sure, lots of guys share women with their roommates and enjoy watching them with someone else. And of course, it's totally fine for a guy to sometimes get off on pretending to force a girl in bed.*

He closed his eyes and groaned softly. He could picture the horrified look on her face. She liked him because he was the nice guy, the literal boy next door. He'd shatter all those illusions. He didn't want that. Part of him really liked how she saw him. But even knowing all that, he didn't want last night to be their only time together. He'd enjoyed every second with her. Maybe he could manage vanilla for a while, maybe...

The bedroom door swung open with a sharp squeak, and Auden's eyelids flew open. Lennox slipped into the room like a cat burglar.

Auden sat up and glanced at O'Neal's still sleeping form.

"What the hell, man?" Aud asked, keeping his voice low.

"Dude," Len whispered, rushing over and crouching down next to the bed. "You gotta get up."

"You can't just walk into my room and—"

"Doesn't your mom drive a white Tesla?" he went on.

That stopped him in his tracks. "Yeah, why?"

"I think she and your sister just parked out front. I was

taking out the trash and saw them turn in. You've got about thirty seconds before they knock." He glanced meaningfully at O'Neal. "I'm guessing you don't want lil' sis knowing you just devirginized her BFF."

Panic zipped through Auden, and he flipped the comforter off himself. "Shit."

"Hmm," O'Neal said sleepily as she turned over.

Lennox stood. "Sweets, Auden's mom and sister are outside."

O'Neal's eyelids flew open. "They're *what?*"

Auden was already on his feet and yanking open a drawer to grab a pair of track pants, his mind racing. His mom had a penchant for surprise visits, but if he didn't hurry, this time he was going to surprise her back. "I'll go. You stay in here."

There was a knock on the front door.

O'Neal sat up, pulling the covers up to her neck, a freaked-out look on her face. "What are they doing here?"

"I don't know. Surprising me with breakfast or something? Spying on me?" he said in a rush. "Having *impeccable fucking timing?*"

"Go answer it. Get them out of here," Lennox said. "If they aren't here for breakfast, take them to one. I'll take O'Neal to my room and drive her home when y'all leave."

"Right." Auden looked to O'Neal after pulling on a T-shirt. He leaned down to give her a quick kiss. "I'm sorry."

She shook her head. "It's fine. Just...take care of it. Please don't let Maya find out. She'll freak."

Auden frowned, another thought hitting him. "If they drove all the way out here, they're going to want to check on you too. Have an excuse prepared if they call you."

She winced. "Crap."

Auden gave Lennox a *take care of her* look and then hustled out.

O'NEAL TOOK LENNOX'S OFFERED HAND AND GOT OUT OF BED, relieved that she'd borrowed a pair of boxers and a T-shirt from Auden last night. She grabbed her phone and swept up her clothes and shoes from the floor. Then, they both hurried out of Auden's room and into Len's.

Lennox shut the door behind them just as she heard Auden open the front door and welcome someone. She pressed her fingers over her mouth, afraid she'd make a noise.

Len gave her a little smile and said softly, "Breathe, Sweets. They're not going to come into my room. Auden will tell them I'm sleeping in. And you didn't drive your car here. You're fine. They can't hear us back here."

Her heart was hammering, her stomach queasy, and her head throbbing. She sat down on the edge of his bed. "Sorry. I just...am not used to this sneaking around thing."

"Yeah, not my favorite thing either." He walked over and turned his desk chair around to face her.

"No?" she asked, surprised. "You strike me as someone who's gotten away with a lot."

He gave her a wry look. "I'll take that as a compliment. And I have, but I've also found I prefer blatant honesty to deception. Both can get you in trouble, though. In this case, a little deception seems prudent."

Nothing about this seemed prudent. For one, she was in yet another guy's bedroom, and shirtless Lennox was super distracting. She found her gaze straying to the scrawled words of his tattoos. She forced her eyes away. What was wrong with her? She'd just slept with his best friend and should definitely not be checking out any part of him at all.

Female voices drifted down the hall, and O'Neal's stomach clenched. Auden's warning came back to her, and she unlocked her phone. She'd turned it on silent last night after texting with Quyen briefly, both of them making sure the other was okay and safe. She had one new message from Maya.

> Maya: Hey, heading up to see the bro. Let's brunch. Miss u!

She groaned and showed the screen to Lennox. "I'm invited."

"No worries. Tell her you pulled an all-nighter, studying, and to give you a time and place, that you'll meet her there, but might be a little late. That should buy you some time. As soon as they leave, I'll drive you back to the dorm so you can change."

"Thank you." She quickly typed out a message to Maya. She set her phone aside and pressed her fingers to her eyes, where the pounding was getting worse. "I don't know if this will work. I know I've got to look like death. They're going to know something's up."

"You look adorably rumpled actually," Lennox said, easy affection in his voice. "And they'll only know something's wrong if you look guilty."

She lowered her hands and gave him a look. "That doesn't help. I *am* guilty."

He braced his forearms on his knees and gave her an evaluating look. "What exactly are you guilty of, Sweets? Last night, you went out with friends and did a little underage drinking— maybe more than you planned—but that's such typical college behavior it's become a stereotype. Then you slept with a guy— safely, I'm sure—whom you know and trust, making a choice as a woman about your own body and enjoying your night. So"— he shrugged—"from where I'm standing, you've committed no crimes."

She let out a breath. "You're forgetting parts. Like what happened in the car."

His gaze darkened a little. "Believe me. I haven't forgotten a second of that."

Her face grew warm, and she stared off to the side, focusing hard on the corner of his desk, embarrassment engulfing her. "That's not, like, normal behavior."

RONI LOREN

"Did you enjoy it?" he asked in a mild tone that could've been used to ask if she liked milk in her coffee.

"That's not the point," she said in frustration.

"It's the entirety of the point, actually," he countered. "As long as something is safe, sane, consensual, who cares what society labels as normal or not?"

She shook her head. "You didn't grow up how I grew up. Literally everything about last night was a crime in my world. Just sitting here with you like this—both of us half-dressed— would give my grandparents a heart attack."

"But that doesn't have to be your world anymore," he said, a gentleness in his voice. "I'm not saying you have to go broadcast that you hooked up with Auden to his mom and sister because that will cause drama neither of you wants, but you also don't have to adopt your family's judgment as your own. Check your own gut. Do you truly feel wrong about last night? Dirty or whatever?"

She frowned and looked down at her hands, processing the words. How *did* she feel about last night? Would she take any of it back? The answer bubbled up as if rising from a deep, quiet place inside her. "I think the drinking too much was dumb. This hangovery feeling is no fun. Zero out of five stars, do not recommend. But what happened with Auden felt..." *Overwhelming. Intense. Amazing.* "Good."

"And me being present for part of it?" he asked, tone careful.

She snuck a glance at him. "Auden asked me the same question."

"Good. He should be checking in with you on things like that," he said with a nod. "What'd you say?"

She inhaled a breath, trying to gather courage. "It was kind of intense, knowing that you'd...liked being there, that it'd affected you. I felt a little bad, honestly, that...you know, we left you that way."

He gave her a little smile. "Don't feel bad. A hard-on is some-

166

thing easily fixed. If any guy ever tries to sell you some story about how painful it is and how he needs relief, show him his own hand." He caught her gaze, a rare shade of seriousness there. "It was hot hearing you and Aud last night. You have nothing to feel bad about. As long as you were into it, I promise both of us were too."

She groaned and put her hands over her face. "I cannot *believe* we're having this conversation. I don't even know who I am right now."

Gentle fingers gripped her wrists, and Lennox lowered her hands. "Don't hide your face, Sweets. You're not some new person. You've just been in lockdown all your life. It's going to take some time and experimentation to figure out which parts of you are *really* you and which parts are other people's expectations of who you're supposed to be. You're not alone in that. That's what college is about for most people. The expectations and family baggage just look different from person to person."

The words were somehow just what she needed to hear. That she wasn't a freak. That even though her background was different from a lot of other people's, everyone was making this journey on some level. To her horror, tears sprung to her eyes again. Lord, when did she become such a crier?

"Hey," he said, voice soft and his thumbs rubbing the insides of her wrists. "What's wrong?"

Embarrassment filled her. She slipped her hands from his grip and pressed the corners of her eyes, trying to keep the tears from falling. "Sorry. I don't know what's up with me. Ignore me. I'm being stupid."

"Nuh-uh, none of that," he said with a frown. He stood and reached for her hand, pulling her to a stand. He put his hands on her shoulders and gave her a purposeful look. "No calling yourself stupid. Come 'ere."

Before she could think better of it, she let him pull her into a hug. He wrapped his arms around her, and she pressed her cheek to his bare shoulder. His body was warm, and the clean scent of his skin filled her nose. Even though they were pressed close and he was shirtless and he'd seen what he'd seen last night, the embrace felt tender and safe, like the hug equivalent of a cozy blanket and cup of tea. She wanted to curl up into him.

"I'm sorry," she mumbled against his skin. "I don't know why I'm crying."

He rubbed her back in a soothing circle. "Sweets, you've been through a major life event in the last twelve hours and then got yanked out of bed in a panic right after. Now you've gotten trapped in a room with an impossibly sexy and charming graduate student, and your brain and body are just over-whelmed."

She snort-laughed against him, the sound a little tear-choked. "A humble graduate student too."

He leaned back, hands on her upper arms, and grinned down at her. "You said *too,* so that means you agree with the other adjectives as well. I'm flattered."

She rolled her eyes and stepped back, swiping at the tears on her cheeks. "You're incorrigible."

"That too."

She sighed and met his gaze. Lennox had a playful nature, but he also had this calmness about him, an openness that made her feel…accepted, like she could say anything to him. Like crying in front of him was totally fine. "Hotness and charm aside, anyone ever tell you that you have a therapist vibe?"

His eyebrows jumped up, and then he chuckled softly. He rubbed a hand over his chest, right over his heart. "Well, maybe that's because I've seen enough of them. You pick up on some things."

She tilted her head, wanting to ask more, but before she could respond, her phone vibrated. She grabbed it from the bed and unlocked the screen.

> Maya: Ugh, all-nighters suck. Aud said he was up late studying too. Who knew Bennette was so hardcore this early in the semester? I'll text you the address where we're going and I'll make sure to order a very potent fancy coffee for you. See you soon!

Lennox cocked his chin toward her phone. "All good?"

"Looks that way. I'll at least have a little time to get ready," she said, typing a quick response. "Auden told his sister he was up late studying too."

Lennox laughed. "So diligent, the both of you. Studying anatomy *so* hard. And so loudly, I might add."

"Shut up," she said with a half-smile.

He winked. "Come on, let's get you to the Greek."

"The Greek?"

He waved a hand. "Movie reference. We'll add that one to your watchlist."

"That's going to end up being a long list." She grabbed her balled-up dress—well, Quyen's balled-up dress—and cringed. Maybe she didn't feel guilty about last night, but the thought of walking through the dorm wearing last night's dress made her want to heave.

"You okay?"

She held up her dress. "I'm okay. Just getting some *Scarlet Letter* flashbacks."

Lennox gave her a sympathetic look. "I don't think your dormmates are Puritans, so you probably wouldn't get a second glance. But don't worry. I've got some gym shorts that you can cinch up that will fit you. Although, one day, I bet you'll be able to walk down those dorm hallways in last night's dress like a boss—giving the finger to the misogynistic concept of the walk of shame."

"Bold thought." She scrunched her nose. "But that day is not today."

"No problem. Baby steps still get you there." He pulled shorts from his dresser, tossed them onto the bed, and then grabbed something for himself to change into. He picked up his phone and texted. When a response came through, he gave her a thumbs-up. "Aud said the coast is clear. I'll meet you out front."

When he had his hand on the door, she said, "Lennox."

He turned his head to look her way. "Yeah?"

"Thanks for this."

"Yeah, sure."

"No, truly, thank you. I know you're helping me out because you're a good friend to Auden, but…I appreciate everything you're doing and for talking me through this. This could've been a really awkward situation this morning, but instead, you made me feel comfortable." She tucked her hair behind her ears. "I don't know how to *do* any of this. I've never had a morning after, but you made me forget to panic. So, thanks."

The warmth that filled his eyes was like a gentle caress. "I'm not doing it just for Auden. Maybe you haven't realized it yet, but I now count you as a friend too." He tipped his head to the side. "Did you not receive your exclusive gold-embossed invitation? I'll have to check with my secretary on why he's slacking off."

Her lips curved, his words filling her with a fizzy feeling. "I'll be sure to R.S.V.P. when I do."

"Excellent." He blew her an air kiss and then shut the door.

Suddenly, her hangover didn't feel so terrible.

# CHAPTER FOURTEEN

"So have you been showing O'Neal the ropes, honey?" The images that filled Auden's brain at his mother's question were obscene enough to make him choke on his iced tea. O'Neal...tied up for him, the ropes making her creamy skin go pink. He cleared his throat and avoided looking at O'Neal who was seated directly across from him at the table.

"Um, a little."

His mom sent O'Neal a pursed-lip look. "Has he been shirking his big brother duties to hang out with his friends instead? You can tell me."

O'Neal's blue eyes flickered with something akin to horror—probably at the words *big brother*—but she covered it quickly. "Auden's been great. Honestly. He's been really helpful. He's shown me...a lot of things."

Auden gave her a look of mild warning.

She picked up her glass of orange juice, giving him a brief, tight smile over the rim of her glass.

"That's good to hear," his mom said with a nod. "I know this first semester can be overwhelming."

"Amen and hallelujah," Maya said from her spot next to

O'Neal. She lifted her fork, a chunk of Belgian waffle dripping syrup back onto her plate. "I have three papers due already, and my reading list is so long, it should have chapters and an index." She popped the bite of waffle into her mouth and glanced at O'Neal. "I thought it was just the rigors of Wainwright, but it sounds like you're being put through the wringer too. All-nighters already? Shouldn't that be reserved for exam time?"

O'Neal shrugged, a stiffness there. "It wasn't for a test. My journalism class has a semester-long project. I need to pick a topic for an in-depth story, and I've been spending a lot of time researching what I might want to write about. The professor said he picks the top two articles to run in the school journal at the end of the semester and chooses one of those people to intern with him over the following summer. That job would come with a stipend, and I'd be able to keep student housing."

"Sounds exciting," his mom said between sips of coffee. "I bet you'll be one of the two."

O'Neal glanced away and shook her head. "Doubt it."

"Oh, don't do that," his mom said. "You're a gifted writer, sweetheart. Be proud of that. And if for some reason it doesn't work out, know that you can always stay with us for the summer. You always have a place at our house."

The honest affection in his mom's tone made Auden want to reach over and hug her. His mom had always expected a lot from him and Maya, and she expected her rules to be followed, but he'd never doubted her love. Seeing her direct that same energy toward O'Neal made him appreciate her even more. When O'Neal's grandparents had failed spectacularly in the unconditional love department, his mom had stepped in.

Of course, he also knew that if her maternal streak had kicked in with O'Neal, she most definitely would *not* appreciate her only son relieving her new surrogate daughter of her virginity and fooling around with her in front of his roommate. His mom had an open mind—but she had her limits.

O'Neal dipped her head a little and smiled. "Thanks, Mrs. Blake."

His mom reached out and patted the spot in front of O'Neal's plate. "Oh, hush with the Mrs. Blake. I know your grandparents wanted you to call me that, but you're an adult now. You can call me Clare."

O'Neal gave his mom a grateful look. "Thank you…Clare."

"Ugh, that sounds weird," Maya said, her nose wrinkling. "So did you figure out what you're going to write your story about?"

O'Neal fiddled with the edge of her napkin. "Not yet. The professor gave us a lot of freedom, which you'd think would make it easier but actually makes it harder. We have to choose one of the types of journalism—investigative, entertainment, sports, political, an opinion piece, that kind of thing—and then go from there. I have a few ideas but haven't settled on one yet. I have to turn in my topic by this Friday, though, so I need to choose soon."

Something about the way she'd said it made Auden frown. O'Neal was lying. No one else seemed to notice, but he could read it all over her body language. He had no idea why she'd lie about something like an assignment, but he made a mental note to ask her later.

"Maybe you should talk about the experience of going from a strict private school to a public university. A slice of life thing," Maya said between bites. "You'd have firsthand experience, and you could interview Auden since he went through that too. There's got to be some culture shock involved, right?"

O'Neal bit her lip and shot a lightning-flash glance at Auden. "There is, but that might be more personal than I want to get. I'm still processing that stuff. I won't have perspective yet."

"Is it very overwhelming?" his mom asked, concern in her voice. "I know Auden had a few growing pains here, but he had more freedom growing up than you did. This has got to be a lot."

Auden watched O'Neal closely, searching for clues that she was panicking about last night. She met his gaze. "It is, but I don't regret the decision I made. This still feels like it was the right choice for me."

Auden smiled, something tight unlocking in his shoulders. He took a long sip of iced tea, keeping his eyes on her.

She blushed.

Maya tapped her hand against the table. "No, no, no. You're supposed to say, *No, Maya, it's horrible and I miss you and I need your annoying roommate to move out ASAP so I can move in and go to Wainwright with you.*"

"Aww," O'Neal said, wrapping her arm around his sister and side-hugging her. "I do miss you so much, and I wish we could be together, but I want a journalism degree and you want Wainwright's killer creative writing program. So it's really the schools' faults."

"Stupid schools," Maya said, stabbing her waffle but smiling a little and leaning into O'Neal. "I can't believe Auden gets to play with you instead of me."

Auden choked a little. "We're not toddlers, My."

Maya rolled her eyes. "You know what I mean."

"I think this will be good for the both of you," his mom said, directing her gaze between O'Neal and Maya. "College is about discovering the kind of adult you want to be. Sometimes that's easier when you shake things up a little. You can hold on to the best things about your younger years—like your friendship with each other—without using those things as a crutch. You'll both be forced to grow. Maya, you're already learning how to deal with difficult people courtesy of your new roommate—a valuable life lesson if I've ever heard of one. O'Neal, you'll get to experience a bigger world than the one you grew up in, which will help you figure out who you are and what you believe is right for you."

"Yes, ma'am," O'Neal said with an appreciative smile.

His mom reached over and patted his knee. "I won't lie and say I wasn't a little worried when Auden first chose Bennette, but look how well it's gone. Good grades, doing great on the swim team, and growing into such a respectable young man. I didn't have anything to worry about after all. I raised him to make good choices and not act like an idiot. Gold star for me."

A ping of guilt went through him, but he forced a chagrined smile. "Your bar was *not acting like an idiot?* Way to set a stretch goal for me, Mom."

"Sweetheart, do you remember your middle school years?" She gave him a lifted eyebrow look. "You only lasted two Sundays as an altar boy because you almost burned the church down while lighting the candles for service. I had to be realistic."

O'Neal laughed and then bit her lip. Maya grinned with little sister relish—always happy to see Auden roasted.

"Hey," he said, affronted, "maybe I did that on purpose because wearing those robes was mortifying. The girl I had a crush on started teasing me and calling me Father Auden."

O'Neal's eyes danced with humor. "Maybe she was flirting."

"She *definitely* was not. Plus," he added, "it was just logistically unsound to have drapes hanging near candles. Major fire hazard."

"The fire hazard was *you,*" Maya said. She looked to O'Neal. "Mom still won't let him light the grill in the summer."

"I'll be sure to keep him away from matches," O'Neal said. "No tailgate barbecues for you this football season, mister."

He dipped his fingertips into his water and then flicked O'Neal with a few droplets. "Go ahead, Shaq, pile it on."

"Hey!" She put up her hands, laughing, and the sound filtered through him like sunlight, putting him at ease.

He and O'Neal had crossed all kinds of lines last night. He'd had his tongue between her legs, had made her come multiple times, he'd been *inside her.* He was still having trouble wrapping his head around everything that had happened and fighting off a little guilt about it too, but being able to joke around with her like they had when growing up smoothed a few jagged spots. Maybe they would be okay. Maybe he hadn't damaged her in some way with his selfish need to touch her.

O'Neal lifted a grape off her plate and gave him a *just try me* look. "Flick water at me again and it's on."

He lifted his palms in protest, laughing, but O'Neal's eyes went wide, her smile instantly faltering. Panic crossed her face.

"No food fights, children," his mom said with amusement in her voice. "I'd rather not get escorted out before I can have another coffee."

She motioned for the waiter, but Auden's attention remained fixed on O'Neal. She was giving him a look that was clearly full of warning, but he couldn't tell what she was panicking about.

He opened his mouth to ask her, but when his mom's and Maya's heads were turned toward the waiter, O'Neal lifted her hand and deliberately knocked her water over in his direction.

"Shit!" Ice water splashed into his lap before he could shove his chair back.

His mom's head turned. "Auden. *Language.*"

"I'm so sorry," O'Neal said, sliding her chair back and standing to come around to his side. "I'm such a klutz."

Auden winced as icy water shocked the warm parts of him. The waiter said he'd grab some extra napkins.

O'Neal was at Auden's side, offering a cloth napkin. He gave her a *what the hell* look that his mom and sister wouldn't be able to see.

She pressed the cloth in his hand and squeezed his pinkie —hard—through the napkin.

*What the—* He almost cursed again, but then it dawned on him. He was still wearing her goddamned purity ring on his left hand. His stomach flipped over. She must've seen it when he raised his hands to block her from throwing the grape.

He let her slip it from his finger, the napkin concealing it, and stood quickly. "I'll be right back."

Relief crossed O'Neal's face.

As he headed to the bathroom, he heard his sister say, "Please tell me you did that on purpose. I can't *believe* he flicked water at you. His *spit* is in there. Gross."

Auden scoffed. His spit was in there? He thought of all the places he'd put his tongue last night. His sister would have a heart attack if she found out he'd done a whole lot more to her best friend than flick a little water at her. She'd outright die if she had any clue about the things he hadn't done to O'Neal yet but had fantasized about.

And that thought made him feel like shit. What the hell was he doing?

When he was alone with O'Neal, he saw the woman she'd become, felt that visceral attraction, wanted to take her to bed and show her all the fun things they could do. But when he saw O'Neal with Maya, it dragged his mind back to all the memories of his little sister and her friend when they were growing up. They'd always been kids to him. Something separate from his world. Seeing O'Neal with Maya reminded him how very young in experience O'Neal was—not just sexually but in life. Yes, she'd consented to what they'd done, said she didn't regret it, but how would he view it if some guy was acting like this with Maya? Not willing to be her boyfriend but sleeping with her under the auspices of *teaching* her about sex? Getting off on calling her good girl?

*Fuck.* The thought made acid burn at the back of his throat.

He'd see it as predatory. Maya was eighteen, but she'd been sheltered. Some smooth-talking guy could tell her the right things and take full advantage probably.

He stepped into the empty men's bathroom and pinched his temples, the reality hitting him. As much of a dick move as it'd be to back off after sleeping with O'Neal, it'd make him a bigger asshole to keep taking advantage of the situation. He could tell himself he had the best intentions, but he didn't trust himself not to take it too far. His fantasies about her were far from sweet. That *teach me* thing she had was too darkly enticing. He'd already crossed lines last night without planning to.

Icy reality settled in his gut.

*Goddammit.*

He had to end this.

# CHAPTER FIFTEEN

O'Neal's eyes were gritty as she skimmed a few more news articles. Most of them said the same thing, but she was scanning for any tiny detail that may give her new information. When she reached the last of the articles and found nothing of note, she rubbed the spot between her eyes, a tension headache forming there, and then glanced at her phone.

The screen was black. Of course, it was. She couldn't deny what that meant anymore.

Auden was officially avoiding her. After brunch two weekends ago, he'd warned her that he'd have a couple of busy weeks coming up with a few papers due and a big swim meet to prepare for, but his lack of texting revealed it was more than a packed schedule. Something about the meal with his mom and sister had changed things, spooked him. Or maybe he'd just decided that what had happened between them had been a mistake. They'd gotten caught up in the heat of the moment or whatever and had made some stupid decisions.

She was trying to be logical about it. It wasn't like they were in love or dating. She didn't need to assign emotional meaning to her first time just because society assigned meaning to that.

She'd relinquished that notion when they'd made their agreement. She'd known, at least on some level, what she'd been signing up for. Friends with benefits or whatever people called it.

But the virginity part wasn't what she was upset about. The friendship part was.

If she'd known sleeping with him meant losing their easy connection as friends, she wouldn't have done it. That would've been too high of a price.

And she couldn't even talk to anyone about it because she was too embarrassed to tell Quyen what she'd agreed to. She didn't want to look dumb and naïve. And she obviously couldn't tell Maya.

O'Neal leaned back in the hard library chair, the wood creaking, and closed her eyes. Her bones felt heavy and stiff, the weight of it all pressing down on her. She'd wanted to learn things from Auden, but she didn't think her first lesson would be how to have a one-night stand and then be ghosted.

If she thought Auden had used her for sex, she could at least be pissed. But that wasn't the vibe she was getting. She doubted Auden had any trouble getting women to sleep with him. He was gorgeous, smart, and funny—not to mention rich. He didn't need to go tricking inexperienced freshmen into bed.

Something else had happened.

She was driving herself crazy trying to figure it out.

The sound of a camera phone startled her, making her eyelids fly open.

"No, stay just like that," said a familiar voice in a gentle whisper. There was another camera click. "I'm going to draw this scene and call it *Overworked Student in Repose*."

O'Neal turned her head, finding Lennox smiling down at her. Well, a version of Lennox she'd never seen. His blond hair was slicked back, and his eyes were rimmed with black liner, making his green eyes as bright as ivy leaves. Instead of his usual jeans and T-shirt, he was in a well-tailored black suit complete with a black shirt and tie to match. For a moment, she couldn't speak.

"Hey, Sweets," he said. "Your roommate said I could find you here."

"Uh, hi," she managed.

He grabbed a chair near her, spun it around, and straddled it. "So what are you up to?"

She wet her lips, still trying to get her bearings. "Working on an assignment. What about you? You look like you're going to the Grammys or something."

He smiled and grabbed the lapels of his jacket. "You like? It's on loan. A friend in one of my classes asked me to pose for a photo shoot. She's doing a series on power."

Her brows lifted. "Like power suits?"

"Well, that was one piece of it. That the clothes can make a man—or woman. But she's also got photos focused on powerful body language, demonstrations of strength, intense emotions, that kind of thing. She took a few of just my clenched fist. Then another couple with my shirt off and my nails scraping across one of my tattoos. Should be interesting."

She snorted softly.

"What?" he asked.

"Nothing. I'm just not surprised that she had shots requiring you to take off your shirt."

He braced his arms along the chair's back. "What do you mean?"

"Oh, come on, look at you. Who wouldn't want you to strip so they can take photos?" The words were out before she could process how they'd come across.

Lennox broke into a grin. "Hold up. Did you just *flirt* with me, Ms. Lory? I'm so proud of you!"

She groaned and pressed her hand over her eyes. "Please shut up."

"Oh no, I'm not good at shutting up, sorry. Libraries literally make me itch with all the quietness." He tugged her hand away from her face and kissed her knuckles before letting her go. "Thank you for the compliment, Sweets. Now, tell me what you're up to."

The easy way he touched her made her breath quicken and temporarily distracted her, so she wasn't able to hide her screen quickly enough. Lennox's attention was already on it. He read the headline aloud, "*Multiple DNA Specimens Found on Victim in Lory Case.*"

"Just researching for my—"

"Lory." He turned to her, eyes concerned.

She cleared her throat, her neck heating. "It's my mom's case. I…I chose it as a topic for my investigative assignment in class."

His expression tightened into concern. "Oh, Sweets, that sounds like a really bad idea. Why would you want—"

"Because I need to, okay?" she said with more ferocity than she'd planned. She glanced around, hoping she hadn't disturbed anyone, and lowered her voice. "I know it sounds morbid to do this as an assignment, but I need this. I've only been told pieces of her story. And the parts I've been told always make my mom sound like…like she deserved it somehow. I mean, they called her the Party Girl. No one should get that kind of label when they're the victim of a crime."

Her hands clenched and unclenched, her voice wavering a little, a mix of emotions trying to fight for dominance. "I don't expect to, like, solve the case or whatever. I don't have that skill set. But I just want to…learn more about what happened, learn more about her. It's like this big chunk of my history that's completely formed from secondary sources, from other people's opinions and interpretations. I want to know her for myself. I want to know who she was when she was here."

Lennox stared at her for a quiet moment and then nodded. "Okay. I get that. But I just…be careful with yourself. You don't know what you'll find or what doors it will open up inside you. Things could get intense."

Her mouth was dry, but she pushed the words out. "I will."

He leveled her with a serious look. "And I don't know if you plan to interview anyone from back then, but don't you dare go poking around people who could be involved in a murder without bringing someone with you."

"I—"

"I'm serious, O'Neal," he said, his tone brooking no argument. "You call me. Or Aud. Or someone else you trust and take them with you. There's a difference between being independent and being reckless. Promise me."

"Len—"

"Promise me."

She huffed a breath. "Fine. But don't sign up Auden for babysitting duty. He doesn't even know I'm doing this."

A line appeared between his eyebrows. "It's not babysitting, it's being a friend, but why haven't you told him?"

She gave him a disbelieving look. "Um, maybe because he hasn't talked to me beyond a basic text in two weeks?"

"He hasn't—" Irritation moved across his features, the eyeliner somehow making him look like an avenging angel. "Are you fucking kidding me?"

"No, I figured you knew."

He took a shoulder-lifting breath and then let it out slowly. "That dumbass. He told me you've been slammed busy, and that's why you hadn't come over." His jaw flexed, and he glanced at his phone, checking the time. "Come on. We're fixing this."

A dart of panic went through her. "What? No. You don't have to—"

He stood and put his hand out. "Yes, I do. You're coming to movie night tonight."

She shook her head and put her palms up. "No way. I'm fine.

It's fine. I don't want to make this even more awkward. He obviously doesn't want me there."

"*I* want you there," he said, still holding his hand out. "And Aud doesn't know it, but I bet he wants you there too. My guess is he's having some crisis of conscience. In his own fucked up way, he probably thinks he's doing you a favor. Saving you from him or whatever."

*Saving her?* "That's ridiculous."

"Agreed, but he's got a hard head. And I've got an idea." He wiggled his fingers at her, asking her to take his hand. "I know I call you Sweets, but do you have any evil hiding under all that sugar? The playful kind of evil?"

She took his hand and stood, intrigued despite herself. "There's a playful kind of evil?"

"Absolutely. Come on. Get your stuff, and let's get outside so we can talk without whispering."

She shoved everything into her backpack and then laced her fingers with his again, letting him lead her out and marveling at how natural it felt to just take Len's hand and trust him. Some deep intuitive part of her felt safe with him.

When they were in the sunshine, the rays warming her library-chilled skin, he guided her to the side of the building under the shade of a sprawling oak and released her hand. He met her gaze. "Come to movie night. As *my* date."

"*What?*"

He smiled. "Then Auden can't protest. You're not there for him. You're there with me. He can stay and watch the movie or go. Twenty bucks says he chooses to stay."

"But what's the point?" she asked, crossing her arms. "It's not going to make him jealous. He said y'all don't do the jealousy thing. And it's not like he and I were dating in the first place."

"The point isn't jealousy," he said, loosening his tie. "The point is that he thinks he coerced you into something because you're too young and innocent to know better. But if he sees

184

that since he couldn't give you what you wanted, you came to me instead, it's going to show him that you're making your own decisions. You didn't fall under some spell of his. You weren't a victim."

"I'm *not* a victim," she said, frustrated at the thought. "Does he really think I'm that unaware of my own mind? I'm the one who kissed him first last year. I'm inexperienced, but I'm not gullible."

"*I* know that," he said. "But that's because I don't have history with you. He's got childhood stuff all twisted up with you. He's got memories of you with skinned knees and pigtails or whatever. It's probably a big transition from seeing you as his baby sister's friend to seeing you as someone he wants in his bed. This could show him that you're not that kid anymore."

She sniffed haughtily and lifted a finger. "First of all, I never wore pigtails. Second of all, I slept with him. If that doesn't alleviate him of that notion, I don't know what will."

Lennox smiled a Cheshire Cat smile. "I do. But it means we're going to have to get real honest and real clear right now."

A shimmer of trepidation moved through her. "What do you mean?"

He lifted his palms like he was trying to calm a horse. "Knowing you won't hurt my feelings either way, on a scale of one to ten—one being, *not at all,* ten being, *back off, you weirdo*—how opposed are you to the idea of kissing me again?"

The question sent her mind spinning, and sweat prickled her skin. "Wh-what?"

"If I bring you to movie night and Auden doesn't immediately see the error of his ways and apologize to you, we're going to have to go through with the bluff that you're there with me. That means making it convincing. Like cuddling on the couch, maybe a little kissing. But I'm not going to go there if you aren't into that." He said it as casually as if they were discussing the weather.

"You're asking if I want to make out with you?" she asked, still trying to process the situation. "I—wait, where are *you* at on that scale?"

"On how opposed I am to kissing you again?" His lips hitched at one corner. "Negative a thousand, Sweets. I thoroughly enjoyed that game last time."

Her breath left her in a rush. "Oh."

"The only reason I haven't made any kind of move on you is because I was giving you and Auden your space." He shrugged. "There's something there between you two that I didn't want to fuck up. But…if he's fucking it up anyway, well then, you can have whatever you want from me in the meantime. Your innocence doesn't scare me." He leaned forward like he was telling her a secret. "It just makes me want to show you *all* the filthy things in great detail."

A hot shiver moved from the top of her head down, making every part of her hyperaware. "Oh."

He straightened and put his hands in his suit pockets, a wicked glint in his green eyes. "So…one to ten, Sweets? Give it to me straight."

O'Neal's thoughts were zigzagging in every direction and crashing into each other. On one hand, she could admit that what she felt for Auden was rooted deep. There was friendship and her long-standing crush and the way he'd looked at her the night they'd slept together. That all was still there even though she was mad at him and disappointed in how he was acting. But some other part of her, some new, daring part, was blossoming and stretching toward the light Lennox was offering.

Lennox didn't see her as shy, sheltered O'Neal Lory, that poor girl whose mom was murdered and who lived under the totalitarian law of her grandparents. He didn't see her with the past superimposed on her image. He saw her in the now. He made her feel…confident in her decisions—to be here, to do what she'd done with Auden, to break away from her family's wishes. He had no desire to wrap her in cotton and insulate her from the world. She believed him when he said he'd show her whatever she wanted. He wouldn't feel awkward or apologetic about sullying her so-called innocence. He wouldn't sanitize things for her. He trusted her to handle it.

Auden saw her as fragile. Lennox saw her as hungry.

Maybe she was both.

Lennox was watching her, a hint of vulnerability in his eyes. She realized in that moment, he expected her to turn him down.

And if she was doing this just to get back at Auden, she would. She'd walk away right now.

But this wasn't for Auden. This...was for herself.

She lifted her hand and raised a single finger. "I'm a one."

Lennox's gaze went to her hand and then slowly traced back up to her face.

She felt the look like a touch, and electricity tickled up her spine. Bravery grew, a small, hot light inside her. "But we have to make it believable. Auden will call our bluff otherwise. We can't look like we're faking."

Lennox stepped forward, gently slid his hand to cup her jaw. "Is that what you're worried about? You think I'd be faking wanting to touch you? Faking wanting to kiss you again?"

Her words left her.

He traced her cheekbone with the cool, rough pad of his thumb, leaving heat traces behind. "We've got no audience right now. How about a chemistry pop quiz?"

"A pop quiz?" She licked her lips.

A wicked gleam flashed in his eyes. "Question one: Do O'Neal and Lennox have believable chemistry? Complete the following activity and evaluate results." He looked down at his open palm like he was reading a document. "One kiss with no one watching."

She bit her lip and nodded.

He gave her a hint of a smile and tilted her face toward him, his gaze searching hers as he drew a little closer. "Still time to drop out of this class, Ms. Lory."

A jolt of resolve went through her. "Shut up and kiss me, Len."

Pleasure flickered across his features, and he lowered his head, pressing his mouth to hers.

Her eyes fell shut at the contact, and her hands went to the lapels of his jacket. His lips were soft and coaxing as they moved against hers, an invitation to a private dance. Gentle. Patient. A match struck inside her. His teeth gently dragged along her lower lip, nipping, tasting, making awareness curl through her like smoke. A little sound escaped her throat.

He *mmm*ed against her mouth, his hand angling her head a little farther back, and then he gently parted her lips with his tongue. His taste was salt and heat and other inviting things that made her crave more. Somehow, it was completely different than kissing Auden but no less exciting. Auden kissed her like he couldn't help himself, like he'd had a test of wills and failed, like he wanted to devour her before his conscience kicked back in. Lennox kissed like he was slipping a drug into her system that he knew she'd get addicted to. Slow. Confident. Potent.

Her grip tightened on his jacket, and their bodies brushed against each other, making a harsh ache open up inside her, but when she whimpered like some needy thing, he eased back. He cradled her face and touched his forehead to hers. They were both panting softly. He inhaled deeply through his nose, eyes closed, almost as if he was saying a silent prayer.

Her pulse pounded in all parts of her body.

After a moment, Lennox took a step back and rubbed his lips together. "Well," he said with a chagrined smile and a flush on his cheeks. "I don't think chemistry's going to be a problem. We just aced that class."

She leaned back against the brick wall of the library, worried her legs had turned to jelly and would no longer hold her up. "We ruined the curve for everyone."

"Fuck yes, we did." He laughed under his breath and unashamedly adjusted the bulge behind his zipper.

The sight of his arousal had her own body revving, a wave of want moving through her. She could step forward, put her hand where his had been, feel him, press against him. But then she met his stare, and now that they weren't touching, all kinds of undefined emotion rushed in behind the arousal. She pressed her hand to her forehead and let out a breath.

His eyes narrowed. "You okay?"

She nodded.

"Nooo," he said carefully. "A nod isn't going to cut it, Sweets. You were good and then you weren't. Your whole energy changed. What's wrong?"

Her chest suddenly felt like she was wearing a corset. "Sorry. I'm fine. It's not—I don't know."

He stepped closer again and put his hands on her shoulders, a soft press. "Look at me."

She forced herself to meet his eyes.

"If you didn't like it or are not into it, just tell me." His voice was cool, calm water over smooth rocks. "You're under no obligation to ever do that again."

She bit her lips together, trying to absorb the calm in his tone, to not panic. "That's not it. I liked it too much. This can't be okay—or normal. I slept with your best friend two weeks ago. Now I'm kissing you and getting all—thinking things—and haven't exactly worked through stuff with Auden. Isn't that what breaks up friendships? What kind of person does that make me, that I'm like"—she lifted her arms out at her sides, searching for the right words—"making out with two different guys who are also best friends and liking it?"

He held the eye contact. "An open-minded and adventurous

person? A person who's been deprived of fun life experiences and is making up for lost time?"

"*Lennox*," she protested. "You know that's not what I mean."

He lowered his hands to his sides and gave her a measured look. "You want me to say it's slutty? Is that what you're asking? You want me to shame you about it?"

The words burned her ears, but she didn't deny them. She looked down at her feet.

Lennox sighed. "Look, O' Neal, the only time I buy into shame is when someone gets off on it."

Her attention snapped upward at that, confusion making her forehead scrunch.

"Yeah, that's a thing," he confirmed. "Some people like being told to do sexual things and then being told how dirty or slutty they are. It turns them on."

Her lips parted, unable to hide her shock.

"It can be a fun game to play, *but*," he said firmly, "I'm not going to stand here and let you feel shitty about enjoying kissing two different guys. You're not committed to either of us. No promises have been made. You don't owe either of us anything. You have the right and freedom to kiss whomever you want. Hell, you could fuck me on the couch in front of Auden tonight, and he wouldn't have the right to say a damn thing about it. He bailed on you."

She gasped.

"Don't worry." His tone softened. "That's not what's going to happen tonight, but if you don't want to go through with this plan, you just have to say no. No harm, no foul."

Her heart was hammering, and his words were running around her head like a dog chasing its tail. Was this really okay? So much of this new life was teasing out which were her own feelings and judgments and which were the ones that had been imposed upon her growing up.

Gut check: did she want to go to movie night with Lennox?

Did she want to do that, knowing Auden would be there and this would be issuing some kind of challenge to confront what happened between them? Did she want to kiss Lennox again?

She took her time, taking a few breaths, and Lennox gave her space, not saying a word.

Finally, she put her hand out. "Let's go watch a movie."

Lennox smiled and took her hand. "You got it, Sweets."

# CHAPTER SIXTEEN

*L*ennox knew he was playing with fire as he drove O'Neal to the apartment. This wasn't how he and Aud did things. They didn't get sneaky. Everything was always up-front and out there on the table. But when Lennox had realized that Auden had just up and bailed on O'Neal, he'd seen red.

What the fuck had gotten into Auden? This was not the guy he knew. He and Auden, no matter who they got involved with, always took care of their partners. Clear discussion before, checking in during, and diligent aftercare. Both of them did everything possible to make whomever they'd been with feel good about what had happened.

If anything, Auden's care and concern with O'Neal should've been over the top. She was a family friend of his, inexperienced, younger than him. That called for a whole different level of being there for someone afterward. But instead, Auden had lied to Lennox about his contact with O'Neal and had left her hanging out on a limb, wondering what the hell had happened.

Unacceptable.

It also was *a tell.* This had been something bigger than a hot night with someone new for Auden. O'Neal meant more to him than he was admitting—maybe even to himself. If this was just about friendship, Auden would've had an adult conversation with her about not continuing to hook up. But he didn't. He ran.

Which meant there was something scary to run from—and Len planned on finding out exactly what that was. Even if it meant Auden was going to be pissed.

In kink terms, Auden was a dominant. He didn't switch like Lennox. But tonight, Mr. Dominant needed a lesson, and Lennox was ready to teach it. He glanced over at the gorgeous woman sitting next to him and smiled. A lesson and a willing partner in crime.

O'Neal kept surprising him at every turn. She was fire trapped under glass. Her upbringing had deprived her of the necessary oxygen, but now that she was out on her own, the flames were starting to grow. She couldn't yet name what she wanted or desired or craved, but she let herself feel things, allowed herself to sink into those feelings when they happened.

Their kiss at the library hadn't been tentative or shy. She hadn't let her fear or inexperience hold her back. The sounds she'd made when he'd deepened the kiss had slid under his skin and singed him from the inside out. She was starved, and for one selfish moment, he'd wanted to be the one to throw all the kindling on that burgeoning fire, every stick and leaf he could find. To show her all the delicious ways that he could make her burn.

But Lennox knew his role.

O'Neal was attracted to him. He had her attention. But Auden had her heart.

Maybe she didn't realize that yet, but Lennox could hear it when she said Auden's name. She said it like a prayer. Plus, he could see it on her face. He knew what it looked like to love Auden Blake. He'd seen that look in his own mirror.

The difference for O'Neal was that she actually had a chance of Auden loving her back.

Lennox parked the car in the driveway and peeked over at O'Neal. "Ready?"

"I don't know how to do this," she said, staring up at the apartment like it was a gauntlet. "How am I supposed to act?"

Lennox squeezed her hand. "Don't worry. Just follow my lead. And if you want to stop at any point say...*water.* That you need to get some, drink some, whatever. That will be your way to say no to me."

"*Water.* Okay. Got it."

He took a breath. Never in his life did he imagine giving a woman a safe word who probably had never even heard the terms kink or BDSM before. He was mad at Auden for breaking the rules, but right now he was tiptoeing precariously close to crossing lines too.

He just had to hope he didn't fuck it up and fall face-first into a bigger problem.

AUDEN SLID THE PAN OF SEASONED GROUND BEEF HE'D COOKED into the oven to keep warm for the tacos and slammed the door shut. He didn't know how to cook many things, but when they got sick of pizza and sandwiches, he pulled out one of the few basic recipes his mom had taught him. *So you won't starve at college,* she'd told him one day when she'd dragged him into the kitchen for lessons. Now, all he needed was for Lennox to get home so they could eat.

Tonight was supposed to be movie night, but they hadn't had one since O'Neal had come over. Just the idea of a movie night made Auden's shoulders bunch with tension. He glanced at his phone sitting idly on the counter.

He should call her. Talk. Explain why they couldn't continue what they'd started.

He fucking *missed* her.

But like every other time he'd looked at his phone, he couldn't bring himself to do it. The thought of saying the words aloud and hurting her made him feel nauseous. He didn't know how to apologize for crossing the lines that he had. He didn't know how to explain why being with him was a bad idea. He couldn't tell her that he was wired differently, that he craved things he'd never ask her to do. That he could never be the kind of guy she'd actually want to be with.

He groaned and grabbed a beer from the fridge, his appetite withering. Maybe he'd just leave the tacos for Len and go to bed. He headed into the living room, and the lock on the front door turned.

The door swung open and Len stepped inside, wearing a suit, which gave Auden pause. The guy could stop goddamned traffic looking like that. But before he could ask what was with the outfit, someone else stepped in behind him.

Auden froze, the sip of beer he'd taken burning back up his throat. *The fuck?*

Len shrugged out of his suit jacket and smiled. "Hey, Aud. Sorry, I'm a little late. I picked up O'Neal on the way for movie night. Hope you made enough for three. Smells great."

O'Neal wasn't smiling. She lifted a hand in a wary greeting. "Hey."

Auden's grip tightened on the beer bottle, a combination of panic and relief rising up inside him and battling for dominance. Panic, relief, and straight-up desire. He tried to ignore the fact that she somehow looked sexy in a loose pair of black cotton shorts and a gray Bennette U T-shirt. He didn't have the right to have those thoughts about her anymore.

"Uh, hey. I didn't know you were coming."

Lennox glanced between the two of them. "Yeah, O'Neal said y'all hadn't been in touch."

"I, uh, meant to call…" he said lamely.

She cleared her throat and set her purse on the table by the door. "It's okay. You said you were busy—but I got the message. You changed your mind. You have that right."

*Well.* Leave it to O'Neal to just say shit straight away.

"I—" He closed his mouth, tried to find the right words, couldn't. "I'm sorry."

"It's okay," she said, the words, crisp, a little cutting. "But I hope you don't mind me crashing movie night. I wanted to hang out with Len. I figured you wouldn't care." She tucked her hands into her back pockets and gave him a look of mild challenge— the version of O'Neal he'd known growing up. The quietly feisty girl next door. "You said what happened wouldn't change our friendship, right?"

Auden frowned. Was she really just going to let him off the hook—just like that? He didn't know how to feel about the vibe she was throwing his way. But what the hell was he supposed to say? He'd been the asshole in this scenario. He wasn't going to make it a thing if she didn't want to make it a thing.

"Right. Yeah, of course. You're obviously welcome at movie night."

She smiled a quick smile. "Great."

Lennox stepped up behind her and put his hands on her shoulders, massaging them lightly. "Is the food ready? We're starved."

Auden had been about to say something else but he pulled up short. *We're?* The word rang wrong in Auden's ear, and his gaze zoomed in on where Len was touching her. O'Neal leaned back into Len a little. The ease between them sent off alarm bells, but Auden managed to keep his expression calm.

"Yeah, everything's ready."

"Nice. Thanks for cooking, man." Len slid his hand to

O'Neal's lower back and guided her forward. "Come on, Sweets. Let's get you fed."

Auden watched them walk by, feeling like he'd stepped into some *Twilight Zone* version of his life. He followed them into the kitchen.

"I can't believe you know how to cook, Aud," O'Neal said as she grabbed a paper plate. "Does your mom know? She'd be impressed."

His mom. The reminder was a needed one. This was why he wasn't walking over to O'Neal and taking back everything he'd said and pulling her in for a kiss. This was why he hadn't called her. She was O'Neal goddamned Lory.

"Mom is the one who taught me, but my repertoire is limited. Don't be too impressed," he said.

She smiled and turned to assemble her tacos. Auden caught Len's eye, trying to convey a *what the hell is going on* look.

Len's expression revealed nothing—which meant Len was up to something because the guy was the most expressive person he knew—but Auden held his tongue for the moment.

They all made their plates and brought them into the living room. Auden took a spot in one of the chairs, expecting O'Neal to take the other, but instead, she sat next to Lennox on the couch. *Close* to Lennox.

"So are y'all doing movie roulette tonight?" O'Neal asked between bites.

Her tone was light, but Auden knew her well enough to sense she wasn't totally relaxed. He took a long pull off his beer, watching. "That's the plan."

"Want to do the honor, Sweets?" Len asked. He grabbed his phone and then scooted closer, draping his arm over her shoulder and holding the phone in front of her. "Hit the button."

Seeing them cuddled up like that made Auden's stomach tighten.

O'Neal sucked a dollop of sour cream off her fingertip,

drawing Auden's full attention, and then touched the screen. "And the winner is...number one hundred and twenty-three."

They both looked over at Auden.

Fully irritated now, he set his plate aside and grabbed his phone to open his spreadsheet. He scrolled down the list. "Looks like that's *Mean Girls.*"

"Ooh." O'Neal's expression lit up. "I've always wanted to see that one. Me and Maya had rented it at one point, but then your mom decided she better call Nana first to check it if was okay. Spoiler alert: she said no." She rolled her eyes. "We ended up watching some Disney movie instead."

"*Mean Girls* it is," Lennox said. "I haven't seen it either, but I'm a Tina Fey fan, so I'm in. Aud, no countertop sex concerns this time? Or any other objections?"

Auden's jaw clenched. "Not a one."

Len smiled. "Cool."

Auden got the movie queued up and then turned off the lights. They watched the first twenty minutes mostly in silence with the occasional laugh from O'Neal while they finished their tacos. Auden paused it when Len got up to throw away their plates. O'Neal pulled out her phone and didn't look his way, blatantly ignoring him.

When Len came back from the kitchen, he handed Auden another beer, and then lifted two bottles in front of O'Neal. "Coke or *water?*"

O'Neal set her phone aside and lifted her gaze to Len, some unreadable flicker of emotion crossing her face. She glanced at Auden and then back to Lennox. "Definitely Coke."

Lennox looked pleased for some reason and handed her the soda. "Excellent choice."

Auden's spidey senses had already been picking up on some weird energy in the room, but now they were pinging hard. Regardless, he couldn't help but watch O'Neal open her soda and then slowly bring it to her mouth. He felt hyperaware of everything. The way her mouth looked, the way she licked her bottom lip to catch a drop. It was like one of those slow-motion soda commercials that was supposed to make you thirsty. He was suddenly fucking parched.

And confused.

She set the drink aside and patted the spot next to her. "Thanks for the drink."

"No problem." Lennox took his spot in the corner of the couch, draping his arm over the back, and then, to Auden's horror, O'Neal shifted over and settled herself against his side as if she'd done it a hundred times before.

"You can start the movie back up," Len said, casual as ever as he twisted a lock of O'Neal's dark hair around his finger.

*What. The. Actual. Fuck?*

Lennox nodded toward the TV, but Lindsey Lohan stayed frozen on the screen. Auden tossed aside the remote. "Okay. I suspected it earlier, but now I know. You two are screwing with me."

O'Neal's eyebrows arched, a mild expression on her face. "What?"

"*You* know what. Since when are you two so damn cozy?" he asked, setting his beer aside and leaning forward, bracing his forearms on his thighs. "You're practically in his lap."

"So?" she volleyed back, challenge in her voice.

That sassy tone did things to him it shouldn't, but he was too irritated to let the feeling distract him. "*So* you two hardly know each other."

"Well, that's not really true," Len said with a little shrug. "We kind of got all the awkward new friends stuff out of the way early. I mean, we've already kissed, and you did some pretty personal things to her in the back seat of the car with me there."

Auden's back teeth pressed together.

"Plus," Len went on, "we hung out for a good while the morning after you two hooked up. Got to know each other.

Connected, honestly." He wrapped the lock of her hair round and round his finger like a taunt. "Then when you decided you were no longer interested in helping O'Neal out on her quest, she came to me to see if I was open to being that person for her."

"The hell she did," Auden said, his gaze pinning O'Neal to the spot. "I don't believe that for one second. That you—O'Neal Lory—went up to Lennox, a guy you barely know and *my* best friend, and asked him to just step into my place and fuck you instead?" He scoffed. "Yeah, okay. Sure you did. You can't even say the word *fuck* without blushing."

Her eyes narrowed. "I know how to say *fuck you* just fine."

Len coughed.

Auden's attention swung back to Lennox. "Don't, dude. You're messing with me. You put her up to this. This has your fingerprints all over it."

"You don't know anything," O'Neal announced. "We've kissed since that first time. I like Len."

"Bullshit," Auden said, getting angry now. "Look, you don't have to do this, all right? I get it. You're upset, and Len's helping you get back at me. Message received. I know I deserve it. I was a dick. But you don't have to continue to pretend—"

Before he could finish, O'Neal shifted on the couch, turning her body and climbing onto Lennox's lap, straddling him. She grabbed his loosened tie and then dipped down and kissed him.

Auden's words died on his lips.

Lennox slid his hands onto O'Neal's hips and held her there as they kissed—kissed like two people who were into each other, two people who had done it multiple times before. The glow of the TV had turned them silver, and Auden couldn't look away.

Part of him was so pissed at himself, so horrified that it was happening. He'd done this. He'd driven sheltered O'Neal Lory to this—whatever *this* was. But another, darker, deeper part of him had a sharp bolt of arousal ripping through him.

And *that* was a big part of the problem.

O'Neal broke away from this kiss, her chest rising and falling with heavy breaths, her hardened nipples visible points beneath her T-shirt. Her focus was firmly on Lennox. Len reached up and tucked a hair behind her ear, tenderness and heat in his eyes.

"I think we've got our audience's attention, Sweets."

O'Neal peeked at Auden over her shoulder, a flash of vulnerability in her eyes, the boldness falling away. Auden didn't know whether to go to her and drag her away from Len or flip the fucking coffee table and leave the room. He swallowed, regret hitting him hard. "I'm sorry I pushed you to this, Shaq. Whatever you're trying to do to get back at me, you don't need to. I feel like shit already. This is my fault. I let you down in the exact way I was trying not to. I didn't want you to get caught up in this."

Her gaze searched his, confusion on her face. She shifted off of Lennox's lap, staying next to him but turning fully toward Auden. "Caught up in what?"

His shoulders were aching from holding himself so rigid. He'd done such a good job of keeping who he was at home separate from who he was here. Bennette was his alternate universe, the place where he could play by different rules. College was supposed to be for experimenting, for getting the wildness out. He figured if he could indulge the darker urges he had during these few years at school, then when he went back home to take over the family business, he could fall back in line. Be normal. He'd have worked it out of his system.

The thought of O'Neal, someone from his life back home, knowing this side of him, seeing those secrets, made him want to fold in on himself. "I don't know, just…everything."

Lennox's expression settled into one of disappointment at Auden's dodge, but he didn't say anything. They weren't his secrets to tell.

O'Neal, on the other hand, was burning a hole in his head with her eyes. "Auden Blake, that answer is a thousand percent not good enough. What are you not telling me?" She put her hands out at her sides, her frustration obvious. "Are you seeing someone else? Selling drugs? Running a crime ring out of the back bedroom? Thought I was really terrible at sex and are afraid to tell me?"

He winced. "Of course, you weren't."

"Then what," she prodded, "could possibly make it okay to sleep with me, your *friend*—act like you enjoyed it—and then literally not speak to me for two weeks? I didn't think you were that kind of person."

He gritted his teeth, holding onto his control by a thread. "You have no idea what kind of person I am."

She scoffed. "Then *tell* me. Stop treating me like I'm some toddler who isn't allowed at the big kid's table. What could possibly make it okay to ghost me?"

"Fine. You want to know who I am? You want to know why I'm doing you a goddamned favor?" he said, his voice rising as he lost all sense of caution. "The night I slept with you was the first time I've slept with anyone in two years where there was no kink or where Len wasn't in the room—or in the bed too."

The words hung in the air—harsh and bright—and then crashed like glass between them. Her lips parted, and she sagged back against the couch as if he'd physically pushed her backward.

"I've been avoiding you since that night not because I didn't enjoy it or because it didn't mean something to me," he went on, unable to stop now that he'd started. "I avoided you because I know myself. Know that no matter how much I liked what we did, I would only be okay with the basics—with vanilla sex—for so long. And to be frank, what we did, wasn't all that vanilla to start. I touched you in front of Len. I got off on playing teacher to your student. I told you what a good girl you were. I took advantage of your willingness—your innocence."

Bright spots appeared on her cheeks like the admission had slapped her.

"And you had no idea that stuff was not, like, typical." He let out a breath. "The temptation to guide you into what I like would be too hard to resist. I already failed that test right out of the gate. I could tell you all of this stuff is normal, and you wouldn't think to fact-check me because you have no experience. Plus, you have the remnants of some schoolgirl crush on me, so you want to please me, want my approval. That's too much power for me to have."

He rubbed his palms along his jeans, his hands sweaty and his heart pounding.

He pinned her with his gaze. "I would *ruin* you, O'Neal. I would take and take and take until whatever notions of normal sex and relationships you may have had the chance to discover with someone else were warped to fit mine."

She was staring at him, her neck flushed even in the dim glow of the TV, a fawn in the headlights of his oncoming car.

"I would like to object to the use of the word *normal* in that speech," Lennox said, clearly annoyed. "Fuck that word."

Auden ignored Len and kept his attention on O'Neal. He could see that genius brain of hers trying to process and piece together what he'd said, to fill in the holes of what he wasn't saying. But she didn't have the reference points to fill in those blanks.

Her voice came out trembly when she spoke. "You're scaring me. What do you mean *ruin* me? What is it you'd want to do? I don't understand."

"I know," Auden said, feeling stripped down and exposed. "I wouldn't expect you to. Forget it."

Her eyes narrowed, and she sat up a little straighter. "Don't do that."

"What?" he asked, exhaustion seeping into him at the soul level.

"Dismiss me." The shakiness in her voice had hardened into a sharp point, her words turning into an arrow shot Auden's way. "That's not fair. You can't tell me what you just did and then pat me on the head and say, *you won't understand, little girl.* You thought I was woman enough to have sex with me—the least you can do is talk to me like I'm one."

"She's right," Lennox said, his voice quiet but firm as a judge's. "And you don't need to be scared, Sweets. We're kinky, not dangerous." He looked to Auden, irritation there. "Auden just hasn't accepted yet that his kink *doesn't mean he's damaged.* Man, your people are big into the shame game. All the self-flagellation. It's *exhausting.*"

O'Neal gave Auden a frustrated look. "Your kink? What does that even mean? I hate feeling this stupid."

Auden let out a long breath and ran a hand through his hair. This was the last kind of conversation he wanted to have with her, but she was right. He owed her truth. "You're not stupid."

"What he's having trouble telling you," Len said gently, "is that he and I like sexual activities that the mainstream would consider alternative and your families would probably consider horrifying."

O'Neal kept her focus on Auden. "Tell me. I want to know."

She wouldn't once she'd heard. She would wish she could rewind time. Whatever nice image she'd formed in her head about him would dissolve into dust. She'd find out he wasn't the guy she should've been crushing on.

He was the kind of guy her grandmother had warned her about.

# CHAPTER SEVENTEEN

*O*'Neal's normally neatly ordered brain was a tornado, thoughts whirling and crashing into each other. She'd thought she'd exhausted every possible reason for why Auden had avoided her after their night together. She thought she'd examined every angle. But this—whatever this was—was so far outside her field of awareness that she didn't even know how to ask the right questions.

She'd heard the word *kinky* before but just assumed it was a way to describe people who liked a lot of sex—like slutty. But Auden's obvious anguish over having this conversation clearly meant she'd gotten the definition wrong.

When he'd said that he'd *take and take and take*—that'd he'd *ruin* her, she'd felt like the words were wrapping around her body and squeezing. Her skin had gone overly sensitive, like every part of her was buzzing, the air around her crackling with energy. Somehow the statement had both scared her and made her achingly curious. What did that *mean?* What would *ruin* her?

She wanted to know. But she also feared the answer to that question.

What if Auden did horrible things to women? What if this

would change what she thought of him forever? His family was all she had now. What if this changed that?

The risk was one she had to take. She was tired of being in the cocoon she'd grown up in.

She met Auden's gaze, steeling herself. "Tell me. I want to know."

After a long, quiet moment, something broke in Auden's expression—the message clear. He was going to tell her, but he didn't want to. There would be a Before and an After and no going back.

Auden glanced at Lennox, who nodded, and then his gaze slid back to her. "What happened in the car is not something most guys would ask you to do. Len and I...share partners. We like to watch and be watched."

She shivered. They *shared?* "Like you take turns sleeping with someone or..."

"*Or*," Auden confirmed. "All three people together at the same time."

The images that popped into her brain made her blush from head to foot, but she kept her expression even. She didn't want to spook Auden, so she managed to simply say, "Oh."

Like *oh, that's interesting* instead of *oh, you've just blown my brain to bits.*

Auden's throat bobbed as he swallowed. "And we like to... play power games."

Her mind was still processing the first part, so this second revelation threw a wrench into her *keep cool* plans. She blurted, "Games?"

Auden laced his fingers between his knees, his knuckles whitening like it was taking everything he had to make these admissions to her. "In kink terms, I'm a...dominant. I like to be in charge in bed, have all the control—with the other person's consent, always with full consent." He looked away like seeing her in front of him was just too much. "Len can switch around.

Most of the time we'll both be in the dominant role. But sometimes he'll submit to me too, will do what I say when we're with someone."

The thought of Auden bossing Lennox around in bed was…a lot to process. Did they do things with *each other?*

*Whoa. Too. Many. Mental. Pictures.* Really, really hot mental pictures.

Did that mean they were gay or bisexual or some different term she hadn't learned yet? Her old operating system was just going to shut down. A blue screen was about to pop up and tell her to unplug and reboot. She peeked at Lennox, hoping he could guide her back, but his poker face revealed nothing. She latched on to the one thing she could manage to say without embarrassing herself.

"You let him tell you what to do?"

Len gave her a brief smile, one that settled her a little. "Sometimes—when he's lucky. I can appreciate both sides of that coin, Sweets, and Auden's good at it."

She absorbed that. *Auden's good at it.* "But Lennox doesn't tell you what to do?"

"No, at least not in bed," Auden said. "Being in control is what…gets me off. I've tried the other side with a dominant woman." His face colored a little, but he cleared his throat and continued. "Didn't work for me. Was kind of a disaster actually."

At least he was looking at her again. "What does telling someone what to do mean exactly? Just like giving them directions? That doesn't sound so bad."

His gaze narrowed a bit like he was slightly pained. "It's not what you're imagining. It's not gentle guidance. More like orders. And sometimes it involves restraining someone. Other times…hurting them a little."

Her stomach plummeted like she'd hit a drop on a roller coaster. "*Hurting* them?"

"With their permission," Lennox added, putting a gentle hand on her arm as if calming a skittish animal. "I know it's hard to wrap your head around when you're new to the concept, but some people get really, really turned on from a little pain—or a lot. We don't do anything too intense in that area—not our kink."

Lennox's touch did soothe her some, though she had no idea why. She shook her head. "I don't get how pain could be sexy in any way."

"No?" Lennox reached out and brushed his knuckles along her cheek, his voice low and gentle like waves lapping against the lakeshore. "Imagine Auden pushing you to your knees, his fingers curling in your hair and tugging until it stung enough to tingle, to get your attention. And while he's holding you like that, he unzips his pants, pulls out his cock, and tells you to suck him off like a good girl."

"*Len.* Jesus." Auden's voice echoed in the quiet room, but the scene Lennox had painted had already splashed across her mental canvas.

She couldn't unsee it. Or move. Heat blanketed her body, and she could almost feel tight, demanding fingers against her scalp. Her nipples instantly went sensitive against her bra, but her full-body reaction confused her. Why would she want to be handled like that—talked to like that?

"Wouldn't that make someone feel degraded?"

She was proud she'd managed to get a question out and not sound as breathless and shocked as she felt.

"Sometimes," Auden said. "Especially if I call them names while they're doing it."

She turned to look at him, frowning at the admission. "And you like making someone feel that way?"

There was grim satisfaction in his eyes now, like he'd accomplished what he'd wanted to. He'd scared her. "Yes. I like it a lot. Sometimes, if a woman cries while it's happening, I get even harder."

Her hands curled in her lap, the answer stunning her, the image she'd always had of good-natured, big brother next door Auden transforming into something else, something alien and unnerving.

"Oh."

"And now you know why what happened between us can't happen again," he said, tone softening. "I want us to be friends. I want us to grab food together or watch movies. I have fun hanging out with you, and the night we had together was amazing and sexy. I feel privileged to have been your first. Even if I probably should want to undo that because it was selfish, I don't want to take it back. But that's where it needs to end. I can't—*won't*—drag you into something you have no business being a part of."

"Unless you want to be," said Len.

Irritation flared in Auden's eyes. "What the hell, Len? *Stop.*"

"No, man," Lennox said, his voice sharper than O'Neal had ever heard it. "You get to make the call on what you want to do, but you don't get to tell her what business she can or can't be a part of. Just because she's inexperienced doesn't exclude her from being kinky. It means she doesn't know yet if she is or isn't."

He shifted on the couch like he was ready to jump up and go toe to toe with Auden.

"And I don't appreciate you describing it to her like it's this twisted, dirty thing," he went on. "You're basically setting her up to feel shitty or shameful about it if she does discover she's into something that isn't Main-Street-approved. Fuck that noise. She's had enough people telling her to feel guilty or wrong about every little thing her whole life. If everyone's consenting, there's nothing wrong with what we do."

Auden growled in frustration and stood. "You don't get it. She—"

RONI LOREN

"Is right here," O'Neal reminded him, angry at being discussed.

"Yes, you are," Lennox said, standing as well, "and you don't have to let him make this call for you." He looked at her. "Tell him again how you felt when he touched you and I was in the car with you because I think he's selectively chosen to forget."

"Don't put her on the spot," Auden snapped.

"He's not," she said, her frustration giving her some confidence. "I already told you I was nervous but I thought it was exciting."

"Beautiful," Len said, pride in his voice. "And how do you feel knowing you've kissed both of us, that we've both seen you kiss the other one? That we both liked watching that happen?"

She ventured a quick look at Auden, feeling his presence like a weight against her skin. He was standing there, arms crossed, watching her closely, but his expression was unreadable. "I don't know. But I liked kissing each of you."

Lennox offered her a ghost of a smile. "You're doing great, Sweets. Honesty will keep us out of trouble with this. Now," he said, catching her eye. "I want you to look at Auden and without editing, tell him what you first felt when you imagined what I said—when you thought about him grabbing your hair, being a little rough, and putting you on your knees for him."

She tensed, anxiety rippling over her skin.

He touched her knee, and she startled. "Easy," he said. "There are no wrong answers. If the thought horrified you or scared you, you can tell him. If it did something else, you can tell him that too. I saw your face. I think I already know the answer, but it's important for you to say it."

His knowing tone had her wanting to cover her face with the couch cushion. It was one thing to admit she was attracted to both of them. It was an entirely different matter to confess how she'd felt when he'd said those words. She *could not* answer this question. She'd die.

210

She shook her head.

Lennox moved his hand from her knee but didn't say anything.

Heat was burning up the back of her neck. *I can't. I can't.*

She dared another look at Auden, part of her hoping he would save her from this, that he'd just send her home and be done with this. But his face had changed, the closed expression now tinged with confusion.

"O'Neal?"

His voice was soft, questioning. He took a step forward.

Lennox stood and backed away, making room for him. Auden's focus hadn't left her face. She felt like he was peeling back the cover of her diary, reading every private word. She dropped her attention to her hands.

"Look at me," he said, quiet authority filling his voice, a tone that commanded.

She shook her head again.

Seconds past.

*One.*

*Two.*

*Three.*

His hand slid into her hair, his fingertips lighting up the sensitive surface of her scalp, and then he tugged, forcing her to look at him and sending a flash-bang of sensation through her body.

The desperate sound that burst from her lips sliced through the silence like a bullet.

Auden's hazel eyes were almost black in the darkened room, but his lips parted with what she could only label as wonder. She liked seeing him look at her like that. His throat worked, and his voice came out gritty.

"Tell me what you felt, O'Neal. Now."

"That it sounded demeaning. That you wanting to make

someone cry sounds wrong." She closed her eyes and shuddered.

"*And*," he prodded, his grip tightening a little and sending sparks downward and across her thighs.

She kept her eyes squeezed shut. "And it made me hot all over. *This* is making me hot all over."

"*Fuck*." His breath cascaded over her like he'd released an inhale he'd been holding forever.

"Good girl," Lennox whispered, pride lining the words. "Honest *and* brave."

The praise fell over her like summer rain. She forced herself to open her eyes and look at Auden. She felt...unmoored. What did this say about her that she was turned on by this? Was Auden right? Did this mean she was abnormal in some way?

"I don't know how to feel about how I feel."

Auden gave her a ghost of a smile. "That's okay. I'm still working on that myself."

"I'm not," Len offered.

Auden's gaze skimmed down her body, his eyes full of barely banked fire. His fingers massaged her scalp, and it was impossible to ignore the growing outline in his jeans. He looked as if he was having some internal conversation with himself. His Adam's apple bobbed.

"I can try to turn off the thinking for you for a little while. We both can. If you just want to get to the feeling part."

Her heartbeat was pulsing low and urgent between her legs. She dampened her lips, gave the barest of nods, afraid she'd chicken out if she spoke.

"Her safe word is *water*," Lennox offered.

Auden's attention jumped his way, his breath a gust of frustration. "How does she already have a fucking safe word, Len?"

Lennox smirked unrepentantly. "Long story."

"A safe word?" she asked, her voice sounding shaky to her own ears.

"You say that word, whatever's happening stops," Lennox said. "No consequences. It's the kill switch. Keeps everyone safe. We can all use it."

She looked back to Auden. "Why not *no*?"

His hand slid from her hair, and he cupped her chin to tip her face toward him. "Because sometimes it's fun to protest. To fight back." He leaned down and put his lips next to her ear. "To make me force the issue. To say no and have me do it anyway."

She shivered, but she couldn't tell if it was fear or rampant, aching curiosity.

He straightened and kept his focus fully on her. She had no idea what he was seeing, but she could sense she was being read like an open book. "Tell me your safe word."

She was trembling. "Water."

"And what happens if you say it?" Lennox asked.

"Everything stops."

"So I guess the question is"—Auden's throat worked—"are you thirsty?"

# CHAPTER EIGHTEEN

O'Neal didn't know much about this world Auden and Lennox were describing, but she did know what Auden was asking her. He was giving her a ticket out. If she said *yes, I need water,* he would back off. They would return to watching the movie. She knew in her gut that he would honor the safe word.

O'Neal also knew, without a doubt, that she was way out of her depth and in over her head. She had no idea what they would expect from her. They lived in a world with kinky, experienced women apparently. She was not that. She would probably mess this up, do something wrong. She didn't even know if she'd enjoy it.

But the sensations in her body, the buzzy feelings that were moving through her, were more powerful right now than logic. She'd peeked behind the *Members Only* door and wanted to know what things were like on the other side. She didn't want to run scared from the unknown. She wanted to *know* and then decide. Evidence-based decision-making, not theory.

She boldly held Auden's gaze, drumming up every ounce of her courage. "I'm not thirsty."

His gaze traced down over her, an obvious hunger there, but wariness remained in his voice. "I need you to be sure. I know you like to skip the intro classes and jump to the advanced ones, but this isn't calculus."

"I know. I'm sure." She pulled her shoulders back a little, made a point to look at Lennox and then back to Auden, and then grabbed onto a thread of gumption. "I trust you. Both of you. And I...want to understand why the thought of you being in control makes me feel...tingly all over."

Auden closed his eyes, inhaled. Then, just when she thought he was going to back out on her, he opened his eyes and pointed to the floor. "Get on your knees, freshman."

She startled slightly at the sharpness in his tone, and she was frozen for a moment.

He lifted a brow—a smug, entitled expression that somehow made her shiver. "Don't make me wait. It wasn't a request."

Her first instinct was to tell him off, but this was the game. He was going to show her what he liked. For better or worse, they were going to try this. She took a deep breath and moved from the couch to her knees, the carpet coarse against her skin.

Auden reached over and flicked on a second lamp. "I don't want to do this in the shadows. I want to see your face when I teach you how to suck my cock."

She automatically winced at the words, the knee-jerk reaction too fast to pull back.

He hesitated. She caught it, but he quickly covered it, smoothing his expression. "Or maybe not just mine. You've never done it before. You probably should practice sucking Len first. Get your technique right before I grant you the privilege of having mine."

She'd be crap at poker. Any chance she had at hiding her shock had been an illusion. She'd grown up in a world where no one cursed, much less talked like this. These words had been sinful, forbidden, punishable in their world. Hearing Auden—

the boy she could still picture in his prep school jacket and tie—
say such things probably should've made her want to hightail it
out of there. Instead some unfamiliar sensation—fear mixed up
with anticipation—was braiding through her. It was making her
breath come quicker and her skin very, very sensitive.

Auden was evaluating her, watching her every reaction. He
crossed his arms, looming over her, his erection a prominent
outline in his jeans. "Take off your top and bra, freshman."

She snuck a peek at Len. There was humor in his eyes, as
usual, but a new heat was there as well. He gave her a *well, we're
waiting* look.

Okay. She could do this. She'd kissed Len. She'd been
touched in front of him. She could let him see her. She reached
for the hem of her T-shirt and pulled it over her head. After she
tossed it onto the couch, she reached behind her back and
unhooked her bra. She slipped it down and off. Her arms automatically crossed over her chest.

"No, you don't," Auden said, voice a little thicker. He reached
down, circled her wrists with his fingers, and lowered her arms
to her sides. "No hiding from us." He traced a fingertip around
her nipple, making her sensitive flesh tighten in the cool air.
"Let us see those pretty tits of yours. Let Len see how respon-
sive you are."

She took a shuddering breath, sensation radiating out from
his touch.

Len stepped closer, his gaze devouring her, and he adjusted
the front of his black slacks. Her gaze went to the bulge pushing
against his fly, and that clear sign of his arousal gave her a thrill.
She had both of them turned on. That felt...*powerful.*

Len reached out, cupping her breast gently and running a
roughened artist's thumb over the tip. "Gorgeous, Sweets. Beautiful inside and out."

"Thank you," she whispered.

"There's a better way to thank him," Auden said, stepping to her side. He tunneled his hand into her hair again, palming the back of her scalp. "Let's show him how eager of a student you are. Unzip his pants."

The slight pressure of Auden's grip made her focus sharpen, everything coming into detailed relief. She rubbed her lips together, nervous as she'd ever been, but not ready to ask for water. She was only going to use that safe word if she felt unsafe or hated something. She would not let herself use it for fear of not getting something right.

"I don't know how to do this," she admitted as she reached for the fly of Len's pants, her hands shaking a little.

"I know," Auden said, voice even. "That's why I'm going to show you. If you do what I say, you have nothing to worry about. You get me as a teacher. Lucky, lucky you."

She snorted softly.

And Len chuckled under his breath. "The ego on this one."

The brief break in intensity was a welcome respite—a reminder that this was still Auden, the guy she'd known forever, and Lennox, a guy she counted as a friend. Her hands steadied some, and she unbuttoned Len's pants and dragged down the zipper. A peek of straining black boxer briefs filled her vision.

Len reached up, undid his tie fully, and started unbuttoning the dress shirt, revealing all that beautiful tattooed skin. A wave of desire rolled through O'Neal as she looked up, taking in the full view. Len's black eyeliner had smudged, and his undone clothes looked rumpled in the sexiest, most enticing way.

He slid his hand into the band of his underwear, and his forearm flexed as he gripped his erection. "Keep looking at me like that, Sweets, and I may start the festivities before Aud tells us to."

Her attention shifted to where he gripped himself, his casual ease ridiculously erotic. Her mind spun to a private place, one where Len held himself just like that, coated himself in something slippery, and stroked. He'd implied that he'd done that the night she'd slept with Auden.

"Tell me what you're thinking right now," Len said. "You just went somewhere. Some place good by the looks of it."

She flinched, caught in the act, and tried to look down, but Auden's fingers were still laced in her hair.

"Oh no, you don't," Auden said. "Tell him. No editing."

She dragged her teeth over her lip, embarrassment trying to choke off her voice. She'd been taught that she wasn't supposed to have impure thoughts. Not *doing* the things wasn't enough. She wasn't even supposed to *think* of them. The nights she'd lain in her bed and weaved fantasies about Auden, her body growing warm and wet and achy… Sometimes she'd touched herself, imagining the possibilities, and then had been swamped with shame afterward. She'd felt like the biggest pervert. That she was broken in some way. But now, they wanted her to speak something like that aloud?

Len touched the tip of his finger to her bottom lip as if trying to unlock the words. "Everything is okay to say. Every single thing. Judgment-free zone. I promise."

"He's right," Auden said. "You're safe."

She closed her eyes at that. *Safe.* After a shaky breath, she opened her eyes and focused on the faint trail of hair tracking below Len's navel. "When you wrapped your hand around yourself, it made me think of what you said about the night Auden and I were together. It made me think about us in one room and the sounds drifting to yours, and what it must've looked like for you to…pleasure yourself."

"And the thought of Len jerking off turns you on?" Auden asked.

She nodded, her cheeks so hot they had to be glowing.

Auden's breath tickled her ear as he leaned down again. "Show us."

She turned her head, blinking up at him. "How?"

He released her hair and then trailed his fingers down her arm, crouching next to her. He lifted her hand to his lips, pressing a light kiss there, and then brought her hand downward, to the waistband of her shorts. He let her palm rest against her belly, and then he popped open the button on her shorts. "I mean"—he took her wrist and guided her hand down along her stomach and beneath the waistband of her panties— "show us how much you liked the idea of Len getting his hand all slick and warm and stroking his cock while he listened to us come. The idea of him shooting all over his chest while imagining he was fucking you."

The image was almost too much to hold in her head, and her body lurched a little with the impact. Her fingers, guided by Auden, brushed the wet, needy heat between her legs, and she gasped at how intense the barely-there touch felt.

Auden's fingers covered hers, curved, led her to the place where she ached most. He made her stroke herself, and she moaned. He hissed out a breath like she wasn't the only one affected and said in a low, grit-filled voice, "Slide your fingers inside, tell Len how wet you got thinking about him. How much you like thinking about his cock."

She closed her eyes, arousal now in control, all other thoughts or worries taking a back seat. She pushed two fingers inside that most private space, and her muscles clenched, seeking more than what her fingers could offer.

"Tell him," Auden cajoled against her ear, his hand still over hers. "Be a good girl and say the words."

For some reason, this was the hardest part. The words. But that was ridiculous. She had one man's hand in her panties while the other was in front of her with his fly open. She could no longer cling to innocence. She was doing this. She...*liked* this.

She gulped past the catch in her throat and honed in on what she was feeling. "I'm so turned on." She forced her eyelids open, her gaze upward. It collided with Len's. His held no humor now, just hunger. She licked her lips. "I'm hot and achy and soaking wet thinking about your *cock*."

Len groaned and squeezed his erection like the words had been painful. "She's going to kill me, Aud."

Auden pressed his lips to her temple, a reward. "Welcome to my world," he said, breath tickling her cheek. "She's been killing me slowly for a long time now. Most tempting woman I've ever met."

She turned her head to look at Auden in surprise.

He gave her a half-smile, the smile of the Auden she knew, and then leaned forward and kissed her tenderly. "It's the truth." He eased her hand out of her underwear and then brought her fingers to his mouth. Without breaking the eye contact, he sucked her fingers clean. He kissed the tips when he was done. "You have no idea what you do to me, O'Neal Lory. You should've already run out the door by now. You're supposed to be appalled. Why are you still here?"

His admission and the wonder in his eyes made more than her body light up. She held his stare and shook her head ever so slightly. "Not running. Not appalled. Guess you better try harder."

"Guess so." His mouth quirked into a playfully evil smirk, and that's when she realized she finally had him. She'd trusted *him* going into this, but he hadn't trusted *her*. He'd expected her to be so shocked she would bail immediately. He'd still had his guard up because he'd expected her to judge him, to be disgusted by what he liked. He'd expected her to act like the world they'd come from, not the world they were in now.

He'd underestimated her.

Auden got to his feet, a new spark in his eyes, and he stepped behind Lennox. He put his hands on Len's shoulders. Both of the guys looked down at her—on her knees, naked from the waist up, shorts unbuttoned—and she tipped her chin up.

"She wants me to try harder to freak her out, Len," Auden said, massaging Len's shoulders.

Lennox smiled. "So it seems. Maybe we're losing our touch."

"We'll see," he said. "Hands at your sides, Len."

Lennox released his grip on himself and shifted his arms to his sides. O'Neal watched, slightly stunned, as Auden's hands traveled downward, tracing down Lennox's chest, and then hooking his thumbs in Len's pants. Auden dragged down Len's slacks and underwear, leaving Len completely bared, his straining erection springing free.

Her focus zeroed in, fascinated at the sight, and her inner muscles instinctively tightened as Len kicked his pants to the side. A bead of fluid glistened at the tip of Len's...*cock*. She made herself think the word. But before she could even absorb the sight of this beautiful guy in front of her, Auden shocked her again.

He spit into his palm and then he wrapped his hand around Len's length, giving his friend a slow stroke.

Her breath hitched and heat flashed through her. She'd considered the possibility that the two of them touched when they were in bed sharing a woman, but thinking it and seeing it were two different things. Her gaze jumped up to their faces.

Lennox's eyes were closed in pleasure. Auden was watching her, clearly gauging her reaction.

Though her family—and even Auden's family—would never explicitly say it, being gay or anything other than straight was not okay in the place they came from.

O'Neal had never bought that line of thinking. She'd had a friend in middle school who'd confided that she liked girls. But that didn't mean her brain wasn't a little scrambled seeing Auden's hand on his best friend.

Her attention drifted back down. She could feel Auden still watching her, but she couldn't help but look. The firm grip, the way Auden spread the fluid at the tip of Lennox's cock down the shaft, the familiarity with which he touched him. If anyone had asked her if she'd ever want to see a guy stroke another guy, she would've said no—*why would I want to see that?* But this...this was one of the most erotic things she'd ever seen or even fantasized about.

The freedom it represented was like a drug. The three of them could do *anything* together. Touch and be touched. Kiss. Taste. No shame attached. No guilt. No one ready to judge the other. It was the opposite of everything she'd grown up with.

She looked up, gave Auden the full unvarnished wonder she was feeling inside, not hiding anything in her expression. "Show me how to make him feel good."

Len peered down at her, his eyes half-mast and his normal lazy smile nowhere to be found. He reached out and dragged his fingers into her hair. "Open that pretty mouth, Sweets."

Nerves quivered through her, but she parted her lips, readied herself as best she could.

"That's it," Auden said, easing them closer. "Good girl."

The words resonated through her like the ringing of a bell.

Auden traced the head of Len's cock along her bottom lip, spreading fluid there. The taste of salt touched the tip of her tongue, and she wanted to explore, but she remained still, waiting to be told. That was the game, and she wanted to play it.

Auden's gaze was heavy on her, a branding iron of a look. "Listen very closely, freshman. You're going to take him in your mouth and use your tongue and lips, no teeth, and prove what a good student you can be. You understand?"

She gave him a barely-there nod.

"Suck his cock like you're hungry for it. Because we know you are," Auden went on, a sardonic note in his voice. "Let's not pretend you haven't been thinking about my best friend way more than you should've been when you were supposed to only be with me."

"I wasn—" she started but at that moment Auden released

Len, and Len tilted her head and eased into her mouth, cutting off her words and making her eyes close.

The velvet heat of his shaft slid across her tongue, filling her with his masculine scent and taste. Len groaned, and a desire to make him do that again, to make him feel amazing, zipped through her. But insecurity was fast on the heels of that urge. Her palms pressed into the tops of her thighs, and she tensed, unsure of what to do. Suck? Lick? Lots of pressure or gentle pressure?

Len let out a shaky breath. "Don't be scared, Sweets. Your mouth feels fucking fantastic. Don't be afraid to move. You won't hurt me."

She instantly pulled back, letting him slip from her mouth, embarrassment flooding her and making her ears burn. "I'm sorry. I don't know how to—what I'm doing. I don't want to mess up."

"Shh." Auden put a grounding hand on her shoulder and moved to the spot behind her. "You're okay."

"I…" she said but didn't know what she was trying to say.

"You're fine. Ask for water if you need it, but you don't have to be scared." The familiar scent of Auden's cologne wrapped around her as he kneeled behind her. His hand spread wide across her stomach, stilling her as he bracketed her against his chest. His voice was close to her ear when she spoke. "You're not going to mess up. I promise. This is an easy A, freshman. It's the P.E. of sexual acts."

She snorted softly, the bit of humor calming her rising nerves.

"Not a secret, but guys really, *really* like getting their dicks sucked. Beyond teeth, there's not much you can do wrong." Auden's lips traced the shell of her ear. "The way your hot, soft mouth is going to feel around him is going to drive him crazy. It's going to take every bit of restraint he has not to grab your head and fuck your mouth like his life depends on it. Think about how you felt when my mouth was on you, when I had my tongue on your clit. What felt good. The heat of my tongue, the pressure of it, the slick slide of flesh against flesh."

Her breath was quickening again, her heart beating between her legs. The tip of Len's cock was glossy in front of her, the head flushed and smooth. She was fascinated by the differences between the men. Len wasn't as thick as Auden was but he was longer with a slight curve upward. As she stared, another bead of fluid appeared.

"Look what you're doing to him. He's leaking for you." Auden's hand glided upward, caressing the underside of her breast. "Taste him, freshman. Trust your instincts on what will make him feel good. I promise, he's going to love it."

Auden's words chased off some of her must-be-perfect qualms. This was sex, not rocket science. She just had to trust what she thought would make him feel good. She looked up at Len, whose face was more strained than she'd ever seen it, and nodded. His grip tightened on her hair, and he slowly guided his erection into her mouth inch by inch. His forearm strained as he gripped himself at the base.

O'Neal closed her eyes and let herself explore, dragging her tongue along the bottom side of his length and circling it around the head, marveling at the buttery soft skin encasing the steel. Len made a guttural sound of appreciation, and confidence grew inside her like vines. She moved her head in a gentle pumping motion, sliding partway down his length and then back, exploring the nuances of this new terrain.

"Fucking hell," Len whispered.

"That's it," Auden said softly, one of his hands cupping her breast and sending tingles over her skin. "Now try and relax your throat. Len's got an impressive cock, but you can take it all if you relax your throat muscles and breathe through your nose. You don't have to use your tongue or do any work, just relax and let him use you for a little while."

The command made her eyes blink open, the thought of taking all of Len hard to fathom. She'd only made it halfway down so far. But she trusted that Auden wouldn't tell her to do something that was impossible.

Len smiled down at her and cupped her jaw. "I'll go easy on you, Sweets. This time. Just relax. I'll always stop if you need me to."

She held the eye contact and tried to soften the back of her throat. Len eased deeper, taking it slow. When he bumped the back of her throat, her gag reflex kicked in and he backed off a bit.

"Easy," Auden said and kissed the curve of her neck. "Try again. You're doing great. And look so fucking sexy doing it." He pressed against her, and she felt his stiff cock against the small of her back.

Knowing she was turning them both on made her want to try again. She looked up to Len, giving him a silent signal. He canted his hips forward again, and this time when the head of his cock touched the back of her throat, she forced herself to release the tension and breathe through her nose.

Len's hand went to her throat and squeezed ever so gently, a shudder going through him. "Jesus. That's…"

She couldn't take her eyes off his face. Knowing she had made Mr. Smooth Talker speechless for a moment was oh-so-satisfying. He rocked back and then plunged deep again, finding his own slow rhythm.

"Look at him," Auden said, so low there was no way Len could hear it. "You're on your knees for him, but he's all yours right now, at your mercy."

A bolt of satisfaction went through her.

"Want to drive him really crazy?" Auden took her hand in his and lifted it toward Len. "He likes this."

Guiding her hand with his, Auden pressed her palm against Len's balls. The tender skin was tight and firm beneath her touch, and Len lost his rhythm for a moment, letting out a whispered *fuck*.

Auden chuckled softly, and O'Neal suddenly understood on some level, the power thing. Knowing you could undo someone was a rush.

"Now," Auden said, keeping his voice low. "Watch him lose it."

Auden left her hand in place to cup and stroke Len, but he moved his back a little farther. She watched in shock as Auden used the tip of his finger to touch a place she would've thought was completely off-limits.

Len's entire body went stiff, and he let out a gritty moan, rocking harder into her mouth and then yanking back abruptly. "*Motherfucker.*"

Before she could track what was happening, hot lines of fluid streaked across her bare chest as Len pumped his hand forcefully and came in a rush.

She stared in amazement at the erotic sight of Len completely lost to pleasure. She'd done that to him. A satisfied *hell yes* feeling swelled inside her.

Auden made a pleased sound and then nipped the lobe of her ear. "Gold star, freshman. Aced it."

After a few seconds to catch his breath, Len gazed down at her with a heavy-lidded look and touched his thumb to her lips. "Screw that pop quiz. We could teach the goddamned chemistry class, Sweets. I usually have more control than that. But, *fuuuuck.*"

She smiled, feeling slightly giddy with how undone he looked. "Didn't Aud tell you? I'm a valedictorian. I don't get Bs."

Auden laughed as he stood and then put a hand on her elbow to help her to her feet. Her shorts fell to the floor, and she stepped out of them, her legs a little wobbly. He turned her toward him and gave her a teasing smile. "Don't get cocky, freshman. You've still got me to deal with." His gaze darkened, a playful glint there. "And some apologizing to do after that stunt you pulled with Len tonight."

"I—"

He shook his head, cutting her off. "It's going to take more than words." He jerked his chin toward Lennox. "Clean up your mess and put that necktie to good use. And don't let her come. She hasn't earned that yet. I'll meet you in my bedroom."

The ice in his voice was like a physical touch, raising hot goosebumps on her skin.

Len grabbed the tie hanging around his neck and grinned. "On it."

After Auden left the room, Len pulled on his boxers and then cleaned her off with a warm washcloth he retrieved from the bathroom. She shivered beneath the rough terry cloth, all of her senses heightened.

"You doing okay?" he asked as the towel grazed over her nipple, making her breath hitch.

She licked her lips, still tasting Len there. "I think so," she said, then rethought her answer. "Yes."

He tossed the towel aside and then leaned down to brush a gentle kiss over her lips. "Thank you. For what you did. I'm honored that you trusted me enough to try it with me. Hottest blow job of my life, hands down."

She rolled her eyes. "Liar. You're just trying to make me feel better."

"Not true," he assured her. "The combo of you being so trusting and willing and Aud guiding you and participating?" He let out a breath. "Fucking mind-blowing. I'm already getting hard again thinking about it." He touched the tip of her nose with his finger. "But how was it for you? Not everyone likes giving head. It's okay if you didn't. Lots of alternatives."

"God, Len." She put her hand over her eyes. "Who even asks that kind of question?"

"I do," he said matter-of-factly and tugged her hand away so he could look at her. "The menu of things that can turn a person on is a long one but a personal one. If you're going to do this kind of thing with us, we need to be open about what you're into and what you're not. I mean, some people get off on being forced to do things they *don't* like. So it's just good information to have."

"I liked it," she admitted. "I liked being taught and kind of... handled, but I also liked that I could bring you to that point and make you lose control. And I really, really liked hearing that I was doing it right."

He narrowed his eyes, evaluating. "Hmm."

"What?" she asked, suddenly self-conscious.

He smiled and draped his tie around the back of her neck, tugging her closer. "And how would you feel if I told you that you're being a very good girl for us? That we're so very proud of you?"

She rolled her lips together. "That should probably make me mad. Sounds patronizing and patriarchal."

"I'm not asking how it sounds," he said, sliding a hand to her hip. "I'm asking how it *feels*."

Her breasts pressed up against his naked chest, and she wrapped her arms around his neck, feeling oddly safe being this close with him. "It makes me feel prickly all over, like in a good way. Even if I feel like anything but a good girl right now. I'm failing *that* test for sure."

"You're not failing at anything, Sweets. You're perfect."

The compliment made her insides go liquid.

He traced his thumb along her hip bone. "And I don't think Auden should have any worries about you being strictly vanilla. It's going to be fun finding all the ways your hidden kinky switches are flipped."

Her mouth went dry at the notion. "I don't even know what switches y'all have yet."

"I bet you're going to figure it out real fast." He gave her a wink. "Speaking of which, we have someone waiting for us in the other room."

She glanced toward the hallway, thoughtful. "You think Auden will actually show me what he likes?"

Lennox's playful expression flattened a little. "Just me and you talking? Probably not. At least not yet and not to the full extent. He'll give you a taste. Feel you out. Edit himself."

She let out a frustrated breath.

"But don't be too hard on him. He hasn't fully come to terms with what he likes, so it's difficult for him to show someone like you, a friend who means something to him, a side of himself that he still feels shame about."

"Should I be scared of him?" The question came out a little shaky.

Lennox's eyes softened. "He would tell you yes. I am telling you no. He always honors people's boundaries and safe words. The guy you know, at the heart, is the guy he is. Kind. Protective. Smart." He smirked. "He's just a fucking deviant in bed."

She laughed. "I love how you say that as if it's the highest compliment."

He shrugged beneath her hold. "It is."

She chewed her lip, pondering. "What can I do to get him to show me the real things he likes?"

Lennox lifted a hand and tucked her hair behind her ear, scanning her expression. "You might not be ready for that."

Well, *that* pushed her buttons and not the good kind. "Don't do that. I can make my own choices. I have a safe word."

Lennox frowned, a pensive look on his face. "Well, if you want to test him out, when we go in there, whatever he tells you to do…"

"Yeah?" she asked.

He leaned close. "Tell him no and see what happens."

A ripple of apprehension went through her. "Oh."

# CHAPTER NINETEEN

*A*uden stared out of his bedroom window, fighting the urge to pace. He needed to get his head together. Having O'Neal submit to him was too big of a temptation. She was so open and willing and eager to please. Whispering instructions to her, watching her take Len's cock down her throat, catching the scent of how turned on she was by it all...the effect was as heady as a drug shot straight into his veins. He needed to rein himself in, take things slow. She was so new to all of this. He had to remember that.

There was a tap on the door, and Auden turned, finding Len leaning against the doorjamb and O'Neal in front of him, dressed in only her pale blue panties, her arms secured behind her back with Len's black tie, her breasts pushing forward. The sharp kick of arousal in Auden's gut nearly knocked him backward. Fuck, she was beautiful. Not just sexy but so...*her.* He didn't know another way to explain it. She had some quality unique to her that captivated him.

Auden crossed his arms over his chest, his dick already getting stiff again behind the fly of his jeans. "Are you ready to apologize to me for that little charade earlier tonight?"

Her lips parted.

He expected her to say yes. To quickly say she was sorry. Then he was going to give her something to do to make it up to him before he let her come.

But instead, she jutted her chin and met his gaze. "No."

The defiant word went through him like a mild electric shock, putting him on alert. He lifted his brows. "No?"

She squared her shoulders, and the look on her face reminded him of the O'Neal he'd grown up with, the quietly stubborn girl who had never been afraid to put her best friend's older brother in his place when he got too bossy. "No. *You're* the one who didn't call *me*. If you couldn't be there for me, then why wouldn't I go to Len? You couldn't get the job done, so I replaced you." She shrugged. "In fact, maybe I'll just go to his room instead. I bet he won't make me apologize."

"True," Len said, mischief dancing in his eyes.

Heat rushed through him like a lava flow, her challenging words lighting up things inside him. The good girl was pushing back. He could play that game too. "Be careful, freshman. I'm not one to play poker with. Let's not pretend you don't want me, that the show earlier wasn't just a big attention grab." He cocked his chin at her. "Get on your knees and say you're sorry, and maybe I won't make this harder for you. Maybe I'll actually let you come tonight."

Her jaw clenched, and she didn't break eye contact.

Part of him wanted her to comply, but another, darker part of him was salivating. "Well?"

Her eyes narrowed. "I said no."

For a moment, a painful, panicked moment, he thought she meant it. That she was going to leave. That they'd taken her too far tonight. But then his gaze tracked downward. The move was subtle, but she was squirming, rubbing her thighs against each other like she couldn't stand still. And that little triangle of blue fabric between her legs had gone nearly see-through she was so wet.

She wasn't saying *water*. She was saying *no*.

Something primal swelled in him. He stepped forward, walking slowly toward her. When he stopped in front of her, he caught her scent and the slight tremor of her muscles. He put his hand to her throat and gave it the barest of squeezes. "I said" —he dipped his head to lock eye contact—"get on your fucking knees, O'Neal."

Her eyes widened and fear flickered, her heart pounding against his palm. That reaction was like a spice on his tongue. A sweet, erotic flavor. But he braced himself for her to knee him in the balls and run.

Instead, to his amazement, her throat flexed against his hand as she swallowed, and then she looked him full in the face and said, "Make me."

Every light on the circuit board inside him lit up, and he sucked in a harsh breath, releasing her throat from his grip. He glanced at Len, who smiled and nodded, their ability to read each other in these situations almost psychic by now.

Len sidled up behind O'Neal, put his hands on her upper arms, and then bumped the backs of her knees with his, bringing her down.

O'Neal gasped as her knees hit the carpet.

Auden smiled and bent down to look at her. "I told you, freshman. Don't get cocky. Len may like you, but he's not going to save you from me."

She was blinking fast now, unsure. He should've probably soothed her. Didn't want to. He went over and grabbed a pillow from the bed and tossed it in front of her. Before she could puzzle out what was happening, he moved behind her, grabbed a hold of the tie between her wrists, and then pressed his hand between her shoulder blades. Unable to fight him with her hands bound, her cheek landed on the pillow, her hips high in the air. She swore softly.

A shudder of pure desire moved through Auden. Even hearing O'Neal curse was a turn-on. "There we go." He tugged her panties down to her knees, binding her legs, and then he smoothed a hand over her bare backside. Goosebumps appeared along her skin. "Ready to say you're sorry?"

There was a pause and then a muffled, petulant, "No."

The word was like candy on his tongue, but he forced himself to double-check. "Thirsty?"

"Now's not the time for a drink, Auden," she said, annoyance in her voice.

He laughed under his breath, fucking delighted, and then he did something he'd never in a million years thought he'd do to O'Neal Lory. He swatted her ass with enough force to make it sting.

The squeak of shock that came out of her proved she'd expected something different. "You *hit* me?"

"Mmm," he acknowledged, rubbing his hand over her reddening skin. "So I did. Maybe you should have accepted that drink."

"You—" she began, but he smacked her on the other cheek, the sound echoing in his ears. "Hey!"

The righteous indignation in her voice was *everything.* She was one step away from asking to talk to his manager. He cocked his head at Len, who looked as entertained as he was. Len sat down cross-legged on the floor next to O'Neal.

"I still haven't heard an apology," Auden reminded her.

She squirmed, and he could sense her considering it—or maybe she was ready to call for water. "Why are you hitting me? This doesn't seem—is this...?"

She didn't know enough to know what to ask. But he could answer her question. He tucked his fingers between her legs and dragged them along her pussy. She was so hot and juicy that the

sound his fingers made was obscene. He wanted to groan, but
he swallowed it back, not wanting to give her the satisfaction of
getting to him yet.

"You're saying a lot of protesting words, freshman, but
you're so fucking wet, you're about to leave a puddle on the
carpet."

"Oh my God," she turned her face into the pillow. "Shut up."

Len chuckled and then reached out to take over where
Auden's fingers had been.

O'Neal moaned into the pillow, and Auden watched
indulgently.

"Ready to say you're sorry?" Auden asked.

"No," she said, muffled.

Damn, she was fantastic. He nodded at Len, who started to
tease her clit in slow strokes, and then Auden went to work.
O'Neal was on the verge of orgasm. He could tell it wouldn't
take much, but he wanted her to feel what the pain/pleasure
combo could be like. He lifted his hand and using short, swift
strokes, he spanked her along the rounds of her ass and the
backs of her thighs, not giving her time in between to recover.

*Smack, smack, smack.* The sound and feel of her made him
harder with each pop. Her skin turned pink and hot. And
watching Len work her pussy, giving her just enough to make
her squirm but not enough to send her over, only added to the
moment. She was theirs to play with, to pleasure, and to give a
little sting.

Auden's gut tightened, his cock begging for release, but the
tug in his chest was even more distracting. He shoved down
whatever that feeling was and focused on the task at hand—
driving Ms. Lory to the brink.

～

O'NEAL DIDN'T KNOW WHAT WAS HAPPENING IN HER BODY. THE initial shock of Auden spanking her was enough to send her thoughts whirling. She'd been a second away from calling for water. But then he'd touched her. There'd been no denying how her body was reacting to this. The thought that he was *punishing* her, *correcting* her, should've pissed her off, but instead, it just made her want to fight harder, to get more from him, to feel all that erotic energy directed her way.

She never got into trouble.

She'd always obeyed. Her whole life.

Until she didn't. And now, disobeying Auden on purpose, even if it was a game, felt...freeing.

Her entire backside was warm and tingling, and the sound of his bare hand on her was the only one in the room. Len's rough-tipped fingers were rubbing against her with deceivingly precise strokes, making it hard to stay in place and not rock her hips toward him to get him right where she needed him.

Auden landed a stinging slap on the back of her left thigh, and Len tucked his fingers inside her. She cried out, all the sensations making her want to beg.

"You say something?" Auden asked, sarcasm in his voice.

She squeezed her eyes shut and forced words out. "I'm. Not. Freaking. Apologizing."

"Damn," Len said with that lazy cadence he had. "Someone's hardheaded. Aud, I don't think she's scared of you."

Auden let out a grunt and the spanking stopped. "She should be."

The sound of a zipper filled her ears, and then strong hands were on the backs of her thighs—Auden. He gripped her hard and forced her thighs wide, dragging her knees against the carpet. She let out a yelp of surprise.

The crinkle of a foil packet sent a dart of anticipation through her. She turned her head to get a peek. Auden was behind her, flushed, his brow dotted with sweat, and a devilish look on his face. His dimple appeared. "If you would've said sorry, I would've let you come first. But now, I'm gonna be selfish."

Then Auden was there against her, hands spreading her, and cock pushing inside. Electric sensation raced up her body from the point of impact to the top of her scalp, making everything tingle. He seated himself fully inside her, her body trying to accommodate him, but this position felt much deeper than the last time. He pulled back and then plunged into her again with none of the gentleness of their first time. She inhaled a ragged breath, afraid the roughness would be too much, that she'd bitten off more than she could chew, but then he found a rhythm, a quick, punishing one, and a new sensation began to stir deep within her. Oh. *Oh.*

"Christ. You're..." Auden yanked the tie, freeing her wrists and not finishing his thought. She braced her forearms on the carpet, giving her more leverage to get to the angle that felt best.

"Yes, she is." Hands stroked her hair, the nape of her neck, her shoulders—*Len.*

Soon, it felt like both of them were everywhere, caressing her, filling her, shattering any fight she had left in her. She didn't want to win the game anymore. She wanted to surrender. Drown in it.

"Aud. *Please.*" The storm was building inside her, the clouds about to break. She was *begging* for the rain. But he knew she was close. He wasn't going to give her just that little extra bit that would send her over unless...

"I'm sorry. I'm sorry, I'm sorry, I'm sorry," she said, the words sounding like begging. "I'm *sorry.*"

Auden's grip on her hips tightened, and a rumble of pleasure escaped him. "I'm not." With that, he angled upward inside her, hitting just the right place, and firm pressure slid across her clit —the heel of Len's hand. Colors flashed behind her eyelids, and a cry wrenched out of her throat as a blinding orgasm enveloped her.

Somewhere in the distance, she heard Auden groan along with her as he came, but she was too lost riding her own waves. Her body seemed to be capable of more than she'd thought, cresting again and again until finally, she collapsed against the pillow, boneless and panting and half out of her mind.

She didn't know how long she lay there, but one of the guys eventually lifted her and deposited her in the bed. She felt the mattress jostle, a blanket pulled over her.

"Time for some actual water, Shaq."

Her eyelids fluttered open. Auden was sitting next to her on the bed, wearing a pair of boxers, his hair mussed. He held out a bottle of water. She shifted to sit up against the pillows, finding Len sitting on the foot of the bed, his eyeliner smudged to hell and an unreadable look on his face. She took the water, swallowed a few deep gulps, startled by how thirsty she was, and then glanced between the two of them.

"Thanks."

Auden brushed her hair away from her face. "Sure. Are you...okay? I know that was a lot." His expression was tender. "But you were beautiful, O'Neal. I can't even tell you—"

"You're a gift," Len finished. "We're fucking honored."

The words were sweet, but she couldn't absorb them yet. Images flashed through her mind. Pictures as if taken from above of what had happened tonight. Her naked between them on the floor, Auden hitting her and her liking it. The things she'd done, allowed to be done to her. Now that the buzz of arousal was fading, panic fluttered to life, threatening to spread through her like a swarm of moths.

She inhaled a deep breath, trying to tamp it down. "Thank you. I'm okay, but can we not...talk about everything right now? I think I just need to...be here. In the moment."

Worry flickered across Auden's face but he nodded. "Of course. Whatever you need."

"Can we be here with you?" Len asked. "In the moment?"

She let the question move through her and allowed her gut feeling to provide the answer. "Yes. I'd like that."

Len smiled and Auden's shoulders relaxed a little.

She made a quick trip to the bathroom, texted Quyen that she was staying over, and then stole one of Auden's T-shirts to wear. When she got back into bed, Auden slipped beneath the covers with her. Len followed suit, claiming the spot behind her. The warmth of their bodies surrounded her, the bed not big enough to leave space between them. She didn't know how to feel yet about the things that had happened tonight, but for now, in the darkness of Auden's bedroom, flanked by these two men, she felt safe and cared for.

She'd worry about the rest in the morning.

# CHAPTER TWENTY

*A*uden was already partially awake, his internal clock primed to get him up before dawn for swim practice, when the smell hit him. He blinked his eyes open, his brain trying to process the anomaly. *Is that...?*

*Shit!* He sat up so fast, he knocked his pillow sideways, sending whatever was on the nightstand toppling to the floor with a crash.

"What the hell?" Len mumbled, voice knotted with sleep.

"Get up! Both of you, come on," Auden said, his words coming at top speed as he jostled O'Neal. "We gotta get out of here. Now!"

O'Neal rolled onto her back and pressed her hands to her face. "What's wrong?"

But Auden didn't have to answer. The smoke alarms started blaring, and her eyes went wide. He hopped out of the bed, grabbed his phone, and then yanked a pair of clean boxers out of a laundry basket.

"Shit shit shit." Len was fully awake now and throwing back the covers. He grabbed O'Neal's hand. "Up and out, Sweets."

The smoke alarms continued their urgent shrieking, and the

three of them hustled out of the bedroom. Auden handed a pair of boxers to O'Neal as she jogged next to him. "Here."

She glanced at the item as if she didn't understand what it was but then the situation registered on her face. She was in panties and a T-shirt. She quickly stepped into the shorts, and then they all rushed out the front door.

The acrid smell was stronger outside, and black smoke curled out a window of one of the bottom floor units—Hunter Brickham's apartment. Sirens wailed nearby, and flashes of red lit up the pre-dawn sky.

"Looks like the calvary's almost here," Len said as they quickly descended the stairs, his hand on the small of O'Neal's back. "Is everyone out?"

"No idea," Auden said. When they reached the bottom, he banged on the door of the unit below them and yelled "Fire!" just in case they were hard sleepers.

But someone called out from behind him. "We're out!"

He turned, finding a small gathering of people in various states of undress at the far edge of the parking lot. Julia, one of the two women who lived in that unit, was waving at them.

A shot of relief went through Auden. He grabbed O'Neal's hand, and they all power-walked over to the group as the sirens got louder. Smoke billowed out of the window, and the occasional glimpse of orange flame flashed inside. Auden did a quick mental check. Julia and her roommate were there, both in bathrobes. The graduate students from the other upper apartment were sitting on a curb, one filming with his phone. And Brickham, or Brick as he was known on the swim team, was glaring at his roommate, a skinny brown-haired guy who was wearing a Super Mario Bros. T-shirt and a guilty look.

No one said a word as firefighters arrived and got to work. O'Neal shivered next to Auden, and he wished he'd grabbed a sweatshirt to lend her when he'd gotten the boxers. Len must've noticed her chill as well because he wrapped his arms around her from behind, trying to warm her. Brick glanced Auden's way, and Auden quickly released O'Neal's hand.

The fire was out within a few minutes, thankfully, and seemed to be limited to the kitchen of Brick's apartment, but the group had been told to wait to get official word that it was safe before they went back in. One of the firefighters was in deep conversation with Brick's roommate.

Soon, the sun was staining the sky with pinks and purples, and Auden worried they'd be stuck out there for hours. He cocked his head at Len and O'Neal, indicating they should get some space away from the group. Once they were out of earshot, he turned to O'Neal.

"You okay?"

"Not on fire, so I'm good." She gave him a wobbly smile, looking far too tempting in his swim team T-shirt. "But should I expect a terrifying surprise every time I sleep over? Last time your mom, now a fire. Is the universe trying to tell me something?"

He sighed. "I *was* planning to surprise you, but by getting up before both of you to grab hot donuts from down the street."

"Donuts?" She lowered her head in dramatic disappointment, pressing her forehead to his shoulder. "That sounds so good right now."

"Instead, we almost got deep fried ourselves," Len said, stretching his arms above his head and yawning, his tattoos flexing in the morning light. "Fun times."

Auden looped his arms around O'Neal and pressed a kiss to the crown of her head. "I'll make donuts happen. I'm just glad you're both safe. Our shitty smoke alarms were delayed. I just happened to be awake and smelled the smoke."

O'Neal lifted her head, a line appearing between her brows. "How did this even happen? Was someone cooking this early?"

"No, my roommate is an asshole," a new voice said.

O'Neal startled and stepped out of Auden's loose embrace, turning toward the voice.

Brick had wandered over to them like he'd been invited. He nodded at Auden and Len. "Blake. Lennox. Glad you're not barbecued."

Auden sniffed derisively in response. Brick was his least favorite member of the swim team with his oversized ego and his shitty jokes, but he held the college's speed record for butterfly stroke so Auden tolerated him. They swam on the same relay team for the medley race, so it was easier to keep the team peace than point out what a tool he was.

Brick smiled and put out his hand to O'Neal. "I don't think we've met. Hunter Brickham, member of the swim team and roommate of the idiot who tried to do a chemistry project for class at four in the morning. I'd like to formally apologize on his behalf for interrupting your...sleep?"

Auden bristled at the way he'd turned that into a question.

O'Neal frowned but took his hand. "No problem. I'm O'Neal."

Brick didn't let go of her hand. "Love the name." He glanced down the length of her body, obviously clocking Auden's T-shirt, and his smile shifted into something sly. *"Swimfan?"*

Auden's neck muscles tightened. The way Brick had said it, as all one word like the movie title, was an inside joke some of the team used. They'd all watched *Swimfan* together last year at some party, and now any girl who showed up at meets or took particular interest in a swimmer got labeled a swimfan, with the implication that they were the type of girl who'd do *anything* in bed just to be with one of the swimmers. But O'Neal had never seen that early aughts teen version of *Fatal Attraction,* so she had no clue he was implying anything.

"What?" She looked down. "Oh. Yeah. Sure."

"Excellent," Brick said, finally releasing her hand. "The best type of person. What's your favorite event? Wait, let me guess. If

you're hanging out with these two..." He glanced over at
Lennox and then Auden. "Relay? Each guy an expert at one
stroke? You should see me swim butterfly."

Auden's fingers curled into fists. He didn't want to embar-
rass O'Neal by revealing what the conversation was really
about, but he was about to punch that smug smile right off of
Brick's face. Whatever penalty Coach would mete out for
breaking the face of a teammate would be worth it.

But O'Neal huffed out a quiet laugh. "Wow. That's...what?
Your, like, *move?*"

Brick blinked. "What?"

"Implying, with your thinly veiled attempt at innuendo, that
because I'm out here with my two friends, wearing one of their
T-shirts, that I what? Let them take turns? That I love swimmers
so much that I want you to join the race too?"

Brick's neck turned red. "I—I, well, no—"

Lennox coughed, and Auden bit his lip to keep from
grinning.

"Let me guess," she said sweetly. "You start the relay, don't
you? Because you don't know how to finish strong?"

"Butterfly always starts!" Brick protested.

"And what a special butterfly you probably are," she said,
patting him on the shoulder. "But a quick piece of advice.
Trying to demean a woman so you can look cool in front of
your bros just lets women know that you're vastly insecure and
probably overcompensating for some major deficit. So thanks
for the heads up to avoid you." She smiled. "Also, extra fun fact
for the road. Why I'm here, what I'm wearing, and who I'm with
is none of your business, so I suggest you go back to your
arsonist roommate. You two seem perfectly matched."

Brick's startled look shifted, his jaw flexing as O'Neal's
words sunk in. "Wow, you're not just a swimfan but a straight-
up bit—"

Auden and Lennox both stepped forward at the same time.

Auden got there first, pushing his fingers into Brick's chest. "I suggest you swallow down that word, Brickham, or you're going to be on injured reserve for the rest of the season."

"Girl can't take a joke, man," he said, voice tight. "I was just messing around. She didn't have to get all personal about it. And I don't know why she's getting on her high horse. She was hanging all over the two of you. It's obvious she's spread for you both."

Auden's fist lifted, but before he could get the satisfaction of knocking those words out of Brick's mouth, Lennox shouldered Auden aside and took a swing.

The sound of a fist hitting flesh cut through the air, and O'Neal cried out. Brick grabbed his nose and moved to swing back at Len, but Auden stepped between them. The scuffle had drawn the attention of everyone else, and a fireman was jogging their way.

Before anyone could throw another punch, the firefighter pushed everyone apart. He lifted a hand. "I don't know what the hell's going on here, but I don't have time for this. You"—he pointed at Brick—"over there. You two"—he pointed at Auden and Lennox—"stay over here. Got it?"

Brick's nose was already swelling but he nodded. He spit off to the side and then cocked his chin toward Auden. "Fuck you, man. Wait till Coach hears about this. He'll bench your ass."

Auden smirked. "I didn't hit you. But even if I had, he'd take my side. Teammates don't insult each other's girlfriends."

Brick glanced at O'Neal and then scoffed. "Yeah, sure she is." He stalked off, his bare feet slapping the pavement.

Only when Auden turned around and saw O'Neal's face did he register what he'd said. *Girlfriend.* Shit. "O'Neal, sorry, I—"

She waved a hand, clearing her expression along with the air in front of her. "It's fine. I know you didn't mean that. But if it gets you off the hook with your coach, use it." She crossed her arms over her chest. "Wow, that guy is a *diiiick.*"

Auden smiled at her emphatic use of a word she would've never said a couple of months ago.

"And you, my Sweets, are brilliant," Len said, shaking out his punching hand and grinning. "The way you took him down? When you asked if he started the relay?" Len laughed. "God, it was perfect. I adore you, O'Neal Lory."

O'Neal blushed bright pink. "Thanks."

Auden's chest squeezed tight. He was so fucking proud of her. She'd stood up for herself with such ferocity, not shrinking at the implication that she'd slept with both of them. He walked over to her and without thinking, pressed a kiss to her mouth. He pulled back and looked down at her, cradling her chin.

"He's right. You were perfect."

She gave him a little nod and let out a long breath, like she'd had to pump herself up to max capacity to survive what had just happened and now all that energy was rushing out of her. A slight tremor went through her body.

Concern washed through him. He released her face and cupped her shoulders, trying to read her eyes. "You okay?"

"Yeah, I just…do people like, know, what y'all do? I felt like he was seeing…everything." She wet her dry lips. "Like I was naked and he was picturing everything I'd let y'all do to me."

Auden winced inwardly, hating that she'd felt that exposed. "It's not public knowledge, but he's…friends with a woman we…from last year. She might've told him some things."

"Right." She blinked, and for the barest part of a second, he thought he saw tears there, but she looked down quickly. "Yeah. So that didn't feel great."

Auden rubbed her upper arms, an uneasy feeling moving through him. "I'm sorry. He's an asshole. I should've cut him off at the pass. But try not to let him get to you. None of it is his business, and you have nothing to be ashamed of. Like you said."

"Like I said. Sure." She made a humorless sound in the back of her throat, and then something dawned in her expression.

She pressed her hand to her forehead and closed her eyes, her whole body curving inward. "Oh God."

"What's wrong?" he asked, worried she was going to pass out or something.

She stayed silent for a long moment but then lowered her hand and looked at him, a haunted expression on her face. "You know, if I had died in that fire, guess what would've been all over me?"

"O'Neal…" Auden said, dread filling him.

"Two men's DNA," she finished.

Len gave Auden a worried look. "Hey, no talk of dying in fires, okay?"

She shook her head and backed away from Auden, her posture closing to them. "I can't believe this."

"Shaq," Auden tried again, trying to pull her out of the spiral he could sense coming.

But she was undeterred. "All that time my grandparents were keeping me on lockdown, so scared I'd follow in my mom's footsteps. All those times I tried to convince them that I wasn't her, that I could be trusted to do the right thing, that I wouldn't let silly things like boys or relationships distract me from my plans." She gave them each a look. "Well, maybe they were right to keep me locked down because look what happens when I'm left to my own devices. Hell, maybe even God has an opinion. I mean…almost dying in a fire is a pretty dramatic warning."

"Don't," Auden said, a pleading note in his voice. "Please don't do that. What happened last night was…"

*Beautiful. Amazing. Perfect.*

"Another kinky college hookup for y'all. One of many," she said, not giving him a chance to finish his sentence. "Another girl for a teammate to tease you about in the locker room. No big deal."

Lennox made a sound of deep displeasure. "O'Neal—"

She shook her head again and lifted a hand. "I'm not mad—well, maybe a little at myself. I'm not blaming either of you. You never sold me a lie. If anything, you tried to talk me out of it. I know what I asked for, and wouldn't take back that decision. I think I needed to maybe…veer off the road for a little while to see what it was like, to be a little reckless. But…" She took a breath. "I'm not built for this to continue. I'm not some cool chick who can brush off guys like Brick looking at me like that and not feel it."

"Fuck, Brick," Auden said, wanting to drag the dude back over here just so he could get the pleasure of punching him too. "Don't let him—"

She looked up at them, the stark look in her eyes cutting him off. "And I'm not cool enough to keep this casual. I already care about the two of you too much. Looking back at last night, I realize I would've done"—her gaze locked on Auden's — "*anything* you asked. Anything to get you to call me your good girl again. I don't even know what to do with that knowledge."

The admission punched him right in the chest and made him ache in a way he'd never ached before. *Anything to be his good girl.* He couldn't even imagine having O'Neal in that way. It was too much to even fathom. A fantasy.

"That's a beautiful thing," Len interjected. "A feature not a flaw. Sweets, we can—"

"Break my heart," she said with a sad smile. "That's what you will do because this has a built-in expiration date. You were right, Aud. I'm too young. Too green for this." She glanced away. "And too in love with you already for it not to do damage."

All the air in Auden's lungs left him—an absolute sucker punch. He opened his mouth to try to speak, but words didn't come.

"Don't say anything. I'm not telling you to get a response," she said. "I'm telling you because it's another reason why this can't go on. I can't remember a time anymore when I didn't love you. But it's an uneven thing. I'm the groupie, and you're the rockstar. No." She gave him a grim half-smile. "You're the swimmer, and I'm the swim fan."

Auden grimaced. "No, you're—"

"It's okay. That's on me. But I can't keep pretending that it won't consume me if I keep doing this with you...and Lennox." She looked at Len. "Because, Len, you would be so easy to love."

Len's expression went blank with shock.

But O'Neal was already continuing, completely unaware that she'd just unraveled him and his best friend. "My mom lost her way here, spending more time getting attention from guys than on her studies or focusing on her own life. It led her down a path she never escaped from. I wish someone would've told her she was enough on her own. Maybe she'd still be around." She pressed her lips together and looked off to the side like she was fighting back tears again. "I need to be enough on my own. I came here to find my own way. I can't keep letting you guys take care of me when things get a little scary."

"Relying on friends isn't a sign of weakness," Len said softly. "It's what friends do for each other."

"And a friend will hear what I'm asking for." Her throat bobbed, resolve coming into her expression. "I need to end this on my terms because it was always going to end." She looked to Auden. "And you know I don't like surprise endings."

Suddenly, a memory flickered to life in Auden's mind. A preteen O'Neal going through all the fantasy and sci-fi books on his shelves and flipping to the end of each. When he'd caught her in his room and asked her what she was doing, she'd had tear stains on her face. Apparently, her teacher had assigned them *Where the Red Fern Grows* for school, and now she was determined to never read another school-assigned book again because *"who gives books to kids where the dog dies?"* Her teacher had told her if she could find an acceptable alternative, she could substitute a book for her book report. So now she needed something fast but wanted to make sure no one important died at the end.

Auden remembered being appalled that she was spoiling all the books for herself but also knew that if his mom had died, he probably wouldn't want to read tragic endings either. So he'd sat next to her and searched through his books to make sure he didn't give her anything that would break her heart again.

Now she was asking him the same favor. *Don't break my heart.*

He ran a hand over the back of his head, the only thing he could say bubbling up and tasting like sour milk in his mouth. "Okay, Shaq. No surprise ending."

She softened like she'd been holding a breath too long, and then came over to hug him. "Thank you."

He gathered her against him, and Len gave him a *what the hell are you doing* look over her shoulder, but what else could Auden say? If he tried to fight for what they had, what did he really have to offer her? A kinky good time for two more semesters? So the fuck what? What did that count for? She loved him. She deserved someone who could give her that kind of love back with no fine print, who could fully commit just to her. Not someone greedy and broken like him. He could never be what she needed or what she deserved in the long term. There were no bookshelves to search for her this time.

He had no story with a happy ending to give her.

# CHAPTER TWENTY-ONE

O'Neal clicked through comments on a true crime forum that had discussed her mother's case a few months ago. Her brain buzzed with a low-level sense of numbness, the comments starting to blend together.

**RTF52:** maybe she turned some guy down and he got pissed and went apeshit

**BeezerRR:** yeah, especially if Mr. Mystery DNA knew she didn't set the bar very high to get with her

**ObzessedwithTC:** I say serial killer, at least two were operating in the state at that time

**BeezerRR:** then his DNA would be in the index

**ObzessedwithTC:** I didn't say they'd FOUND those serial killers

**RTF52:** then the DNA would've at least matched another crime. I say jilted dude

**steeeeveAF:** who cares, this case is boring. Drunk college chick hooks up with the wrong guy, the end. Check out this dismembering case in the PNW!

O'Neal rubbed the pounding spot between her eyes. She'd thought doing some research would get her mind off of her break-up with Auden and Lennox—if she could even call it a break-up—but this was just making her feel worse. Not only did she have to see people tearing down her mother, but she wasn't any closer to having an answer as to what happened than she was before.

Across the room, Quyen stretched out on her bed, hanging her head upside down off the end of it, and groaned. She kicked the notebook she'd had open on the bed to the floor, and a pencil went rolling under the desk. "Why, oh why, do I need to learn all the math when I'm planning to be a therapist?"

O'Neal closed out her screen and smirked at the inverted pink-haired woman across from her. "Because reasons?"

"Ridiculous reasons." She opened her eyes. "They just make us take these things so we have to stay here longer and then they can charge our parents more money. How will knowing how to solve for $x$ help me treat someone's anxiety or whatever?" She lifted her head and rolled over so she was facing O'Neal upright again. She sat her chin on her folded arms. "$X$ is giving *me* anxiety. Stupid $x$."

O'Neal gave her a sympathetic look. "Maybe the math will help you count all the money you're going to make when you become the best therapist there ever was."

She sniffed. "That's what I'll hire an accountant for. It's important to know what you're not good at."

"I'm pretty good at math if you want some help," she offered.

Really, anything to get her mind off of what had happened with the guys two weeks ago would be good. Anything to save her from replaying everything over and over again. Sometimes, she was lucky and all that would replay were the steamy parts, the "before" parts. Those memories usually hit late at night when she was alone in bed and half asleep and her body got antsy. But those sexy memories were quickly eclipsed by the painfully embarrassing ones. Like her blurting out her love for Auden like some starry-eyed preteen. *Ugh.*

And lately, the most popular scene that her brain liked to play on repeat was what had happened with that guy Brick. The way he'd looked at her, had talked to her. Even knowing that the guy was an idiot hadn't saved her from feeling what he'd wanted her to feel.

Diminished. Desperate.

When Brick had looked at her, he hadn't seen some woman coming into her own and making adult decisions about her relationships and her own body. He'd seen some gullible freshman with a childhood crush who'd do anything the older guys wanted to get some attention. A plaything. An amusement.

She knew in her heart that Auden and Lennox hadn't used her that way, at least not consciously, but some of the things she'd done with them…

When she was with Auden, she didn't want to say no. She wanted to *please* him, to get that praise from him. What she couldn't figure out was if she had let things go that far because she'd truly wanted to experience it or if she'd done it because part of her was still that girl with a crush, that girl who idolized her best friend's big brother, the girl who wanted to be seen as more than a kid in Auden's eyes, who had something to *prove.*

If another guy had asked her to do those things, would she have said yes? If another dude had told her there was no way he could be her boyfriend but he could definitely sleep with her and order her to her knees and share her with his roommate, would she have agreed or would she have run screaming in the other direction?

The answer made her stomach hurt. Which was why she hadn't called Auden or Lennox or taken back anything she'd said to them, no matter how much she missed them.

She'd made the right call.

"O'Neal?" Quyen's voice was a record scratch to O'Neal's spinning thoughts.

"Uh, sorry. What?"

"I said, thanks, I'll take you up on the math tutoring later but not right now. I need a break." Quyen eyed O'Neal's laptop. "How's the investigative reporting going?"

O'Neal set her computer aside and stretched out her legs. She'd confided in Quyen, sharing what had happened with her mom and what her project was about. She'd been nervous at first to open up about it, but Quyen had been nothing but supportive. "It's mostly mind-numbing, often soul-crushing."

She pushed her lip out in an empathetic pout. "I'm sorry."

"It's okay," O'Neal said, bone-deep exhaustion making her feel like she was wearing a weighted blanket. "I don't think I'm going to be able to get anything worth writing unless I talk to actual people. I'm trying to psych myself up for that."

"Who would you talk to? The police department?" Quyen sat up, her interest obviously piqued.

"Yes, though I don't know how excited they'd be to talk to me or how much they could even share with me." She picked at the corner of her quilt, an internal debate waging. "I also found out that one of the guys she was...seeing at the time still lives around here."

"Seeing? Whoa, wait, like one of the DNA matches?" Quyen asked, already shaking her head. "No way. No interviewing potential murder suspects. I do not want to be a future interviewee on a true crime doc. *She really was the best freshman roommate a girl could ask for...*"

O'Neal's lips lifted at the corner. "You sound like Lennox. He said the same thing. I'm not going to put myself in danger. The guy's not a potential suspect. He was cleared. Two of the three matches were cleared with solid alibis. The third one is still unknown. Most people think that's the killer." She massaged her temples, trying to chase off a headache. "But it could've just been another guy she'd hung out with that night. There's still so much they don't know."

Quyen rubbed her arms, a frown line appearing between her brows. "Either way, if you decide to talk to him, don't you dare go alone. I will kill you."

She snorted. "You would kill me to save me from being killed?"

"Absolutely."

Her concern warmed O'Neal. "I wouldn't go by myself. And I don't know if I have the guts to do it anyway. I want to know what happened to my mom, but I also…"

"Are afraid you'll find out stuff you don't want to know?"

O'Neal sighed. "Yeah. I have very few memories of my mom, and my grandparents have filled in the rest, but I just…" She paused, that familiar anxiety unfolding inside her. "I have so little of her. I don't want to…taint that. This research is already threatening that."

Quyen's head tilted in sympathy. "I get that. And you know, it's okay if you decide not to do this project or to just put together what you know and not push further. Your mental health is more important than an A on a paper."

"I know. I'm not doing it for the A. I think being here, starting college, has just made me miss her more—or at least the idea of having a mom." She pulled her knees up to her chest, hugging them, wistfulness for what could never be moving through her. "Every time I hit a new milestone, I want to pick up the phone and call her, ask her all these questions." She scoffed. "Which is an unrealistic thought anyway because I can't imagine that if she were here, I'd really call and say, hey, Mom, so I slept with our neighbor's son and then told him I loved him and then bailed..."

"Hold up," Quyen said lifting a finger and making a screeching car brake sound. *"You told Auden you loved him and didn't tell me?"*

O'Neal's lips parted. "I—"

Quyen launched a pillow at her. "These are things you tell your favorite roommate. Oh my God!"

O'Neal batted the pillow away and laughed, the over-the-top reaction lightening her heavy mood a little. "I try not to advertise the most embarrassing moments of my life to anyone."

Quyen was still wearing her shocked face. *"Dude.* Like, I *love* you, love you? That was fast." She winced. "Sorry. I don't mean that in a judgmental way. Just...wow. Is that why you two stopped hanging out? Did he freak out and bolt?"

O'Neal sighed and grabbed a pillow to hug, unsure how much to tell Quyen but wishing she could say it all. "No, he didn't bolt. I didn't give him the chance. I basically said I love you and I have to break this off. So, technically, I was the bolt-er."

"Why did you have to break it off?"

She ran her fingers along the pillow's edge. "Because he doesn't feel the same way. I knew that before I slept with him, and I don't regret doing that. I just, I couldn't let myself get in deeper than I already was. I have a lot of things I want to do here at school, and I don't want to spend my time crying into my pillow because I went and got my heart broken. I didn't come here for boys."

Quyen stared at her in wonder. "Damn. I cannot believe my sweet, super-sheltered, couldn't-be-alone-with-a-boy room-mate not only got rid of her V-card before I did but also sent the guy packing afterward so she could focus on her own goals."

She pressed her hand to her chest. "That took a shit ton of confidence."

O'Neal rolled her eyes. "Don't be too impressed. This wasn't confidence. This was reading the writing on the wall. Things with me and Auden were only going to end one way. Might as well get there by the quickest route. I'm sure he's relieved he didn't have to be the one to break it off."

The words tasted sour on her tongue.

Her brow lifted. "You sure of that? He seemed pretty into you from what I saw. Maybe you broke *his* heart."

O'Neal huffed. "Not a chance."

"Why not?"

She glanced toward the darkened window. "Because he didn't put up a fight. And he hasn't called. Or texted. Or anything at all."

Everything had just…ended.

Maybe their friendship had too.

Maybe she'd ruined everything.

Quyen frowned and then swung her legs off the bed. "All right, enough homework and sad topics for the night. We need pizza and ice cream and a scary movie. Come on."

O'Neal blinked. "Like now? We're already in our pajamas."

"There is never a bad time for pizza and ice cream." Quyen slipped her Vans on, not bothering to change out of her unicorn pajama pants. "And the film club is doing a marathon of scary movies leading up to Halloween. Tonight is *Gremlins* so nothing too terrifying."

O'Neal's heart squeezed. Instinctually, she knew that Quyen wouldn't be suggesting the movie if they were playing a slasher. Nothing that would remind her of murder or true crime. And she also heard the unsaid words in between the offer. *I see you're sadder than you're letting on. I've got your back.*

O'Neal had no idea how she'd gotten so lucky. She'd heard so many college roommate nightmare stories, but instead, she'd gotten Quyen. Her belief system had been turned on its head lately, but in that moment, she sent up a little thank you to whoever watched over her.

She got up from her bed and crossed the room to hug Quyen.

Quyen smiled. "What was that for?"

"I'm a newly converted hugger."

"Excellent." She hooked her arm with O'Neal's. "Now, let's go. On the way, I'm going to get real nosy about this whole virginity thing because if I hold in my questions for much longer, it's going to kill me."

O'Neal shook her head and laughed.

"No, I'm serious. You're going to have to give me the unvarnished truth about this hymen situation—like on a scale of one to ten, one being having a bandage yanked off and ten being impaled on an iron fence, how much pain are we talking?"

"*Quyen.*"

"This is vital information I need to know!"

O'Neal smirked and grabbed her shoes. "I'll tell you everything."

But of course, she wouldn't. Couldn't. Because if Quyen knew the real truth, O'Neal would never be able to look her in the eye again.

She wasn't the confident woman Quyen was imagining. She was the girl with the desperate crush who'd been willing to do anything for that boy's attention.

# CHAPTER TWENTY-TWO

*a*uden glanced over at the clock on his bedside table—not even five a.m. yet—and sighed at the awake state of his mind and the stiff state of his dick. He lowered his head back down to the pillow in defeat. Since the night with O'Neal and Len, he'd been having painfully vivid erotic dreams interspersed with straight-up nightmares about not getting out of the fire in time. It was like his brain couldn't decide which punishment he deserved more—to be constantly hard up or to be terrified.

O'Neal had told him that she loved him and then had walked away. Well, she *thought* she loved him. He suspected it was just feelings arising from him being her first. But even so, he'd barely been able to focus over the last few weeks. His swim coach had pulled him aside and asked him why his times were slipping. He could just imagine what Coach Collins would say if Auden admitted it was a girl.

But how was he supposed to focus? First, he'd had a fantasy delivered straight to his doorstep. The night with O'Neal and Len had been...perfect, the experience more intense than any he'd ever had before. He'd even enjoyed sharing the bed with the two of them afterward, something he and Len hadn't done with anyone else.

The whole thing should've been a win. All three of them having fun, all three on the same page. Sexy. Casual. Comfortable with each other in a way that went beyond basic chemistry.

But he'd been delusional. He should've known better. O'Neal hadn't been ready for that. She'd said she was. She'd consented. But he should've known better and protected her. That was his job. He was the older, more experienced one.

Instead, he'd thrown her into the deep end, selfishly chasing his own desires and ignoring the warning bells. Ruining their friendship. And pissing off Len too. Because Len had wanted him to put up a fight, to not let her walk away like that. But Auden had no weapons. O'Neal had been right to call it off.

Now, he didn't have O'Neal, and Lennox was barely talking to him, always conveniently out of the apartment when Auden was home. He'd fucked everything up.

Auden closed his eyes, trying to fall back asleep, but his brain was now in overdrive. With a groan, he flipped the covers to the side and climbed out of bed. He opened his door quietly, trying not to wake Len, and headed toward the kitchen to get some water. But when he stepped into the living room, he saw that his stealth mode hadn't been necessary. Len was hunched over his drawing table, the muscles in his back bunched, his desk lamp burning bright on the paper in front of him. The soft sound of Len's drawing pencil scratching against the paper was a soothing, familiar sound.

Lennox was so lost in what he was doing that he hadn't heard Auden come in. Auden crossed his arms and leaned against the doorjamb for a minute, just watching. Len drove him crazy sometimes, but after the days of near silent treatment, Auden realized just how much he missed being in his orbit. The guy was a brilliant artist and the best friend that Auden had ever had. People usually wrote off Len as the never-serious, good-time guy, a what-you-see-is-what-you-get kind of shallow. Lennox cultivated that image—maybe even believed it sometimes himself. But Auden knew better.

Len could glitter like the surface of the ocean, but if you got past that, you could drown in the depths below. He'd seen Len vulnerable, stripped down, all artifices torn away. He'd seen how deeply wounded Len had been by the loss of his mom, how scarred he was from the rest of his family abandoning him afterward because he'd been the child of an affair, not a real member of their family anymore. Auden was one of the only people Len had trusted to see that side, to know those things, but right now, he felt completely shut out. Alone in a way he hadn't felt in a long time. He wanted to fix it. He wanted to say he was sorry.

He wanted…

"Couldn't sleep either?"

Len's voice broke the silence like a thunderclap, startling Auden from his thoughts. Apparently, he hadn't been as stealthy as he'd thought, but he was just happy that Len was talking to him at all.

"Had a dream."

Len glanced over. "Good kind or bad kind?"

Auden shrugged. "Both? I guess. My brain is a sadist."

"All of you is a sadist." Lennox spun the chair to face him, expression flat, his blond hair sticking up like he'd been scrubbing his fingers through it. "It's because you made a bad call. Brains like to haunt us when we do something stupid."

Auden sighed. So they were going to do this now. Hash it out. Fine. At least they were talking.

"You can be pissed all you want, but I made the right call." He rubbed his jaw, tension making his teeth hurt. "Actually, I didn't make a call at all. O'Neal did. I'm respecting her wishes. I wish you could do that too."

He grimaced. "Is that what you're telling yourself? That

you're doing the right thing?" He twirled his drawing pencil between his knuckles, staring at him with disdain. "What a fucking joke. I hope you're holding on tight to the reins of that high horse you're riding."

As much as he wanted to mend this fence with Len, irritation broke through Auden's calm façade. "What the hell is your problem, man? Remember that whole consent thing we live by? *She* walked away from *us*."

"This isn't about consent, and you know it, so don't throw that in my face. My *problem*," he said in a hard tone, "is that when a smart, beautiful, kinky woman tells you that she *loves* you and you actually feel *the same fucking way about her*, you're supposed to grow a spine and tell her you love her back and then show her why you're worthy of her love. You don't say, *Okay, cool story, bro. Have a nice life*."

Auden's ears were ringing, his anger swelling to full song. "There is so much wrong with that statement, I don't even know where to start."

"Try," he demanded. "Because I need something, Aud. Something that explains why you acted like that."

Auden gritted his teeth, part of him wanting to tell Len to take a damn walk, that it wasn't his business, but of course, it was his business. He'd dragged Len into this too.

"One, she's not kinky," Auden said. "We guided her into that."

Lennox looked to the ceiling and laughed without humor. "Bull fucking shit." His gaze drilled into Auden. "You think she *faked* her reactions?"

Auden winced at the thought.

"Nothing about that was fake. She was into everything we did or would've safe-worded if she wasn't. She loved it. And she doesn't have the vocabulary to name it yet, but she's got a praise kink a mile long." He lifted a brow in challenge. "Or did you forget the part where she told you she'd do *anything* to hear you say *good girl*? Come on, dude. She's inexperienced but not vanilla. You uncovered something that was already there. You didn't put it there. But now she won't have anyone to help her process that or help it flourish. You did the same thing to her that your upbringing did to you—left her to feel bad about it, to think how she feels is wrong."

Auden's fingers curled. He didn't want to hear this. Didn't want to remember what O'Neal had said, what it'd done to him, how much he wanted to be the person to feed that craving in her. "Even if she has kinks, it doesn't matter. You heard her. She loves me. I can't give her what she wants. I care about her, but I'm not in love with her."

Lennox stood and tossed the pencil onto his desk. He crossed his arms. "Say it again."

Auden let out a frustrated huff. "I'm not in love with her."

Len stepped forward, his green eyes burning holes into him. "We've always had one rule between us. We don't lie to each other. Look me in my goddamned face and tell me you don't love that woman, that the thought of her with someone else doesn't drive you nuts, that you don't want to show her all the things in bed but also curl up with her on the couch and hear what she thinks about movies and life and what she wants from it."

Auden's neck muscles tightened to the point of pain, cold dread moving through him.

"Tell me," Len went on, "that she was just another girl to you."

Auden turned his head, breaking the eye contact. His gaze landed on the drawings on Len's desk. There were postcard sketches of O'Neal laughing and Auden looking at her with affection. A sketch of all three of them intertwined in twisted sheets, naked and sated, sleeping peacefully. He swallowed thickly as the images turned into full color in his mind, the night rushing back to him. He closed his eyes.

"Fine," Auden said softly. "She means something to me. A lot. But it's not that easy. Loving her isn't enough. It's complicated."

Len let out a long, audible breath. "Thank you. Finally, we can talk about this like grown-ups." The weight of his hand landed on Auden's shoulder, and he gripped, shaking him a little. "It doesn't have to be complicated."

"Right. Sure. It's totally simple," he said derisively.

"It could be," Len went on, voice quieter now. "It's okay, you know?"

Auden opened his eyes, a hollow tiredness overtaking him. "What is?"

Len's expression was unreadable. "We've been ignoring the very handsome and charismatic elephant in the room since she told you that she loved you." He put a hand on his own chest. "*Me.*"

Auden frowned. "What are you talking about?"

"You know what I'm talking about." Len crossed his arms. "I know how things have always been, but that doesn't mean they have to stay that way. She loves you. You love her. The math of that is pretty obvious. I don't have to be involved. It can just be you two. Cut out the complication."

Auden tensed, thrown by the suggestion. "Cut out the—you mean, cut *you* out?"

Len gave a half-hearted shrug. "I mean, yes, I've developed feelings for O'Neal too, and that night together was…as great a night as I've ever had. But I've known from the start that she's not just another woman we're having fun with. I'm not blind." He met Auden's eyes, vulnerability there. "She's special to you. You look at her in a way I haven't seen you look at anyone before. I'm pretty sure you were already halfway in love with her when she stepped onto campus."

"Len—"

He lifted a hand. "I'm just saying, I haven't forgotten our original agreement."

Auden's words left him for a moment.

Their original agreement. The one where they promised that if either of them ever met someone they wanted to be in a committed relationship with, the other would back off with no hurt feelings. Panic was edging in.

"*Len.*"

"As your friend, what I want most is for you to be happy," he said, a strained note in his voice. "I know what you're going back to at home. All those expectations. I know these last few years are just your experimental ones. I've always known what we're doing is just a college thing for you."

*A college thing? Experimental?* Auden's ears began to ring like he'd stepped out of a loud concert. "Are you being serious right now?"

"Come on, Aud. If that wasn't the case, you'd be a film major, not a film minor," he said, no ire in his voice. "You're going to go back home and help run your dad's company and be the boss one day and live in a nice big house in a nice fancy neighborhood with your loving wife and family behind you. I'll be that weird, artsy friend from college you sometimes see when you're in town."

Auden couldn't speak. The hum in his ears grew louder, more insistent. *Stop. Stop. Stop.*

"Part of me wanted to push you away from that, to challenge it," Len said, "but that's because I thought you couldn't be yourself in that life. But I was wrong. Seeing you with O'Neal, I saw that I was wrong."

Auden pressed his fingers against the now throbbing spot behind his brow bone. Something deep inside him had gone frantic, panicked, ready to shatter.

Lennox gave him a resigned smile. "O'Neal is fantastic. And, she *fits.* You love each other. She's kinky. You'd make your family happy, bringing home a smart, respectable girl they already like." He sniffed. "Well, your sister may murder you first.

But when she got over that, you could have a storybook life there when you're done with school, while still getting what you both need behind closed doors. Best of both worlds. No one disappointed."

*No one disappointed? What the actual fuck?* His brain came back online in a rush, too many responses surfacing at once, and he made a garbled sound of disbelief. "When have I *ever* given you the impression I'm looking for a storybook life back home?"

"Come on. You're going to go back home. You always were. You and your family don't agree on everything, but you love them too much to hurt them." Len rubbed at the pencil smudges on his fingers—a tell. He wasn't as chill about this as he was trying to project. "All I'm saying is that O'Neal is…she's good for you. And I think you could be good for her. And not just in a 'makes your families happy' kind of way. In a real way. She's got the image you need for your outside world, but in private, matches up with the parts of yourself you keep secret. She also isn't afraid to go toe to toe with you—which you need, believe me. You two make perfect sense."

Len glanced up, resigned.

"So right now, *I'm* the only complication in this equation. I don't doubt that O'Neal cares about me on some level, but what she did with us was *for you*. So she may be running in part because she's too nice to hurt my feelings or she's overwhelmed by the thought of managing two guys. She wants *you*. So simplify the math for her. Leave me out of it and get the girl. Get the happy ending."

*Leave me out of it.* The words made Auden's skin go clammy. He'd never had a panic attack, but he imagined this was what the beginning of one felt like. He breathed through the anxiety.

"What and you just go on your merry way?" Auden asked. "Go hop in other people's beds? Just be our friend who comes over for movie nights?"

Len made a dismissive sound. "I mean, I guess. Long term,

it's not like it could turn out any other way. Whether it's O'Neal or someone else down the line, that's where this was always going once school ended. Your dad's business is waiting. Your family is waiting. You're their golden boy. You're not exactly going to roll into town with a harem. You couldn't even roll in with a boyfriend. What we've been doing always had an end."

Auden sat on the back of the couch. Len's speech had knocked the wind out of him. The things Len was saying were, of course, thoughts he'd had before. He knew what kind of life was waiting for him at home. Who he was here couldn't be who he was there. But he'd never let himself think about how this would end. Hearing it come out of Len's mouth, imagining Len just being some friend he saw on occasion sent a wash of deep, sickening grief through him.

"Lennox…"

"I'm just the third, Aud," he said, a somber edge to his voice. "Expendable."

*Expendable.*

*Expendable?*

"The fuck you are," Auden blurted.

Len gripped the back of his neck with both hands, his tattoos rippling with the movement. "Don't make this harder. I'm trying to be decent here. I can't compete with what you could have with O'Neal. I won't. I care about you too much to get in the way of that. You and O'Neal both deserve to be happy."

Auden's gaze drifted over Len's face, down his bare torso to the tattooed words from the W. H. Auden poem, and an ache went through him. "And what do you deserve?"

His lip curled. "I'm already playing on house money. I've gotten more than I ever expected. I'm not going to press my luck."

"She has feelings for you too, you know?" Auden said, tone careful. "Hell, sometimes I think she likes you better than me."

Lennox laughed softly. "Well, can't blame her. You can be a dick. And have you seen me?"

The joke took some of the edge off the sadness moving through Auden. "I have seen you. And she's not wrong."

Len's gaze flicked to his, wariness there.

Auden gripped the top of the couch, trying to steel himself for what he needed to say. "I'm not going to lie. My head is completely scrambled with all this. But I do know a few things for sure." His throat was on fire, the words burning there. "One is that you're not expendable to me."

"Aud—"

"You're fucking *non-negotiable.*"

Len's nostrils flared, but his gaze remained guarded.

"This big plan you have is utter bullshit," he said, voice hard. "Because if you walk out of my life or just become some old college buddy I see every now and then…it will punch a hole right through me. One that would never be able to be stitched up." He blinked back hot tears that were trying to form and looked at his best friend with as much honesty as he'd ever shown him. "So stop fucking acting like you don't matter to me."

Len's natural fidgeting stopped, his body going stock-still.

Auden's throat felt like it'd narrowed to a pinhole, and he tried to clear it. "I know things are…complicated. I'm not going to pretend there aren't expectations for me back home or that a solo relationship with O'Neal wouldn't be a tidy answer to all that, but it's not an honest answer. That's why I had to let her walk away. I can't give her a one-on-one relationship. O'Neal is…amazing. And she's surprised me at every turn. But one of the reasons I'm feeling what I feel for her is because of the way she feels about *you.*"

Len's face slackened.

"And I know I've made that murky. I've been…guarded when it's just you and me. I've drawn weird lines…but it's not because I don't think the thoughts or feel the want. Or more than that."

Len's lips parted, but then he shut them again like he was afraid Auden wouldn't go on if he interrupted.

"It's there. All of it." Auden had figured out a long time ago that he wasn't straight. He was attracted to the person, not the gender. But crossing that last line with Lennox, that one-on-one line, had always seemed like an epically bad idea. They lived together. It would change things and could be a one-way ticket to destroying the most important relationship he'd ever had in his life. But he couldn't let Lennox go on thinking he was just some dude he sometimes invited into his threesomes.

"It's there, Len. We both know this is more than a friendship. And if what I feel for O'Neal is love, then I'm feeling that partly because of how she is with *us*, not just me. She could love the guy I already love."

Lennox stared at him for what seemed like eons and then let out a whispered, "Fuck." He leaned back against his desk and ran a hand over his face like he was in pain. "*Fuck!*"

Worry filled Auden. "What?"

Lennox straightened and then stalked his way, his eyes darkening. Auden got to his feet, bracing for a punch based on the look on Len's face.

"Aud," Len said, his voice edged with rusty razor blades. "You better walk the hell away right now if you don't want me to kiss you. Because otherwise, that is about to happen, and you're just going to have to deal with it."

Auden froze.

Len stopped in front of him and poked two fingers into his chest. "Better run, roommate. Because, surprise, I love you back. And this shit's about to get romantic if you don't get out of my fucking face right now."

The words were terrifying but, in that moment, it would've taken an earthquake to move him. "I'm not going anywhere."

"Don't say I didn't warn you." Len grabbed Auden by the back of the neck and kissed him.

Auden's hands went to Len's biceps, an automatic move of residual panic, but then Len's tongue parted Auden's lips, and a groan escaped from a place deep inside him, a place that had been on full lockdown for a long damn time. *Fucking hell.*

Auden dragged him closer, letting himself have this. They'd deal with the consequences after. Len kissed like he did everything else, with utter goddamned confidence and a threat of wildness, like one tiny break in restraint and they would tear each other to pieces. Auden kissed him back, and his ass landed on the back of the couch again. Len stepped between his knees, not even trying to hide the fact that he was getting hard against him.

When Auden's body responded in kind, he didn't fight it. This was Len. His cocky, frustrating, amazing best friend. Maybe giving into this would burn what they had to the ground, maybe it was a mistake, but Auden was tired of pretending this part of their relationship didn't exist.

Auden pulled away, breathless and hard and a little crazed. He caught Len's gaze. "Len...."

Len backed up. His pupils were dark, ominous. "Is this the part where you tell me you were just kidding?"

Auden shook his head. "No, it's the part where I tell you it's late. I should go to bed."

Len's jaw flexed, his expression shuttering. "Right."

Auden stood and cocked his head toward the hallway. "You coming?"

Len blinked and then laughed. "Holy shit, did you just throw a line at me?"

Auden gave him a droll look. "Don't act like it's not going to work. You're hard as a rock already and apparently love me."

Lennox scratched the back of his head, suddenly looking unsure of himself. "Look, both those things are true, and I want this. Have for a long time. But let's not pretend this isn't a big deal or that it isn't new for you." He lifted his brows. "I mean, you're basically a virgin in this arena. I don't want you to feel like just because we've decided to open up this door that I expect you to be instantly on board with anything and everything. We can take it slow."

Auden's first instinct was to deny, to brush off his concern. He was so used to being the one in charge, the one who knew what to do, that admitting anything different felt uncomfortable. But he held his tongue. Lennox was right. He nodded.

"Okay."

"Good." Lennox smiled, the playfulness coming back into his expression. He stepped close to Auden again and reached down, wrapping his hand around Auden's cock over his boxers. Auden closed his eyes as pleasure glittered through him. "How about we start with this? We go to bed. You show me exactly how you want to be stroked?"

Auden inhaled deeply, absorbing the feel of something brand-new and yet comfortingly familiar. "Let's go to bed, Len."

# CHAPTER TWENTY-THREE

*L*ennox's heart was pounding so hard he feared Auden would hear it as they made their way to his room.

Never in his life had he been so scared to go to bed with someone. Even when he'd been a virgin, his mind had been too clouded with horniness that first time to let worry in. But this, being with Auden, felt like walking a tightrope over a field of landmines. So much could go wrong.

For the last couple of weeks, Lennox had been preparing himself for the end of this. When O'Neal had said she loved Auden, Len had felt the truth of her words and had seen the reciprocation on Auden's face. He'd been thrilled for them even as it'd broken his own goddamned heart. The two of them were perfect for each other. Of course that was the answer to the equation he'd tried for so long to solve—how to make Auden happy.

Lennox hadn't expected what O'Neal had said to him, though. *You would be so easy to love.* No one had ever found him easy to love, and hearing it from O'Neal had made him want to pull her into his arms and not let go, to tell her, *back at you, Sweets.* But he knew that wasn't a realistic option. Not in most worlds, but especially not in the one O'Neal and Auden were going back to. He and Auden couldn't both have her. So Len had been crushed for himself but determined to make Auden get his head out of his ass and see that he could have something beautiful with O'Neal.

That was going to be his parting gift to his best friend. Here she is, Aud. See her. Love her. Be happy.

Len could've accepted that outcome, knowing they both had each other.

But then Auden had to go and screw up Len's gorgeous, selfless plan by admitting he had feelings for him. That he wanted him, *loved* him.

Now Len was feeling less like a martyr and more like a hungry dragon, selfish and greedy and wanting all the treasure for himself. Mine.

*Mine. Mine. Mine.*

Because now he wanted them both. Damn the torpedoes. This would have to be a secret. And secrets blew up lives and they blew up families and he hadn't wanted to do any of that because he'd been the secret that'd blown up his family, the surprise baby of an affair. But now he couldn't help himself.

He was in love. And he wanted this. They were all fucked.

Auden stepped inside his room and turned around, his calves touching the bed. He gave Len a chagrined smile. "I'm used to being in charge but…"

Len shut the door behind him and moved closer. His gut tightened at the sight of his normally confident best friend looking vulnerable and *so fucking hot.* He rarely got to really *look* at Auden, always afraid he'd reveal too much on his face, but damn the guy was gorgeous, all honed swimmer's muscles and smooth skin. He couldn't believe he was going to get to touch him without restrictions.

Len slid his hand onto the back of Auden's neck and touched his forehead to his. The clean scent of Auden's soap was somehow making him even harder. "One day, I'll let you do whatever you want to me. You can order me around however you want," he put his lips next to Auden's ear "Because for you, Aud, I will do *all of it.*"

Auden shuddered in his grip and whispered, "Fuck."

"But for tonight, let me lead," he said, lifting his head. "If you want to stop at any point, just say so."

Auden met his gaze and nodded. "Okay."

Something unlocked inside him. Auden didn't trust easily and he didn't cede control. Holding that trust in his palm was a precious gift. He needed to be worthy of it. He leaned in and kissed Auden again, one, because he'd wanted to do it for so long and now was marveling at the access, but also, he wanted to get Auden's mind out of analytical mode and into sensations.

Auden's stiff posture relaxed as their tongues met, and he put a hand on Len's hip, drawing him closer. Len groaned as Auden's hardened cock brushed against his. Man, the guy made him feel like a virgin again, like he could go off at any second. He put a hand on Auden's shoulder and pressed him back, guiding him down to the bed. Auden went willingly, and they never broke the kiss as Len crawled over his best friend's body.

Len's braced himself above him, his hips rocking slowly, their cocks grinding gently against each other as they made out. Len was about to ask if that was okay, but before he could, Auden's hand slid up the back of Len's thigh and then gripped his ass, positioning him so that things were harder, rougher.

Auden made a sound into Lennox's mouth, and a hot shiver went through Len, raising goosebumps. *God.*

He'd promised that they'd take things slow, but right now he didn't want to stop being this close to him. He broke away for a breath. "I need you naked."

The words had slipped out, and Lennox feared he'd moved too fast, but Auden didn't flinch. "You too."

Lennox rolled off briefly and shucked his boxers, tossing

them somewhere, and Auden did the same. Len reached for a bottle of lube he kept in a drawer in the nightstand. When he turned back toward Auden, his breath caught. Auden was stretched out, hand around his cock, and eyes on Len. Hungry eyes. The impact of it was like a shot of a drug. He'd never seen Auden look at him like that. Like he was ravenous for him.

Lennox inhaled the feeling and then drizzled lube into his hand. "Need some help with that?"

Auden's teeth dug into his bottom lip, and he cocked his chin at Len. "You first."

The offer surprised him, but he tossed the bottle to Auden. Aud slicked his hand up and then beckoned him forward. Once Len was straddling him, Auden's fingers slid along Len's cock with a firm, confident grip.

"Christ," Lennox breathed, tilting his head back.

Auden chuckled and gave him another stroke. "You're making this easy. Who's the virgin again?"

Lennox snorted and then reached between them and wrapped his hand around Auden's thick erection, giving it a good pump.

Auden's hips lifted and he gasped.

Len laughed. "Takes one to know one, asshole. You're easy too."

The little bit of teasing melted the rest of Lennox's nerves away. This was Aud. Yes, this was a big deal, but this was still his best friend. If he didn't do everything just right, it would be okay. He just needed to follow his gut.

He rocked his hips into Auden's grip a few more times while slowly stroking him, but he felt Auden's restlessness. It mirrored his own. *Not enough. Never enough with him.* He dipped his head next to Auden's ear. "I know I promised slow tonight, but I want to feel more of you. Can I?" Instead of articulating what he wanted, he showed him. He moved his hand away and nudged Auden's, then their cocks were against each other, slick and hot and hard. He dragged himself against Auden, the feel of being skin-to-skin like an electric shock through his system.

Auden moaned and joined in the rhythm, his hands reaching to grip Lennox's ass. "Fuck yes."

The hard grip of Auden's hands made Lennox grunt, and he ground against his cock, the heat between them making him dizzy with desire. He lowered his mouth to Auden's and sucked and bit at his bottom lip. Auden's fingertips teased low, touching the base of Lennox's balls and then tracing upward, slowly, slowly, until he was teasing the outer rim of that oh-so-sensitive place and slicking him with lube.

An embarrassing whimper escaped Len, the feel of Auden touching him so boldly almost too much for his body to process.

Auden's dominant instincts kicked in at Len's obvious plea-sure, and he rolled Lennox, pinning him beneath him, taking control of the rhythm, and rutting against him as he slid two slippery fingers inside him.

"You'll let me have anything, Len?" Auden was breathless, panting, the sound of their bodies slick and needy against each other one of the most erotic soundtracks Lennox had ever heard.

Len tried to find his breath, the combo of sensations short-circuiting his brain. "You know I will."

"*Fuck.*" Auden's expression tightened into one of erotic torture. "Want you."

"Got me."

Auden didn't need more discussion than that. With swift movements, he yanked open the drawer, sheathed himself with a condom, and glossed himself and Len with more lube.

The brief break in contact made Len feel almost frantic. His body was aching for Auden's hands, his cock, his mouth.

But he didn't have to wait long. After a few toe-curling

strokes of Aud's fingers, he settled himself above Len and entered him with a slow, purposeful pump of his hips.

Len's nerve endings sizzled with pleasure, and he almost lost himself to the sensation, but he forced himself to keep his eyes open. The feel of his best friend filling him was almost enough to send him over the edge, but the look on Auden's face was what had him disintegrating into ash. Aud hadn't closed his eyes either. He was looking right at Len, showing him everything he'd apparently kept hidden until this point.

Desire. Possessiveness. More than that. *Love.*

Len gripped the base of his own cock and squeezed. "Gonna. Fucking. Come."

Auden chuckled, though it sounded breathy and broken. "I certainly fucking hope so. My ego would never recover." He pumped his hips again, dragging his cock backward nice and slow, and then burying even deeper. He closed his eyes and trembled above Len. "And don't judge me on staying power this time either. You feel so fucking good."

"Deal," Len choked out.

Auden shooed Len's hand away from where he was gripping himself and Auden took over instead, stroking Len's cock as he moved his hips. Len's back arched, and he moaned, the dual sensations rolling like a thunderstorm through his body. He forced himself to watch every moment, to not get lost in his head, and for a crystallized moment, he couldn't believe this was happening, that his best friend was on top of him, that they loved each other. That Len could have something this...*good.* Maybe more.

Auden's breaths and movements sped up, his rhythm turning almost desperate, and Len couldn't hold onto the view anymore. He closed his eyes, and everything morphed into pure feeling. Auden's hand on his cock, his body stretching tight with him, their hearts pounding together.

Auden let out a loud, strangled sound, a sound of release and triumph and pain and pleasure all mixed into one, and his cock swelled inside Len. That was all it took to break the last threads of Len's control. His muscles jolted and a gritty sound escaped his throat, the rush of orgasm almost too much. The warm fluid of his own release hit his chest as he came along with Auden. He reached out, digging his fingers into Auden's bicep, half afraid that he was going to launch them both right off the bed.

They rode out the waves of their orgasms until they had nothing left to give, and Len's muscles decided to quit working. He melted into the bed, sated and possibly dead, and Auden eased off of him and rolled onto his back, sucking in air like he'd run a marathon. Lennox dragged in deep gulps along with him as he lay there in the dark next to him, his body humming and his heart soaring.

But when things stayed quiet for too long, anxiety began to well. Lennox had fooled around with guys who'd claimed to be straight before and had witnessed how quickly regret set in once the horniness faded. How fast a guy could grab his clothes and make you promise to never tell anyone. He couldn't handle Auden doing that to him. That might kill him.

"Well, that happened," Auden finally said.

Lennox tensed and stared at the slowly turning ceiling fan in the dark. "It did."

"Give me a sec." Auden was up and out of the room before Len could say anything. A rabbit high-tailing it out of the den.

*Well, shit.* Len rolled on his side and turned on the lamp, readying himself for the backpedal.

But Auden came back. He'd cleaned himself off and had a fresh pair of boxer briefs on. He also had a wet washcloth in his hand. He cocked his chin at Len. "Sit up."

Len lifted a brow but followed the order.

Auden sat next to him and ran the warm washcloth along Len's chest and abdomen, cleaning him up with a tenderness that surprised him. "We made a mess."

"Dudes are messy," Len said, helping with the cleanup process and then pulling the blanket to his waist.

Auden's gaze flicked up to his, and he tossed the washcloth aside. "*This* is messy."

Len exhaled. "Yeah. I know. And if this went too far, if in the heat of the moment—"

"Shut the hell up, please," Auden said, a little smile softening the firm tone. "I know I don't have the best track record, but I'm not saying that to take back what I said. Or what we just did. My attraction to you isn't new."

The words were like a thunderclap in Len's head.

"This has never been an I'm-afraid-I'm-bisexual thing," Auden said, a tired note in his voice. "I kept the lines drawn because two guys who live together and have threesomes can still be called roommates. Two guys who are living together and also sleeping with each other are in a relationship. And neither of us is good at those." He glanced toward the darkened window and squinted. "And I…"

Lennox was still processing the first part when Auden's words drifted off. "And what?"

Auden sighed and looked back to him, a pained expression on his face. "And this makes me feel like a dick but…just you and I, I mean…"

Awareness dawned and Len smirked. "Aud, are you trying to tell me I'm not enough?"

His nose wrinkled. "That's not what I—"

Len lifted a hand, cutting him off. "Stop. I know it's hard to see past that truly enormous ego of yours sometimes, but you do realize that I wasn't doing threesomes with you just to get the chance to touch your dick every now and then, right?"

He blinked.

Len snorted. "Aud, I love you. And you're fucking hot, and sex with you is great. But we're poly. Both of us know how many

things light up on our circuit boards when we share a woman."
His heart sank as a wave of melancholy hit him. "Well, not just *a*
woman. I don't think that's going to work as well anymore.
Nothing lit us up like being with *her*. *You* were different with
her. Fully yourself in a way you aren't with other women."

Auden scraped a hand over his jaw. "Believe me, I know.
Even when we were kids, she always had this way of seeing
right through my bullshit. Like I'd put on this I'm-the-older-
brother act around her and my sister, and she would just cut me
off at the knees. She didn't let me get away with anything." He
groaned. "And she was *such* a goody-goody. Once, when I was
like thirteen, we were at church camp together, and she caught
me trying a cigarette with this girl, who of course, I was trying
to impress. God, O'Neal would've been like ten or something,
but she was *so* pissed. I was terrified she was going to tell on me,
so I promised her I'd give her anything to keep it a secret. The
chocolate bars I'd smuggled in from home. My Nintendo. She
could name her price."

Lennox laughed. "What'd she ask for?"

Auden's gaze went soft, and a little smile played at his lips.
"She wanted me to teach her to swim better because she was
getting beat in all the relays, and the other girls were teasing her
about it."

"Ha. That tracks. That one has a competitive streak."

"Yeah, and she knew it was a big ask but that she held all the
cards," Auden said. "So every morning that summer, when I
should've been sleeping in, I woke up at the crack of dawn and
went to the lake so I could teach her. She was lapping the other
girls in the races by the end of camp." He gave Len a wry look.
"And a few days after we got home, she left one of those big
yellow mailing envelopes on my bed. She'd printed out all this
stuff about what smoking does to your body and gross photos
of cancer. She'd put a note on top that said, *You scared me. Don't*

*do that again. If you die, who else is going to teach me the backstroke next summer?"*

"Damn."

"Yeah, I felt like a complete ass. She'd lost her mom, and now I was doing things that she saw as life-threatening." He shook his head. "And it worked. I never smoked again. Hell, anytime I've been faced with some decision like that since, I think of her. I never wanted to scare her again. I wanted to like, make her proud or something."

Len's chest filled with warmth. "Did you teach her the backstroke the next summer?"

Auden rolled his eyes. "Of course I did. Even without blackmail hanging over me. I'm such a sucker for..."

"Her."

Auden sighed. "Yeah. For her. She's...*dammit.*" He gave Len a helpless look. "I really do love her."

Lennox breathed in the admission. *Thank God.* They were finally on the same page. "Yeah. Glad you caught up, genius."

"And I fucking miss her. Not only in our bed but just *her,* in my life." The words were spilling out of him now. "Our lives."

"Agree, one hundred percent," Len said, some of the weight he'd been carrying over the last few weeks lifting off his shoulders.

"But we can't do this to her," he finished.

*Annnnd we're back.* "Do what? Love her? Take care of her? Be great boyfriends? Give her great sex?" Lennox asked. "Because I think we damn well can."

Auden met his hard stare, his frown deep. "She's a freshman in college. I've already taken a bunch of firsts from her. She needs to have room to have others, to experience life. To date. To try different things. She can't even know if she's vanilla if all she's ever been exposed to is salted caramel sundaes."

Len gave him a droll look. "There's a joke in there about salty things, but I'm not going to touch it."

"I'm being serious. This. Us." He pointed between the two of them. "Is a lot."

"We are. I get that and I bet she does too," Len said. "But she's not that ten-year-old anymore. She's a grown woman. A woman who was smart enough to look at us and go, 'Wow, that was fun, but these dudes are a mess and are going to let me down.' *Because we fucking were.*"

Auden flinched, the truth stinging.

"On some instinctual level, she recognized that we weren't ready for her. We didn't deserve her trust yet," he went on. "You couldn't admit your feelings. You and I had all this unsaid shit between us. Based on the evidence she was working with, she made a damn brilliant decision to walk away and save herself the heartache."

"So you're saying you agree with me letting her walk?"

Len pressed his lips together, frustrated. "What I'm saying is that she has to make her own choices. That's her job. But making sure she has the right information to do that? That's our job. Right now she's working with bad evidence."

He stretched out beside Len, propping his head on his fist and looking exhausted. "Bad evidence."

"She ended things because she's scared. And that asshole teammate of yours pushed some shame buttons for her, confirming her fears. He made her feel young and naïve, like her desire to please you was about her being gullible, not about her being kinky. And we did nothing to talk that through with her. We both let her walk away believing she'd been just a fling for us or disposable, and that we didn't have feelings for her. And then you haven't called her, and I didn't feel like I had the right to."

Auden closed his eyes. "I've completely screwed this up."

Len rolled on his side to face him. "We both have. But maybe there's still a chance to fix it." He slid a hand onto Auden's chest, marveling at the fact that he could do that now.

"I mean, speaking from experience, you're kind of hard to say no to."

Auden cracked an eyelid open to peek at him, a little smile tugging up the corner of his mouth. "Is that right?"

Lennox's heart flipped over. "You're a fucking menace. Use your powers for good, man."

Auden laughed and reached up to pull Lennox against him. "Define...*good.*"

# CHAPTER TWENTY-FOUR

O'Neal was walking out of her history class when her phone buzzed in her pocket. She hiked her backpack higher on her shoulder and grabbed her phone.

> Auden: Hey. Can we meet up and chat?

Seeing his name on her screen sent a hollow pang through her, and she halted, frozen. Someone behind her nearly collided with her and barked out an "ugh, watch where you're going."

O'Neal stepped off the path and took shelter under a nearby oak tree. She stared at the text, unsure of what to do.

She wanted to say *yes, yes, yes.* Scream it. Not talking to Auden and Len these last few weeks had left her grief-stricken in a way she hadn't anticipated. She hadn't just lost a physical connection with them. That was hard enough, but she was used to being alone in that department. The loss of the friendship had been much more gutting. In the short time she'd been at school, the three of them had developed such an easy connection. Every time something interesting happened in her day, she wanted to pick up her phone and tell one of them about it. She wanted to hear Len joke with her. She wanted to listen to Auden break down a movie in his nerdy, passionate way. She wanted...

*No.* She grabbed a bottle of water out of the side pocket of her backpack and tried to ease the sudden tightness in her throat with a quick gulp. She was not going to cry in the middle of campus. And she was not going to keep doing this to herself. She forced herself to answer how she needed to.

> O'Neal: You don't have to do that. I'm OK.

Because that had to be what this was about. Time had passed. Reality had set in, and now he was back to being Auden. Feeling guilty and worrying about her. This was a big brother check-in. She needed to let him off the hook.

*Look, I'm okay! I'm fine! Everything's great! I'm totally not ready to cry in the quad.*

Three dots appeared on the screen and then disappeared. Then popped up again.

> Auden: I'm not

The two simple words didn't register at first, and then they had her sagging back against the thick trunk of the tree. *I'm not.* He's not okay.

Another text popped up in a separate thread.

> Lennox: I'm not either.

She pressed her lips together, her gaze watery now.

> Auden: We just want to talk. Please?

O'Neal sat down in the grass, feeling exhausted all of a

sudden. Did she really want to talk about this? Did she want to sit there and have them mansplain about why love couldn't be a factor in this? About how they'd warned her from the beginning about what this was? Or how her feelings weren't really love but just a silly crush? She didn't know if that would give her closure or just make it worse.

Saying no would be the smart thing. She needed time, space to grieve this and move on. But she couldn't make her fingers type the word. What she'd been doing since she'd walked away from them hadn't been working. She'd planned to focus totally on school, but thoughts of them were still a constant distraction. This was still an open wound that she hadn't been able to close. She needed real stitches to stop the bleeding, a real end, an honest talk. And it wasn't like she could avoid Auden forever. She was staying at his family's house for Thanksgiving break in a few weeks. They needed to clear the air before then.

She quickly typed a reply before she could chicken out.

O'Neal: OK, when, where?

Auden: You're done with class for the day, right?

The fact that he still knew her schedule made her stomach ping. God, she was hopeless.

O'Neal: yes

Auden: now? Our place?

Their place. The last thing she wanted was a reminder of the time they'd spent together. That was going to hurt. But if they were really going to talk about things, she definitely didn't want to discuss such personal stuff in the middle of a coffee shop.

> O'Neal: OK. I'm going to drop off my stuff at my dorm and will head over after

> Auden: Thank you, see you soon

She took a deep breath. "You can do this. You can totally do this."

*I CAN'T DO THIS.* HALF AN HOUR LATER, SHE WAS STANDING ON their doorstep, trying to get herself to knock and failing miserably. Just when she was about to turn on her heel and give up, the door swung open.

Then Auden was there in the doorway in a pair of faded jeans and a dark green T-shirt, looking even better than she remembered, which was saying something because her memories were damn vivid. She cleared her throat.

"Um. Hi. I was about to knock but…"

His eyes crinkled at the corners a little, almost as if he was pained. "It's okay. I heard you on the stairs. Thought I would make it a little easier. Doors are hard."

O'Neal felt glued to the landing. Her instinct was to hug him. Auden, her friend. Auden, the boy she'd loved for longer than she could remember. But that option had been swept off the table, replaced by a banquet of awkwardness.

"Thanks."

Auden cleared his throat and stepped back. "Come on in."

She made herself follow him in and to the living room. Lennox was there, standing behind the couch and offering a small, tentative smile. His blond hair was messy, like he'd been running his hands through it. She wanted to smooth it for him.

"Hey, Swee—O'Neal."

The correction was like a little stab in her side. "Hi."

"Do you want something to drink?" Auden asked.

She shook her head, her stomach turning. She'd been right to not want to knock. This was too awkward. Too painful. "No, thanks, I'm okay. You know, maybe this wasn't a good idea. I think I might just—"

"Please don't." Auden grabbed her hand, a desperate note in his voice.

The move and his tone shocked her. She glanced at their linked hands. "Aud…"

"Please, Shaq."

She closed her eyes. The sound of her nickname, of their shared history echoing through the word, tore through her like a jagged knife. She'd messed this all up. She should've never taken that step with him, never pushed to cross that line. A crush had been manageable. A crush meant she still had him as a friend in her life. Now she had neither friend nor lover. Now she couldn't have him at all. "Please don't make me do this," she whispered. She opened her eyes and looked at him. "I know you probably think it will make it better. But please don't make me sit here and listen to why I was right to end this. Please don't big brother me."

"I'm not your brother," Auden said, voice gruff.

"Auden…"

"I'm not your brother. Or your keeper. Or your old friend from home." He laced his fingers with hers and then got down on one knee. "I'm just fucking *yours.*"

She sucked in a sharp breath, the words and his position scrambling her brain. "What are you doing?"

Len walked over, and to her amazement, he knelt next to Auden, looking up at her with those beautiful green eyes of his. "We're doing what we should've done that morning of the fire. Begging for fucking forgiveness for being absolute jackasses. Begging you not to walk away."

"I—" She shook her head. "I don't understand."

"That day," Auden said, his hand still holding hers, "you told me you needed to end things because you loved me."

She winced.

"And that you were scared and ashamed or embarrassed that you'd do anything to hear me call you my good girl," he continued. "That feeling that way must mean something was wrong with you, like you were fulfilling some genetic party girl legacy."

Her face burned at the memory.

"But"—he pressed a kiss to her palm—"you're wrong, Shaq. I should've told you that then, but I was too scared to say the truth back to you that day. What I should've said is that I know exactly how you feel when I call you my good girl because it's how I feel when you submit to me and let me. Like I've won the goddamned lottery. Like I'm the luckiest fucker in the universe. Because, wow, beautiful, brilliant, badass O'Neal Lory is looking at me and giving me this gift." He touched her cheek. "You would do anything for me to say *good girl?* Well, I would do *anything* to have the privilege of being the man in your life, to be worthy of that kind of trust from you, to be worthy of your love."

She was shaking, his words like an earthquake rumbling through her and upending her life.

"I don't know if I ever will be that worthy, but I asked you to come here today to tell you that I want to try if you'll let me," he said. "Because I should've never let you walk away and let you think for one minute that you didn't mean the world to me or that there was something wrong with liking what we did. I love you. And I've been a fucking wreck since you left."

*I love you.* The declaration was like a sonic boom in her brain, in her heart. Auden Blake *loved* her. Her knees literally went weak. She'd always thought that was just an expression, but it was as if her muscles had liquified. She put her hand on Len's shoulder, afraid she would fall.

Len placed his hand atop hers and cleared his throat. "I can't top that speech, and I know we don't have history like you and Aud do, but Sweets"—he met her eyes—"you unravel me. What the three of us shared was special. I've never seen someone so inherently brave and beautifully, naturally kinky. I fell a little more in love with you every day we spent together."

Tears filled her eyes. Auden and Len. Both of them on their knees in front of her, telling her they loved her. Even in her wildest of fantasies. She hadn't dared to imagine this.

"I...I don't know what to say."

Auden's throat bobbed like he was nervous. "You don't have to say anything and you don't owe us a thing. We just needed you to hear what we had to say, to have all the information before you made a decision. We know this is complicated. We're still figuring it out ourselves. But we didn't want you going another day thinking that what we had was just a fling, or that you leaving didn't destroy us. We want a relationship with you. We love each other and we love you." Auden's eyes were misty now. "And I'm so fucking sorry it took me this long to see you for the woman you've become. One who knows her own mind and her own heart and doesn't need some guy telling her what she feels."

Her tears spilled over, and she sank to her knees in front of them, the weight of the last few weeks falling off her shoulders like a heavy wool coat. How in the hell was she ever going to find the words to respond to all of that?

Auden and Lennox were quiet now, and both seemed afraid to move, like they truly expected her to hear all of that and then hand their hearts back to them and say no thank you. She slipped her hands from theirs and then leaned forward, wrapping her arms around both their necks and pulling them to her until her head was sandwiched between both of theirs, their cheeks pressed together. *Auden. Lennox. Hers.* A sob choked her.

"I don't know how to do this. I didn't even know we *could* do this. But"—she smiled through her tears—"I did wait a really long time. I was alone…a really long time. Maybe I *do* deserve two of you."

Len laughed and Auden joined in, relief ringing through it.

"You definitely do, Sweets." Len kissed her temple. "You deserve it all."

She closed her eyes and absorbed the words, inhaled their scent, and then she released them. *Mine.* She stood and they followed her up. She stepped back a little so she could look at both of their faces. "I love you too." She took each of their hands. "Both of you. Aud"—she twined her fingers with his— "yes, you're bossy, always have been, but you're wrong. You always saw me. You may have been the only one when I was growing up. And I've loved you for so long that it's become a part of me."

He leaned forward and pressed a soft kiss to her lips, the connection warm and perfect and *right.*

"And Len," she said, turning to him. "You have the biggest heart of any guy I've ever met. You make me feel safe and heard and cared for. And I love the way you love Auden."

"Thank you," Len said, his voice catching. He brushed her hair away from her face and kissed her with tender affection. When he pulled away, he turned to Auden and kissed him.

O'Neal's thoughts stuttered and then burned away as she watched Auden's lips part and accept the kiss from Len, his hand going to Len's hair. *Whoa.*

Her skin went hot and her heart took flight. A little squeak escaped her throat.

Auden broke away from the kiss and turned to her, a tentative look on his face. "Um, yeah, so that happened while you were gone. I don't know how you feel about me and Len, uh…"

Delight fizzed through her, and she pressed her hands against her heart. "Oh my God, I am so happy right now I can't even tell you."

Len laughed. "I called it. Dirty voyeur hiding in there."

"Well, yes, probably," she said, based on how hot her blood was running just seeing them kiss, "but I'm happy because you two…"

Auden lifted a brow. "What?"

"Were so obviously into each other," she finished. "And having lines drawn between you when we were all together was kind of weird."

Len snorted. *"Someone* took a while to see that."

Auden rolled his eyes. "Fine. I'm a little slow on the uptake, all right? We got here eventually, didn't we?" He gave Len a sweetly conspiratorial look and then turned back to her. "So I guess this means you're not leaving us?"

She grinned and swiped the tears from her cheeks. "Nope. You're stuck with me now. Well, until your sister murders you."

Auden groaned. "We'll cross that bridge when we get to it." He reached out and slid a hand onto her waist. "I'm not going to pretend I know what I'm doing here or what the fallout might be if and when we decide to tell anyone. This is new territory for all of us. Complicated territory."

She nodded, the gravity of the situation still a steady weight in her gut. "I know."

"We may…lose people," he said. "And I hate that for you."

"I hate that for both of you," Lennox said with a scowl. "Why can't people just mind their own damn business? We're not saying they have to be bi or kinky or polyamorous. They can be as boring as they want to be."

She took a deep breath, looking at the both of them, and then squeezed Auden's forearm. "I've already been disowned just for wanting to go to a state school. I'm not going to lie. It hurts. But also…I think I'm kinda done with having people in my life who only love me if I fit into the mold they made for me. That's…not love. That's control." She gave them a sly smile. "And apparently I only give up control in very specific circumstances to two very specific people."

Auden's lips curved into a slow, evil grin. "Is that right, Ms. Lory?"

A shiver ran across her skin at the shift in his tone. "Yes, Teach."

He gave her a heated look. "I love it when you call me that. And it's appropriate right now."

"Oh really? Why?" she asked.

She expected one of them to make a move.

What she did *not* expect was what Len announced. "Because we have a slide presentation!"

She blinked, the screech of car brakes sounding in her head. "You have a what now?"

Auden smirked that dimpled smirk of his and grabbed her hand, kissing her knuckles. "My dearest Shaq, once upon a time, you gave me a stack of research about smoking."

She closed her eyes in mortification. "Oh my God, are you seriously bringing that up right now?"

"Yes." He guided her to the couch. "Because we're doing this the right way this time. We're not going to give you ammunition to run away again." He picked up a remote and the TV came on. "We're giving you what your hungry journalistic brain needs before we take one step more."

He clicked a button, and a PowerPoint slide came up titled *Praise Kink and Why It's Awesome.* There was a cartoon sketch, no doubt Len's handiwork, of Auden and Len giving a thumbs-up.

She laughed and pressed her hand over her mouth. "Y'all didn't."

Len stepped up next to the TV and put on a pair of glasses like he was some hot professor. "Oh, we did. We did it real good, Ms. Lory. There are statistics and graphs. A whole section on polyamory. A breakdown of BDSM roles. I hand-illustrated some slides with filthy art."

"We *cited sources for deeper reading,*" Auden said low against her ear, like he was whispering where he was going to touch her. "There may be pop quizzes. And rewards for good grades. Punishments for wrong answers, though, so you better pay attention."

To her chagrin, she shivered in anticipation. She pressed her hands over her face. "I hate you both."

Auden laughed. "Why?"

"Because this is totally doing it for me. I am ridiculous," she declared.

"No," Len said. "That's the point."

She lowered her hands and he was standing in front of her. "What is?"

He squatted down in front of her and cupped her chin. "You're not ridiculous. You're perfect."

Auden sat next to her and put his hand on her knee. "Perfect for us. We love you exactly as you are. We wouldn't change a thing." He leaned over and kissed her behind her ear. "Because you're such a very. Good. Girl. *Our* good girl."

Yes. That.

She closed her eyes and let the blissful feeling of their praise and love roll over her. Maybe they were right. Just because it was complicated and different didn't mean it was wrong.

In fact, she'd never felt so right inside as she did at that moment, like the combination to the intricate lock inside her had finally clicked into place and the safe had opened, revealing the most private, precious things about her. Things that they adored and would cherish.

She didn't have to pretend with them or put on a façade or be someone they wanted her to be. She'd performed on some level her whole life, keeping things bottled tightly, keeping things neat, never being a bother, a burden. She'd been a good girl in the worst way, the way that had allowed those around her to lock her into fulfilling their expectations while ignoring her own. *Good* in her grandparent's world had been a trap.

That had started to unravel that day in the kitchen with

Auden. He'd seen past the polished exterior and to that secret place inside where her desire lived, where she had dreams of her own, where the fire of who she could be burned hot but quiet. *Why can't you?* He'd thrown that bomb into her world. Why can't you have what you want? Why can't you be who you want to be?

*Why can't you?*

With them, she finally could.

And she was going to be so very *good* at it.

# CHAPTER TWENTY-FIVE

*A*uden woke up with a smile on his face. Since the night of the fire, he'd been waking in the middle of the night as a pattern but this time it wasn't from nightmares. He blinked into the darkness, the remnants of his dream fading, and heard Len's soft snoring beside him. At first, this threw him, but then the night rushed back to him. *Lennox. O'Neal.* All three of them spending the night exploring, making love, keeping the kink to a minimum for the moment and just celebrating that they'd all finally gotten out of their own way. Part of him worried it had all been a dream.

He reached out for O'Neal but found Lennox's bicep instead and no one between them. The empty space made his gut clench. Was she okay? He didn't think he could bear it if she was having second thoughts. Careful not to jostle Len, he climbed out of bed, grabbed a T-shirt from the floor, and tugged it on as he headed out of the bedroom.

When he stepped into the darkened living room, he could make out a silhouette in the chair near the window, the sight giving him a rush of relief. O'Neal was wrapped in a throw blanket, knees to her chest, and was scrolling through her phone. He cleared his throat, hoping not to startle her.

She looked up, the blue light of her phone revealing her surprised expression.

"Hey," he said quietly.

She shifted in the chair to turn toward him, a gentle smile on her face. "Hey. Did I wake you?"

"Nah." He walked over to the spot on the couch nearest her and sat. "I've developed a habit of middle-of-the-night waking it seems. Everything all right?"

Her phone screen went dark, leaving only the moonlight coming in through a crack in the curtains to illuminate her. "Yeah. I woke up and couldn't get back to sleep." She gave him a self-deprecating smile and tapped her temple. "Busy brain."

"Bad busy or good busy?"

"Good busy, I guess, but..." She scrunched her nose. "Also a little—probably a lot—embarrassing."

"Oh." Well, that piqued his interest. "Why's that?"

She looked to be debating for a moment but then sighed, unlocked her phone, and turned the screen toward him. "I might possibly be working my way through your references in your presentation."

He blinked at the screen and then a delighted laugh burst out of him. His studious Shaq had been up doing her research. He loved that her first instinct was to learn *all the things* about kink immediately. She'd probably be able to write a dissertation on it by next Tuesday and teach them some things.

"And how's that going for you?"

"Good. They're actually really helpful links." She glanced away. "And I just...like to know stuff."

"I love that you want to research everything. Don't look apologetic about it. I just want to make sure that..." He searched for the right words.

"What?

"That you know you don't have to get an A in this," he said gently. "We can all figure this out together as we go along. The universe of kink is vast. Some of it will work for us, a lot won't."

She chewed her lip. "I know. But I also know that y'all have a lot more experience and are used to...other people who do too. I don't want to—"

"Stop." He took her phone and placed it on the coffee table, turned on a nearby lamp, and then beckoned her with his hand. "Come over here."

He scooted over on the couch, making room.

She pursed her lips, looking adorably defiant. "Why?"

"Because if we're going to have this conversation, I want you next to me. Come on." He patted the spot beside him.

She huffed a sigh, shrugged out from under the blanket, and then joined him on the couch, cross-legged and facing him.

He turned to face her fully, trying to ignore the fact that she looked as enticing as he'd ever seen her—hair mussed, face washed clean, and wearing only a pair of panties and his T-shirt. He wanted to pull her onto his lap and make her feel good again, kiss away that wrinkle in her brow, but he could see the vulnerability in her eyes. This wouldn't be fixed with a make-out session.

"First," he said, holding her focused stare, "I can't deny that there were other people before. But, I can promise you that there has never been anyone like you. For me or for Len. That fact has been plaguing me since that day you kissed me in the kitchen. I was done for. You're special. We love you."

She gave him a small smile. "I love you too."

He leaned closer and, in a conspiratorial tone, said, "And I'm not saying that to exploit your exceptionally hot praise kink."

She snorted. "Shut up. I'm still trying to figure out why that does it for me so much. You don't want to know all the answers I've come up with in the last hour," she admitted. "Those are some dark hallways."

"I know. I get it." He reached out and tucked a loose hair behind her ear. "And I can't answer your whys for you, and Lennox would tell you we don't need to, that some things just are and it's okay. But for what it's worth, knowing you like me calling you my good girl and that you want praise from me? Knowing that you like being shared between us?" He licked his lips, trying to find the right words. "*Undoes me.*"

Her eyes flared with heat.

"So did you fighting back that first night we were all together. Because I know part of that was real. I really didn't deserve an apology that night. I was the one who'd fucked up." He shook his head. "But goddamn, O'Neal. The way you—I can't think about it too much because I'll just get hard again."

Even in the dark, he could see her cheeks darken. "I don't know how *not* to feel a little embarrassed about that. The whole faux force thing. That I…liked it. I'm reading up on it, but my inner feminist is very confused."

He nodded. "I'd argue that it's pretty damn feminist to own whatever it is that turns you on instead of letting society dictate what's acceptable or not. But like I said, I get it. I promise you I can top you on the don't-want-to-admit-to-that-out-loud scale of what gets me hot. You have no reason to be embarrassed."

Her lips curved wickedly. "Well, now you gotta tell me what you're afraid to admit to. I mean, it's only fair. We're dating now."

"Nuh-unh." He shook his head. "Nope, not a deal I made, Ms. Lory."

She tilted her head in challenge. "Wow. Don't make me do the chicken dance, because I will."

She raised her hands to make them into little beaks, threatening the dance she, Maya, and he used to do as kids when one of them chickened out on something first. No one wanted to be the subject of the chicken dance.

He laughed. "You wouldn't."

She cocked her chin at him. "Start talking, Aud. You'd want to know my secret fantasies."

He sighed. She was right on that account.

"Okay," he said, feeling a little queasy at the thought of saying this out loud to her, but if they were going to be together, they had to trust each other. He wanted to be her safe place, but now he had to be brave enough to let her be his too. He cleared his throat. "Want to know what dream I had when I first fell asleep tonight?"

She nodded, her gaze not leaving his. "Tell me."

*Just say it*, he chastised himself silently when the words wouldn't come. *Jump in the cold pool. One, two, three, go!*

"You on your knees in your high school uniform calling me *daddy* and asking me to teach you how to use sex toys," he said in a rush. "So if you want to talk about dark hallways, I've got some. Because *what the fuck* is that?"

Her eyebrows shot up. "Whoa."

"Yeah. You're telling me." He ran a hand through his hair, feeling more than a little exposed. "You turn dials in me I didn't even know I had. I don't have a thing for high school girls in real life. I know I'm not a creep. But you're so good at being an eager student, and it's…inspiring all kinds of fantasies. You melt my brain, Shaq."

She groaned and put her hands over her face.

"What?" he asked warily. "You're completely horrified and want to dump me immediately?"

"No," she said from behind her hands. "I'm groaning because that praise thing must be especially potent for me, because right now, even though it seems completely bizarre in theory"—she dropped her hands to her lap with a huff—"I just want to call you daddy to see what it does to you."

His body zipped with electricity. *Fucking hell.* "I swear to God, O'Neal. Don't draw weapons because I will draw mine."

She bit her lip, wicked glee in her eyes. He remembered this

O'Neal look. When they were young, it was the look that meant he was about to be dunked in the pool or have his ice cream cone stolen. "I've never met my dad, so you know I have no sentimental ties to that word. It's no big thing."

"It was just a sex dream I was sharing with you," he said, trying to sound calm and in control even though every cell in his body seemed to be vibrating. "I wasn't making a request."

She leaned close to his ear and whispered, "Sure thing, daddy. I'll be good and won't say another word about it."

Auden closed his eyes as the tabooness of the word raced like wildfire down his skin. His cock flexed against his shorts. He didn't feel like *daddy* was the right fit for them, but the fact that she was willing to say it just to play with the fantasy was like sugar on his tongue. It showed she felt safe with him to try things, that this private space between the three of them could be free of judgment. But more than that, it made *him* feel safe. O'Neal wasn't scared of his dark hallways.

But that didn't mean he was going to let her get away with manipulating him that easily. He could play this game too.

He reached out and cupped the side of her head, giving her his best adoring look, which wasn't a stretch because dammit, he did fucking adore her. "My little overachiever. Always going for the extra credit. You know you can make me hard just being near me." He mapped her cheekbone with the pad of his thumb. "You should see how irresistible you look right now. Rumpled and well-fucked but still wanting more. Your nipples already hard and begging for my attention." He let his gaze trace over her, slow and lewd. "I bet those panties are getting damp again because you just love taking whatever I want to give you. My fingers, my tongue, my cock. My best friend."

She closed her eyes, a quiver going through her. "You're playing dirty."

He smiled, loving that he could do this to her. "So are you." He

300

brushed his mouth behind her ear, kissing her there. "I bet you'd do whatever I asked you to because you're such a good girl." His hand slid down to cup her between her legs. "*My* good girl."

She whimpered and arched against his palm. "Damn you."

He chuckled darkly and rocked the heel of his palm against her panties. "I love this about you, freshman. You're so hungry all the time. I should feel bad you haven't had anyone but yourself to take care of that ache for you, but man, I really don't." He pushed the fabric aside, and all his blood rushed downward when he found her slick and burning hot. "We're going to take good care of you. Make up for lost time."

"Yes," she said, breathless now.

"Anytime. You have a thought, a fantasy, an urge. I don't care what time of day or night. You need to be touched, you have us," he said, his voice going gritty as he dipped two fingers inside her, and she clamped around him. "You don't have to take care of it alone anymore. All you've got to do is be our good girl and ask nicely, understand?"

Her head dipped down, pressing into his shoulder as she rocked against his hand. "Yes."

"Yes, what?" he asked hoarsely. "Call me what feels right. Whatever you want."

"Yes...*sir.*"

*Sir.* That did it. She'd dug into her research tonight. No way she'd chosen that term out of the ether. But knowing that she'd picked that name instead of him assigning it, knowing that it was what felt right to her, made it into the most erotic word he'd ever heard.

"Good girl," he whispered, the words catching in his throat.

He slipped his hand from between her legs, and she made a sound of protest.

"Don't worry. I'm going to take good care of you, love." He pressed a kiss to her forehead and reached for the drawer in the side table. "Take off everything and kneel on the couch, legs spread."

"Yes, sir," she said, like it was automatic, natural. Then she did as she was told, tossing his T-shirt and her panties aside and looking like a goddess in the moonlight with her perfect breasts and her wet pussy.

He yanked his shorts off and got a condom on in record time. He stretched out on the couch and then patted his thigh. "On my lap, freshman. Take me. Slowly. So I can watch."

Her eyes were open now, but the haze of arousal was there, no shame, no reluctance. She straddled his lap and then took his cock in her hand. The feel of her grip almost did him in, but then she guided him inside her. He watched with rapt attention as every inch of himself disappeared into the sweet, hot clutch of her body. He shuddered hard and reached for her hips, holding her there, drowning in the sensation of it all.

"Touch yourself," he said softly. "Use me how you need."

She dragged her teeth over her bottom lip and looked down at where they were joined, but just when he thought she might get self-conscious and back out, she drew her hand down her belly and slid two fingers along the sides of her swollen clit.

O'Neal Lory, the girl who'd stolen her first kiss from him in his parents' kitchen, the girl he'd always seen as off-limits, was riding him, touching herself, showing her most private side to him in a way she'd done with no one else. Trusting him. Loving him. The sight was so intimate and erotic, he could barely believe he'd landed here. How had he gotten so damn lucky?

He settled back against the arm of the couch and watched the roll of her hips as she rode him, the dance of her fingers. Her eyes were closed, and her hair cascaded down, teasing the tips of her breasts as she panted softly, lost to the sensations. He prided himself on his staying power, but she already had him fighting off orgasm.

"You ever touch yourself like that thinking of me?" he asked gruffly.

She didn't open her eyes but she nodded.

"Tell me about it," he whispered, reaching out to caress her inner thigh.

"Can't."

"Why?"

"Too many times. To count," she said between breaths.

The answer pleased him immensely. He slid his hand higher and rubbed his thumb along the place where they were joined. "Is that right?"

She let out a little gasp and then she finally opened her eyes and looked down at him. She smirked, some of the snarky girl he knew sneaking into her expression, even though she was clearly on the edge of coming. "Not that your ego...needs to know this..." Her hips continued to pump, driving him mad. "But you were always...my favorite fantasy, Aud. From the very first time I thought a dirty thought. "

The words wound through him like a song he'd never tire of hearing. "I'll try to live up to the hype."

She laughed but the sound cut off as soon as he moved her hand away from herself and took over, lifting his hips and angling inside her to hit just the right place. She moaned and tilted her head back.

God, she was beautiful. "Come for me, freshman."

As if all she needed was to hear his permission, she broke apart above him, crying out and her inner muscles spasming around his cock so intensely that he couldn't hold back any longer. He called her name, the sound rumbling from deep in his chest, and he spilled into the condom as he lost himself in the pleasure of her body, her sounds, her words.

When both of them had coasted down from their highs and were quietly catching their breath, Auden lifted her hips, removed and tossed the condom, and then guided her back to lay against him. She melted against his chest, tucking her face against his neck.

He stroked her hair as he listened to her heart beating against him.

"You definitely live up to the hype," she murmured.

He smiled. He didn't have a praise kink but he certainly loved hearing O'Neal tell him that he'd taken good care of her. "I wish I could get into your head and see what you imagined back then."

"Not this," she said, humor in her voice. "I didn't have the reference points for any of this."

He combed his fingers through her hair, staring at the ceiling. "Why was I the lucky one to get the starring role? I was always giving you a hard time when we were kids."

"That's just it," she said, lifting her head and propping it up on her fist so she could look at him. "You were the only one who didn't treat me like I was made of glass. You saw me, not the girl with the murdered mom, not the girl with the strict grandparents. Just me. It made me want to show you...everything. Still does."

Her words wound around him and made his chest squeeze tight. *Mine.* He kissed her softly. "I love seeing your everything."

She let her hand trail down his stomach. "Your everything's not so bad to look at either."

He kissed the top of her head. "I just love you."

"Same." She was quiet for a few minutes, and he thought she had fallen asleep against him, but then her voice cut through the silence. "So, you and Len, huh?"

He kept his eyes closed, his fingers trailing down her arm, and a blanket of contentment fell over him at the mention of Len. "Yeah. That's a recent development."

She murmured an acknowledgment against his chest.

"Are you comfortable with that?" he asked, tone careful. This was probably something they should've discussed last night before falling into bed. "I know we were taught—"

"If I believed everything we were taught, I wouldn't be here in the first place." She snuggled deeper into his hold. "I love that you two are together in all ways now. That feels right. I want us to be free to be with each other in all those different permutations. No jealousy stuff."

"Agreed," he said, relieved that she felt the same way he and Len did. "I want you to be able to have that kind of one-on-one relationship with Len as well."

"I want that too." She let out a happy little sigh. "He's pretty great, isn't he?"

"Yeah." Auden smiled in the dark. "He's the best guy I know."

She turned her head to peek up at him. "Let's go back to bed, okay? I don't want him waking up alone."

Her affection for Lennox warmed him in a way that had nothing to do with his libido. During so much of this, he'd worried that he was pushing O'Neal into the things he liked or manipulating her toward his kinks, but being with her now, seeing her obvious love for Lennox, he realized Len had been right all along. They didn't create this in O'Neal—they'd unearthed it. She was perfect. Perfect for them.

He kissed the tip of her nose. "Yeah, let's go steal his covers."

# CHAPTER TWENTY-SIX

*W*hen O'Neal woke up late the next morning, she rolled over and was disappointed to find an empty bed. She grabbed her phone to check the time and a text was waiting for her.

> Auden: early swim practice, didn't want to wake you, love you

There was a kiss emoji at the end, which made her smile. She wouldn't have suspected Auden to be the kiss emoji type. She quickly checked her email to make sure the meeting she'd set up tonight had been confirmed and then got up.

When she wandered into the bathroom, she found a folded towel, an unopened toothbrush, and her clothes sitting on the counter. There was a note on top in Len's handwriting. His letters were these quick scratches that somehow looked like art.

*Morning, Sweets! Shower's yours. Clothes are washed. I'll be under headphones working in the living room. Please don't jump-scare me. I hate that.*

She laughed. Lennox had initially intimidated the hell out of her. Tattooed grad student, obviously gorgeous, and just so

smoothly confident that he could melt the butter right off your
toast. But now she knew how sweet and tender he was at the
core, and she just felt enormously thankful that she got to love
and be loved by him.

She showered quickly and used the new toothbrush that
looked to be a freebie one of them had gotten after a dental
visit.

When she walked into the living room, she found Len
hunched over his drawing desk, barefoot in jeans and a black T-
shirt, a pair of wireless earbuds tucked in his ears. His head was
bobbing softly to whatever he was listening to, and he was
sketching with quick, precise strokes. She let herself watch him
in profile for a moment. The look of concentration made her
wish she had the talent to draw *him*.

Knowing she would for sure startle him if she walked over,
she reached out and flipped the living room light switch off and
on. He immediately straightened and turned. When he saw her
standing there, a wide smile broke through. He pulled his
earbuds from his ears.

"She lives! We didn't kill her with the sex!"

O'Neal laughed. "Yeah, sorry. I can't believe I slept in this
late. I'm typically an annoying early riser, but I think y'all wore
me out."

He chuckled as he set his pencil down and then spun his
chair to face her. "I think you and Aud's after-hours meet-up
might've been the kill shot. Y'all didn't come back to bed for a
while."

The words made her tense. "I, uh…"

"Oh shit," he said quickly. "Don't get that look. I'm not, like,
saying that in some jealous way. I'm glad you two got some time
alone."

"Yeah?" she asked, relieved.

Len exhaled and stood to come over to her. "Of course." He
cupped her face and pressed a tender kiss to her lips. "We're all

in this together. That's the beautiful thing about it. We'll figure out all the different versions of it as we go. You should have some couple time with Aud. I know I came into the picture as supporting cast, so our relationship is newer and will take a little more time. That's okay."

The words crashed like off-key notes in her ears.

"Um, no, actually it's not okay."

He gave her a questioning look. "Uh…"

"Supporting cast?" She made a face. "That's not how I see you at all. I object to that term."

He laughed and touched the tip of his finger to the corner of her mouth where she must've been frowning. "I appreciate the righteous indignation, Sweets, but I'm fine. Truly. We all love each other. None of this is a competition. And if it were, I'd be seriously outgunned anyway. You had a mad, long-standing crush on the dude. There's history. There's been *pining*."

"I have not *pined*," she said with a huff.

His eyebrows lifted and he gave her a knowing look.

"Ugh, fine. There was much pining."

"Ha." He tugged a lock of her hair. "Nothing to be ashamed of. Passionate people pine. I pined for him too. And I was pining *for you* when you left." He stepped past her to head to the kitchen. "Now how about breakfast? I'm starving."

She crossed her arms and followed him, frustrated not just that he was teasing her but that he was somehow okay with not having a starring role, that he didn't think he deserved more.

He turned and held up a white bakery bag. "We've got plain and everything bagels. Plus chive cream cheese. Pick your poison."

"Len," she said.

He lowered the bag, looking wary all of a sudden. "What?"

"You know I'm serious when I say I love you, right?" Her words weren't elegant but they were honest.

He smirked his trademark smirk. "Of course."

But she wasn't buying the confidence this time. She walked closer and then hoisted herself up to sit on the counter in front of him to get eye to eye. "No, I need you to really hear that. I know I have history with Aud and all this childhood crush stuff, but the times you and I have spent together? The things we've done? I didn't do that for Auden. Or even because you're melt-my-eyeballs hot—which you are, by the way. I did that because you're funny and smart and interesting. I did it because I like who I am when I'm with you." She pressed her finger to his chest. "I did it because I was falling in love with you."

His Adam's apple bobbed, his gaze as stripped down and open as she'd ever seen it. "I love you too. Had those feelings even when I wasn't supposed to because you were supposed to be his."

"No. I wasn't supposed to be his. I'm supposed to be *both of yours*," she said with a conviction she felt down to her bones. "You're mine too, and I'm not settling for you having less than a starring role in my life. So you better get over that inferiority complex you're throwing at me real quick because—"

She didn't get a chance to finish what she was going to say because Len cupped the back of her neck and kissed her. It started out sweet and gentle, but when she reached out to curl her fingers into his T-shirt, the bag of bagels hit the floor. He stepped forward, fitting into the space between her knees, and held her there as his tongue dipped into her mouth.

She sighed softly at the connection and flattened her hands against his chest. His heartbeat was quick against her fingertips as he whispered her name against her mouth and then deepened the kiss. She hooked her legs around his waist, the heat of him pressing against her, and got lost in the feel of him.

When he finally broke away for a moment, he gave her a look that made her stomach somersault. "I promised myself I wouldn't touch you this morning, but how am I supposed to resist you when you look at me like that? Say things like that?"

"Why no touching?" she asked, confused.

Concern creased his face. "Because last night was a lot and you could probably use a break and I need you to know I love you for more than just what we do in bed and—"

"Lennox?"

"Yes?" he asked, looking slightly miserable.

"You have nothing to prove to me," she said. "Over and over again, you tried to stop me and Auden from blowing this whole thing up with our insecurities. You fought for this. For him. For me. For *us*. You didn't let us hide. You"—she splayed her hands against his chest—"made this happen. You loved us enough not to give up."

He blinked, his eyes shiny. "Sweets."

"Plus"—she gave him a saucy smile—"yes, last night was a lot, but I was a virgin for nineteen years and felt guilty about every sexual urge for most of that time. I think I've earned a little overindulgence, don't you?"

At that, a laughing smile broke out on his face. "Hell yes, you do. Not touching was a terrible idea. That was very stupid of me. Please forgive me."

She laughed. "Forgiven."

"God, I adore you." He dove back into the kiss with more purpose now, and need pulsed through her. Before she realized what she was doing, she'd grabbed for the hem of his shirt and tugged it upward. He helped her along and tossed the shirt aside. Then she was kissing down his neck and nipping at his collarbone. She had the urge to run her tongue along every part of him, to explore each tattoo, to see which spots made him feel good. She started by sucking his nipple between her teeth, having no idea if that was okay, but letting her instincts take over.

"Jesus," Lennox gasped, tipping his head back and letting his hands slide into her hair as she sucked and licked. "Fuck bagels. I'm going to eat *you* for breakfast."

The declaration made her thighs clench. She licked over the words scrawled along his ribcage, ready to do whatever he wanted, and then boldly let her hand travel down between his legs. She gripped him through his jeans, his cock already like iron against her palm.

He let out a strained sound and then reached for the button on her shorts. Before she could take two breaths between kisses, he had her shorts and panties off and her legs spread.

"Your counter," she protested, remembering what he'd said after *Fatal Attraction*. "You're anti-counter-sex."

But Len braced his hands on each side of her thighs and leaned in to kiss her again. "You're changing my mind on a lot of things. Hold on to the edge, Sweets."

She did as she was told and watched with a held breath as Len lowered down to his knees. The counter wasn't too high, and his height put him in exactly the right place. Sunlight streamed in through the window over the sink, a nearly sheer curtain the only thing keeping this private.

"You're fucking gorgeous, O'Neal," he said, voice ragged as he dragged a finger down from her navel, his gaze following the path with rapt interest. "I want to draw you just like this one day. Every line and curve."

She shivered, the sound of her real name on his lips doing something to her. This wasn't playful Len anymore. He was focused on her with palpable intensity.

He traced his fingertip down the center of her folds, spreading her curls and brushing over that sensitive little bundle of nerves just enough to make her gasp. He circled there, barely grazing her clit each time, teasing her as he painted her with her own slickness.

Her neck arched. "Please. More. I need..."

His gaze lifted to hers, a flicker of something wicked in his eyes. "I have an idea. Something that will make this feel even better for you."

She looked down at him, nervous anticipation filling her. "Yeah? What?"

"Do you trust me?" he asked.

She licked her lips. "Yes."

"Excellent." He smiled and rose to his feet. He wrapped her legs around him and lifted her. "I have a different counter in mind."

A few minutes later, she was sitting naked atop a towel on their bathroom counter. The water was running warm in the sink next to her, and her heart was hammering as she tried to piece together clues to figure out his plan.

"What are we doing?"

Lennox ran a hand along her thigh and kissed the spot behind her ear. "You know how good it feels when we put our tongues on you? How sensitive everything gets?"

Her nerve endings prickled at the memory. "Yes."

"Imagine if there were no barrier at all, if every inch of skin was so sensitive"—he scraped a blunt nail along her labia—"that even a warm breath could feel like a touch?"

She swallowed hard, sensation shooting through her.

His breath tickled her ear. "I want to shave you, Sweets."

The words shocked her. She'd had no idea what his idea for the bathroom was. She'd thought maybe a shower, but this hadn't crossed her mind.

"I…"

Lennox straightened so that he could face her. He brushed her hair away from her eyes, and she could only imagine what her expression must be saying. He gave her a gentle smile. "You're perfect just as you are if you don't want to, but I can tell you from personal experience that everything gets more sensitive that way. And Auden's got the good stuff to do it because he has to shave everything for swimming."

"I b-believe you," she said, her pulse racing, "about the sensitivity. But I mean, I can take care of it. I didn't know I was supposed to—"

She'd always taken care of her bikini line, but was this another thing she'd been left out of the loop on?

He shushed her with a kiss. "You're not *supposed* to do anything. Some girls do, some don't. Some guys do, some don't." His hand massaged her thigh. "I'm not offering as a favor, Sweets. I'm offering because I'm hard as a rock thinking about being the one to make you bare. To be the first one to taste you that way."

Her inner muscles clenched and her clit ached. This sounded insane, but suddenly she wanted nothing more than to experience what Len was promising. Flesh against flesh. Heat against heat. She tried to wet her lips but her mouth had gone dry.

"Okay."

"Good girl," he whispered and kissed her again.

The words were the perfect balm, relaxing her muscles and evening out her breathing.

Len stepped away for a moment to grab a few things from the cabinet, then he wet a hand towel under the stream of warm water. When he pressed it between her legs, she leaned back against the mirror and closed her eyes. Len didn't say a word as he got down on his knees and spread her wide, but he kept a grounding hand on her at all times, soothing her nerves.

He kissed her inner thigh and then his fingers were on her, smoothing the shaving cream over her and touching her in the most intimate places.

"Stay very still for me, Sweets," he said, voice husky, and then the cool press of the razor scraped slowly across her skin.

It should've been terrifying—man with a sharp blade on her vulnerable flesh—but Len's movements were so tender, so precise, an artist's hands, that a moan escaped her throat. He completed another slow swipe, and another, and the cool air that chased over the newly bared skin sent a wash of arousal through her.

She opened her eyes to peek at him. His blond head was bowed in concentration, his full attention on what he was doing to her, but there was a flush in his cheeks and his pulse was visibly beating at his neck. This was turning him on as much as it was her.

She dared a glance at the spot where he was working. She watched with rapt attention as he patiently worked his way around every delicate part of her. Seeing his hands on her, the care he was taking, made her even hotter, and she had to fight hard not to squirm, her body wanting relief. Finally, he eased her open with his thumb and then drew the razor along the tender inner flesh of her labia, smooth, pink skin appearing and tingling sensations following the razor in its wake.

She must've made some noise because he peered up then. The fiery desire in his eyes nearly burned her to the ground. Without breaking eye contact, he dropped the razor into the sink and cleaned off the rest of the shaving gel with the warm towel. The brush of the terry cloth against her bared skin made her groan.

"You okay?" he asked, voice gruff.

She shifted on the counter, instantly bereft at the loss of his touch, and nodded quickly. "So, so, so okay."

"Thank God because if I have to wait another second—" He tossed the towel aside, and before she could take another breath, he lifted her legs over his shoulders and buried his face between her thighs.

Her entire body jolted at the sudden onslaught of sensation and she cried out. She'd expected him to tease her, to lick her slowly, tasting each new section of exposed skin, because Lennox was a guy who had a plan, who didn't get rushed. But some other version of him had taken over his body. He was a man possessed.

His fingers dug into her thighs and the flat of his tongue licked up her center in a flurry of hungry, hot lashes. The feel of it was like nothing O'Neal had ever felt. No longer was there one sensitive spot but a million. Every touch of his tongue felt electric, sensation radiating out to every part of her, lighting things up she didn't know could be lit up. Her breasts ached, her thighs quivered, even her scalp tingled.

She reached out to grip his hair, needing something to hold on to, and she pulled him even closer, spreading her legs wider and losing all sense of self-consciousness. Len made a desperate, sexy noise against her and got even greedier with his mouth, devouring her like she was his last meal on earth. Nose and lips and tongue driving her wild, his stubble scraping against her. She gasped for air, afraid her body was just going to crack apart. Her hips rocked, searching for a way to get even closer. He plunged two long fingers inside her, pumping his arm and sucking her clit between his lips.

Every nerve cell inside her detonated. A scream scraped past her throat, and her head tipped back against the mirror, her entire body going rigid.

The waves of orgasm stole her capacity for thought for a few long seconds, and all that was left was sensation and the slick sound of Len's magical mouth and fingers.

He held on to her, keeping her from sliding off the counter, and he softened his movements as she started to come down from the high. When her brain came back online, he was already standing up and lifting her. Her bones felt liquified, and she pressed her face into his neck.

He kissed her hair. "God, Sweets. That was…"

"Need you," she whispered. Because she did. She didn't know if she had another orgasm in her, but she had a visceral need to be close to him, to feel him inside her.

"Yes, baby. Same."

She didn't open her eyes but knew he was carrying her out.

Soon, he laid her on his bed. Her eyelids fluttered open, and she found him shucking his jeans, his gorgeous backside giving her the urge to bite him. When he turned around, his hand was wrapped around the base of a straining erection, the head flushed an angry red.

"Please tell me you want this." He rubbed himself, watching her. "I'm trying to play it cool here, but I'm not going to lie. That was one of the hottest fucking things of my life, and I may actually be dead right now. I might be a ghost."

She laughed, feeling slightly delirious.

"But you can say no. I can take care of things myself." His gaze raked over her, ravenous hunger there.

She lifted her hand to him. "Come to bed, Len. Stop being such a gentleman."

Relief washed over his face, and he yanked open the bedside drawer to grab a condom. In a blink, he'd rolled it on and climbed onto the bed. He dipped down to kiss her, giving her a taste of her own arousal. She groaned softly, her body already revving anew.

He lifted his head. "I've wanted you since the first time I saw you—even when I really, really wasn't supposed to. I'm so glad it's now."

The words warmed her in more than the sexy places. She licked her lips and whispered, "Same."

That seemed to break something in his restraint, and he gripped her behind her knee, opening her to him and then plunging deep. Her back arched with pleasure, the feel of him different than Auden, deeper, but no less mind-blowing. The sensation of being so filled up by someone still made her heady with arousal, but not just someone. *Him.* Lennox saw her in a way that made her feel powerful and sexual and brave. He always saw the woman, never the girl.

And he was sweet.

So. Very. Sweet.

Which was why she wasn't scared when she looked up at him and said, "Show me exactly how much you want me."

The flare of satisfaction that lit his eyes and the indulgent smile were rewards in themselves.

He grabbed her wrists and lifted them above her head. "Hold on to the headboard and don't you dare let go."

With that, she latched onto the wood rails and his long fingers spanned over her hips, tilting her just so, and then he slammed into her until he buried to the hilt. The headboard hit the wall and the mattress squeaked and the place he was rubbing inside her was driving her up the mountain, but that wasn't what had her close to coming again. She was enraptured by the man above her, the ferocious beauty of him losing himself to the moment. He was glistening with sweat, his eyes closed, and his abs were flexing with the power of his thrusts. He wasn't holding back or being gentle for her. And she loved it.

When his breaths started to quicken, he slipped his hand between them, finding her clit and circling it. Everything was hypersensitive, but he seemed to know to put just enough pressure. A moan escaped her and she clenched around him.

He made a strained sound in the back of his throat like he was trying to eke every last bit of pleasure out of the moment. "Come for me again, Sweets. I feel you squeezing me. I know you can. Milk me dry, baby."

The filthiness of the request was like lighting a match to her libido. Another orgasm, sharper than the first, crashed into her, and she yelped in surprise at the suddenness of it.

Len let out a choked shout and sunk deep, grinding into her as he came in long, hard shudders.

When they were done, he collapsed onto his forearms above her, both of them panting like they'd run a marathon. She finally let go of the headboard and circled her arms around his neck. When he kissed her this time, slow and sweet, she felt her heart turn over in her chest.

317

He lifted his head and smiled down at her before kissing her nose. "Be right back."

He rolled off of her to dispose of the condom but before he could leave, there was a swift knock at the front door. The sound made her jump.

He frowned, looking toward his bedroom door. "I wonder if Auden forgot his key. He's usually not back this early."

"Maybe it's a package or something," she said, pulling the covers over her.

"Maybe." He tugged on his jeans sans underwear. "Give me a sec."

She listened to him head to the front and open the door, but when she heard a familiar raised voice, she quickly grabbed a T-shirt and a pair of Len's boxers. She hurried out to the front, trying to smooth down her hair.

"I'm not leaving until you show me proof," the visitor said. "Let me in, dude, like right the hell now."

"I promise she's fine. She's in the shower. She's—"

O'Neal walked into the living room in view of the front door. Quyen was standing there, arms crossed and expression determined. When she caught sight of O'Neal, she did a double take.

"Oh. Hey. You *are* here."

A shirtless Len opened the door wider and turned toward O'Neal and mouthed, *Sorry.*

O'Neal cleared her throat, discomfort flooding her. "Yeah. Hi. Um, what are you doing here?"

"You didn't text me this morning to check in. We're supposed to do that. You know, our system."

O'Neal cringed. *Crap.* She and Quyen had agreed that if they stayed over somewhere or would be out late, they would tell the other the address of where they would be and they would check in the next morning. She'd done the first part but had forgotten the second.

"Oh God, Quyen. I'm so sorry. I...lost track of how late it'd gotten."

Quyen gave Lennox a suspicious once-over, pausing at the unopened button of his jeans where a line of hair disappeared. She looked back to O'Neal. "Are you okay? Where's Auden?"

"I'm fine. He's at swim practice." Her mind was scrambling for what to say, trying to come up with a logical explanation for why she was here with a half-dressed Lennox.

Quyen's eyes narrowed and she gave Len a look. "I'm gonna need you to leave for a minute," she said. "I need to talk to O'Neal alone."

Len lifted his hands. "No problem. I'll be in my room."

Lennox walked past O'Neal, giving her another apologetic look, and then disappeared down the hallway. Quyen came inside and shut the door behind her. She rushed over to O'Neal and put her hands on O'Neal's shoulders.

"Look me in the face and tell me you're okay. If he's done anything to you and—"

O'Neal winced. "I love you for this. But I really am fine. I swear."

"Then what the hell is going on?" she said in frustration. "I was knocking forever. I saw your car out there and got scared."

Her stomach dropped. She hated that she'd caused Quyen even a moment of worry. How would she feel if Quyen had done something like this to her? "I'm so sorry. I'm a terrible friend. We...didn't hear."

Her eyebrows shot up. "*We?*"

"I—"

"As in you and Auden's ridiculously hot, currently half-naked roommate?" She gasped. "Holy shit, are you sneaking around with his roommate? I thought you said last night that you made up with Auden?"

O'Neal had never wished more for a trapdoor or a magical portal. She wanted to *poof!* disappear. But as she stared like a deer in headlights at her friend, she realized the way Quyen was looking at her didn't scream judgment or disgust, or Brick's *swimfan* look, it screamed desperate curiosity. The relief that filled her was palpable. She could trust Quyen. She glanced back toward the hallway to make sure Len was out of earshot and then looked back to her friend.

"It's...complicated. I have to get back to our room to change and stuff, but why don't we meet up for lunch?"

Quyen gave her an eager nod. "Yes, let's because...*girl*. I'm literally dying with questions right now. Pizza or salad?"

O'Neal was so grateful for her in that moment, she wanted to cry. "It's definitely a pizza day."

"Agreed."

They made quick plans as O'Neal walked her to the door. But before she let Quyen step out, she reached out and hugged her. "Thank you."

Quyen stepped back with a smile. "What? For rudely interrupting?"

"No, for checking on me," O'Neal said, truly touched by her friend's concern. "Not everyone's lucky enough to have a friend who has her back and who was about to challenge a guy twice her size to a fight."

She laughed. "He's lucky you walked in when you did. I could take him. I know how to tase and I aim low."

O'Neal grinned. "See you soon."

After O'Neal shut the door, Lennox came back into the living room. He'd pulled a shirt on and buttoned his jeans. "Sorry. I didn't want to not open the door to her, but I should've given you a heads-up first. I didn't mean to put you in an awkward position. You can tell her we both just overslept—in separate rooms."

"It's okay." She walked over to him, and he pulled her into his arms. "We're going to meet for lunch and talk. I think I'm just going to be honest."

He looked down at her in surprise. "Really?"

"Yeah," she said, her confidence in that decision growing. "I don't want to lie to her. And I get the sense that she's...open-minded."

"Wow," Len said, smiling. "That's great. I'm glad you have that kind of friend."

"Me too." She pushed up on her toes to kiss him. "But I'm going to have to skip those bagels and head back so I can change and get ready."

"Sure, no problem. I've selfishly stolen your morning already."

"You weren't *all* selfish," she said with a smile as she stepped out of his hold. "In fact, I found you exceptionally generous."

He kept ahold of her hand for a moment longer. "Thank you for this morning. It was...fucking spectacular."

Her cheeks warmed. "It was."

He kissed her knuckles. "Love you, Sweets."

"Love you, Len." She squeezed his hand. "Do you actually believe me this time?"

He pulled her in for a hug and kissed the crown of her head. "Yes, ma'am. I truly do."

She smiled. "Good boy."

He laughed and hugged her a little tighter.

# CHAPTER TWENTY-SEVEN

Q uyen stared at O'Neal as she took a bite of pepperoni pizza. The friendly inquisitor. She flicked her hand in an *out with it* motion.

O'Neal took a giant bite of her pizza slice instead so her mouth was too full to talk. Being open and honest with her roommate had seemed like a good idea at the time, but now that they were in the bright light of the restaurant face to face, O'Neal's resolve was wavering. What if Quyen was disgusted? What if she thought there was something wrong with O'Neal?

"Are you going to tell me what's going on or am I going to have to play Twenty Questions?" Quyen asked.

"Sorry," she mumbled, annoyed that, as far as she'd come, she still was having trouble saying this out loud. Nineteen years of training to be quiet and discreet died hard.

Quyen pursed her lips, eyes narrowing. "Okay, fine. Twenty questions it is. Let's start with an easy one. Did you sleep with someone last night?"

O'Neal swallowed the too-large bite and nodded.

"Are you being safe and using protection? Because that's

truly the only thing I'm going to lecture you about." She lifted her palm like she was taking an oath. "I swear."

O'Neal's shoulders loosened a little at that. "Yes. Condoms and I've been on the pill since I was sixteen."

Quyen looked surprised. "Your super strict, you-can't-talk-to-boys grandparents let you get on the pill?"

"Oh, hell no," O'Neal said, nearly laughing at the idea. "I had really terrible periods, and my doctor said birth control could help. My grandmother said absolutely not. I mean, she wouldn't even let me use tampons because she thought that could mess with my virginity. But afterward, the doctor spoke with me alone and offered me a prescription and the name of a clinic where I could get it filled without them notifying anyone." She took a sip of her iced tea. "I knew I wasn't getting it for sex, so I didn't feel guilty getting it, even back then when I was still believing most of what I'd been taught."

Quyen's face scrunched up. "No tampons? Poor baby teen O'Neal. I wish we would've been friends back then. I would've snuck them to you."

O'Neal smiled. "Thanks. I wish we had been friends too." She stirred her tea with her straw, stalling, but then got irritated with her own behavior. Quyen was great. She wasn't here to criticize her choices. She just wanted to know what was going on. O'Neal needed to grow a spine and trust her friend. "So, yeah, I'm being safe." She cleared her throat. "With both of them."

To Quyen's credit, she kept her expression poker-face smooth. "Okay." She nodded. "So both. That's…something. I mean, I know you and Auden had a fight, and if no one has made any promises for exclusivity and you want to explore options and—"

"They both know," she said quickly before Quyen could skip down the wrong path.

323

"Hold up." She shook her head as if trying to clear it. "They both *know?*"

"Yes." She glanced around to make sure no one was too close and lowered her voice. "Because, last night, I got back together with Auden…and Lennox. And I was with both of them…at the same time."

Quyen's slice of pizza froze halfway to her mouth.

O'Neal rolled her lips together, bracing herself. Her friend's expression was a still-shot photo, but she could almost hear Quyen's internal screaming, so she kept talking. "They're, *we're,* uh, polyamorous. So. Yeah. That happened. It's a long story, but we're in a relationship now."

With very precise movements, Quyen set her slice of pizza down and smoothed the napkin in her lap.

O'Neal was sweating beneath her T-shirt.

"I see," Quyen said, nodding almost to herself. "Okay. So I may need a minute. My brain…and possibly my ovaries just exploded."

A choked laugh burst out of O'Neal, relief flooding her.

"So what you're saying," Quyen said, as if summarizing a lecture back to one of their professors, "is that you're now dating Mr. Hot Swimmer *and* Mr. Inked Artist, and they are both, you know, at your sexual disposal. Singular or together. Like you could call one or both right now and get a nice big dose of Vitamin D?"

"Quyen!" O'Neal's face burned. "Well, I wouldn't say it like that. And it's not just about sex. We love each other. But, also, yes, I could."

Saying that aloud felt empowering as hell. Yes. She. Could.

"Whoa." Quyen considered her. "This is…" She waved a hand in front of her face. "I think this may have literally blown my mind. This is not what I expected this conversation to be about. So. Many. Questions."

O'Neal pulled a slice of pepperoni from her pizza, watching

the cheese stretch. "You can ask. Some things are private, but I can probably answer other stuff."

Her eyes lit. "Really? I can ask?"

O'Neal swallowed her bite and nodded, the ability to talk about this with someone she could trust like a beautifully wrapped gift. "I reserve the right to pass on some."

"Of course." Quyen sat forward in her seat, pizza forgotten. "Okay. So first, is it as hot as it sounds or is it, like, intimidating?" She frowned. "Or exhausting? I mean two older guys and all that testosterone and Auden's an athlete, all that stamina, that's a lot of—a lot to handle. Literally and figuratively, I imagine."

"Quyen!"

"O'Neal! We cannot have this conversation without me least acknowledging that there are two penises present." She grabbed two breadsticks from the basket between them and held them up. "That's a lot to deal with!"

O'Neal laughed and took the breadsticks from her, setting them back in the basket. "Fine. Yes, I *am* exhausted. It *can* be intimidating, especially since they have a lot more experience than I do." She bit her lip. "But it's also been really, *really* hot."

"Yay!" Quyen did a little fast clap, and then a thought visually dawned on her face. "Wait, are they with each other too?"

"Pass." That was their business to share, not hers. She had a feeling they wouldn't mind Quyen knowing, but she didn't want to say anything without their consent.

"Whoa." She closed her eyes and muttered. "I will not objectify your boyfriends. I will not objectify your boyfriends."

A rush of joy surged through O'Neal. *My boyfriends.* She loved the sound of that.

When Quyen opened her eyes again, she looked more serious. "Do you feel safe with them? Because that's a lot of boy parts but also a lot of muscle, and you're all by yourself."

A soft smile touched her lips. "One thousand percent. Honestly. They're...the best. And very sweet."

Quyen literally squeed and pressed her fingertips to her mouth. "Oh my God, I am so happy for you. After what you've been through, you deserve like a hundred beautiful guys lined up to worship at the altar of O'Neal. Get it, girl."

She rolled her eyes. "I wouldn't go that far, but thank you for not gasping in horror and calling me crazy. That means a lot to me."

Quyen had no idea how much. O'Neal had had a lifetime of judgment. Harsh, black-and-white, no-gray-area judgment. To have a friend who simply accepted her and how she was feeling without trying to lecture her felt like a miracle.

Quyen snorted. "As if I'd ever. I'm shocked but in a good way." She took a long sip of her soda. "As long as it's what you want to do and you weren't, like, pressured by them or anything. Did they pressure you?"

"No." She took a bite of pizza, chewed, and swallowed. "If anything, Auden tried to push me away. That's why things have been so complicated lately. He didn't want me to know that he was this way. That first time, the night we went dancing at that club, it was just me and him."

"That's good. I mean, about not pressuring you," Quyen said, finally remembering she had food in front of her. She folded her second slice of pizza in half. "So you said love. Like *love* love."

O'Neal nodded, the word electric in her ears. *Love.* "Yeah. It all feels...very real. And right."

"That's amazing," she said. "I'm going to sit here like a good friend and pretend I'm not wildly jealous." She gave her an overly bright smile and pointed at her face. "See, totally not jealous. Totally not thinking about how every date I've been on lately has turned out to be a spectacular dud."

O'Neal gave her a wry look. "Well, don't get too jealous. I've been disowned by my family, and will probably get disowned by my adopted one if they find out I'm sleeping with their son and his roommate, oh, and I'm doing a project on my dead mother so…"

Quyen's expression turned contemplative and then she nodded. "Yep. You're right. I can be patient. You deserve the two hot guys. The universe owes you a pretty big debt." She cleaned off her fingers. "Speaking of which, how are you feeling about tonight's meeting?"

The shift in conversation made O'Neal's stomach churn. "Nervous. But ready, I guess."

Quyen gave her a sympathetic look. "Did you tell Auden and Lennox about it?"

"Not yet." She hadn't wanted anything to rain on the happiness of last night.

"Maybe you should." She picked up her phone and checked the time. "If they're free, I bet they would come with us. Couldn't hurt to have more people watching your back. I mean, I'm prepared to tase this guy if he gives me any weird vibes at all, but more people, especially two big guys, would help the cause."

She shifted uncomfortably. "I don't know if I want to drag them into this. I already feel bad dragging you into it."

Quyen reached out and put her hand over O'Neal's. "You're not dragging anyone. It's called letting people be there for you." She tipped her head toward O'Neal's phone. "Come on. Call your dudes. They'll for sure want to come along and be there for you." She gave her a look. *"Let them."*

O'Neal sighed, knowing that both of them would come without question. They'd probably be mad if they found out later that she'd gone and didn't ask for them to be there with her for support. She would want to be there for them in this situation, so maybe she should stop trying to shoulder this all on her own.

"You're right."

Quyen perked up with a smile. "I usually am."

~

A FEW HOURS LATER, O'NEAL WAS SITTING IN ANOTHER
restaurant, this time in a Thai place, and a man who'd known
her mother was sitting across from her at the round table.
Flanking her on each side were Auden and Lennox, and Quyen
was next to Auden, poised with a notepad—and probably a
weapon at the ready.

Jason Hazelwood was tall and friendly-looking with a casually styled head of red hair and the faint remnants of childhood
freckles across his nose. O'Neal had only exchanged a few brief
emails with him, but she'd done enough research to feel as if she
knew him at least a little. He'd been a junior in college, majoring
in pre-med, when he'd known her mother. Now, he owned a
small veterinary clinic in a quiet suburb about half an hour
from the college that had a 4.5 star rating on Yelp.

When she'd reached out to him through his Facebook page,
he'd been guarded and had made her go through steps to make
sure she was who she said she was. Apparently, true crime
podcast people hounded him on the regular. But once he'd
confirmed O'Neal was Katie's daughter, he'd been open to
meeting with her.

They'd gotten to the restaurant a while ago and had already
done quick introductions, made awkward small talk, and
ordered their drinks, but now Jason was waiting with a slightly
wary look on his face—probably because Quyen was giving him
a look that said she was capable of carving his heart out with
her butter knife if needed.

O'Neal knew she was supposed to start talking, but her vocal
cords felt paralyzed.

"So," Jason said after clearing his throat, apparently deciding
he needed to be the one to break the ice. "I'm not sure how

much help I can be, but if you have questions, I'll do my best. You said you're doing a project?"

O'Neal forced her voice past the constriction of her throat. "Yes, I'm a journalism major. But I'm also her daughter. I just... want to know more."

"Of course you do." His eyes were sad but kind. "And I wish I had a lot of answers for you or had something that would help solve Katie's case. Believe me. I've racked my brain and memories over the years trying to find anything I missed. She...meant a lot to me. I still can't believe she's gone."

O'Neal took a shaky breath, his obvious affection for her mother making a mix of emotions well up in her. Her mother had been a person in his life. Not a name on the news. Not a cold case. She'd once had friends. Lovers. Hopes. A life here.

"I really appreciate you meeting with me even if you can't answer all my questions."

"Sure," he said. "To be honest, I wanted to meet you too. Katie used to show us photos of you. She was really proud. Said you were the smartest, most adorable kid on the planet." He gave O'Neal a somber smile. "You look a lot like her."

O'Neal pressed her lips together, her eyes already burning with unshed tears. Auden put his hand on top of hers under the table. A thick lump was growing in her throat.

"Thanks."

The word came out as a croak.

"So what were your questions?" he asked, clearly sensing that he was venturing into make-her-cry territory if he kept up with the sentimental stuff.

O'Neal inhaled deeply and sat up taller in her chair, trying to find the burgeoning journalist inside her instead of the grieving kid. "I guess my first one is were you two dating? Some of the stuff I've read says yes, some says no. Most make it sound like it was a hookup in a night of hookups."

The waiter brought their iced teas and waters and then

slipped away, obviously sensing they weren't ready to give their orders.

Jason took a quick sip of his drink and adjusted in his chair, glancing between the four of them. "It wasn't a hookup. The news media paints Katie like she was some wild child, like she was partying with a bunch of guys. But that's not accurate."

"Okay." O'Neal's leg was bouncing beneath the table. "So what was accurate?"

He sighed. "Katie wasn't at school to party. She was on a mission to get her degree so she could get a job and..."

"And?" Lennox prompted.

"And get away from her family," Jason said, looking at O'Neal as if to gauge her reaction. "She wanted to be able to support herself and you and to live her own life without having to live by your grandparents' rules. She felt very... smothered is how I remember her describing it, but she couldn't say anything because they were raising you while she went to school. They wanted her to find a husband because they didn't think it was good for a child to be raised by a single mother."

"Find a husband?" O'Neal asked, thrown by the knowledge but not surprised that her grandparents would think that way.

"Yeah, and she was determined not to do that," Jason continued. "She said she didn't want the distraction of a relationship. Plus, she had you. She didn't want to bring some college guy into her kid's life. So we weren't dating. We were good friends."

"But you were sleeping together. The DNA," O'Neal said, proud that she'd been able to say it so matter-of-factly.

He ran a hand over the back of his head. "The night she went missing—sorry, this is a little weird telling her kid."

"I'm nineteen," she said. "And I already know what the DNA meant."

"Right." He nodded. "Well, that night, she was with me and a friend of mine. All of us...together."

Auden, who'd been taking a sip of water, choked a little and set down his glass. Quyen gave her a wide-eyed look

"Oh," O'Neal said, her brain spinning.

Jason rubbed his thumb along his glass. "It wasn't a regular thing. That night was the first and only time. Katie was good friends with both of us, and I think she suspected that I…"

"Suspected what?" Len asked, obviously impatient.

"That I was in love with my friend," Jason finished, a touch of chagrin in his voice. "But I wasn't out at the time. Not even to myself really. And we were all hanging out and drinking a little, and I think she thought she would help break the ice between me and the friend. It started as a silly truth or dare thing but ended up turning into more." His lips lifted at the corner, his eyes distant. "And it was a gift. Because with her there, we were all able to let our guards down. Turned out that the friend felt the same way about me." He looked up. "After that night, we dated for about five years."

O'Neal gasped softly, the story knocking her back in her chair. "She had a threesome with you *to play matchmaker?*"

He laughed self-consciously. "Looking back, it was a very Katie thing to do. She didn't want a husband, but she definitely had a romantic streak. She liked to see other people happy. And she wasn't afraid to meddle a little to make it happen."

*A very Katie thing to do.* The words made O'Neal wish he could give her a long list of *Katie things*. Maybe this was a start.

He met O'Neal's gaze. "I know it probably sounds sordid, especially with how the news media has painted her, but it really wasn't like that. It was this really beautiful, comfortable night between friends. My only regret is that I should've insisted she stay the night with us." His brown eyes went shiny. "She told us she couldn't stay and had an early morning class, but I think that was an excuse. I think she figured she'd give us some alone time to figure things out. But I should've demanded she stay. Instead, I walked her to her car and let her go."

O'Neal felt warmth on her cheeks and only then did she realize she was crying. *I walked her to her car and let her go.* She could picture it. This man walking her mom to her car after this intimate night, her mom feeling good about what she'd done to bring two friends together. Her sweet, beautiful mother walking away with a smile but unknowingly heading to the end of her short life.

"You couldn't have known."

Jason nodded, his hand pressed against the tablecloth. "That doesn't make it hurt less."

"What do you think happened?" Auden asked, a solemn note in his voice, his hand still on O'Neal's. "Do you have a theory?"

Jason blew out a ragged breath and shook his head. "I've thought about it so many times, but I can't come up with anything besides it being some crime of opportunity. Maybe she had to run some errand before she went home and a stranger found her by chance. She wasn't seeing anyone. And after the night we'd had, I can't imagine her going out anywhere or to bed with anyone else that same night."

He got a far-off look and was quiet for a moment.

"It wouldn't make any sense," he said finally. "She was visibly tired when she left, ready to go to sleep. She'd washed her makeup off. Every indicator was that she was going straight home. We had lunch plans for the next day." Sadness filled his expression. "Then she was just...gone. All that light she carried with her, gone."

O'Neal swiped at her cheeks with her napkin, and Lennox put his arm around her. Quyen was crying now too.

"God, I wish I had something that could help. I want them to find who did this," Jason said, anger coming into his voice. "I'd actually like an hour in a room with him and my surgery tools if I'm honest, but there's just...nothing. And I've listened to the shows and podcasts about her case to see if maybe anything jogs something loose in my memory, but I just end up getting mad about how they talk about her. Even if she had been a party girl, whatever the hell that's supposed to mean, she didn't deserve what happened to her. The world is a darker place without Katie Lory, and whoever took her from it and you needs to pay for it."

O'Neal continued to cry silently, her chest hurting. "Thank you for being a friend to her. It sounds like you had a special relationship."

Jason's expression was full of empathy as he looked at her. "Your mom was a wonderful, kind-hearted person, and she *adored* you. She was never shy about telling people she had a daughter. Your photo was on her keychain, and she showed it to everyone."

O'Neal smiled a wobbly smile.

"I know she'd be proud that you're trying to find justice for her," Jason said. "But I hope that you can get to a place where her memory isn't only about how her life ended. She was a person who wanted others to find their joy, whatever that looked like. She'd want you to find that too, to remember her happy. Because she *was* happy. Her teen years had been rocky, but she'd let go of the past and had really come into who she was here at school. Her end was tragic but her life wasn't."

O'Neal squeezed her eyes shut, the tears flowing freely and not so quietly now, but she could feel Auden's hand entwined with hers and Len's arm around her shoulders. Quyen's support was radiating across the table.

If her mom was looking down on her right now, she hoped that she could see it all. That her daughter missed her. But that she was surrounded by love. That she wasn't alone. That she was finally figuring out who she was.

And, yes, that she was happy.

# EPILOGUE

"*A*ll packed up?"

"I think so," O'Neal said, handing her duffel over to Auden and stepping into the apartment. She gave him a quick kiss. "I mostly brought casual stuff. I figured we'll be spending most of the time hanging out at your parents' house. If I'm remembering right, your mom is way into the holiday spirit and has things pretty planned out."

Auden smirked as he set her bag aside and shut the door behind her. "Yes, there will be much board gaming, cooking, and Christmas caroling. Mom turns into a sentimental holiday monster at this time of year."

"I'm so looking forward to Blakes-mas," Lennox said, walking over to O'Neal. He pulled her against him and planted a hot kiss on her lips. "Though two weeks of pretending I don't want to touch both of you all the time is going to be a high-level test of will."

"Hey, you two will be sharing a room. I'll be locked away in Maya's room," O'Neal said, leaning back and giving him a pointed look. "Highly unfair."

Auden snorted. "Don't be jealous, Shaq. Len and I will be

taking turns sleeping on the floor. There's not a chance in hell I'm taking that kind of risk this week. We're keeping our hands to ourselves. All of us. I'm only prepared to deliver one shock this week. We'll tackle the others down the line."

O'Neal smiled and turned, putting her back against Len's chest. "We're proud of you, you know?"

Lennox sat his chin on her shoulder. "Ridiculously so. You're much hotter as an official film geek instead of a closeted one."

Auden crossed his arms over his chest and gave them a wry look. "My family will probably shit a brick, but what's done is done."

Warmth suffused through O'Neal. Auden was trying to play this cool, but she could see the sparkle in his eyes. As of nine this morning, Auden Blake was officially a film major with a minor in business instead of the other way around. It was going to mean an extra year of school, but he was prepared to take out loans to do it. He was going for his dream, and over the break, he was going to tell his family about it.

"Poor O'Neal," Len said, a pitying note in his voice. "She thought she'd fallen for the heir to a business fortune, but now she's stuck with two artsy types." He kissed her cheek. "You know we're insufferable."

Auden came over to them, putting his hands on Lennox's shoulders and caging her between them. "And often poor."

She laughed. "I'm not looking for a bank account. I can make my own money. But I've heard the artsy types are good in bed. Real creative, you know?"

"Right." Auden touched his forehead to hers. "And kind of intense."

"And pretty filthy-minded," Len added and then kissed the side of her neck, sending a shiver downward. "And insatiable. They'll want you all the time."

She closed her eyes. "Sounds terrible."

Auden slid his hands along the lapels of her long coat. "How are we supposed to go two weeks without touching you?"

Goosebumps broke out along her skin. She didn't know the answer to that question. Since they'd decided to be together, they couldn't seem to get enough of each other. Not just in bed but simply being with each other. When they'd eventually chosen to be out with their relationship, at least at school, the freedom was like a drug. Never in her life had she felt so in her own skin. With Auden and Lennox, she felt fully herself. Nothing to hide or be ashamed of or apologize for.

"We better get our fill tonight," Len said against her ear. "Make the memory last a while."

"Agreed." Auden went in search of the button on her coat, and her heartbeat picked up speed. Her plan suddenly seemed risky. Maybe it was a bad call. Maybe it was weird.

Too late now.

Auden opened her coat and froze. Her gaze jumped up to his as she braced herself for his reaction.

His breath whooshed out, fluttering her hair. "O'Neal. *Shit.*"

She scrunched her nose. "Is it bad? Too much? Is it—?"

"What the hell is going on?" Len asked, stepping from behind her to see what Auden was looking at. An instant smile lit his face. "Well, hello there."

Auden reached out and pushed her winter coat fully off, letting it pool at her feet. He took a long, lingering glide of a look from head to foot, taking in the school uniform she'd dug out from the bottom of her boxes from home complete with a plaid skirt, white Oxford shirt, and blue blazer.

He ran a hand over his jaw like he was in actual pain. "I'm seriously going to hell. I'm a terrible, terrible person."

She licked her lips and tilted her head, nervous but getting the sense by the look on his face and the growing thickness at the front of his jeans that she hadn't missed the mark. "Um, Merry Christmas?"

"Fuck yes, it is," Len said.

Auden visibly swallowed and he stepped closer, sliding a hand onto her waist. "I know I shouldn't be turned on by this, but I think my brain might literally be liquefying as we speak. You look..."

"Like a very good girl," Len finished, moving behind her again and tracing a fingertip along her collarbone. "*Our* very good girl."

She smiled and cocked her chin, confidence rising in her. "I am. I got straight As this semester, despite some very big, very handsome distractions."

"Mmm," Auden murmured as he moved closer, trapping her between them, and opening the top button of her blouse. "So smart. I'd give you a sticker but I'm all out. Guess we'll need to reward you in some other way."

"An orgasm for every A sounds fair," Lennox suggested.

She bit her lip, a ripple of anticipation shimmering across her nerve endings. "That might kill me. I got a lot of As. But I'm willing to sacrifice myself to science to find out."

Auden laughed and leaned in to kiss her deep and slow. When he pulled back, he cupped her jaw. "You're my favorite student. Always so eager to learn."

"What should we teach her tonight, Aud?" Lennox asked, his hand tracking up the side of her thigh and then beneath her skirt. He traced a line along the seam of her ass over her thin cotton panties. "Maybe a little multitasking?" He pressed gently against that sensitive, private opening. "There are two of us after all, and so many fun places to visit."

She inhaled a sharp breath, her body reacting as if he'd pinched her.

Auden's gaze darkened, his eyes searching hers as his thumb caressed her cheek. "Hmm, I think you scared our freshman a little, Len."

O'Neal's tongue pressed to the back of her teeth. Her heart-beat was suddenly thumping in her ears.

"Her expression looks vaguely horrified. But..." Auden tucked his hand between them, lifting her skirt. With a raised eyebrow, he slipped his fingers inside her panties. The slippery heat that greeted him had her moaning and him smiling his evil Auden smile. He tucked two fingers inside her, making her muscles clench, and stroked. "But she's melting like butter at the thought of taking both our cocks at the same time." He shook his head at her and made a *tsk*ing sound. "I'd say that's a good girl fail, freshman. What dirty, dirty thoughts you have."

*Taking them both.* The one thing she'd thought about way too often since they'd been together. The thing that both intrigued her and intimidated her. She shivered and said the first thing that came to mind. "I don't know how to do that. Y'all would have to teach me."

Auden's nostrils flared at the request, and Lennox buried his face in her hair and breathed her in.

"You are so fucking sexy when you want to be taught," Auden said, his voice full of gravel. "And this uniform only makes me want to do it that much more."

Satisfaction flashed through her. She was nervous about what they were suggesting, but seeing their reactions, knowing that she could push their buttons like this, felt sexy and power-ful. No longer did she have to hide in the dark and feel shame about her fantasies or her urges. She was safe with them to feel what she felt, explore what she wanted to explore. She didn't have to worry that wearing her school uniform could have creepy undertones. With them, it didn't. Because they knew each other's hearts, the love at the core of this. Fun could just be fun. Kinky could just be kinky.

And if they were going to try this, she knew it'd either be great or she could tell them to stop and that it wasn't for her. Either way, she'd be okay.

"I don't even know where to start," she said with a teasing smile.

"Guess we have our work cut out for us tonight, then." Auden moved his hand from beneath her skirt and then reached past her. "You up for a lesson, Len?"

She turned her head to watch as Auden took his slick fingers and painted Len's lips with her arousal. When he leaned in and kissed him, pinning her between them, she damn near went up in flames.

Len eased back and licked his lips and smiled. "Class is in session."

Before she could respond, Auden wrapped his arm around her and then hoisted her over his shoulder. When she wriggled in protest, he delivered a swift smack to her ass. "Stay still, freshman. I don't want to have to punish you before class has even started."

"I do," Len said as they headed toward Auden's bedroom. "Keep at it, Sweets. Spanking you in this skirt is a new life goal."

She laughed. "Deviants, both of you."

"Absolutely," Len said as he walked beside them. "You should probably run far and fast."

She smiled against Auden's back. She wasn't going anywhere.

Auden deposited her onto his bed with a squeak of bed springs, and before she could say another word, he flipped her skirt up and pulled her panties down and off.

"That's better." Len sat next to her on the bed and dragged cool fingers along her pussy. She'd kept it smooth since that day he'd shaved her and she still marveled at how sensitive every touch was. Her hips lifted against his hand, seeking more.

Auden unbuttoned the rest of her blouse and opened it wide. She'd worn a lacy white bra beneath and instead of taking it off, he pulled the cups to the side, forcing her breasts to spill out but stay plumped together. He circled her right nipple with a fingertip, making her flesh tighten and tingle.

"Gorgeous."

He stepped away for a second to get something out of his drawer, and O'Neal's gaze went to Len. He was sitting beside her on the bed, facing her. His blond hair was a little mussed already, and his pulse was beating quickly at his neck. His fingers lazily drew paths along her inner thighs and pussy, making her arch, her thighs opening automatically, seeking more, but his focus was on her face.

He smiled an almost wistful smile. "Damn."

A little spark of self-consciousness went through her. "What?"

He shook his head. "Nothing. I'm just amazed I live in a world where I get to have this. You. Auden. *Us*. It fucking blows my mind still. I must've done something right in a previous life."

She sat up and reached for him. He came willingly but continued to stroke her. She dragged her fingers through the hair on the back of his head and then kissed him, their tongues twining in a slow dance, matching the rhythm of his fingers. When she finally pulled away, she rubbed her nose against his.

"You earned it in this one, Len. No previous life needed. I love you."

He closed his eyes and pressed a kiss to her forehead. "Love you too, Sweets. Now lie down so we can cuff you up and do bad things to you."

She laughed and lay back on the bed, arms above her head.

Auden was at the ready, a devious smile on his face as he put leather cuffs on her wrists and then hooked them to the head-board. They'd used these a few times before, and she'd learned she liked the whole restraint thing, but butterflies fluttered in her stomach, knowing what might happen tonight.

After he'd secured her, Auden pulled off his clothes, giving her an eyeful of tan skin, lean muscle, and an erection that made her mouth water. Lennox followed suit, stripping down completely and stroking his cock, a teasing touch that made her ache to feel him between her thighs.

"Where to start? Where to start?" Auden pondered, a wicked gleam in his eye as he looked down at her.

"How about we start with everywhere?" Len said.

Then the mattress was dipping with their weight as they climbed into bed with her, blanketing her with their mouths and tongues and hands, their cocks rubbing against her and making sensual promises she knew they'd fulfill.

She couldn't keep her eyes open. The onslaught of sensation short-circuited her brain. There was so much maleness and touching and sensation that her skin felt like it was literally buzzing. And when one of them found her clit, rubbing it with lubricated fingers, and the other sucked her nipple between his teeth, O'Neal exploded with an orgasm, the headboard banging the wall with the force of it. She thought she'd get a reprieve after that first one, but they had no interest in letting her rest.

Almost immediately they started ramping her up again, but now, there was no relief in sight. They'd bring her to the edge and not let her go over. So close and then no. Right there and then no. At one point, they were both going down on her at the same time, and she thought she was going to shatter, but then as soon as she arched her hips to get them to just the right spot, they backed off, leaving her to moan in desperation.

Auden's teeth tugged at her earlobe. "Not yet, freshman. We're going to make you so desperate for it that you'll let us do *anything* to give you some relief."

"Please," O'Neal pleaded. "I'm ready. Anything. Please."

"She's so pretty when she begs," Lennox mused. "Let's make her do that some more."

"Traitor," she muttered.

Len laughed and then he slid a vibrator inside her just long

her. She could feel *everything*. Her body had become a circuit board fully lit up—signals coming from every direction.

"There you go," Len said, his voice like a lullaby. "Push out when I push in. We're going to make you feel so good, Sweets."

O'Neal swallowed, her body revving again, desperate, on the edge. The head of Len's cock pressed against her opening, and for one panicked moment, she thought there was no way it was physically possible for this to happen. They were both too much, too big. She was definitely going to break. But then she did what he told her, and the thick, full feeling of Len burying inside her made her moan.

Oh *God.*

"That's it." Auden's focus was fixed on her, and his fingers were stroking her with expert precision, sending her nerve endings into a frenzy. She breathed, tried to find calmness, patience so she wouldn't detonate immediately. But then they both began to move, a coordinated rhythm that dragged them against each other inside her and filled her up in a way she could've never imagined possible.

"You okay, Shaq?" Auden asked, strain showing on his face as he clearly tried to stave off his own orgasm.

She tried to hold on to her thoughts. She felt drugged, drunk, drowned in sensation. But she managed to nod quickly. *I'm okay. Possibly disintegrating into atoms but okay.*

He gave her a loving look and started moving quicker. Len groaned behind her, his own thrusts picking up speed.

"Ready?" Auden asked.

She nodded again. *Yes. Yes. Yes.*

"You can let go now," Len said, his voice full of jagged rocks. "We've got you. We've always got you. Come for us, beautiful."

*We've always got you.* She closed her eyes and let herself fall into it, to really feel every bit of them, being between these two men, her body filled with them, and her heart overflowing. She didn't know how her life had led her here, but maybe there was someone up there looking out for her after all. Because from the outside, this might look salacious, but in her heart, she knew exactly what it was.

It was love.

Tears streaked down her face, and every inch of her body exploded with pleasure as she took what these two men were offering her. Their trust. Their hearts. Their everything.

She wasn't alone in the world anymore.

She'd found her way home.

THE END

*Read on for a bonus scene!*

# BONUS SCENE

Maya dropped a peeled sweet potato into the big bucket of water they'd set on the porch and then scraped the peelings into the trash can they'd placed next to it. When O'Neal, Auden, and Lennox had arrived at the Blakes a few days ago for Christmas break, Mrs. Blake had assigned them all tasks for the week like a drill sergeant preparing for battle.

Auden and Lennox were out with Mr. Blake on the hunt for the perfect Christmas tree because it was their tradition to put the tree up the week of Christmas and then leave it up until New Year's. O'Neal and Maya were on vegetable prep because apparently, it was also their tradition to go starch-wild having sweet potato casserole, scalloped potatoes, *and* mashed potatoes. But O'Neal wasn't complaining. The Blakes had welcomed both her and Lennox like family for the holidays, and she was happy to help however she could.

The only hard part was going to be keeping their relationship a secret. She, Auden, and Lennox had decided that one day they would tell Auden's family, but that Christmas was not the time. Plus, Auden was going to drop the bomb that he was switching to a film major, so they figured one explosive revelation per holiday was more than enough.

O'Neal stared out at the sparkling pool. The winter had been unseasonably warm so far and the Blakes hadn't drained it yet. She'd caught Auden swimming laps this morning even though the temperature of the water had to be pretty bracing. He'd said it was his equivalent of cold showers.

"I forgot to ask you how your project about your mom turned out," Maya said, grabbing another sweet potato and breaking O'Neal from her thoughts. "I feel like we've barely talked this semester."

"I know. Things have been crazy." O'Neal dragged the paring knife along her white potato, trying to keep the peel in one long curl. "I ended up switching to a different topic. The case is still open and the podcasts are bringing fresh eyes to it, so I'm hoping they'll find new clues. But I have so little of her that I realized I didn't want my memory banked filled up only with information about how her life ended. I want to remember her as she was when she was alive. And I want to learn more about her, the person not the victim." She looked over at Maya. "I found one of her close friends and we've been exchanging emails and talking on the phone. He has all these stories about her and photos from college. It's been...good to get to know that version of her. She was pretty great."

Maya smiled. "I bet she was. I'm glad you're focusing on that part instead. I was worried about you."

The concern in Maya's voice made O'Neal's gut twist a little. Maya had been her best friend for as long as she could remember, but since they'd started college, she'd basically shut her out. She didn't know how to navigate their friendship when she felt like she'd changed so much. She didn't know how Maya would feel about this new version. "Thanks. I'm sorry I've been bad about keeping in touch. I haven't been the bestest of best friends."

Maya shrugged and then cocked her head. "Is that possibly because you're most definitely doing it with my brother?"

O'Neal's potato dropped right out of her hand and landed on the porch with a wet thud. She scrambled to pick it back up and then tossed it in the trash pile. "Um, what?"

Maya sliced a peeling off and gave her a look of challenge. "That day we went to brunch, he was wearing a ring on his pinky. I thought he'd developed some really awful fashion sense. But then later, it was back on *your* hand. Your purity ring."

O'Neal opened her mouth, scrambling for a reasonable explanation, but her cheeks were going hot and thoughts wouldn't form. "I—what?"

God, she was a terrible liar.

Maya sighed, set her sweet potato aside, and wiped her hands on a dish towel. "My mom didn't catch it. She has no idea. But the way he was looking at you?" She shook her head. "He's got no poker face."

O'Neal stared at her friend for a moment, panic like a fluttering bird in her chest, but then her shoulders sagged. She couldn't keep lying. Not to Maya. "Okay. Yes. I'm sorry I didn't tell you, but you know why I couldn't."

"Oh my *God*. I'm *right?*" Her nose scrunched but she laughed. "I cannot believe you've, like, done naked things with Aud! I'm horrified. *It's Aud!*"

"Shh," she said, glancing toward the house. "Let's not announce it to everyone."

"No one can hear us out here. But seriously, *Auden? Really?* You do remember my brother right? The boy who used to put orange juice in his cereal? The one who'd silent fart on road trips and then blame it on me?"

O'Neal laughed. "You've got sister blinders on. Auden is..." She took a breath, gathering courage. "I'm like super in love with him. Had a crush on him for a long, long time."

Her eyes widened, a different level of awareness dawning.

"Whoa. Like *love* love? It's that serious? Does he *know* you love him? Because he doesn't exactly have a great track record with—"

"I don't have a great track record with what?" a deep voice interrupted.

Both Maya and O'Neal startled and turned. Auden was walking up the garden path in the backyard, his red T-shirt streaked with what O'Neal assumed was tree sap. He joined them on the porch, bringing the wintry scent of pine with him.

"Oh, Aud. Hi!" Maya said brightly. "Wow, you look like you've been in a fight. Did you have to wrestle the tree to the ground to capture it?"

He crossed his arms over his chest and gave his sister a look. "Dad picked a Griswolds' size tree and it took some creative engineering to get the thing secured to the top of the car. Mom wouldn't allow me in the house. Len's grabbing me a change of clothes."

"Fun," Maya said, still using that too-bright tone.

He glanced at O'Neal and then back to Maya. "So what exactly do I have a bad track record with?"

"Nothing. Girl talk," Maya said dismissively. "Wasn't talking about you."

He glanced at O'Neal and she sighed. "Maya knows about me and you. Figured it out at brunch that day. I think she was about to tell me your track record with relationships ain't great."

"Is that right?" He sat down on one of the porch chairs, placing himself next to O'Neal and across from Maya. "Glad to know my lil' sis is putting in a good word for me."

Maya gave him a *don't even* look. "I'm just stating observable facts. I love you, but O'Neal is my best friend. She should know."

Auden exhaled slowly and reached out to take O'Neal's hand in his, but he kept his gaze on his sister. "My, I appreciate your protectiveness, but I assure you, I'm in love with O'Neal and I plan to treat her very well."

The words still sounded like music to O'Neal every time she heard Auden or Lennox say them. *Love.* She squeezed his hand.

Maya glanced between the two of them, a hint of surprise on her face. "Wow, you mean that."

"I do," he said.

Maya grinned. "Oh my God, does this mean we'll *be actual sisters one day?!*"

O'Neal laughed and lifted her free hand. "Tap the brakes there, sister. No white dresses anytime soon. I don't know if I even believe in that whole marriage thing."

Maya's brows crept up.

"But you're like my sister no matter what," O'Neal finished.

Maya put her hand to her chest. "Aww. Same." She looked to Auden. "So, are you going to tell mom and dad?"

"Not yet," he said. "I'm telling them I'm changing majors on this trip so I need to space out the big announcements. Plus, it's a little more complicated than it appears."

O'Neal tensed and gripped his hand a little tighter.

"What do you mean?" Maya asked.

Auden glanced at O'Neal as if to ask permission. Her blood was rushing in her ears, but she gave a little nod. Sharing only part of the truth meant another part remained a lie of omission. If they were going to be honest with Maya, she deserved to know all of it.

Auden cleared his throat. "You have to promise you won't say a word to anyone."

Maya leaned forward in her chair, her attention rapt. "Of course, what is it?" Horror flashed across her face. "Oh man, you're not pregnant, are you?"

"*What?* No! Definitely not," O'Neal said, shaking her head.

Maya put her hand to her forehead. "Thank you, Jesus. I could just see your grandparents putting up an *I told you so* banner across the front of their house. I'd hate to give them that satisfaction."

"No," Auden went on, his tone measured. "Not pregnant. It's just that we're in an unconventional relationship. It's not just the two of us. It's me, O'Neal, and—"

"Hey, I've got fresh clothes for the guy who fought a Christmas tree and lost. I couldn't find your socks though, Aud, so you can borrow my reindeer ones." Lennox froze at the edge of the porch when the three of him looked his way. "Oh, uh, sorry, am I interrupting?"

But the silence stretched too long for Maya not to put together the equation.

"Holy. Crap." Maya's voice was hushed, maybe a little awed.

Len smiled in that unsure, awkward way someone does when they're left out of a joke. "Did I miss something?"

Maya blinked like he'd spoken an alien language, then she looked to O'Neal. "You're with...?"

O'Neal bit her lip and nodded, bracing herself.

"Oh," Lennox said, catching on. *"Oh."*

Auden coughed. "Yeah. So Maya knows."

"Holy crap," Maya said again.

O'Neal could almost hear her friend's brain processing the new information at high speed. It wasn't going to take her long to—

"Hold up." Maya pointed back and forth between the two guys. "Are you and Lennox like dating each other too?"

Auden's Adam's apple bobbed. He nodded. "Yeah."

Maya pressed her hands over her face, her head shaking back and forth. "I can't even believe..."

"Maya—" O'Neal started, ready to mitigate as much as she could.

But then Maya lowered her hand and the hugest, biggest smile broke over her face, her glee outshining the afternoon sunlight. Then the laughing started. She started quietly but soon she was full-out belly-laughing, holding her stomach, and tears escaping the corners of her eyes.

O'Neal looked to the guys in mild panic. "I think we broke her."

Maya laughed harder, bending forward, and her shoulders shaking.

"My," Auden said, reaching out to put a hand on her arm. "Are you okay? What are you—"

Maya lifted a hand to stave him off, mirth in her eyes. "No, it's fine. I just." She couldn't seem to catch her breath. "I just cannot believe the holiday gift you just gave me. Christmas is early."

"What are you talking about?" O'Neal asked.

Maya swiped at her eyes and tried to rein in her laughter. "Y'all. You have no idea how happy I am to hear that you've gotten yourself into some kind of threesome love story. I mean, I can't tell you how much I've been stressing these past few weeks, worried about something I have to tell mom and dad one day soon. And you three just saved me from that spotlight. Because wow, my thing is going to pale in comparison to yours."

O'Neal stared at her friend. "What thing? Maya, what's going on?"

She collapsed back in her chair, her eyes still smiling, but her posture exhausted. "O'Neal, you haven't been the only one avoiding conversation. I was too afraid to get on the phone with you and not spill the beans. I thought you might...not what to be friends anymore but—"

"What beans?" Auden asked.

Lennox leaned against the porch column, looking rather delighted at the turn of events.

She lifted her palms in a *what can you do* motion and gave them a resigned smile. "So this semester, I fell completely head over heels...for my suitemate."

*"What?"* Now, it was O'Neal's turn to be stunned. "You go to an all girl's college."

"Yep," Maya said, emphasizing the hard *p* at the end of the word. "Turns out, I like girls. One in particular. Which I thought was going to be an earth-shattering announcement for the fam, but my news sounds downright pedestrian now. You three are definitely going to steal the stage."

O'Neal felt fizzy with delight for her friend. "You're in love?"

"I think so," she said, excitement in her tone. "Alexis is the literal best. You're all going to love her, too. She's majoring in classical music, but she's also got this indie rock band thing on the side. And she's really funny. And—"

Auden leaned forward and pulled his sister into a hug. "I'm so happy for you, My. That's fantastic."

"Happy holiday news all around," Lennox agreed.

Maya hugged her brother back. "Thank you. All of you."

When Auden released her, O'Neal reached out and squeezed Maya's hands. "You could've told me. I love you. Whoever makes you happy is who I want you to be with."

Maya gave O'Neal a hug, too. "I could say the same to you. I don't exactly understand the whole three-people thing, but that doesn't mean I'm not open to hearing about it or being happy for all of you." She leaned back and gave her a look. "Though if you give me any dirty details about my brother, I will literally vomit."

Auden groaned. "Yes, please, no sharing of that."

O'Neal laughed and raised her palm. "Promise."

Maya sat back in her seat and let out a long breath, her attention honing in on Auden. "This is going to be a lot on Mom and Dad. Do you think this is going to blow up our family?"

Auden glanced at the house and pondered. "Well, we didn't plan on telling them about our relationship quite yet, but maybe we just need to lay it all out there and see how it goes. Stand by each other, owning the truth. All four of us."

Maya's brow wrinkled with worry.

"Mom and Dad love us," Auden said with a little more confidence. "And I think it will take them a while to understand, and we need to be patient with them on that, but I don't see them cutting us out of their lives." He looked to Lennox and then to O'Neal before sending his sister a contented smile. "But even if they would, are you willing to give up your own chance at happiness to keep the peace?"

A resolute look came over her face. "No." She looked at O'Neal, her eyes going shiny. "My best friend showed me that standing up for who you are is worth it even when it's scary."

"She taught me that too." Auden took O'Neal's hand and reached out for Lennox to grab his other. "They both did."

"I'm glad, truly, that you're happy," Maya said. "And I guess if our parents go nuts on the four of us, then we at least have each other, right?"

Warmth rushed through O'Neal, her love for these three people making her feel more like part of a family than she ever had in her life. "Of course."

"Always," Auden said. "Family."

"Group hug!" Lennox announced.

They all laughed at the break in seriousness and stood, huddling up like a football team around the pile of potatoes.

"I hope we all really like each other," Lennox said, "because with all the sap on Auden's shirt, I think we might be permanently attached now."

*Permanently attached.*

To the guys she loved. To her best friend. To a family.

That didn't sound so bad to O'Neal at all.

# ABOUT THE AUTHOR

Roni wrote her first romance novel at age fifteen when she discovered writing about boys was way easier than actually talking to them. Since then, her flirting skills haven't improved, but she likes to think her storytelling ability has. She holds a master's degree in social work and spent years as a mental health counselor, but now she writes full-time from her cozy office in North Texas where she puts her characters on the therapy couch instead.

She is a two-time RITA Award winner, a HOLT Medallion winner, and a *New York Times* and *USA Today* bestselling author. She is also the co-host of the RAD Reading podcast.

**Hang out with Roni via her interactive Happy for Now newsletter where she shares what she's reading, watching, and other things she's excited about: roniloren.substack.com**

facebook.com/roniloren

twitter.com/roniloren

instagram.com/roniloren

goodreads.com/roniloren

# ALSO BY RONI LOREN

# ACKNOWLEDGMENTS

First, a big thank you to you, dear reader for picking up this book. I hope you enjoyed it! *Good Girl Fail* was a passion project. A story that I was having a little affair with for two years in between working on my traditionally published books. When I'd get blocked writing the other stories, I'd come back to O'Neal, Auden, and Lennox to just have fun and remind myself that writing can simply be for the joy of it. I hope you found some joy in this story too!

As always, there are many people to thank because writing is not a solo journey. Thank you to my husband and parents for always being supportive no matter which job I do or which kind of story I write. Thanks to Dawn Alexander, my friend, podcast co-host, and editor of this book for being rad! Thanks to Jessica Snyder for a great copyedit and for catching my subtle *Dirty Dancing* references. And thanks to my agent, Sara Megibow, for always being a fantastic cheerleader and business partner in this publishing journey. I'm a lucky girl to have so many people in my corner!